# THE SEVEN DEADLY KINS SERIES

## Presents:

### BOOK 1 – The Top Dog

## Part 2

# Written by Tiana Laveen

Edited by Natalie Guillaumier

Cover Layout and design by Travis Pennington

*A Romantic Suspense Series*

## THE SEVEN DEADLY KINS SERIES

The Top Dog – Lennox (Book 1) – LUST: *Part 1* and *Part 2*
(Double novel)
The Black Sheep – Roman (Book 2) – GREED
The Lone Wolf – Kage (Book 3) – SLOTH
The Lion's Share – Phoenix (Book 4) – PRIDE
The Elephant in the Room – Maddox (Book 5) –
GLUTTONY
The Eagle Eye – Journey (Book 6) – ENVY
The Dark Horse – Ryder (Book 7) – WRATH

Blood and Rhinestone Cowboy Productions Presents:

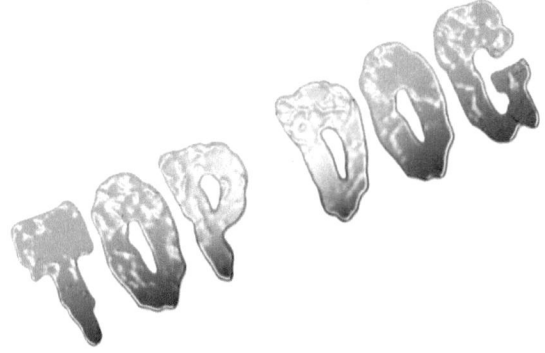

In the heart of Texas, the Wilde family dynasty conceals a dark secret society. Ruled by money, debauchery, and the iron fist of their patriarch, seven rebellious grandsons refuse to bow to their powerful grandfather's will, bringing dishonor upon the family name. As each cousin grapples with their own demons and desires, their journey of defiance leads them on a path of revenge, self-discovery, and unexpected love. From the shadows of power to the depths of passion, join the Seven Deadly Kins as they challenge tradition and forge their own destinies.

*This is PART 2 of Top Dog's story.*
*The finale.*
*Beware. He's escaped the kennel...*

# BLURB

**Someone should have let this sleeping dog lie…**
**Now, Lennox "Top Dog" Wilde, is out of the**
**doghouse, and he's not returning without a hunk of**
**flesh.**

## BOOK 2 and Part 2 of the 7 Deadly Kins Series

Lennox Wilde is determined to protect Nadia 'Velvet' Deere from unforeseen danger, lurking in every corner. As he battles family demons and Nadia wrestles with her pain and paths to healing, their love for one another grows. Nadia must choose between her past and her present, while Lennox is set administering the perfect revenge, securing the keys to his freedom, and offering Nadia the loyalty and love she's never had. Their greatest challenges are yet to come.

*From USA Today bestselling author Tiana Laveen comes Book one of the 7 Deadly Kins series. Come along for a dark love story packed with suspense, revenge and passion. 'The Top Dog – Lust' is an exciting friends to lovers, second chance, destined for love, possessive alpha hero, bad boy, sexy, contemporary romance. It's the first installment in the series, but can be read as a standalone double novel. It has no cliffhanger, and has a HEA (Happily-ever-after). This book includes mature themes and content that may not be suitable for all audiences; reader discretion is advised. Please look inside BOOK 1/PART 1, under the 'Trigger Warnings' for possible topics that may be deemed personally objectionable.*

# COPYRIGHT

Copyright © 2024 by Tiana Laveen
All rights reserved.

Print Edition

ISBN: (eBook) BOOK 1/Part 2: 978-1-962451-03-1
ISBN: (paperback) BOOK 1/Part 2: 978-1-962451-05-5

# TRIGGER WARNINGS

**These double novels contain adult content. Please look at book one – Top Dog: Lust, under Trigger Warnings for further details. Thank you.**

**Please note:** This book contains a guest appearance from a Tiana Laveen fan favorite. He is the hero from the 'Saint Series', Dr. Saint Aknaten. If you are unfamiliar with the 'Saint Series' and this particular character, then prepare to be shocked! Dr. Saint Aknaten's character portrays that of a licensed clinical psychotherapist, sex therapist, and psychologist who specializes in human sexuality, family counseling, and romantic relationships. He is also a psychic and empathic healer, but doesn't advertise that. He uses unorthodox methods to assist his clients. This can include crude, profane language, sexually charged statements, and unconventional therapeutic practices.

# TABLE OF CONTENTS

# CHAPTER TWENTY-TWO

## *Soul Sister*

XXTENTACION'S, 'VICE CITY' punched through the club amplifiers. The bass hammered and pulsated within the atmosphere, making one feel alive. Lennox glanced at his iWatch, noting the time, then headed towards the other end of the club. He and several other bouncers made their usual rounds, rotating stations every now and again.

Wearing a black sports jacket and matching pants, he caught his image in a mirrored wall, gleaming with reflected flashing lights. His black hair had grown out a bit and was brushed back from his forehead, exposing his lowbrow, thick eyebrows and the fire in his satin gray eyes with gold flecks. Darkness flashed in his vision, in his soul, and in his heart, but there was light at the end of the tunnel. He could feel the black heat on his heels, as if something invisible but wicked was shadowing him within each step he took. Yet, he didn't run.

Nevertheless, something had his dander up. Something unseen and unheard. *Nadia should have called me back by now. Hasn't she left yet?* He glanced at his iWatch once again, then stood by the bar sizing up the inebriated and high people swaying on the dance floor. He tried desperately to stay focused on the job at hand, but it proved to be far more difficult than he imagined. It wasn't like Nadia to not call him when she got off work, and with all of the shit going on as of late, he was resolute to keep tabs on her. After all, this was her last night at the gentleman's club—and afterwards, she was to go home. They'd agreed that he would meet her at her apartment after he got off work.

His phone buzzed, signaling a text message. Hoping it was her, he reached into his pants pocket and pulled out his phone, but was disappointed to see it was some random email. He figured it was spam, but opened it and read it anyway. His face warmed with happiness once he got to the final sentence of the message.

Tonight wasn't so bad after all. He sat on the good news for a few moments, relishing it, then sent Nadia a text message inquiring about her whereabouts so he could tell her, too. He waited a few minutes. She didn't respond.

Concern welled in his throat forming an itchy knot, and he couldn't speak. What was he to do with these feelings that were clouding his good spirits? And then it hit him. Back in the day, there was someone he always contacted when he had good news. Someone who'd been a friend from the day she'd been born—and one of the few people he trusted. Someone he missed dearly. Was this a good time to mend fences? Would he be ignored as usual? Or would good luck strike twice in the same night?

He radioed to another bouncer.

"Hey, Steve." Static erupted on the walkie-talkie. "Can you hear me? Over."

"This is Steve. 10-4. Hey Lennox. What it do? Over."

"I gotta make an important call. I'm leavin' my post, but will be back in a jiffy. Over."

"Copy that. Do what you need to do. Over and out."

Lennox made his way into a little office at the back of the club. The large metal desk was covered with files, crunched up receipts, and various papers, some of them stamped with the words, 'Invoice'. He proceeded to make the call, remaining standing in the middle of the room, amid all the mess. Muffled music drifted to the room, the song indistinguishable as he called a number from his contacts that was etched in his memory.

He was startled when he heard her voice, not expecting for her to answer.

"Silva?"

"Yes? Lenny? Is this Lenny?"

"Yeah… it's me."

"Is… is something wrong? It's late." She yawned, for a split-second sounding like her old self.

He realized she was probably still somewhat asleep, and picked up the phone without even thinking about it. He'd hoped she *did* in fact see that it was him calling and answered without hesitation, but he knew deep down that was unlikely. She'd probably have let it go to voicemail. Why would tonight be any different?

"…Something's been wrong for a long time, Silva. I, uh,

miss you. Regardless of the tension and messed up shit between us, I wanted you to know that your prayers and encouragement worked."

"My prayers? Prayers for what?" She sniffed, sounding a bit stopped up. His little sister always did struggle with her allergies.

"I got the bank loan to start up my own fitness center. I even eyed some property, and now I can go 'nd buy it and get started with renovations. An old car dealership over there on Barker's Landing."

He was met with her silence, and only the stifled noise of the music from the dance floor.

"Well, that's good, Lennox. I'm, uh, I'm really happy for you," she said in a flat voice.

He briefly broke the awkward conversation and looked around his boss' cramped office—at the old-fashioned beat-up gray metal file cabinets, and a half empty bottle of booze near a dead plant. After a deep breath, he decided to take his chance.

"Just to catch you up on a few things in my life, I also decided—"

"Lennox, this isn't a good time for a chit chat. It's late. Maybe call me later in the week?" The words rang fallacious, devoid of feeling. This was no true invitation, just something to toss to a starving dog, so one could make it past the mutt in peace. He took a deep breath and looked down at the floor. His leather Burberry dress shoes looked back up at him.

"…Why do you hate me, Silva?"

He heard what sounded like her shuffling about in the

bed, perhaps tossing sheets aside, then he heard her husband mumbling words he couldn't quite understand.

"No, everything is fine, Tony. It's Lennox... No, he's not... Okay... I'll take it out here. Go back to sleep." He heard her walking in what sounded like slippers. A door opened, then closed. "Okay." She yawned. "I was waking Tony up so I left my bedroom. Headin' to the living room. About what you said... Lennox, I don't hate you, okay? I could never hate you. It's just that—"

"Well, Silva, from where we come from, our household with our mama, love is an action word. Actions tell me how somebody feels. Not words."

"I... I don't want to argue with you," she said in a whispered—almost pleading—tone. "It's just that you changed a lot when Mom died, Len, and you didn't listen to anybody. You were so... so angry! So rude. Closed off. You lashed out at me. At Dad. At everyone."

"That was years ago. We were still talkin' a bit after all of that."

"Yeah, we were still talkin', Lennox, but I never forgot your behavior. It scared me. I never got an apology, and when you accused me of being weak like Dad, that was the final straw for me. I had to cut you loose."

The office smelled of liquor and old-fashioned cologne. He inhaled the odor while he mulled what she said, playing those old conversations back in his mind. He vaguely recalled saying such a thing to her, and though it wasn't nice, the comment had merit. Regardless, it was now more than obvious he'd hurt her, and he wanted to make things right.

"You never told me you felt that way… you never gave me a chance to have this conversation."

"Because I know you, Len. You'd just defend what you said. Double down on it. You're stubborn, and you were… mean. I know it sounds a little babyish, and maybe I'm too damn sensitive, but I had never experienced that from you. I didn't want to experience it again."

"First, I want to apologize to you for that. I mean it, Silva. We had a pretty bad argument the last time we spoke, and a lot of things were said out of anger. I said you were weak because you chose Grandpa's money and prestige over what Mama taught us about life, and about *him*. I was angry with you because it was like all of that went out the window when she died. It was like you were his favorite little granddaughter, and you didn't want anything to change that."

"Mama tried to keep me away from Grandpa, and I resented her for it. I didn't see the mean old man you and she painted him out to be, Lennox, and I can't vouch or cosign for something I did not experience!"

"Silva, listen to me. We're having this talk, so let's air it all out. It's long overdue. I would've never said you were weak if you did all of that but we still stayed close. You instead allowed Grandpa to slander my name and lie on me. He turned us against one another, and he used you to do it because you were the most susceptible to his manipulation."

"Len, not this again. Grandpa didn't turn me against you."

"Yes. He. Did. If he had never gotten in your ear, we

wouldn't even be havin' this conversation right now, and all this time wouldn't have passed with you ignoring my calls, ignoring me when I stopped by your house to speak to you in person, and then you sending me a long ass, awful text message tellin' me to basically fuck off and go to hell. Yeah, you share some of the blame because you actually fell for it, but he got the ball rollin'."

"Nonsense. He opened my eyes, Lennox. He told me what you did!"

"Oh, really? Well, did he tell ya how I told him that he was using and abusing our father to the point that Dad gets piss drunk far too often? Dad's a functional drunk now! Had to hide his grief over Mama and drown his sorrows in a bottle. Did the old man tell ya how he threatened my life?! Whatever it is that you think I've done, Silva, it's a walk in the park compared to the shit Grandpa has either orchestrated or carried out with his own two hands!"

"Grandpa would never hurt you and you know it! He—"

"Listen to yourself! Think about me, the *real* me, and who I am! Yes, I was an asshole after Mama died. I own that! But you know my fuckin' heart, Silva! You know that wasn't the person I wanted to be, I was going through some things and it became too much. I was too young for that kind of pressure. Some of that pressure came from the old man. He wanted me to be an enforcer. A score settler—to run the revenge show! Do you have any idea what that is and what it would entail?"

"He'd never do that to you! Grandpa is—"

"A MOTHERFUCKIN' DEMON WHO HATED OUR MOTHER! He's toxic! You don't know him! Don't you remember what Mama said? She said he was dangerous, Silva… Why can't you believe that?"

"Mama said that, but she was stubborn, like you, and she was paranoid, Len. Do I think Grandpa is perfect and was a great guy to her? Of course not, but I can't deny how good he's treated me my entire life! Because of him, I am runnin' a successful furniture design business. No loan was needed." He knew that was a little dig at his good news, but he let it go. "He gave me the investment money. Tony has the awesome job he has in real estate because Grandpa pulled some strings. I'm grateful, and there's nothin' wrong with that!"

"When Satan gives us a gift that will cost us our sanity and soul, should we be grateful for that, too?" He heard her suck her teeth and imagined her rolling her eyes. "Anyone who gets in Grandpa's way is bulldozed over. Shot in the head. Tied up and tortured. Set up and sent to prison for a crime they didn't commit. House burned down to the ground. Do something to piss off old man Wilde? Boom! Kiss your life goodbye. HE. HURTS. PEOPLE!"

"And so did you!"

He swallowed, shut his eyes, and rested his forehead against the closed door. Placing his hand on the smooth wood, he waited for the other shoe to drop.

"He told me about you doing those… those things!" she spat.

"What *things*?"

"Contract kills!" she whispered. "My brother is a murderer! How *dare* you sit on a high horse!"

He rolled in the silence, his heart galloping to the point

of pain. He stood straight and sighed.

"It's complicated, Silva."

"No, it's quite clear, big brother. You killed people for money. How *could* you?!" Her tone was rough with angst. "I would expect that from some people in our family, Len, but not you... not you. Grandpa tried to help you out of that mess because I also know Daddy begged Grandpa to help keep you outta prison, and it worked. Grandpa put up the money and advocated for you, and now you betray him by not only talking badly about him, spreading lies and blaming him for all of your problems, but you didn't even give him a chance! All he wanted you to do was help with his security company."

He burst out laughing. "You can't be serious. That's like Hitler sayin' he didn't mean any harm, and he just wanted a few Jews to teach him how to make a matzo ball soup." He started laughing all over again, not believing his damn ears.

"Oh, is this funny to you? Well, it's not funny to *me,* and I'm dead serious. The dead part you seem to know a lot about. He showed me the proof of your dirty deeds. The police had suspected you, and they were going to charge you with these crimes! They talked to Dad, who called Grandpa in a panic. Grandpa stepped in and saved the day, but the fact that you could do that... the fact that you could raise a gun and kill someone... *many* people... Oh my God, you're a monster... You had been so loving and caring when we were growin' up. You changed. People's mothers die every day, and they don't turn around and become killers. You broke my heart, Lennox."

She was crying now.

He grabbed his forehead and massaged it. As this was transpiring, he saw a text flash across his phone from Nadia that simply read:

*Had an eventful evening. Bittersweet*

*Sorry I couldn't call you back. I love you*

*See you at my place in a little bit*

"Silva, I hear what you're saying. There's a lot you don't know or comprehend. It would take a long time to break it all down, but I'm going to address a couple of things right now, so that you have a better understanding because I can't just let you say these things, then hang up."

"Don't waste your breath. It won't change anything."

"You need to hear the information I have to share before you determine that. You believed Grandpa with no pushback, didn't you? Didn't challenge him. Didn't ask no questions. His words were bond, right? Yeah… I thought so. Now, the least you can do is give me the same damn courtesy."

"Fine, Lennox, but just know that I find what you did unforgivable."

"And I find the fact that you turned on me so quick is almost unforgivable, too. Now you listen here, and you listen good. I don't have a lot of time right now. Also, you're tired, and from the sound of things, highly misinformed." She sighed. "I made a lotta bad choices after Mama died. I was hurtin'. You were hurtin'. Dad was hurtin'. Dad told me while I was tryna finish my classes that money was tight. He didn't tell me right away why. It didn't make any sense, but I was determined to finish that business degree. That meant I needed some money, and fast. Since Dad didn't tell us why money was tight, I did some diggin' and found out. Now I had two more reasons to get cash, Silva.

"Dad needed the dough. Come to find out, Grandpa and he had gotten into it right after Mama died. Dad blew up on him big time, said he disrespected Mama their entire marriage, and he'd never forgive him. Grandpa cut him off 'cause our father, for once in his life, stood up to him. Told him the truth. Grief had brought it on, Silva. Dad had lost—"

"The love of his life."

"That's right. We were living in that big fancy mansion, all the cars, expensive clothes and shit. Dad got fired, but those bills were still rollin' in. I made a stupid decision to solve our problems. I got my hands on some fast, big money, doin' the devil's work. I admit that. I did it to help myself, you, and our father. The opportunity seemed to show up out of the blue, and right when I needed. A lot of the savings were gone because the bills were so damn high. Come to find out, too, Daddy was helpin' others out as well, Silva. A lotta people relied on his assistance. He was generous and charitable, but it cost him a lot of the money that he had in reserves."

*I figure in some strange way, Daddy and Mama giving to all of those charities made him feel better about workin' for such a horrible person: his own father.*

"So, I stepped up to the plate, Silva. To this day, Dad doesn't know *I* was the one payin' the mortgage." He pointed into his chest. "He thought it was Grandpa."

"Oh… well I'm sure Grandpa corrected him and—"

"No, Grandpa didn't correct his assumption. I know because when I told Dad after the cops came nosing around about my extracurricular activities, I then had to explain to him what I'd been doing, and why. That's what got them talkin' again—and then they mended their relationship and Dad was his accountant all over again… back under his thumb. All for greed. Did you even once, Silva, stop and think about why the police were talkin' to Dad?"

She cleared her throat. "Well, he's the father of a suspected murderer, and you still lived at home, so—"

"No. I was an adult. Grown. They came to him before they even came to *me*. He wasn't my guardian. No interview. No ride down to the police station. Because they knew what family we come from, Silva! Cops get paid peanuts for the jobs they do! They wanted Daddy to give them some cash so they could make this shit all go away. It was blackmail! Besides, Grandpa has a reputation to uphold, right? He wants to be big time and come across as some messiah. Swoopin' in to save the day. Dad didn't have the money, and he didn't want me to go to prison partially on account of me tryna help *him* out. The guilt would've eaten him alive. So, he went runnin' to his daddy."

"I don't get this. I can't understand this!"

"You *can* understand it. You just don't want to, Silva. Grandpa doesn't want me to help with his security company. He wants me to do *exactly* what you called me a monster for doing, only on his command this time around. He's made several threats to get me to fall in line. He said if I don't work for him, he's gonna expose that Mama worked as an escort before she met our father. He's going to tell her family, our grandparents back in Lebanon, and you know what that'll do. Destroy them." He heard what sounded like a cork popping. Then liquid pouring into a glass. "I'm going to send you a copy of the letter Grandpa gave me when I hang up from this call with you, so you can see and read it for yourself. I'm *not* makin' this shit up, Silva."

"But didn't Grandpa *still* help you? I mean, let's say all of this is true. He didn't have to." Her voice quivered, as if hanging by a thread.

"Grandpa didn't help me out of the kindness of his heart, Silva. He did it so I would owe him. Something to wave over my head. And all that so-called help? He threatened to undo it… said he'd call some folks and have those murder cases reopened, and I'd be pinned to them. The same money that paid 'em to be quiet is the same money that could pay to make them take me down. Knowing Grandpa, he'd even have some crimes I had nothin' to do with pinned on me, too. So yes, he told *part* of the truth, Silva. A rich guy I went to school with, and who knew what family I came from, propositioned me. An offer to make some money. Initially I turned him down, but a few weeks later, I approached him and asked if the offer still stood. I did it."

She sobbed in a quiet whimper.

"I used that money to keep us in that fuckin' house that you loved so much, to go to college so I could take some business courses to fulfill my dreams, and the rest of the money went to pay off all of Mama's hospital bills and Dad's debts. I didn't have hardly a dime afterwards, but I was okay with that. Dad was back on his feet, but because I had rejected Grandpa yet again, I was kicked out of my own house. You thought I just moved out, but I didn't. Grandpa made him do that to me. Instead of groveling though, I got a job and lived my life on my own terms. That's why I was workin' at that hole in the wall restaurant, makin' barely minimum wage. I needed to take care of myself, *without* Dad's blood money."

"This… this is so horrible! I don't know who's tellin' the truth and who's lying, Lennox."

"Think about the timeline, Silva. Think about everything I shared with you tonight, and you will see that I'm tellin' the truth. I never wanted it to come down to this. I never wanted to hurt you, for you to know, but since Grandpa opened that floodgate, I'm going to tell you the ENTIRE story, and not just the bit that makes me look good, the way Grandpa handles delivering information. He's extorting me. He's blackmailing me. He's interfering in my life! He now has someone following me around. Not every day, not consistently. But I know what I feel, and I know what I saw. He's called our mother a whore to my face!" Silva wept louder now. "He never said it in front of you. He was careful, but he said it to me and Dad plenty of times.

"He's tried numerous times to ruin my aspirations of runnin' my own fitness center, like tryna keep me broke, using scare tactics and the like. You know that's always been my dream, since I was like fourteen years old. He even interfered with financing a few years ago when I tried to open one up, so I had to use a foreign bank this time and do everything secretly, without telling a damn soul. I'm tellin' you right now, Silva, not because I trust you—I don't completely anymore, and I'm sure the feeling is mutual— but at this point if it gets back to Grandpa that I've got what I need to get started, I'm ready for him."

Even in the heat of anger, he felt an overwhelming sense of calm come over him.

"I am tired of his shit. He has destroyed our friendship. He has weakened my and our father's bond, too. He's like a virus, starving all the good cells and feeding the bad ones. This isn't just about me workin for him, Silva. It's about control. Because I said no. I stood up to him. Do you *really* think someone like Grandpa can't get someone even better for whatever fucked up position he wants to use me for? Just think about that! He *wants* me because I don't *need* him! He's just using you! You're a pawn in this game, something he can rub in my face. He knows it hurts me that you wouldn't speak to me, just as he'd planned. And he knows that I blame him for it. He wants *all* the credit and accolades for destroying our nuclear family."

"I don't know what to say. I feel like I'm trapped in a bad dream… a really bad nightmare."

"Well, imagine that nightmare being my true reality. Because it is. You *know* me, Silva. I've done some really messed up shit, I'll admit to that, and I was wrong for how I treated you after Mama died, but we all grieve differently, and sometimes grief ain't fair. It ain't pretty. I'm tryna make an amends with you because I love and value you as a person who means the world to me. What Grandpa told you about me was partially true. He failed to give you the reasons why, and that should be something that just doesn't sit well with you. He took what he told you out of context. On purpose. I would *never* lie to you about this, girl." She blew her nose, and he could tell her tears and pain were becoming more intense. "You and I have been through a lot together, baby sister.

"Losing our mother was catastrophic," he sat down at the messy desk as he felt a bit lightheaded, "but we held onto one another. I miss... I miss my friend." She started sobbing loud and clear. "Look, I, uh... I took enough of your time and I'm at work, so I gotta go." He blinked back his emotions. "I'll be showing you the letter Grandpa sent me, where he details the ultimatum of a lifetime.

"You can say it's fake or I made it up, Silva, but just ask some of our cousins that Grandpa had his eye on if they got somethin' similar. They did. Call Kage, okay? He knows the specific details of my situation. He'd have no reason to lie on my behalf. It doesn't help him to lie about this for me, in any shape, form, or fashion." She didn't respond, but he could hear her breathing. "I'll... I'll call you back later sometime. Despite everything, I love you, Silva. More than you'll ever know."

With that, he quickly disconnected the call. More loud music thumped all around him. His mind spun with the unpleasant memories and dug up the dusty recollections of bad dreams that used to haunt him as a child. He sat there and took several deep breaths, then went to his photos on his phone and grabbed the scanned letter he'd saved, the one Grandpa had drafted, then texted it to her. There was no guarantee Silva would be convinced that his character had been framed, his reputation assassinated, and she'd been used due to her naivety, as well as their closeness, but he had to tell the truth. The truth was always better than a lie, and he had faith that it would prevail.

Getting on his feet, he texted Nadia back:

*I love you. I'll see you soon.*

He slid his phone back in his pocket and opened the office door, leaving the stuffy room and entering into the cool corridor. It was a long walk down that darkened hallway, him just alone with his thoughts before his entire body was glowing with flickering lights, his ears drowning in loud chatter and boisterous laughter from the patrons. He reached the main dance area and stood back by the bar, merging back with society. Crossing his arms, he scanned all the people dancing and having a good ass time. It was interesting how people benefited from others' hard work, folks behind the scenes, but these people having a good time rarely seemed to take into account what was done to ensure it.

There were construction workers who were often underpaid, at times risking their lives to build the structure these people danced and chased ass in. They didn't consider or ask themselves: who was keeping the lights on? Paying the celebrity DJ who'd spent a long time perfecting his craft. Who was making the wine for them to devour? Months, sometimes years, would be spent aging it to perfection all for them to slurp it down with little to no deliberation. It was hard work for the guys behind the scenes…

Like the men and women in small offices who had desks covered in overdue bills and unpaid bar tabs because they refused to cut any staff. The top dog was often once the underdog… Someone had to take the heat and hide the secrets. Someone had to do the contract kills to keep the lights on in the big house, the little sister in oblivious bliss, and the inner rage at bay… Someone had to do the heavy lifting and the dirty work. Someone had to get down low and claw at the ground. Someone had to be the Top Dog and dig into the cool soil, burrowing deep, digging a huge hole, a perfect hiding place for the dead bodies of life's mishaps.

A place to conceal a father's sins and weaknesses, cover the dark shadows with light to protect a mother's secrets and shame. A place was needed to bury the dirty bones of the wicked… All so everyone else could bask in the sun, live a peaceful life, and have a good ol' unaware time, never knowing about the monster under the bed and the boogeyman in the closet. Someone had to do it, and that someone would do it all over again if it was guaranteed that his family would be at peace. *After all, that's what a top dog does.*

*HE PROTECTS. SUPPLIES LOYALTY. PROVIDES UNCONDITIONAL LOVE. Even if it means no one ever sees him, acknowledges him, or says, 'Thank you.' He doesn't do it for praise. He does it for his master: Love.*

# CHAPTER TWENTY-THREE

## *Brown Sugar*

IT BEGAN TO rain before she could get home. Nadia pulled into the parking lot of her apartment building and debated on just how to tell Lennox about yet another man that had attempted to do her harm. Only this time, it was worse. *Much* worse. This was his own flesh and blood. There was no way that Lennox wouldn't be compelled to act.

She wasn't sure she could muster the words. How much more could Lennox take before he cracked? This would certainly make him lose his composure—he was a mere step away from diving off the cliff. *First it was my dumbass ex-boyfriend threatening me through text messages that he'd seen on my phone. Then it was that fool Dice who'd followed me from the club. Now this...*

She sat for a while in that parking lot, gripping the steering wheel and gritting her teeth. Mountains made of adrenaline soared inside her, and her anxiety had sprinted so high during the shower altercation that she now had a pounding headache and was on the verge of an anxiety attack.

*If Lennox hears about this, he's going to jail for murder… Period. Point blank. I know he won't be able to control himself. Shake beat that mothafucka's ass, but I know that would be nothin' compared to what Lennox would do. I wonder if this guy or his grandfather contacted him and told him what occurred? I can't imagine them doing so. This was supposed to be on the low-low, and they probably would want to see if I say something first. I can't believe this shit.*

She debated on calling a friend, but thought better of it. She didn't want anyone worrying about her. Besides, the fewer people that knew what happened, the better. After a while, she stepped out of her car, gripping her gun, and walked to her apartment building. Once at her door, she entered and locked the door behind her. She stood there for a long while. She enjoyed the peace and quiet of her place, with only the sound of the central air running.

Making her way to her bedroom, she slipped her duffle bag, Dolly, and purse off her shoulder and set them on the desk. She removed Parton, checked both of their chambers to ensure they were full of murdering kisses, then secured one in her upper nightstand drawer, the other beneath her bed. She had a third smaller pistol that she kept in a cookie jar in the kitchen. Easy access in case something else jumped off before the night was complete. Slipping out of her sneakers, jeans and shirt, she tossed the clothing on the floor, not giving a damn where they landed.

She sat on the bed in the dimly lit room, rubbing her

shoulder. What should have been a nice final act of service had turned into a nightmarish finale. As she replayed the events in her mind, she decided on another shower. She hated that the fucker had been so close to her. She needed to rinse off the grit and grime, along with the memory of the poignant interaction. The water was piping hot and steamed up the bathroom quickly as she listened to soft jazz playing on her cellphone and lathered herself from neck to toe. When she was finished, she quickly rinsed off, brushed her teeth, then slipped into a cool burgundy satin gown with matching robe.

She put out a bottle of red wine on the counter, along with two wine glasses, the latter an old birthday gift from a girlfriend of hers back in Atlanta. From her guest bedroom, she grabbed her laptop and brought it into her bedroom. She set it on a small corner desk and opened it, then paused as Dr. Saint Aknaten's new paperback book that she'd recently purchased online drew her attention. '50 Shades of Blackness – *The Melaninated Queen*.' As she flipped through it, a sentence jumped out at her... '*A friend of mine in the psychology research department once said, 'Saint, women are like guns. They don't blast you unless triggered. Men's recklessness is often the activation. No bullet flies without a cause. It doesn't just jump in the air and soar across the room on its own volition, striking the target. Something from the past or present caused it.*" She quickly closed the book. *Well, that was strange how I landed on that page like that. If I start reading that now, I will never put it down. Let me stay focused.* She turned the computer on and pulled up one of her playlists.

After she turned on some music—'Already knew,' by

Ro James XIX—she went to spritz some Victoria Secret, 'Very Sexy Orchid Eau de Parfum,' behind her ears. At that moment, her doorbell rang.

She practically raced to the door, desperate for his touch, needing to look into his storm-cloud gray eyes that bequeathed her wellbeing with a mere glance. Needing to be held in his big, strapping arms. Needing to feel his fortress of a body all over her. Desiring his soft lips delivering a rough kiss to every inch of her body…

She snatched open the door and his eyes raked her as if she were hot coals…

*Does he know?!*

He burst into the apartment, tossed his overnight bag onto the floor, slammed the door and locked it, and picked her up in his arms, spinning her around as he flattened her lips in a searing kiss. The smoldering flame in his eyes startled her for it was unrelenting, even in the midst of his lavish affections.

"I hope you don't have on any panties under that lingerie… I'm just gonna rip 'em off."

The pit of her stomach tingled with desire as he cradled her close, walking her back to her bedroom with slow but steady steps. Each step he took made her jostle in his grasp. He was a big giant, his body like steel against her silky skin.

Laying her horizontally across her bed, he stood before her and began unbuttoning his black dress shirt, his eyes never leaving hers. She sat up, hurriedly removed her robe and tossed it aside, then gathered the soft fabric of her gown and discarded that, too. A lurch of excitement surged within her when he was fully undressed. Hovering over her body, he stood with his pecs jumping and his necklace swinging—an onyx canine tooth hanging from a black and silver rope chain.

He dropped on all fours, boxing her in from all sides. She was in a beautiful prison cell—the ceiling, his face, and the bars, his arms and legs. She felt like his favorite prey, and prayed that tonight she'd get licked and sticked. Taught a firm, hard lesson.

In awe, she looked up at one of God's most supreme creations, her heart pitter pattering within her and her pussy already seasoned to perfection with anticipatory juices. She reached up and stroked his hard jaw. His short black beard felt good against her fingertips. He leaned into her touch like a wounded animal in need of love and attention. For a split second, he was meek and mild. For a split second, he was vulnerable. He took her hand, kissed the inside of her palm, then flattened her against the bed, pressing all of his weight against her body. A rush of heat from his harsh breathing bathed the side of her neck as Ro James belted, 'Take It All.'

"You smell so good, baby." A deep inhale. A loud exhale. "Why's your heart beatin' so fast?" He fashioned the words around a deep chuckle as he ran his hand along her bare breasts.

A flash of the shower... the gun on the fucker's hip... the hellish look in his icy blue demonic eyes. Her eyes, straining in the semi darkness of the shower room... her pistol pointing to an adversary's skull... the drops of water getting louder as they splashed onto the tiled floor... the shower spigot trickling. Plip and plop. The rain... the

RAIN... A storm of misery... *I hate the rain...* MORE FUCKING WATER.

Water was trauma... wetness... drowning in the past... generational curses wrapped tightly around abusive men who lied, gaslit, beat, raped and occasionally tried to kill their women... A triggered reminder of what *was* and what would be... a black Sunday for a harsh baptism...

*Tighten the fuck up, girl. Get yo' shit together. Don't tell him right now!* She was thinking the words, but could hear them being said in her mother's voice. *I'd risk him being sent to prison for killin' someone if I say it now. I'd lose him. He won't be able to stand it! You know this man so well, don't risk it. You know how he operates. He has to think this through and if he flies off the handle tonight, the plan will be null and void.*

*I don't care how much therapy and introspection Lennox has had. Lennox is STILL a WILDE. It's in his blood to be a terror out in these streets. Wilde men are ruthless. These men go off! And his family has the money to cover their dirty tracks. No, you be quiet and hold it close to your heart. I'm going to tell him, just not this second. Wait until a little time has passed—don't cooler heads usually prevail?*

She shook the thoughts from her mind and wrapped herself around her man.

"My heart is beating fast because I'm just happy to see you is all, so glad that you're here." It wasn't a lie—she was truly happy he was there, with her. More than he would ever know.

He dispensed wet, needy kisses all along her collar bones, then trailed them up her chin, her lips. The taste of peppermint on his breath made her mouth tingle. A big hand skated beneath her back, and up past her shoulders. Long, wide fingers sprawled against her scalp as he gripped the back of her head and brought her closer as his tongue dove deeper into her mouth. Her heart hammered in her ears when his other hand wedged between her thighs, forcing them farther apart with a rough shove.

"I should've brought a priest and an extra pillow with me." His deep, rumbling voice so close to her ear made her whole body tremble.

"Why's that?"

" 'Cause I'mma make sure that your screams wake the dead, and I put your pussy to sleep."

Her senses leapt to life.

He swept his fingers in a fluttery motion against her pussy, soft strokes that became faster with each second, building carnal momentum.

"I was worried about you tonight." Her stomach clenched at his words. His eyes darkened. The grip around the back of her head seemed suddenly tighter. He cocked his head to the right and peered into her eyes, as if trying to look inside of her very soul. Licking his thumb, he ran the wet pad of flesh against her clit in slow, torturous circles. "You always let me know when you're leaving work. Why was tonight different?"

"There was a lot going on." She swallowed. Careful not to lie… careful not to give the whole truth, either. "Bittersweet ending. Like I said in my text to you tonight. Some of those people I'll never see again. That's for the best I suppose but some of 'em I'll miss like Lydia, Sunshine, Danielle, Shack, just to name a few."

He kissed her forehead, the sweetest, tenderest gesture. She fought a wave of guilt.

"Are you happy you quit dancin' and OnlyFans, or do you have regrets?"

"Yeah, I'm glad to be done with it. It was a big part of my life though, so it'll take a second or two to adjust to just bein' a full-time student." He nodded in understanding. "I'm excited about school and my future with you." She mustered a smile.

His gaze softened, and he pressed his lips to hers. His fingers moved faster against her soaking wet love. A bit harder, too. Administering pressure against her neck, he sucked the side of her throat then drifted lower and layered her shoulder with sensual kisses.

Her body heated as he worked his way down her sensitive canvas, his taut tongue leading the way, leaving a slick trail past her cleavage and along her stomach. When he got to her garden, he wrapped his hard, muscular arms around her legs and pulled her so her ass pressed against his chest. He buried his face in her wet pussy, devouring her like a ravenous animal. Smacking, licking, and sucking his way to her glory.

She bucked and writhed against his long tongue and soft lips, feeling the warmth from his mouth and nose—a rhythmic burst of heat like that from a raging bull.

"Mmmmm, baby, you taste amazing. I could eat your pussy with no breaks for days…"

His subdued voice and the sexy words he uttered sent her even more over the edge. His tongue sprang up and down the creases of her slick folds, slow and easy as if he were trying to paint the perfect picture. She melted into his touch until she felt that special feeling creeping through her body and surrounding her love. Gripping the sheets with both hands, she stirred against his mouth that eagerly drank from her.

At last, she came in short bursts, her body relaxing then stiffening as she called out his name. Through groggy eyes, she looked up at him while her orgasm subsided, leaving her a satisfied, wet, beautiful mess. Light smoldered in his gold-flecked gray eyes. Traces of moonlight illuminated against half of his face, competing with the flickering candles and blue nightlight. A remix of Glorilla's, 'Yea Glo!' started to play, a smooth jazz version mixed with Twista's, 'So Sexy.'

He bit his lower lip in such a sexy way, it made her shudder.

Aftershocks.

He slowly slipped his finger inside of her and curled it, making a come-hither motion between her walls. Her eyes rolled as he scratched that itch, jolting when he slipped another finger inside her ass. He moved them both in rhythm, slow and easy, until she broke into a full body shiver, her orgasm a sensation of her floating out of her body.

When she relaxed, he laid her down against her pillows, wrapped her up in his arms, and kissed her with the tenderness of a flower petal falling to the ground. She saw her reflection in his eyes, and her heart pounded in thundering, erratic beats. He gently grabbed a few strands of her hair and wrapped them around his finger, playing with them as a smile slowly grew across his face.

"I got some good news tonight, baby." He kissed along her neck then looked back into her eyes.

"Really? What? Tell me."

"I got the loan. I'm buyin' that old building. The car dealership. Going to knock down a wall. Make it bigger. Big plans. I'm finally gettin' my fitness center."

She pushed back a wayward strand of his dark hair and looked into his beautiful eyes. "Of course you did! I'm so happy for you, baby. We'll have to celebrate soon."

Taking her hand, he brought her fingers to his lips and kissed them.

"I've renewed my certifications. Things are movin' forward." He nodded, for that was an obvious weight off his shoulders. "Things are finally lookin' up."

He ran his hand slowly against her breasts, then bent down and kissed her left nipple. She stared at the ceiling, her heart pounding with excitement on his behalf. Shifting, her pussy pulsed as he drew on her nipple and sucked it slow and hard, bringing her back into the moment.

"Shit... yeessss... Baby, you know I like it when you do it like that... ahhhh... Len, don't stop..." She grinded her hips against him as he went to the other breast, giving the same tender loving care. Running her fingers through his hair, she welcomed his touch. He massaged one breast while sucking on the other then changed, loving on them equally.

"...I used to fantasize about bein' with you like this, Nadia. I used... I used to look at you sometimes in the restaurant... in your little pink and white skirt and crop top, your hair in a ponytail, and I would imagine gettin' you in that back room where we kept the supplies. I would think about me layin' you down on those huge industrial-sized bags of brown sugar, taking your clothes off, one piece at a time, while that old country music played, that register rung up, and that coffee percolated... and I could imagine those customers talkin'... eatin'... drinkin' out front... and us tucked away from them, while I had you down on that concrete floor, your long, pretty, legs spread wide open for me...

"And I'd think about how I'd get on top of you... kiss you... push my dick deep inside of you, honey... and cover your mouth to keep you from screamin'..." Her breathing became sporadic the more he spoke. "I'd put my hand over your mouth tighter 'cause you'd be hollerin'... stoppin' you from gettin' us busted, and I would keep on... movin' faster and faster... and faster..." Len was breathing harder, too... "...my nuts slapping against your wet, fat pussy lips each time I'd shove my dick in and out of your drippin', warm, soft, pretty refuge... and you'd hold onto me tight, baby... so tight, your body sliding up and down along that floor as I fucked you real hard and real good, darlin'. But then, somethin' would happen. We'd hear our boss callin' for us, asking people where we were... but we wouldn't stop. I'd keep on holding you, fucking you, and you'd keep wanting it... taking it... I wouldn't let you go until you came... Determined to make you feel good all over... And you'd cum for me, baby. You'd shake, just like you do for real. You'd scream so loud but it would be muffled from my hand still on your mouth... I'd look down and see pussy juice all over my dick… drippin' on some of the brown sugar bags… sticky with your nectar… and then, it would be my turn to cum.

"You'd let me cum inside of you, baby. I'd climax so hard inside of you, honey, I'd have to bite my bottom lip to keep from yellin' 'cause it felt so damn good… I'd fill that tight, sweet, pussy of yours with my hot cum…And then we'd lie there. Kissin'. Promisin' each other we'd always be together no matter what…"

"That was your fantasy?"

"It sure was. I used to have that fantasy of us a lot, and I never forgot it. I prayed one day it would come true. It came true alright, and the first time I slid inside of you, it was even *better* than my fantasy, baby. Each time we make love, it blows my mind. My fantasy is no longer *just* pretend. You're my dream girl. And now, you're a dream come true."

Pure joy bubbled within her.

*Whatever I did to deserve this man, God, thank you, thank you, thank you…*

"I love you, Len. I see you had a real dirty mind back then." She smiled.

"I 'spose so, but I loved you, girl." His gaze turned real serious. "It was more than just a sexual fantasy. I wanted you to be my girl. At the time you didn't seem to realize just how beautiful, funny, and smart you were. But I did. I saw it. That's why I would call you brown sugar sometimes at work back then."

She'd forgotten all about that. *That's right. He did.*

"You'd laugh and think it was somethin' racial. A silly

pet name. You'd call me 'White boy,' as a response, and I'd laugh, too. But naw, baby… that's not why I called you brown sugar. It was because of *this*… because I wanted to make love to you in the pantry of the Red Rooster. The place where you cried the most—by the flour and brown sugar. I wanted to make you feel beautiful, and give you happiness in your body and soul, the same place where you expressed so much pain in your heart. I wanted to fill that hole inside of you. Literally and figuratively. I wanted to be your *some*thing because you were *every*thing to me…"

She came beneath him, completely taken off guard by her unexpected orgasm, created by his confessions and sexy words. Her back arched as he breathed close to her ear. Janelle Monáe's, 'I Like That' started to play. Moisture dripped from her pussy, trickling down onto the bed as she writhed and rose against his chest, her body a fleshy roller coaster made for only one man to ride. He lay against her, his heavy frame a fort protecting the queen. They stayed like that for a long while, his heart beating against hers.

"I ain't never been in love like this before, Lennox." She ran her fingers along the side of his neck. "Never fell so hard. So fast. So deep."

"It ain't fast if we started fallin' ten years ago."

"You're right." She enveloped his earlobe in her mouth and sucked on it softly. Moments later, she maneuvered from beneath him, crawled off the bed, and turned up the music. Kelly Rowland ft. Lil Wayne's, 'ICE' serenaded them. "I've got one more dance to perform tonight. It's time for you to have a VIP private show, baby."

He slowly sat up, a slick grin on his face as he slipped

his arm behind his head and leaned against the headboard. She began to rock her hips from left to right, slow and easy, dancing to the beat of the music, swaying her body as he eyed her, the sheets bunched around his waist, and one of his feet sticking out from the bottom. She danced around the room, bending at the waist, turning away and shaking her ass at him. Twerking so fast, every cell in her body felt as if it were being shaken up. He clapped and laughed, then whistled, yelling dirty, sexy things, encouraging her to continue.

"…I wanna see *more* of that! Spread that pussy open for me, baby!" He dog whistled.

When she drew close enough to the bed again, he lurched towards her so fast, she jumped. She burst out laughing as he hopped out the bed and grabbed her, lifting her from the floor with the greatest ease. She lay a slow kiss on his lips as he held her to him while walking her over to the wall.

"You know how to do a handstand?"

"Of course I do."

"Do it." She threw him a curious glance. "Come on. Do it right where I'm pointing at the floor." He pointed downward.

She grimaced, not certain what he was up to, but decided to comply. She did a handstand close to the wall. He circled her real slow, and she watched his long, fat dick jump as he sized her up, then leaned against the wall. Just as she was getting ready to ask what this was about, he leaned forward, bent at his knees, situating himself just so, then grabbed her ankles and pushed his dick inside her.

"Oh my God…" Pressured warmth filled her body and her pelvic muscles began contracting.

"Just relax, baby," he spoke softly. "You can take it easy. I'm holding you up. You don't have to balance yourself anymore." He plunged in and out of her.

The floor was now her ceiling. He dove deeper inside of her. Her eyes fluttered as the blood rushed to her head and her body rocked with his slow thrusts. Her pussy felt so full. Her world was upside down, but her heart was right side up.

"That feel good, baby?" He was driving her crazy.

"Damn it, yes…"

He sped up, tightening his grip around her ankles. Miguel's, 'Sure Thing' serenaded them this time. She rotated her hips, meeting his thrusts, shuddering when his hands drifted to her ass, pushing her into his plunges. Holding her tightly to his body. She felt him practically in her stomach. In her heart. In her mind. Taking over her soul.

"Grab me, baby," he commanded as he wrapped his arms hard around her legs and squeezed, lifting her so she dangled a few inches from the floor with his dick still inside of her, fucking faster and harder. She flailed for a second then wrapped her arms around his calves and held on tight. Her body felt light and airy as he took control. She looked up and watched him going in and out of her, banging into her pussy with each pass.

"I LOVE YOU SO FUCKIN' MUCH, NADIA! FUCK! UHHH!!!"

She grew excited for he was clearly at the edge of explosion. She screamed when he somehow flipped her back right side up. She wrapped her arms around his neck and her legs around his waist. He walked her back to the bed, threw her down onto her back, and slid nice and easy back inside of her within seconds.

Holding her down, he began to rotate his hips from left to right, then in circles, driving her mad. His pelvis bumped into her clit, over and over. His hands at her lower back, he propelled her into his menacing plunges. Her joyous screams overlapped his raucous grunts and groans. Sweat broke all over their bodies, making the tremendous fucking slippery and soaking wet. He dripped on her breasts, his hair a sopping mess. Loud clapping echoed alongside the beat of the music as his balls slapped against her swollen pussy lips.

"LENNOX, OH GOD! OH GOD! OH GOD!" He was so damn deep, it was like he was committing a beautiful murder: pussy homicide. She pushed her palms against his rocking pelvis, trying to control his pace and depth, but he slapped her hands away and pinned both of her wrists to the bed. That only turned her on more…

"Stop it! You're a big girl, you can take it! TAKE THAT DICK!"

She shivered and came again, this time harder than the last. Each time he dove inside of her, he managed to thrust at that perfect angle and hit her G-spot. The man fucked like he was a professional gigolo, and she simply couldn't get enough.

His body began to spasm, his complexion deepened, the vein along his forehead protruded, and she braced herself. A deep, guttural groan emerged from him, so poignant its echo flowed through her body. His hips bucked and jerked hard as he climaxed, shooting his warm semen within her. Her pussy pulsed and squeezed his nature tight as his long, thick rod throbbed within her. His high plateaued. He swallowed hard. Eyes closed. Sweat streaming down his face. One more involuntary spasm of his hips. A small jerk of the thighs. He fell down onto the bed beside her, his legs hanging off the edge.

As they lay side by side, their hands found one another and intertwined. No words were spoken. Only breathing. Rest. Sexy music.

And love.

She glanced over and saw his dick was semi-hard, though he seemed oblivious. She rolled over on top of him, took his cock into her mouth and sucked on it softly. He groaned and gently massaged her head as he fell once more into the pleasure. When he was nice and hard, she climbed on top of him and slid down his rigid shaft. He held her loosely around the hips as Usher's, 'Glu' played its beat for them.

Pivoting up and down, she fought tears as she looked into his eyes. Happy tears. Sad tears, too. He smiled up at her—a slightly forlorn smile, matching her mood. He appeared to be reading her mind. He always seemed to know her next thought, even before she completed it.

His lips partially ajar, he began to thrust upward inside of her at an even pace.

"Something's not right." He seemed to choke out the words. "You're holding back."

"No, I'm pleasing you as much as I can."

"No, baby. Not the sex... this feels fantastic. *You* are fantastic. I'm talking about something being on your mind.

Whatever it is, you don't want to tell me, do you?"

Her pulse quickened, but she kept riding him. Her hands pressed firmly against his chest as she rose up, then came down.

"It's not that I—"

"Shhh…" His brows knitted, he gripped her hips tighter, pumping shallowly within her. "I know whatever you say right now won't be the entire truth. Don't say shit at all if you're not going to give it all to me. I will never be satisfied with just pieces of you, Nadia, or pieces of the truth. Just like the other day when you told me about that motherfucker that followed you home!" His voice got harsher and his thrusts became sharper.

"And look what happened? I told you, and you threatened to kill him, and then you doubled down on that shit later. I don't give a fuck about that guy, but I do care about your sanity, and you stayin' outta trouble!"

"Don't worry about me or that situation." His eyes drew darker. "I want you to come at me correct, or not at all. I want from A to Zebra, not A to Give-a-fuck. If I can't have the whole fuckin' alphabet, just keep it to yourself until you can tell me… only make sure you *do* tell me. I know you, so I am sure you have good reason for not sayin' anything. I'll give you a little time and some grace for whatever it is. But I want to know, and I want to know in a timely manner. Do you understand me?" His voice was deep and timbered, his tone unyielding.

She chewed her upper lip, then nodded. A tear rolled down her cheek. He had a way of bringing her to her knees. Of commanding her to listen. Of not allowing her to run away on the inside.

He reached up and wiped it away.

"Don't cry, sweetheart."

"Okay." Her voice cracked as she sniffed, fighting her emotions.

"You know I'd do anything for you, girl."

"...I know, baby. I love you so much, Lennox... so, so much."

"I know you do, Nadia. You want to protect me, just like I want to protect you. Whatever is going on, the truth always comes out though. It don't have to be tonight, but it's gotta come."

"I know... I know..."

He sat up and leaned against her. Their gazes locked, eye to eye. She kept riding him, and he kept pivoting upwards inside of her until she fell into a million orgasmic pieces, him following close behind her. Crisscrossing his arms around her body, squeezing her to him and kissing her hard, he shuddered as he climaxed. His moans came out hoarse, loud and choppy. Gruff and strained from exploding ecstasy.

They soon gathered under the sheets, and he wrapped his body around hers so damn tight. She held onto him, surrendering, then falling asleep pressed against him. She dreamed of them as they had been ten years prior... at The Red Rooster singing songs off key. That had been the day she realized she was falling in love with her friend. The day love came knocking. She didn't answer the door right away. She answered it years later, perhaps almost too late. Or maybe it wasn't late at all? Maybe, it was right on time...

# CHAPTER TWENTY-FOUR

## *What in the Sam Hill happened?!*

"...YOU'VE GOT TO be shitting me. How could you let this happen? You stupid idiot."

Grandpa grabbed the arms of his lawn chair, clutched the top of his cane, and got to his feet. He stood beneath a gray canopy, listening to Elvis Presley's, 'Burning Love' while dark clouds gathered above his head. A storm was brewing and the air was tinged with the scent of a pending downpour. He tossed his cane across his verandah, and it landed far into the immaculately cut green grass. A white dot in the distance. Sitting in a black lawn chair beside a large stone white lion was the most disappointing spawn of his bloodline to date.

Grandpa peered down at his grandson, Samuel, who now sported slumped shoulders, making him feel nothing short of pure, undiluted disgust. "Why in the hell would you approach her without your gun already up and ready to use if you were going to be so stupid as to flash it?! That was a threat!"

"'Cause she was in the shower. I figured she didn't have one," he answered sheepishly. "I mean, she walked down the hallway butt naked, ya know? Ready to shower. Who would think she'd have a gun in the damn shower, Grandpa?" He sulked.

Sam's clothing was in bad shape, all torn up, and his face was a bruised and bloodied mess. A fleshy canvas in colors of marbled purple and streaks of blue. He'd complained that he could barely lift his right arm over his head and it hurt something awful. It would probably need a cast. Some Goliath type brutes had slammed the guy's limb in his own car door before sendin' him on his way to drive with only one useable hand after the beat down of the century. Sam's thin lips were triple their normal size, reminding Grandpa of an innertube. *He looks like a damn duck. A goofy duck. Donald Duck. Good God...*

"That's not the question I asked you! You had no business flashin' a weapon! I told you to watch out for this cunt, didn't I?" He gritted his teeth and kicked a stone across the ground. It landed in the bird fountain. Plop. "You got her dander up prematurely. I told you to call me before you made a move, but what did you do? Try and be Roy Rogers and save the day! This ain't no episode of Gunsmoke, gotdamn it! No TV show or movie. You were on *her* turf! That bitch is no dummy. She's a shark!"

"I called ya, Grandpa. I called ya and told you that she was in her dressing room. I figured that was enough when you said okay, let 'er come out."

"And I told you that when Dodie pretended to be a

belligerent drunk in there, it would be a good cover for you to sneak in the back where she'd go to get freshened up. She does the same thing each and every time. We had her routine down pat! It was a sure deal! Glen told us they typically have two or three security guards there on any given night. That melee would keep 'em busy tryna throw Dodie out the club. As soon as the commotion broke out, you were to dip in the back. They don't like cameras in there, so we found out the cameras on the outside of the place are real, but the cameras on the inside, with the exception of one pointed towards the bar, are decoys.

"Once Dodie did his part, I said that's when you can make your move, just be sure she was alone or someone would blow the whistle. I showed you the blueprint of the place and everything so you'd know *exactly* where to go, and to follow everything to the letter until she came outta that dressing room. Why?! You were not to say one single gotdamn word to her until you had the go ahead from ME!" He leered at Sam, pointing to himself. He wanted to spit at the dumbass. Stomp him into the ground. Sam was young and kinda stupid, but he'd figured he surely could handle something simple like this. Besides, he was good lookin'. Sluts liked good looking men. Saw them as far more interesting.

Sam blinked hard, then folded within himself like a crab. His eyes watered, and it made Grandpa sick to his stomach.

"I thought it would be easier than it was."

"Ain't nothin' easy about this lady, Sam, except for the way she gives up her pussy. This woman was at a gun show in Atlanta a few years back, on video, shootin' two Colt

M1911s at the same gotdamn time, then spinnin' them revolvers around her fingers like she was some stuntwoman in an action-thriller flick. Does that sound like a sitting duck to you? This is not some silly little damsel in distress. She's been teaching those whore dance classes too that I told you about, proving she's quite quick and agile. The whore can climb a fuckin' pole faster than a rabid squirrel, and slide down fast like a fireman. I told you to not let her pretty face fool you. She's wild and untamed!"

"But why would Lennox want a wild and untamed woman?"

"Who gives a fuck!" He raised his arms to the sky and shook his fists. "Look, Sam. This bitch is just like Lennox's mama. Some men have a thing for women that remind them of the pussy they came out of." He shrugged. "Some Freud thing, I think. Every man on this planet has somethin' that titillates them about women though, and maybe you're just too young to understand that, but I tell you this much: If a certain woman we find attractive has that 'thing', whatever that 'thing' is, then we want it. And we want *her.* The point is, she's sneaky, like Lennox, and you found that out the hard way. Walked right into her trap.

"Now, because of this complete debacle, Lennox, who is normally fairly easygoing, is going to be thirsty for blood, like the mutt that he is! He's unpredictable from this point forward, and I'd like to thank *you* personally for that. When Lennox is in this crazed mind state, he is treacherous. I've seen it with my own eyes. You can't reason with him. You can't bargain with him. You can't do anything but fight him! I've worked hard to avoid this—to push him yet so far at any given time—but now, the cat is out of the bag."

"Huh? When did you see him like that? I've known him my whole life, Grandpa, and he never came across that way to me. Lennox barely raises his voice."

"That's because you weren't in the fucker's crosshairs, and you have the observation skills of a deaf and blind one thousand-year-old hairless mole!" he huffed. Then he took a deep breath, trying to regain his composure. "Look, Sam… I've seen it a couple times over the years. One time it had to do with the death of his mother. You were too young to witness it. He went on a murdering spree. You've only got one body under your belt. Lennox is in the double digits… You don't know your cousin like you *think* you do."

"A murderin' spree? Lennox? Why?"

"Because he was a mama's boy and he completely lost his fuckin' mind when she kicked the bucket. I saw an opportunity open up because of that…" He reached into his suit pocket and pulled out a cigar, then lit it. "I needed to see if Lennox had the grit I believed he did, Sam. I knew he was strapped for money at the time because I had turned off the currency faucet for his father after we'd had a fallin' out." He hawked a loogie on the ground, then looked out towards his vast backyard. "The whole family was in a bad way after their matriarch perished… that little slutty, know-it-all Muslim bitch. The good doctor…So, I found some punk in one of his little college classes," he stated dismissively. "Told him to solicit Lennox for some dirty work. See if Lennox would take the bait.

"In return, the decoy would get paid nicely. I'd get some

folks out of here who I needed eradicated in the process, too." He shrugged. "Lennox could get some cash and blow off some steam. Be none the wiser that he was workin' for me actually—just through a middleman. Everyone would be happy."

"Did it work? Did the decoy accept the offer?"

"Of course the decoy took the deal. He buddied up with Len and offered him cash for kills. Showed him the money I gave him in advance. He was to act like a rich bigshot. We'd planned it for weeks. And for the record, I told your Uncle Scott that Len didn't need no damn college, anyway!" Smoke eddied from the side of his mouth as he replayed those old tapes in his mind. "It would put silly ideas in his head... like this dumb gymnasium he wants to open. He took business classes for it. Anyway, the point is, all of these bastards want to link up with a Wilde boy, Sam. Getting a decoy is easy, but you never befriend them. So many people want to be our friends. Be around us." Sam nodded in agreement. "If they're broke, they wanna get close to our money. If they're boring, they want to ride our coattails to look big and tough and get some excitement."

"Yeah... yeah... did Lennox do the deal, too?"

"Lennox was depressed and angry. He was sitting in those classrooms feelin' sorry for himself and pissed at the world because his mama was in the grave, and this was even waaaay after her death. He took it real hard. He was easy pickings. He rejected the deal at first, but then, he accepted it. Did it in a heartbeat. I got him at his weakest. He had bloodlust. You could see it in his eyes. I tell you what," he giggled, "I was impressed with Lennox's God-given talents, boy.

"He wasn't a skilled hitman, not by any stretch of the imagination, and yet, he managed to do it so damn easily and without leavin' any evidence behind. Damn… he was so good at it too, Sam. A natural. He could kill with not a care in the world…" His voice trailed as he lamented over the crimes. His heart beat harder and faster when he saw the crime scene photos from the decoy. Lennox is a beast. Too remarkable to pass up.

"This is all about Lennox not taking your offer, Grandpa, but it baffles me because why wouldn't he want to work for you? All of his money problems woulda been solved, and he would've been safe."

"Sam, Lennox has refused to work for me since he was in his teens. I approached him at seventeen to just get the lay of the land – nothin' criminal. He refused. I approached him at nineteen. Learn the business. He refused. I approached him at twenty-one. Get trained for the Zoo. He refused, and so on, and so on. He's got a nasty stubborn streak. He declined politely at first, but then he became more aggressive as I put the heat on him. It was his fucking mother. She poisoned him, turned him against me!"

His voice echoed, reverberating in the outdoors as hot rage coursed within him. "Regardless, in the end I found out what I needed to know. The plan was going well. Of course it wasn't long before his father came runnin' to me after I called the police anonymously and reported Lennox as a suspect in the murders I needed done."

"What? Why would you do that? I thought you wanted those guys killed anyway?"

"I did… Let me explain. My son Scott, Lennox's father, wanted my help to get Lennox off the hook for the crimes he'd committed. In his mind, somehow, the police had found out and were lookin' for a payday to keep quiet, knowing that Lennox was a Wilde. Well, I did in fact use my money and influence to get him off the hook. I hoped Lennox would then be grateful for my generosity, but he wasn't." He sighed. "Things went downhill. He was still tryna finish school, and eventually he picked up a job at some little hole in the wall restaurant. How embarrassing." He tsked.

"What about the decoy? Were you ever worried he'd squeal?"

Grandpa turned to him and chuckled. "You eat and never leave crumbs, boy. The decoy was silenced with a bullet right between the eyes." He gleamed as he pointed to his forehead. "You never allow anyone who isn't family to hold your secrets, Sam. Don't ever forget that. I've only made one exception to that rule, and Jasper is a longtime friend of mine who has proven his loyalty."

He walked back and forth, smelling the freshness of the day, and then glanced up to see the sky filling with streaks of light. "Everything is royally screwed up now, boy. You've helped create the perfect recipe for disaster, and now he's linked up with a bitch just like him. They're a two-headed monster, and I have to deal with the fallout."

"GRANDPA, BUT I—"

You've single-handedly," he eyed the guy's fucked up arm, "created double the trouble. What part of 'don't let your guard down around this trollop' did you not understand?!"

"I'm sorry, Grandpa," Sam looked downright wretched. "What are... what are we gonna do now?"

"There's no '*we*', Sam, and I don't know just yet what *I* am going to do, but I can tell you what I damn sure *shouldn't* have done. I should have never sent an amateur to do a pro's job. This is my fault." Sam hung his head. "Let me think about this." His brain fired from all cylinders as he played with various scenarios. "If that woman told Lennox what happened, and I imagine she did, it's not a matter of *if* he tries to come after me, but *when*. He is not to be allowed anywhere near this property. I'll tell security, and you tell the family. Do you hear me?!"

"Yes, sir."

"Tell everyone to be on alert, but no one is to follow him right now, either. It's too risky." He paced out into the backyard, thunder striking the sky, booming. Racing through the soft, vibrant green grass, he grasped his cane and made his way back to Sam who kept playing with a bag of ice he'd been using on his head and mouth for the past hour.

He slipped his phone out of his pocket and called Jasper.

"Yes?"

"If anyone on this property sees my grandson, Lennox Wilde approaching my estate, I'm to be told immediately!"

"Understood." Jasper ended the call.

He looked up at the sky once again when he felt a raindrop.

"...And Jesus wept..." he whispered. "Sam, dangerous

men aren't always born. Sometimes, they're created. He'll be armed, and he'll arrive intent on hurtin' everyone involved if he shows his face here."

"Okay, I understand what you're saying, but you just said yesterday that Len had turned a new leaf, that he cares about family, and that he didn't—"

"A leopard never changes his spots. He just hides them under the brush! Lennox is a dog, Sam. Do you understand me?! He *pretends* to be obedient and on some 'give peace a chance' crusade, but that's not who he *really* is, deep down. He masquerades as a poodle. He's always wanted to live up to what his mama wanted him to be, but inside he's a ruthless and cruel pit bull who will tear anyone who pisses him off to shreds! By the time you hear him bark, it's too late! Those crime photos are stained on my brain! He went above and beyond the call of duty!

"It was beautiful..." He couldn't help but smile as the rain got a little more intense. "He has a viciousness like many have never seen, but it must be activated. And that takes time. He's a killer to his core." *He's a true Wilde child.* "Why in the hell did you think I wanted him in my Zoo subdivision? Why would I be so insistent if he were just mediocre? He's a devious mama's boy, his only but biggest flaw, but he also happens to be vengeful killer. Go figure.

"Oh, here's a funny story." He chuckled. "He once shot a man in both hands for stealin' money from some old lady. An old lady he barely knew, mind you, so imagine what he'd do for someone he's in love with?" His eyes narrowed on Sam and their gazes hooked. The world was getting smaller... the walls closing in. *He's not going to just let this shit go. And neither am I.*

"I have a question."

Grandpa looked at his grandson and shook his head. He placed his hand on his hip. "What could you possibly wish to say at this point?"

"Wouldn't Lennox have been mad either way?" Sam shrugged, his voice a bit wobbly, as if he were afraid to ask. "I mean, even if your strategy went according to plan, wouldn't he have wanted to get at you because she would have called him, like you said, and broke up with him?"

"I think your mother dropped you on your head as a child, or was drinkin' moonshine during the pregnancy." Sam grimaced and gave a black layered look. "Sam, of course he would have been furious—that was the whole point! But the outcome would have been different, and the ball would have been in *my* court. She would have left him either because she was scared to death of the consequences, not wanting all the drama that comes along with dealin' with a Wilde boy, or didn't want him to get hurt on account of her, and lastly, I thought she might just want the money and didn't give a damn in the first place. Either way, the odds were in my favor, three to one. I would have effectively ended his relationship, but been able to bring her back if he agreed to work for me.

"All I would have had to do is call her, pretend I made a grave mistake, allowed her to keep the money, and perhaps offered more as a peace offering of sorts, and bring them right back together like the two fucked up love birds they are. It also would have reminded him what I'm capable of by taking what was most important to him away within minutes. I already threatened to contact the police regarding his previous crimes, but naturally I wouldn't want to do that because it could put me in jeopardy as well. I am more than willing to expose his mother though—that's still on the table. A card to be played.

"The best-case scenario however was getting that girl away from him. It would have been perfect if she took the money. It would be evidence that she is just another gold digger, willing to take the cash and toss him aside. Finally, I'd have him to the point where he'd be miserable and realize that there was no way out of this. Regardless of her reasoning—whether for love, protection, or greed—she would have been gone! Mission accomplished. He would in no way, shape, or form be happy without her, Sam…

"She was our golden ticket. With that situation, and his mother's side of the family being shunned, he'd finally fold after all of these years. But instead, none of that happened, now did it?" He shoved his hands in his pockets and rocked back on his boot heels. "Because you fucked it up!"

"She wouldn't have fallen for it either way, Grandpa! This isn't all my fault!"

Grandpa marched swiftly up to Sam and grabbed his fractured arm, squeezing it.

"AHHHH!!!!"

"You dimwitted fool." He wrapped his hand tightly around the fucker's shirt collar and lifted him from his seat. Sam's complexion deepened to a blood orange, and he struggled to breathe, gurgling as his feet ran against nothing but air. "Since you decided to use the threat of violence to ger your point across, you should've done it *right*! If you'd had your gun pointed at her gotdamn head as soon as you walked into that fucking shower room, she would have done whatever the hell you told her to do. She chose *him* over the money and additional funds to pay full college tuition only because she'd gotten the upper hand on you! That's the only reason why this shit fell through!

"You never let a bitch get the best of you, and you never let a bitch get one over on you! She would have complied to save her own pathetic, miserable life!" He released him, tossing him back down into the chair, and took a couple of steps back. Sam sighed in pain as he rubbed the side of his reddened neck. "Now, Lennox is going to dig his heels in even harder. He knows for sure that she's loyal down to her bones. Like him! Like a gotdamn dog! She's a *real* bitch!" He laughed dismally.

"… I wish you would've just let me kill her! I coulda just gone in, put the silencer on, and shot her. No conversation needed! No negotiations! No nothing!" Sam's face balled up with regret as he peered from the corner of his eye, still rubbing on his neck.

"I told you that I don't kill women unless it's absolutely necessary. And besides, she's the dangling carrot. You don't kill the carrot, Sam. You use the carrot to nab the rabbit. Lennox is the prey, not her. She's the bone. He's a dog to his core, and he only serves one master. First, it was his mother. I got lucky and his mother died. Then, it was complete loyalty to his sister. I got Silva away from him with no issue, but he still wouldn't budge. Now, it's Nadia. She's the new leader of his heart. I *need* that master seat. I deserve it."

"Still, you just shoulda let me kill her, just shoulda killed 'er!" Sam blubbered under his breath. His face streaked with angry tears as he repeated the same ol' delirious mantra.

"Not only is your body bruised, but so is your ego." Grandpa sighed.

"I'm sorry, Grandpa."

"Yeah? Well sorry doesn't help, now does it?" he scoffed. "In some strange way though, I kinda appreciate her boldness, her grit, and will to survive."

"It all happened so fast." Sam threw him a blank gaze.

"I imagine it did. Yeah, I hate to admit it, but that harlot is definitely a rare one, isn't she?" He shrugged. "Admirable in this day and age. I underestimated her, it seems, and I take full accountability for that."

The corner of his lip twitched, and flashes of her face from his investigation photos flooded his mind. She angered and astounded him all at once. "I studied her, as I always do in these cases. She'd proven how money hungry she is for many years. She charges an arm and a leg for her OnlyFans live cam videos. Had, at one point, a bunch of little businesses going in Atlanta, like under the table legal advice for strippers, somethin' like that." He began to pace slowly back and forth. "All the signs were pointing to the likelihood of her caving.

"She didn't appear to be morally sound in the least. First and foremost, the Jezebel is a complete tramp." He laughed mirthlessly. "She's had more boyfriends than you can shake a stick or dick at. No daddy in the picture, a workaholic mother who was barely home, from what I could gather.

She didn't grow up in the best neighborhood, either. A lot of gangs, violence, and drugs were around her community. She's also a college dropout. The odds were in my favor and yet still, she didn't fold on Len." He shook his head in disbelief as Neil Diamond's, 'Song Song Blue' played. "She's got balls, that's for damn sure."

"I don't know about that, Grandpa." He looked at his grandson curiously. Sam was slumped over and nursing the side of his head with that bag of ice. "I don't think she's one of them transgenders. She has a pussy actually. I saw it. I know they make 'em now, but this looked real. In fact, her pubic hair is shaped like a heart, and she's got small hands and feet like a chick, big titties that look natural, and her—"

"Gotdamn it! I *know* she's a biological woman! Why do you take so many things literally?! You know what? never mind." He closed his eyes and tried to regain his composure. His grandson was a lost cause. He'd taken him on due to the pleading of his damn father. He never wanted Sam with him, and he now saw he'd been right and should've trusted his better judgment. He loved him though, in spite of himself. "Sam, I gave you a chance, and you blew it. You did well on the first couple of assignments last year, but this is a major blow."

"I know you said you're finished with me, but I promise I can make it right! Just let—"

"No. YOU'VE DONE A-FUCKIN' ENOUGH, BOY! Your father said you were havin' trouble with employment. Couldn't keep a job. Frederick *begged* me to let you work for me, but I didn't want no part of it! My son Fred does good work, so I went against my gut and tried to do what I could.

Whenever I do that, I usually live to regret it. Well, here I am. Full of regret. I will take care of this from here on out, Sam. You went to get somebody but got got! You were supposed to lay down the law and let her know you meant business, offer the deal, then leave. Five minutes tops!" He held up his hand. Fingers sprawled.

"I think I might need to go… to the… hospital…" The boy's eyes rolled.

"Instead of doin' what you were tasked with, you come bustlin' in here at three in the gotdamn mornin', smellin' like cheap beer and perfume, and practically in need of a blood transfusion! Bleedin' all over my good rugs! You go and lay down in one of my guest suites, probably left blood all over the gotdamn sheets and pillows, then I'm told right after breakfast this morning that you're here to see me. Now here we are. She made a fool of you. You turned around and let that boy take your gun and whoop up on you! He called a couple of his pals to help him out, and the first thing out of your mouth when you hit my door, according to Jasper, was about me suing on your behalf! I'm not suing any gotdamn body! This is embarrassing, and you know I don't like my name mixed up in things like this. You were at a place of ill repute! A den of sin! A lust lair! I have a reputation to uphold!"

"…Yeah, but you sent me to the strip club, Grandpa. I wasn't there by choice or to look at the girls."

"You wasn't there to see the little stripper girls?" He rolled his eyes and huffed. "Seems to me, you saw *plenty*! You know all about her big, bouncy titties, and the little black curly Q's growin' out of her beaver, cut into a damn heart like it's fuckin' Valentine's Day! You got distracted, and in that split second, that Black succubus fucked you up good!"

Sam now looked as if he were on the verge of wanting to take his own damn life.

"This was a mess, boy." He gently patted Sam on the back, then ran his fingers jokingly through the bastard's short blond hair. The young man was trembling, his eyes square on the rifle by his side. "Relax, boy. Grandpa ain't gonna kill you for this. You're human after all. Young. Naïve. But you will *never* work another day for me from this moment forward." Sam's eyes sheened over, then he exhaled. "You're a liability, and you're just not cut out for this business, boy.

"I shoulda sent Jasper, but your father wanted me to give you more responsibilities so you could move up the ladder. Be made. Go in the house and see Jasper about gettin' my private doctor to check you out to make sure you don't have a concussion or worse. After you get a look over and cleaned up, I want you to go home. To your own house."

"…Yes, sir."

"I'll pay you your salary until the end of next month, but then, you're on your own." They remained in silence for quite some time, with only the sound of the wind whistling through the trees and birds chirping, breaking up the mounting tension.

"Do you… do you want me to leave now?"

"What the hell do *you* think? I can't stand to look at you another second. Sam, I'm trying with everything within me not to punch you in your damn throat." He clenched his fist. "I need peace and quiet. I need time to think. Go on. Get!"

Sam slowly got to his feet, hobbled past him holding the ice to his temple, and entered the house. The door slammed behind him. Grandpa stood outside with his semi-automatic rifle, surveying his acres of land.

*Lennox used to be one of my favorite grandchildren. Now, he's my enemy. He's gonna race over here halfcocked, guns loaded. Wanting my head on a platter. I understand… Can't blame a hound for feelin' frisky when his bitch is in heat and someone interrupts the fuck fest. That's fine, but I'll be ready. Even in my seasoned age, I can still learn new tricks. I'll put him down like the dog that he is…*

# CHAPTER TWENTY-FIVE

## *Flat as a Pancake Dinner*

H E DECIDED TO leave while she was asleep…

Lennox managed to slip from beneath his slumbering baby. Nadia was snoozing so deeply, he imagined her as Snow White, only able to be awakened by a passionate kiss. He smiled down at her as he quietly got dressed, each of his movements measured and deliberate. He pulled his jeans up each leg, careful to not make any gestures that would force the fabric to kink against his skin, creating unnecessary friction and noise.

He carefully pulled out a white T-shirt from his overnight duffle bag and slipped it on. Keeping Nadia in his sights, he flashed a mischievous grin that he felt down to his bones. He was so proud of his handiwork in putting that pussy to sleep, just as he'd promised, killing it softly. *My dick is like NyQuil.* He chuckled within, but more importantly, he was pleased that her body had a habit of telling on her, revealing the secrets that roamed the hallways of her mind.

What her upper lips wouldn't say, her lower ones would. As he'd made love to her the evening prior, her movements, facial expressions, and the relaxing and rigidifying of her body let him know that she was holding something painful inside. Trying to hide it from his prying eyes. Something awful and foul.

They were the same facial expressions she'd make when they'd worked at the restaurant so many years ago. The ones she'd produce when she was troubled about her father standing her up for another daddy-daughter visit, or her brother not wanting to come home and his whereabouts unknown. Maybe she'd gotten into a heated argument with her mother, but whatever the cause, that was the face she wore. Sometimes she didn't want to talk about it. A shaken bottle of bubbly about to burst—only it wasn't for a happy occasion but yet another crack in the foundation of her heart. Another loss of trust. Another blow to self-esteem. Another dream slipping down the crude coated drain of life.

But sometimes, those bad days he could make better. He treasured those moments. When he could turn her frown upside down.

He felt useful. Of service. That's when he was at his best. She gave that to him, wanting nothing more than a little of his time. When she did want to discuss her problems, he'd listen. Sometimes he'd offer a bit about himself too, as much as he safely could so she'd feel more comfortable. He didn't want her to know what his surname meant in their town. He wanted his family and past to fade away like days on a calendar, and for her to see him for *him*, to understand that he was her friend purely out of enjoying her company, and his love for her.

He hated when she cried. She struggled often to hold back the tears, and then they'd pour down her velvety cheeks, making his heart break into a million pieces. He'd hug her, offer encouraging words. As he'd shelter her in his arms, her body would be stiff as a board, then it would loosen, unravel like a string of yarn as she released her pain against his frame.

And now, here they were. Ten years later. He realized when it came to how Nadia processed disappointment, nothing had changed. She wore her feelings on her sleeve only if she trusted you, and he was grateful for that. He knew without a shadow of a doubt that this woman was indeed his soulmate, for he was the same way—and their connection was deeper than any words uttered, in any language known to man.

There was nothing she could hide from him, even if she were invisible. Moreover, he understood that if she was being quiet—she felt it was for good reason. Not to be spiteful or duplicitous, but to protect the innocent, or plan retribution towards the wicked. He gave grace and forgiveness for her not being forthcoming, but he was determined to get to the bottom of it, nevertheless. With or without her admission.

*Nadia, you sleep tight. I have some responsibilities to tend to.* Once he had his shoes on, he grabbed his duffle bag, now filled with his clothes from the evening before, and other odds and ends.

He crept towards the bedroom door, opening and closing it slowly behind him. Walking to the front door of the apartment he completed his silent exit. Once he was in his truck on the highway, he turned on some music at high volume: Shaboozey's, 'A Bar Song.' Soon, he arrived at his first stop. The junkyard. He was in and out in ten minutes. Getting back in his truck, he arrived next at the thrift store he'd Googled. It wouldn't open for another five minutes. He took that time to reach for his Daniel Defense H9 in the glove compartment.

Setting it on his side, he patted it like he would an old friend, then tucked it out of sight. He clenched his teeth until his jaw ached, although the music provided a little distraction to the dark mood he was falling in bed with.

An employee unlocked the front door of the thrift shop. Just as he was about to get out of the truck, his phone rang. Ignoring it, he made his way inside the store. He was back out in four minutes. Getting back in his truck, he turned the music up high. He pulled onto the street and headed to the highway. Just then, his phone rang again. He glanced at the caller ID on the Bluetooth dashboard of his truck, expecting it to be Nadia ready to lay into him about sneaking off, but much to his surprise, it wasn't.

He turned off the music, then pressed the 'Answer Call' button.

"Hello…"

"Jesus." Silva exhaled loudly on the other end. He could hear what sounded like the outdoors. Birds. Wind. Even a wind chime. Perhaps she was standing on her deck with a cup of coffee. That was how I imagined her anyway.

"Mornin', Len. This is my second time tryna reach you this morning. I had hoped you were still an early bird."

"I am. I don't sleep much. Mornin', baby sis."

"Yeah… so, uh, I've had some time to think, and that thinkin' got me to thinkin' some more. You should remember how I am when somethin' don't sit right in my spirit. Keeps me up until I get to the bottom of it."

"Well, baby sis, to be honest wit' cha, I wish you'd felt that way about mendin' our relationship, but it seems I was the exception. You know what?" He laughed and waved his hand. "I'll refrain from attackin' you… I'm just still a lil' riled up is all. I missed you. You called. That's all that matters."

"I understand your position. I get why you feel the way you do. I imagine I'd feel much the same way and though you may not think I deserve it, I would like for you to give me a moment here. I'm still processing this shit. I've been down a rabbit hole and can't see the forest for the damn trees. So I don't want to get sidetracked, alright? I got somethin' to say, if you'll allow it."

"Mmmm hmmm. Go on 'head."

"By the way, I haven't smoked in years. I'm on my third cig since we spoke. Stole it from Tony's stash."

"I reckon your nerves are in a knot." He casually switched to the fast lane.

"Somethin' like that. I called off work today. Said I was sick. Tony's at work, and I'm home alone. It's for the best because I don't want to have to explain this mess to him. At least not while I'm tryna get my own hands around it. Look, uh… things are pretty fucked up."

"Indeed they motherfuckin' are… Hold on… I'm behind some slow fuck. MOVE!" He honked his horn at someone in a Corolla in the fast lane going forty miles per hour.

"I meant what I said about your horrible attitude, Lennox, and your road rage right now shows you still got it in ya." She chuckled. "But regardless of all of that, I still owe you a big apology. You were right. I took Grandpa's word at face value, not believing he had any reason to lie to me, when he had *every*thing to lie about accordin' to that there letter. I've read the letter several times. The one you said Grandpa sent you… did a little exploration, too.

"Initially, I was tryna convince myself that you wrote it yourself. A scheme of yours. Then I realized that's not even your style, and the letter is written out just how Grandpa speaks when I'd hear him on the phone with Daddy. I'm a 'details' girl. I notice stuff like that—but I guess it took Captain Obvious to make me see what was right in front of my damn face."

"Well Silva, when we love and trust someone, it's easy to think everyone else is the bad guy, 'cept for them. You didn't trust me anymore. That's how he was able to keep this charade going."

"That's right. I have to deal with that reality, too." She exhaled loudly, and he heard what sounded like slow walking. Pacing back and forth, maybe?

"Where are you?"

"Outside on the deck." He smiled at that. "With a cigarette 'nd coffee." Now he was laughing. "I'm faced right now with the fact that a man I adored, practically worshiped, is nothin' like what I thought he was. I feel like my whole damn childhood was a lie. In my effort to prove you were full of shit, I did call our cousin."

"Which one?"

"Kage. Problem was, he didn't pick up when I called. Or he might have me blocked."

"What makes you think he'd block you?"

"Because I cursed him out last Thanksgiving. He'd been drinkin' and acted a plum fool. You weren't there, of course. You haven't come by Grandpa's in a long while."

"No, not voluntarily. Anyway, Kage wasn't invited, Silva. Kage isn't even allowed on the property anymore from what I understand."

"Oh, he showed up all right… smashed and ready to rumble. He was escorted away. That's a polite way to put it. As security was draggin' him out the door, I gave him a few choice words. He jerked his head in my direction, and he sported the evilest look on his face, Len, paired with a sick smile. He told me he hoped I'd get what I deserved and some other crap I'd rather not repeat. He was real offensive. On purpose, naturally."

"…Naturally." He stifled a desire to burst out laughing.

"I don't know if it was the booze talkin' or truly his thoughts of me, Lennox. Something tells me it was the latter." She exhaled loudly. "That was that."

"Yup. Sounds like Kage." He sighed. "His patience is a hell of a lot shorter than mine, and Grandpa has taken him through the wringer."

"Kage is no angel, but I can only imagine. So, since I couldn't get a hold of him, I called Roman." Roman was another cousin on the outs with Grandpa. He'd been a Marine, but his record was marred with petty crimes, elaborate schemes, and other offenses instead of his great military service to the country. On top of it, Roman had a strange ability to memorize practically anything he laid eyes on. It helped him cheat in Vegas, and win big. His face was now on posters to never allow the bastard back into several casinos. "Have you spoken to Roman any time recently?"

"Yeah, I have actually, but we didn't get too deep. Roman prefers to be the class clown, so to speak, so he wouldn't really let on how he was feelin' about all of this shit to me. I don't even know if he's takin' it seriously, to be quite honest, but I damn sure hope so because Grandpa truly hates his guts. Makes everything even more ironic if you ask me. Anyway, what'd he say?"

"Well, he corroborated everything you said regardin' the letters. Said y'all all got them, and were essentially abducted and required to have a meetin' with Grandpa, the seven of ya. Said it was a real shitshow." Silva went on to recap what had gone down, and he offered a nod here and there. What sounded completely absurd was in fact what had transpired, and only his family would do and condone such a thing. The Wildes were wild. Amen. "…And so, that's that. I've been such a damn fool." She laughed dismally. "You always told me, even when we were kids, that I was too naïve… your codeword for stupid."

"Nah, I called ya stupid sometimes, too. No codewords needed."

"Oh, okay. Thanks. I appreciate you clearin' that up." They both had a good laugh at that.

"I'm sorry, well, kinda, but it's obvious why. You've got a trustin' heart, Silva." He stroked his beard as his thoughts weaved together like a basket. "You believe people at their word unless they make you think otherwise. It makes you susceptible to attack from people with ill intentions is all."

"Gullible? Well, I guess sometimes I can be."

"It's just that you're a real good person, and you don't see evil in the world because well, people like you have a hard time wrapping your head around the fact that such wickedness exists in the first place. To you, that type of shit only takes place in movies, ya know? I mean, despite the dysfunction in our extended family, what was goin' on under our roof was good. It was wholesome. We had two parents who loved one another. They loved us, too. We never wanted for nothin', and Mama taught manners and respect. Dad was funny, Mama was about business—but she was kind, too. After we walked out of that front door though, Silva, it was an entirely different world. Mama dyin' was the first brick to fall. Then the whole damn thing came crashin' down."

She was quiet for a spell. "...He really did all these horrible things, Lennox? Don't respond, 'cause it's not a question. It's me sayin' it aloud. We're talking 'bout the same Grandpa who cleaned my scraped knee when I fell ridin' my new bike he bought me on my 7th birthday. The same Grandpa who told me I could be anything I wanted to be when I grew up, then introduced me to a lady who was one of the first female firefighters in all of Houston... He taught me how to ride a horse, then bought me a pony for God's sake! I still have the picture of him holding me when

I was born. He was actually cryin' tears of joy like he'd just won the lottery.

"He was like... Santa and Mr. Rogers rolled into one person, only he was my grandfather, and I loved him... I loved him..." She sniffed – fighting emotions he didn't get a chance to have in life. *Grandpa hadn't claimed her for his evildoings. He marked me with the letter of the beast.* "My mind knows the truth now. It's my heart that's broken."

"Yeah, finding out the hard, ugly truth tends to do that."

"I knew that, uh, Grandpa had dirty dealin's in the business world. How could I not?" She chuckled miserably. "...But I didn't think he'd do anything like this to family, you know? Not to Daddy. Not to my brother." She cried for a bit, then cleared her throat. He didn't interrupt, just let the dust settle. "I gotta mourn who I thought he was, and accept who he *actually* is. I need to get on a plane and go to Mama's grave again. Visit her. I know she's been seeing this... I have to apologize to her for me thinking she was bein' dramatic."

"No you don't. She knows you were still a kid back then, Silva. You didn't know any better."

"...But *you* did. We're only three years apart, and I'm an adult now. I should have known better. How could I be so blind?!"

"Three and a half, but who's counting?"

"You know what's so crazy to me? Roman said it so matter-of-factly, you know? What happened... Like he was describin' a bad job interview with a negative CEO. Like it was no big deal. It showed me just how traumatized he was,

Len, and he doesn't even know it. Showed me how traumatized y'all are, really. 'Cludin' Kage. I wanna tell you that I'm sorry. Sorry won't fix this, all this time we've been estranged, but I'll say it all the same because it's long overdue."

"Thank you. I accept your apology. It wasn't *all* your fault, though. I could've been nicer. I made it easier for Grandpa to drive a wedge between us because I had been actin' up. If we'd not been bumping heads at the time, it would've been harder for him to pull us apart."

His sister was quiet on the other end for a long time. He gave her that space. That silence. He figured it was a lot to take in.

"So, I guess I shoulda asked you this at the beginning of the conversation, but I've been up all night, runnin' on fumes. Not thinking straight. Sleep deprived ever since I spoke to you and Roman."

"What do you want to ask me?"

"What have you been up to? How's life been treatin' you?"

"Life's been difficult at times, baby sister, but it's got some really pretty silver linings, if I say so myself." He glanced at his reflection in the rear-view mirror. He was all smiles.

"Yeah? The gym, right? I can't wait to see your plans for it. You know I want to help with design and things like that—if you need me of course."

"Yeah, that's an idea that's worth exploring. The fitness center is definitely one of the things going right, but there's something else, too. I ran into an old friend. Girl from when I worked at The Red Rooster. Always had a yearnin' for her."

"Oh, really? This is more than a fling, huh? You were always a ladies man. I used to hate when my friends would gush over you when they'd come over. *'Oh, your brother is so dreamy!', 'Lennox is sooo cute!'* I'd say, *'Gross!'* To me, you were the same big brother who'd fart in my face and would run off laughin', leave the kitchen a mess and watch a bunch of gross, gory movies at high volume, and then laugh about all the killing. Let's not talk about your porno DVD collection. Must've been hundreds of them. You were disgusting." She giggled, and he couldn't help but follow suit.

"Yeah, I guess I was kinda gross back then. This is the real deal, though."

"What's her name?"

"Nadia. We met about ten years ago at the restaurant. Both of us worked there. You might remember me talking about her sometimes."

"The name does ring a bell, but I can't picture her."

"Well, she moved to Georgia, and then about four or five months ago we saw each other again. I was workin' one night at the club, and she came in. We've been inseparable ever since. She's always had my heart. The one that got away."

"Oh my goodness, that sounds so romantic." He could hear the smile in his sister's voice.

"That's my lady. My baby. We're, uh, we're in a relationship now."

"Oh my goodness, a lot *has* changed, hasn't it? My brother is now the settlin' down type. I love that for you. I always thought you'd make a good husband and father... You were usually pretty responsible. Reliable." Her voice trailed towards the end. "...I guess that's why I couldn't so easily dismiss the fact that you'd been paying the bills when Grandpa had fired Dad. I never knew anything about that."

"I know you didn't. Yeah, well, I always knew that eventually I'd get married, too. Have some kids. Just wasn't sure when. I wasn't picky enough sometimes about who I slept with, but definitely was picky about who I was serious about."

"I can't argue with that. Nadia... Nadia... yeah, I definitely remember you mentionin' her a long time ago. Your work buddy."

"Yeah, but over time, we both liked each other more than just as friends. Everything worked out. She's the one, Silva... I'm in love, baby sis. Gonna ask her to marry me soon, too." His heart pounded damn near out of his chest at the thought of it all.

"Well hell! I *have* missed a lot!"

"I doubt she'll be surprised when I pop the question though because I already told her early on that she was gonna be my wife. She knows I mean what the hell I say."

"Wow. I have to meet her."

"You will."

"So... what are we gonna do?"

"What are we gonna do? About *what*?"

"About Grandpa, Lennox?!"

He smirked at that. "What are *we* gonna do? We're going to do *nothing*, Silva. *I'm* doin' something though. You best believe that. You just stay out of this. I don't want you gettin' hurt."

"I'm as hurt as I can be already, Lennox. I wanna help. I *have* to help. I can't let him do this to you and just sit back and do nothing."

"Nope. It's not up for discussion."

"Mama would roll over in her grave if she found out I fell for his tricks. I just feel so damn stupid. After all the terrible things he said about Mama, you have to let me help make this right, Len!" The woman's voice shook, as if she were on the verge of a nervous breakdown. "He never said those things to me about her. I knew they didn't care for one another too much, but Grandpa was certainly not disrespectful in my presence, and then to find out he is willing to destroy our grandparents' lives for *this* shit?! All because you disobeyed him? NO. I won't have it, Lennox!" He bit down on his lower lip while gripping the steering wheel a little tighter. "When I didn't know the information, I had an excuse to keep wearing blinders. Now I know the truth, and it's so dreadful... Daddy drinks himself into a stupor, and is being manipulated. Just like I was, I suppose."

"Dad made his bed. He can lie in it. He had the nerve to tell me to give in and just accept the job. All so he could get the pressure off his back and for things to return to the status quo. Spiteful business as usual. Somebody needs to sell some damn spines on Amazon, eBay, or Etsy so that our father can buy himself one. Fuckin' jellyfish."

"Len, he grew up in this shit. Cut him some slack. He has it worse than we did... You know he loves you. Daddy is just lost is all." He sucked his teeth. "You were dealin' with this all on your own, and that's what I wanna focus on. That's over. Not anymore. He has to be stopped, Lennox."

"Yeah, he does have to be stopped, but like I said, you aren't part of the plan. Now I want you to relax and stop thinkin' about all of this. I've got some business to tend to. Let me holler at you later, okay?"

"Do you promise to call me back?" Silva sounded so pitiful. It made his heart ache.

"Of course I will. In the meantime, when it comes to Grandpa, keep actin' typical. That's what you can do for me. It's important that he not know that we've made up and you've been filled in on what actually went down. Act like you don't even know the truth, okay? Keep smilin' in his face, and whatever it is you two normally do."

"It'll be hard, but I'll do it. Lennox, I'm not going to have you—"

"No, Silva. Whatever you are going to say, the answer is no. I don't care how much you beg. He doesn't care who he has to take down to get his way. He just wants to destroy me, make me suffer, and he wants me to live to endure it. Death would be too easy and forgiving in his mind. I'm the guardian, not you. I've always protected you, even when you hated my guts. Nothin' is gonna change."

"It's too late to protect me from this!" Her tone was piercing. "He's *already* hurt me! The lies on top of lies, on top of lies! I know you thought I was stickin' to him like glue because of all the money he gave me and Tony over the years, and the strings he pulled for our careers, but that's not true at all. You didn't say it, but I know how you think." He couldn't deny that initially, it definitely crossed his mind. "He's tryna ruin my brother's life and destroy my mother's legacy by bringing up her past, which we know in her community back in Lebanon is a reputation destroyer."

"He still might do it. Problem is, he now knows that won't deter me."

"Shit! We know how Mama's culture is in the old town. The entire family over there will be shunned."

"And somehow the old man knows that."

"What a sickening thing to do. She's dead, for God's sake! I felt sorry for myself when it first hit me that you were tellin' the truth, Len, and then, I felt nothin' but rage. That's my mama, too! I'll do what you asked for now, but not forever. I'm in this whether you like it or not!"

Lennox took a deep breath. "Don't tell Tony about this. We'll discuss it further later."

"Sooner rather than later. This ain't right, and I need somethin' done about it. NOW. I owe it to you. I owe it to Mom. I owe it to Dad. I owe it to myself." The call ended before he had the opportunity to respond.

He sat with their conversation for a few moments, re-playing it in his mind. Soon, he pulled into a lot full of construction vehicles. Richmond Premier Rentals was the name of the place. He took note of the black and white sign, the letters faded. The gate was open so he drove through, parking next to a dump truck that appeared to be receiving mechanical services, seeing as how the hood was up and one of the tires was missing.

The sounds of big machinery could be heard moving all around the dirt pathways. He slipped his gun into his back pocket, then grabbed his duffle bag and phone. He opened his photo library, selecting a recent video he'd been sent. He watched it again, and again, and again...

His life of being a blue-collar worker who'd worked all sorts of jobs proved to be invaluable after all. It had taught him about people, about life skills and human frailty. He'd never been afraid of a hard day's work. He kept replaying the special video on his phone, memorizing the sounds, the light, the darkness...

His thoughts drifted in and out of sanity... He lamented over the scene in the video, tag teaming with thoughts over the careers he'd had in his lifetime that helped make him who he was today. His thoughts drifted back to working the land. He'd done a lot of odd jobs, even getting his trucker's license at one point, and was employed in warehouses using forklifts, too. For over a year, he'd worked a construction job. He didn't believe any labor was beneath or above him. He sat there and pondered why his woman would leave the club, on her last day of work of all days, and behave in such a manner. No call. No text. Short replies and conversation. Stiffness in a hug. Want and need in her eyes. Her body bent toward him. Cried out. Nadia was a creature of habit but only those who knew her well understood this.

To an outsider, she appeared to be a fly by the seat of her pants type of person, when in actuality, everything she did was calculated, planned, and well thought out.

*This isn't like her. Something messed up happened. When we fucked, I could feel it... I'm right. I just know it. Who did this? It had to be that bastard who followed her home and damaged her car. Maybe it was the ex-boyfriend who'd threatened to come into town and hurt her over that money? Nah. There's no way it could be him. It's got to be the club dude.*

He was going to keep digging around in the ground until he got to the root of it all and uncovered the truth, and then he was going to yank it up by the stem. Expose it. The evening before he'd arrived at Nadia's apartment, he'd followed up on a prior inquiry. It was time to find out if the information he'd been seeking was now available. He'd been waiting a while. Before quitting time at the club the night prior, he followed up on his lead. He got into his truck and dialed the right number. Spoke to the right person. He needed more information before he made his move, but he needed it fast. Time to pull the trigger. Nothing would stand in his way.

One of the issues to deal with was a fucker named Dice. Nadia's graphic police report detailed a night of horror: A man who'd attempted to follow her home and used his vehicle to intimidate her in order to cause her emotional and physical harm had been arrested, but some fucking way, released on bond soon thereafter. The police had it all on film. There was no denying it. And yet, he'd walked away. He flipped through scanned images of a police report, too, then replayed that video.

*You deserve to be eatin' dirt sandwiches, motherfucker...* The anger and fear in his baby's eyes tore through his soul—the way her car jerked forward so hard, it was a wonder she didn't go flying out the windshield... *You wanna play bumper cars? It's your time to shine, bitch...*

She'd told him all about the incident, but seeing it on actual tape brought it to a whole new level. He had a sneaking suspicion that Dice may have shown back up at the club her last night of performing.

*She didn't tell me because she's afraid of my reaction. Afraid I'll get in some trouble tryna track him down and make him pay for this. Well, that's too damn bad...*

Thanks to utilizing the resources of a highway patrol officer he trained at the gym, he had a copy of the footage now, too. He watched it right before he drove to her apartment the evening prior, then replayed it several times that morning as he stood next to her refrigerator, brewing not only coffee, but contempt. Each time he replayed it, his mood became a little darker. His thirst for revenge, untamable and sharper. He had a plan. And it was a good one.

It fueled him to make a move. The fucker had to pay. Eye for an eye. Dog tooth for a dog tooth. He got out of his truck, slipping on a pair of sunshades and a dark brown skull cap. He entered the rental office, noting how chilly it was inside the cramped place that smelled of burnt coffee. A timeworn radio sat on the hostess window shelf, playing deep-rooted rhythm and blues songs.

A middle-aged white lady with sallow skin sat behind the counter, her thin-rimmed silver glasses practically dangling off the end of her tiny, pointy nose.

"Hello, may I help you?" She peered at him with small hazel eyes. Dainty gold hoop earrings gleamed from her lobes.

"Yes ma'am. I called earlier 'bout rentin' a bulldozer for some of the contractors over yonder. They're one short and I don't want that to slow anything down. We're on a tight schedule. I won't be personally usin' it, but I'm licensed to drive it over to the property for demolition work. Tryna save them a little time."

"Oh yes, you must be Mr. Williams, right? Called this mornin' at the crack of dawn?" She chuckled.

"Yes, ma'am. Like I said on the phone, I recently bought some property that needs tendin' to." He pulled out his alter-ego ID and passed it to her. The guy in the picture looked somewhat like him, but to a discerning eye, there were enough differences to question it. She looked at it from over her glasses as she drank what appeared to be water from a small green paper cup, taking her sweet time.

"I know you said you won't be doing the work, Mr. Williams, but you requested to drive it over." She handed him back his driver's license.

"That's right. All those guys are busy and I figured I could help them meet their deadline if I just grabbed it myself."

"Alright, that's fine, but in the state of Texas we can't let you just go off with a bulldozer without the proper licensing."

"Of course not. I completely understand. Ma'am, I'm accredited and authorized to drive that machine."

"Can you give me the construction company's license number please, and I need to see a copy of your certification and CDL, too."

"I sure can. No problem." Lennox reached into his wallet and pulled out a tri-folded piece of paper with detailed information from a random contractor, as well as his CDL information too, in Mr. Williams' name.

She took the papers, looked them over, then got to her

feet and walked away. She made copies of the documents and returned to the desk, handing everything back to him. Taking a noisy sip of her water, she got to typing on the computer.

"Looks like it's gonna rain today, don't it?" she questioned as her short dark pink painted nails hit the keys of her dated machine.

"It sure does. I figure we need it though. My grass is lookin' mighty dry."

"Mmm, hmmm. Yeah. Mine too. Lord knows it costs an arm and a leg to water our grass now. Rain will probably help. My poor petunias need it, too." She turned away and started fiddling with a clipboard she had lying off to the side. "Okay, Mr. Williams, I've looked over everything, includin' your certification, and it all looks fine and up to date. Please read, date, and sign this paperwork."

With a nod, he did as she asked while another blues song played. Once it was all done, he handed her his credit card, also in the name of a Mr. Williams. It was interesting the crazy things you could learn to do by being a Wilde grandchild... *Grandpa's little tips of the trade come in handy every now and again, and the things I learned back in the day to cover my tracks after a kill are useful, too.*

She offered him a silver key.

"Here's the key to lot number fifty-two, Mr. Williams. Your rental is for two days, per the paperwork. Should you need an additional twenty-four hours, you can just call us and we'll charge your card on file accordingly. Any more than that and you'll need to return the vehicle, and sign an extended contact for re-rental, along with paying an additional fee."

"Yes ma'am, understood. My truck is parked back this way," He pointed to the front door. "Is it okay if I return to get my truck in an hour or two?"

"That shouldn't be a problem. Just make sure you pick it up before we close today, or it'll be locked inside. We close promptly at five P.M."

"That's plenty of time. I'll be back in a jiffy."

They parted ways and he made his way to parking spot fifty-two, finding the bulldozer parked next to several others—all pristine, clean and in a row. Pulling a pair of surgical gloves out of his pocket, he slipped them on. He could barely curb his enthusiasm as he hopped in the correct machine, started it up, and felt the rumble and shake from the powerful piece of machinery. He hadn't been on a bulldozer in years, and he kind of missed it.

Off he went from the lot then, tossing a glance at his parked truck as he made his way onto the street. According to his calculations, the place he needed to be was about twelve minutes away. That was why he'd specifically picked this rental place. It was closest to the sweet spot. Before he arrived at his destination, he pulled over to the side and opened his duffle bag. *Time to get to work.*

He pulled out a can of temporary hair dye spray and covered the machine in dark brown spots, strategically placed all over the bulldozer, creating simulated stains that resembled rust and corrosion. Some stains were big, others small. Then, he pulled out two sizable pieces of tire tread, cut them into smaller sections with a Steelman tire knife, and placed them on the bulldozer tires, adhering them with tire glue and vehicle cement to create confusion regarding the tread pattern of the vehicle. Junkyards were amazing for that sort of thing. Tires of all sorts. Most of them flat. He then reached back into his bag and put on a bright green jacket, as well as his sunglasses.

He tucked his necklace into his shirt, and switched hats, plopping an old, beat-up baseball cap on his head with the logo of a team everyone knew he hated: The Dodgers. It was amazing what you could find at thrift shops in the wee hours of the morning. The best fifty-nine cents he'd ever spent.

Getting back onto the bulldozer, he drove to his destination. It was still fairly early in the day, and not everyone was out and about. Wasn't much traffic, either. Rather quiet, in fact. He drove up to the address he planned to party at, and sure as shit, he spotted what he was looking for...

A white Mitsubishi Eclipse, parked in the driveway of a modest brick house with blue curtains in the windows. *You're some big-time local rapper, huh? Well, I've got a rap song for you, too...* He parked onto the street near the driveway, then turned the bulldozer off. Getting out of the machine, he checked the license plate on the car. *Yup. It's the right one.*

He got back into the Cat C27 844 Model Dozer, fired it up, and pulled up to the Mitsubishi like a man about to fuck his favorite whore. He idled behind it for a few seconds, his adrenaline rush intoxicating, then put it in drive and crushed the damn car like a sardine can, rolling over it with the greatest of ease. A loud crunching, smashing noise ensued. The perfect lyrics to the perfect song. The perfect revenge, to a night gone wrong.

Glass shattered and tires were popping like corn kernels in high heat. He jerked the bulldozer in reverse and repeated the process. What a thrill! His face felt tight with a manic grin as elation flowed through him like the very blood in his veins. He kicked it in reverse once again as he heard nearby doors opening and witnessed a couple of people gawking from partially drawn windows.

He casually made his way back onto the street and headed in the opposite direction he'd come. The bulldozer didn't drive very fast, 1,800 r/min, but he'd planned everything out just fine. Not a care in the world. If the fucker had come to the door and tried to interrupt him, he'd have been shot. Simple as that. Since he didn't, the bastard could thank his lucky stars that he got to live to see another day.

Less than a minute later, he spied the old library. It was boarded up, just as seen on Google maps. He looked around and noted there appeared to be no cameras, either. *No need for plan B, then. Perfect.*

He parked behind the defunct library and made quick work of removing the fake rust stains with the cleaning solution and cloths he'd brought in his bag. He removed the glued-on tire treads, too, which had made for a slightly bumpy ride. Then, he quickly took off the jacket, hat and glasses, folded them up and shoved them in his duffle bag, then covered the bulldozer with a large, dark tarp. *I'll keep it for two days. If I return it right away, that'll draw suspicion.* Making his way back towards the street, his gloves off and duffle bag in tow, he trekked the thirty-two-minute walk back towards where his truck was parked. Instead of going to retrieve it, however, he headed to the diner across the street.

He'd worked up quite the appetite. When he sat down at the counter, he was still on a high from his little adventure. An older guy with thinning wheat-colored hair approached him, asking what he'd like. He opened the menu and scanned it, then placed it quietly back down onto the counter.

"Three scrambled eggs. Bacon, extra crispy. A servin' of buttermilk pancakes. Home fries with onion 'nd peppers, and coffee. Black."

"You got it."

Keith Whitley's, 'When You Say Nothing at All' played through scratchy speakers. He bobbed his head to the song, a favorite of his father's. Looking around the establishment, he realized the place looked a lot like the one where he and Nadia used to work. He felt his phone buzz and pulled it from his pocket. Two missed calls and a text from Nadia.

Nadia: *Boy, where the hell are you?!*

Lennox: *Had to take care of a few morning errands. I have to make a couple more stops too, but I'll be back soon. I didn't want to wake you.*

He was fine with that. He'd told the truth. They were in fact errands, and he definitely did not want to wake her.

Three dots popped up in response, then disappeared. A couple minutes later, all she wrote back was: *OKAY*. Soon, his food and coffee arrived, and he took his time to savor it. He added a bit of salt and pepper to his eggs and potatoes, then ordered a glass of orange juice. He liked it served with a little ice. After he was finished, he paid the bill and left a nice tip. Walking the rest of the short distance, he crossed the road to retrieve his truck, whistling 'Sitting on the Dock of the Bay,' by Otis Redding. Once he got to the construction vehicle rental spot, he kept a low profile and didn't speak to anyone. He'd been gone almost two hours, just like he'd said.

Hopping in his truck, he turned on the radio. Brent Faiyaz's, 'Pistachios' played as he drove the back roads. Once he was almost at his next destination, he pulled over to the side of the thoroughfare in a desolate area of town. This last task had to be done before he made it to the heart of the damn city where all the cameras, glitz, and people would be.

He ripped away two fake confederate dixie flag decals from the back of his truck he'd snagged late last night at a gas station, took down the naked lady air freshener he'd obtained from the junkyard, too, and removed the fake license plate he'd placed on the back of his truck. He always kept a spare license plate, just for occasions such as this. He slipped the license plate in a black trash bag, followed by everything else, including his surgical gloves, and tucked the rubbish neatly under his driver's seat. Everything except for his truck—the clothing and all would be burned up later in a sweet bonfire.

He got back behind the wheel, and drove with determination.

*Next order of business: See the marine.*

It was time to pay Roman Wilde, the black sheep cousin, a much-deserved visit...

# CHAPTER TWENTY-SIX

## *Standing on Business*

GRANDMAMA TOLD ME *one time that hurt people hurt people. Mama told me one time that Black folk are always lookin' for a messiah. Someone to save us. Swoop down and rescue us from the evils of racism and poverty. That's why we're so susceptible to fake preachers, pimp mentality, toxic culture, and so-called leaders of the Black community that don't do nothin' but exploit us, peddle pipe dreams, and sell snake oil. Sometimes, I think the situation is more complicated than that. Other times, I think we as a people make it too complicated our damn selves. Things aren't always so simple but sometimes, they aren't so tough and hard to understand.*

*As a kid I used to wonder why it seemed like other races that went through terrible things, like Jews during the Holocaust and Mexicans fleeing gang infested cities, would come over here and fare better than us. Mama said it was because the White man gave them loans and more opportunities. Grandma said it wasn't that but because they banded together, and held each other accountable. I bet it was all of those reasons, and probably a few more, too.*

*When I think about me and Lennox, I see the struggle—I see the fight. I see the reasons why we drifted apart, and the reasons why we drifted right back together. Some things, like struggle and survival, are just in our makeup. They make us who we are. They are just meant to be. That man is my other half. We are amazing alone, incredible together. This morning, I thought I was waking up next to my soulmate. He made love to me so good, I slept like a rock.*

*I woke up this mornin' happy, but soon, I was just confused. I feel like my man is hurt and wants to hurt someone else. I feel like he took my not speaking to him about the terrible thing that happened as some sort of a challenge. I may have made things worse... by just trying to protect him. Lennox doesn't want protection from a woman or even another guy, and he isn't a very patient man. I've learned that the hard way. Seems he wants to save me from the world, but I'm not makin' it easy on bein' saved. He wants to make my life like heaven, but now I am wondering, 'Where the hell is Lennox?!'*

Sitting on her comfortable cream loveseat in the living room, Nadia kept her phone close to her ear as she waited for her brother to get back on the line. Nelson put her on hold. He always had this spastic energy, never able to keep still. He wasn't much of a phone talker either, but he'd try.

It was a bit dark in the room, just as she liked it, but she had turned on one floor lamp with a purple light, to keep it somewhat dim. She yawned, digging her toes into the plush cream carpet, then noted the time. Lennox still hadn't returned. Her troubled spirit beat drums and screamed. In her heart, she knew it would be awhile. They needed to talk, as soon as possible.

"I'm back," Nelson stated, followed by a cough. "I'm watchin' on old game from last year and needed to find the remote to turn it down. I could barely hear you."

"What game?"

"Boston Celtics playin' the Dallas Mavericks." She could hear the basketball game playing in the background, but it didn't seem like he'd turned it down at all.

"They're always neck 'n neck most games, ain't they? I haven't followed in a while."

"Yeah, pretty much. They both play hard."

"Hmmm. I haven't watched sports of any kind in a long while. What are your plans tonight?"

"Cherrie 'sposed to come by soon with some chicken wings."

"Oh, y'all talking again?" Cherrie was Nelson' ex-wife, but they seemed to spend more time together *after* the divorce than before.

"Yeah, we *been* talkin'. She can't get enough Nelson the Great!" He cackled, causing her to roll her eyes. "That lil' piece of paper don't mean nothin' to me. I get more pussy from her now than I did when we was in so-called wedded bliss."

"Where is she getting the wings from? Got my mouth watering now, too." She glanced at her front door, distressed that she still hadn't heard the bell ring or a knock.

"Wing Boss."

"Nice. Uh, Nelson, Mama brought you up this morning. She sent me a text message. Now, I ain't gonna say what it said, but she basically implied that you are ignoring her calls. I know I have my nerve because I ignore her calls sometimes, too. Regardless of that, when was the last time you spoke to Mama?"

"Oh, I'd say… shit. Let me think. Uh, probably three days ago. Naw… it was five days ago. Yeah, it was five days ago. I've been working double shifts so the time has gotten away from me. Duty calls. Ain't nobody else gonna pay this mortgage but me." He was an EMT, and still helped financially with his ex-wife's daughter from a prior relationship. Nelson was all about saving money though—they had that in common. "Mama don't care about me comin' there or callin' her no way."

"Nelson, now you know that's not true."

"I bet if I sat right in front of her face at the kitchen table this very second, she wouldn't even look up from her newspaper to know I was there. Who the hell still reads a damn newspaper? Mama. That's who. Maybe when I was a lil' boy, I shoulda asked God to be reincarnated as a newspaper so she coulda paid attention to me, too." He laughed even harder, a forced sound this time—to cover the pain. She knew all about that. "You done asked all this shit about me, then about mama. What about *you?* What's been goin' on with my sister since you left the club and all of that, school girl?"

"Nelson, I told you I've been making some changes in my life. I'm a work in progress. Yeah, I stopped dancin'. I'm back in school, and yeah, but I'm determined to finish this time."

"You okay on money? I can help you if you need it." She smiled at that.

"I know you would, but I've got enough savings to sustain me. I do work a part-time home job doing customer service a few hours a week, too. Just for little extras I might want so that I don't dip into my savings for frivolous stuff, things like that."

"Mmm hmm, okay. You know I got you if you come up short. I'm proud of you." He sounded like Grandma when he said that. "You know I support just about anything you do. You know that, right?"

"I know, Nelson, and I appreciate that. I appreciate *you*. We don't talk all the time but when we do, the love is definitely there. With all of this, you know, the changes I'm makin', I have accepted that I need to get therapy to get over my hatred of my father, and to come to terms with Mama's attitude sometimes. Hell, I struggle to describe it, but you know what I mean. Sometimes she's—"

"Cold-hearted, mean as a starvin' rattlesnake. Everything is black and white … ain't no such thang as a gray area, suck-it-up-buttercup recommendations, I'll cook for you so you can forget about me cussin' you out for havin' feelings, and your mouth will be too full from eatin' to keep yappin' about yo' problems, don't nobody betta bring me no bad news havin' Miss JoAnn. That's how you describe her damn attitude." He huffed. "Mama loved us from a distance, even though she was standin' right there. Guess we shoulda moved next door and gave her some space. She's an electrician. We know she woulda kept the lights on, and the stove hot at least."

They laughed together, even though none of this was particularly funny.

"She tried, Nelson. Mama is complicated. I've come to realize that when a bowl is broken, it can't hold a lotta stuff. It can try, but whatever you put in it will just run out. Like water in a shattered glass. It ain't the bowl's or glass's fault that it's cracked and can't hold nothin', and it ain't the water's fault that it fell through the cracks."

He drew quiet. She could hear him turn the television off as silence took over.

"Yeah. Yeah," was all he offered.

*He could use some therapy, too, but he has to want it.*

"She loves us, Nelson. It's—"

"I know that. You ain't gotta to tell me that."

"I am aware you know that. You cut me off before I could finish my sentence. She loves us—it's just that Mama has a problem expressin' her feelings. I kinda realized that recently. I mean, I always knew, but I finally put it into context."

"Well, goody goody gum drop for yoooouuuu."

"Nelson don't be ugly." She smirked, fighting between wanting to laugh, and wanting to curse him out. "I've been mad at her for a long time. She is who she is, and all we can do is tell her how we feel about it and let it go."

'Mama has a problem expressin' her feelings, huh? Jo-Ann don't have no problem expressing anger though, now does she? She do that shit mighty well." His words cut like hot iron to metal. Before she could respond, her phone rang.

"Nelson, somebody callin' me." She glanced at the caller-ID and realized it was Sunshine, her stripper associate from the Sweet Soiree Gentleman's Club. *What she doin' calling me this early in the day? Matter of fact, Sunshine rarely calls me, period.* "Let me click over right quick. It's one of my old friends from the club. Hold on, okay?"

"Alright."

She glanced at the ID once more, then clicked over. "Hey, Sunshine. What's up, baby? Everything okay?"

"Giiiirrrrl! Did you hear what the fuck happened?!"

"Huh? About what? With who?"

"Somebody crushed Dice's car with one of those big construction cars! What do they call 'em? A backhoe? No! A bulldozer! Yeah! A mothafuckin' bulldozer, girl! Rolled it flat as a pancake. It looks like a metal rug!"

The blood drained from Nadia's body. Her skull began to pound. She pressed her body against the edge of her seat, bracing herself for the second shoe to drop.

"...How... how do you know that this is true? Did he just say so?"

"No! Dice ain't been in here since he got banned for followin' you home. Shake 'nd dem made sure of that. I'm at the crib right now and saw it. It's been all over the news this afternoon. You know that car of his was his prized possession. Now it's just a cookie sheet. He better get to baking!" Sunshine hooted.

"Oh my..." Nadia stood to her full height, feeling a wave of lightheadedness.

"They keep showin' the footage and it's funny as hell, girl! Somebody backed up, rolled over it, then did it again. They did it twice. Talk about standin' on business. More like rollin' on business!" Sunshine's shrill laughter echoed over the line. "They see me rollin'! They hatin'! Tryna catch me riiiidin', diiiirty!" She sang, laughing hard now. "He was an asshole, but my God, that's extreme! He was cryin' on the news about it, too, girl. That was the icin' on the cake."

"Oh, they interviewed him?"

"Mmm hmm! His voice was crackin' like my grandma-ma's knees! See how karma works? God don't play about you, Nadia."

"...Yeah, it, uh, it sure seems that way. Um, Sunshine, I'm on the phone with my brother. Let me call you back, okay?"

"Okay. Oh, and we miss you, girl! Come visit!"

"I miss y'all, too." Nadia struggled to end the call, trying to sound unmoved and pulled together, but finally managed. She clicked back over to her brother, but he'd already hung up. Reaching for the remote control, she turned on the television, her hand shaking. The first news channel had on the weather report, so she switched to another station. She waited a few minutes, then felt her body go hot.

A black reporter wearing a dark red shirt and black slacks stood in front of a brick ranch home, a slightly distressed look on her face. "... It happened around seven this morning, according to a neighbor who wishes to remain anonymous. They were awakened by a loud noise, like a dump truck running over glass, she said, only to discover that someone on an old excavator had compressed their neighbor's vehicle. The neighbor added that initially she thought that perhaps the car owner wished to have it demolished, and this was some do-it-on-site service being provided, but moments later when the homeowner came out of the house and screamed, then dropped to his knees, she realized that wasn't the case."

The news coverage then showed an earlier clip of the crushed car being loaded onto some sort of long flatbed attached to a tow truck. There Dice stood beside it, in his robe, his eyes watery as he screamed into the microphone and looked angrily into the camera.

"I TOL' Y'ALL (BLEEEEEP!) I DON'T KNOW WHO DID THIS (BLEEP)! BUT I'MMA FIND OUT AND THAT MOTHAF-(BLEEP) BETTER COUNT HIS DAYS! I'M DYNOMITE DICE, DAMN IT! I'M WIT' THE (BLEEP!)," Dice went on ranting, screaming at the top of his lungs. His voice cracked repeatedly, and he looked pitiful and wild about the eyes. At the end of a pair of long, skinny legs, his feet were clad in a pair of beat-up fuzzy blue slippers reminding her of Cookie Monster, as his robe swung widely, revealing his small pot belly with jail tattoos scribbled all over it.

Nadia picked up her remote and rewound the footage. She did it again, and again, until tears streamed down her face from laughter—so much she was on the verge of choking. After she'd gotten her fill, she got to her feet and called Lennox. She wasn't surprised when she got no answer. Instead of sending a text message, she left a simple voicemail: "I know." She ended the call, then poured herself a glass of water. She actually wanted liquor, and lots of it. Grabbing her phone to make another call, she took several deep breaths as she mustered up the courage.

"We're sorry. The number you have reached has been disconnected."

Surprised, she then dialed another number.

"Hi, Marie, it's Nadia."

"Nadia! Oh my goodness! I haven't heard from you in so long, baby! How are you? Your mama and brother?"

"I'm doing fine, honey. Everybody is well." Marie lived in Atlanta, and was the aunt of her insane ex-boyfriend, LeRon. She was a good, big-hearted woman who'd also warned her while she'd been dating her nephew, who she helped raise, stating that LeRon was a waste of her time— she urged her to cut him loose, for he would only cause misery. Nadia lived to regret not heeding that advice. They'd formed a friendship of sorts, and stayed in touch off and on since she'd moved back home to Houston. "How have you been, Marie?"

"I've been good! About to take Kyla to the grocery store to get some school supplies for a project she's workin' on."

"Ohhh, how old is Kyla now?"

"Fifteen! Can you believe I have a fifteen-year-old granddaughter now? Time flies."

She and Marie caught up for a little bit, and then, she asked the pressing question.

"Marie, have you heard from LeRon?"

"I saw him a couple of days ago at his apartment, but I couldn't stay long. He was with his physical therapist."

"Physical therapist?"

"Yeah, he was finally released from the hospital about a week ago." Nadia's heart began to race.

"…The hospital? For what?"

"What? You didn't know? I figured since he keeps your name in his mouth so much he woulda used it as a guilt trip, and told you as soon as he gained consciousness." She heard the woman suck her teeth.

"I don't know anything about any of this."

"Well, that definitely shocks me, 'cause one thing LeRon is gone do is throw a pity party and expect a full house."

"In fairness, I asked him to stop callin' me, and he—"

"I know you told him to stop, but he refused, so I figured this would be no different."

"Well, he hasn't called me in a while. I... uh, I needed to ask him something today, and when I unblocked his number and tried calling him just now to do so, I found his phone was disconnected."

"Nadia, the phone is probably just cut off 'cause he ain't pay the bill. He got another one though, but it ain't that fancy iPhone. Hell, he ain't been able to talk properly for weeks. Mouth all messed up." Her stomach began to clench. "Some guy got LeRon, and got him bad. Probably someone he stole somethin' from or did wrong! I tol' that boy to quit fuckin' wit' people!"

"Did he get into a fight? What happened?"

"Honey, it was far from a fight. More like an ambush. LeRon said it was a big ol' burly dude dressed in all black, drivin' a black big rig truck. Said the guy jumped out of the rig and broke several of his ribs, and both of his knees, with a big ass baseball bat!"

Nadia held onto the kitchen counter for support.

"Oh... oh, my goodness. That's terrible." *LENNOX!!!! GOT DAMN IT!!!*

"Did the police arrest anyone?" She cleared her throat, trying to pull herself together.

"Nope, and I doubt they will because nobody saw it happen."

"Oh, man... that's crazy. No cameras or anything to

corroborate what he said happened?" *Please! Please! Please!*

"Well, here's the crazy thing about that. Some strange way, the two cameras that were pointed in that direction were disabled, accordin' to the police."

"Damn. Where did this happen?"

"It was over there in Sugar Hill and you know LeRon has a criminal record, so the police ain't checkin' for him with all the mischief he's been in. They claimed to have tried to retrieve the footage, or so they said. Nobody knows either way. So that means it's just his version of what happened. He basically described the Grim Reaper wrestler, girl! Oh, I mean the Undertaker. That was before yo' time. It just sounds crazy. The police probably think it was drug or gang activity, but I actually believe his ass about this. He seemed genuinely shook up."

"Wow... this is crazy. Does he know the people who did it?"

"It was just one person, he said. He ain't get a good look at 'em. How it happened was, he said he had left a party, and about ten minutes into the drive, this big truck was blockin' the road at like two or three in the mornin' at the end of the street. He kept honking and they wouldn't move, so he got out of his car. That was mistake number one! His dumb ass got outta that car, and it could have ended up like a scene in a horror movie, Nadia! I done taught that boy betta than that. If it had been *me*, I would have put my car in reverse and found another way home. But not my nephew. LeRon's dumb ass approached the truck to tell whoever was in there to move, and this big guy opened the cab door, dressed in all black with his face covered with some Vendetta Guy Fawkes type mask, jumped out with a big ol' baseball bat, and beat the brakes off my nephew.

"Beat him down until he turned to jam! Blackberry molasses on bread that taste and look like pavement! Stomped him like his name was Kirk Franklin! One doctor said his knee was split so bad, it's a wonder he'll ever be able to walk again on it without a knee replacement. He's gonna be like the tin man from the Wizard of Oz. Squeakin' and sqawkin' when he walks. He's got many months of rehab ahead of him. A long road indeed."

"As much shit as LeRon put me through, I'd never want this for him. That's too bad."

"Yes, it is. And as much as LeRon has made my sister's life miserable, and been in his share of shit, I cried when I first heard about this attack. I just want him to get his life right, you know? Too many crazy people out here in this world to be just walkin' up to any ol' body. I hope this teaches him to appreciate life more 'cause baby, he almost lost his!" Marie went on to discuss other things. Nadia half-listened, but pretended to be completely invested in the conversation. Once they parted ways, she picked up her phone and dialed Lennox once again.

This time, he picked up. The sounds of 'Not Like Us,' by Kendrick Lamar, played in the background. Lennox let out a lazy laugh, while another voice, a man's, was talking in the background. *He seems to be having a mighty good time. Especially for someone who was cosplaying as the Incredible Hulk and did a Hulk SMASH earlier in the day! THIS MOTHAFUCKA RIGHT HERE!* She grabbed a fistful of her nightgown and squeezed it, trying to control any potential outburst that may roll off of her tongue.

"Baby," she said in a sing-song voice. "How's every-thing?"

"Oh, it's lovely, honey. Just lovely."

"Did you get my voicemail?"

"I didn't check it yet. I'm over my cousin's house. About to leave from here in a bit, swing by my father's, then come back to your place."

"We need to talk. I tell you what, you finish your... errands, as you called them, and go on back home. I will meet you at your house later tonight instead."

"Oh, so *now* you're in the mood to have a chat? Last night you were on mute. Wanna talk to me about shit, huh?"

"I sure do, Mr. Bob the motherfuckin' Builder, also known as V for mothafuckin' Vendetta. You like big rigs too, don't you? Goin' from state to state like you some big-time performer on tour! I heard the devil was down in Georgia..."

She was met with a pregnant pause. Then a burst of manly, raucous laughter.

"I will go *wherever* the fuck I have to go, even Jupiter, your Majesty, to make a left thing go right."

"Well, seems to me you definitely hit it out of the ball-park, and flew into outer space. Seems to me that you were a baseball player in a past life, and that you like big ma-chines best, too."

"The bigger, the better. Ain't that right, baby girl? I *love* construction work. I prefer to work with my hands, If you know what I mean."

"You do? Well aren't you handy! Speaking of Bob the Builder and construction, I feel like deconstructing some shit right about now. Like yo' damn face. What do you think about that?!"

He snickered. "You should be thanking me."

"Thanking you? No, I should not! I am worried now. What if the authorities find out? That would be it. Call it a wrap! How could you do this?! I love you! Why would you put yourself in jeopardy like this?!"

"I love you, too… that's why I took care of business."

"I don't want anything to happen to you! You are playing these dangerous games. You apparently wanna be up under the damn prison, Lennox. You just out here runnin' amuck!" She waved her arm about, wishing he could understand. "You have to be strategic about this sort of thing! I'll give you credit for makin' it harder for things to be pinned on you—you at least put some thought into it— but it *still* doesn't mean you covered all of your tracks!"

"Actually, I did. It's amazing how simple it is to mess up tire marks so that they're untraceable."

"…This is insane. I can't believe what I'm hearing. This ain't the wild west!"

"Oh, but it *is* the zoo… I'm a handler. I handle shit." He chuckled—just as easy as he pleased.

"I bet you do, mothafucka. You're not The Incredible Hulk!"

"I don't know what to tell you, baby, and I don't know what you expected me to do, Nadia." He yawned, as if getting bored of the whole discussion. "They let that dumb

Dice fucker out of jail with a slap on the wrist after he terrorized you, and practically destroyed your car. That LeRon the Con idiot kept callin' and threatening you nonstop, even after several warnings. You think I was going to wait around to see if he made good on it? Something had to be done! I'm the top dog, baby. Throw me a bone. Every dog has his day! WOOF! WOOF!" He burst out laughing, like he was at a damn comedy club. She heard a man in the background following suit, too. Both of them giggling like school girls.

*OH, SO HE HAS SOMEONE CO-SIGNING THIS SHIT. THAT'S ONE OF HIS CRAZY ASS COUSINS. THESE FUCKING WILDE MEN... THEY ARE NUTS!*

"I will see yo' ass this evening at ten, boy."

"You do that, sexy. I look forward to it. Oh, and wear something pretty. I wanna smash. AGAIN." He and his demented cousin erupted in laughter once more, but she cut them short. She angrily disconnected the call and began jumping around in place, stomping and screaming.

"HE'S *STILL* DESPICABLE! HE'S *STILL* DOIN' THE SAME SHIT! Therapy my ass! He told me he had a trainers' meeting a while back, but I bet that's when he took his ass to Atlanta." Flashes of when he beat up that man at the restaurant raced through her mind. *Talking about he's reformed now... PLEASE! He's just a better monster...*

She stormed out of the kitchen, made her way into the master bathroom, and started the water. After a long, hot shower, she calmed down a bit. When she stood in front of the mirror combing her wet hair with a shampoo comb, she glared at herself, hating what looked back at her. Her stark reflection.

And she couldn't stop smiling…

ROMAN SAT ACROSS from him, his bare chest exposed and his long legs covered in expensive white linen pants. Bare feet patted against the floor to a drum-filled beat of, Khruangbin & Leon Bridges', 'Texas Sun.' Roman had eclectic musical tastes—that fit him perfectly. The mysterious dark twinkle in his light cinnamon eyes and twisted smirk was his usual expression. It rarely left his face, regardless of his mood.

Lennox studied his cousin's apartment in appreciation. Roman enjoyed the finer things in life. The man's downtown Houston digs were high class and fit for the wealthy, with an edge. The modern loft boasted high ceilings, ribbed pillars, Greek replica statues and a kitchen fit for a chef. It was a huge brick-walled structure with multiple rooms, some of them behind lock and key. An open space with wall-to-ceiling windows showcased the city skyline.

Roman tapped his cigar into a large amethyst ashtray. Tilting his bare chin towards the rafters, he clicked his tongue. "It's funny when they get mad at us for doin' what we need to do, right?" His eyes narrowed, growing dark.

"Of course. Most women don't understand Wilde men, and the women that do understand us, we don't want 'em."

Roman laughed at that, then pointed to his empty glass. "More whiskey?"

"Nah, I'm straight. I'll be leavin' soon anyway."

"Well, I appreciate you stoppin' by, even if it's not for the best of reasons."

Lennox set his glass down and nodded.

"Lennox, I wish when we were younger we'd spent more time together. I was usually with Phoenix and Ryder, and then I went into the Marines, and—"

"It's okay, man. Our parents had alliances. Drawn lines in the sand. There was a hierarchy." Lennox shrugged.

Roman nodded as he smoothed out an imaginary wrinkle in his pants. Taking a swig of his brandy, he set the empty glass down. He leaned forward, and there was that look again—an unspoken hatched-up, devious plan was on the horizon.

"Lennox, I know you're worried about me. Want me to be proactive and take Gramps seriously... I am. I just refuse to let him see me sweat."

Lennox was not certain how to respond. Roman often said things that weren't true—he was a poker player, after all. A good one. No, great.

"I just want you to be careful and most of all, safe. Grandpa can't entice you with money. You've already got it. He can't cajole you wit' a fancy gig or popularity. You're an ex-Marine and now a successful investment banker. But, you have a past. As we all do."

Roman offered a subtle bow, then grinned. "Yeah, I do. The Black Sheep is what grandpa named me, right? An embarrassment to the Wilde family name." He cackled.

"Well, bein' a successful and proud outlaw in his mind I guess can do that, but I think it's remarkable how you thrive, in spite of it all. You keep your cool... I think that's what Grandpa likes about you. He thinks he can use that part of your personality to his advantage."

"Eh, it's more than that... You know that. He wants me to make some illicit moves on his behalf. Jeopardize all I've worked for, now that I'm keepin' my nose clean."

"He wants access to the accounts in your care, and insider trade information."

"And you know this!" Roman gestured as if his hand were a gun, and he was pulling the trigger. "The fucker is so greedy, his billions aren't enough, Lennox."

"It's not the money. It's not the dollar amount, Roman. It's the control."

They rested in a brief moment of silence.

"He won't be happy until he destroys everything I worked so hard for. But," Roman grimaced in a nonchalant sort of way, "I'd expect nothin' less from him."

"Just be ready. That's all I'm saying." Lennox grabbed his keys. "Well, I better get goin'. I gotta swing by my dad's house, then go get cussed out by my lady." They both got to their feet, laughing at the same time.

"She's lucky you didn't kill them. You went easy on 'em, far as I'm concerned," he said in a somber tone.

"Exactly. This is the Kumbaya version of myself." He pointed at his chest. "The elevated version. She thinks I just popped off, but she has no fuckin' idea."

"I remember the old you. You definitely weren't shy around some revenge. Life did a number on you though. I get it."

"Life did a number on both of us, Roman. But yeah... The old Lennox woulda had both of those motherfuckers six fuckin' feet deep. This was a favor."

"Pre-fuckin'-cicely. She should be happier than a pig in shit."

They bumped fists. Roman walked him to the large industrial looking door equipped with about five locks and a security system mounted to the wall beside it. Lennox went to undo the first lock, and Roman reached for his wrist.

"It's been a while since I've been in the Marines. Some believe, once a Marine, always a Marine, Lennox." His throat constricted and a dire expression crossed his face. "If you need any help with finishing this shit off, if you need backup, you holler at me, you hear me? He's closin' in on you, and he's gonna go after that girl."

Lennox nodded in agreement. "Thanks. I will definitely call you if I need to."

"Grandpa doesn't expect us to band together. He expects us to stay separated, like how some of our parents tried to do us, because of his influence, while growin' up. He'd purposefully cause division. Create cliques and confusion in the family. Messy, devious shit. Almost everyone says Kage is crazy. But Kage was the only one who was man enough, at the age of thirteen, to do what all of them were too chicken shit to do as full-grown adults."

"I can't argue with that. Kage has some problems, but his instinct and bullshit detector is trigger happy, and scary accurate."

"Kage used to make fun of me." Roman smiled sadly. "Call me 'Pretty Boy,' things like that, but he was protective of all of us, too. He took the role of oldest cousin seriously.

So, since you say you're communicatin' wit' him, and now with me, I say we stay as a united front. The three of us at least. People outside of our family can't understand this. Can't get how one man can control a business, a family, and a whole damn city the way he does, but when you grow up the way we did, we get it. I got you, man." He patted his back.

Lennox took him into his arms and hugged him. Roman was the cool and collected clown. He was damn good with numbers. A slickster. Hard to pin down and read at times, too. Daring and arrogant. When he offered himself to you, that was a compliment. He was stingy with his time, and even more stingy with his advice.

They hugged one more time, said their farewells, and he walked away, slowing when he heard all the locks sliding into place. Roman stated that before Grandpa had sent his goons to grab him, he had three locks on the door. Now, he had five and a big ass loaded rifle hidden in the umbrella bin, right by the front entrance…

# CHAPTER TWENTY-SEVEN

## *Granddaddy of them All*

L ENNOX STARED AT the missed call number. He didn't know who it was, but they'd called multiple times. No voicemail. No text. He chose to ignore it, but not block it just yet. He arrived at his father's house after such a busy, and somewhat fun-filled, day. He was looking forward to this evening, too—even though he realized it more than likely involved plentiful arguing.

Nadia had made it clear how she felt about his recent goings-on. He had no regrets. The butting of heads would ensue. He pulled up into his father's long, winding driveway. The estate was just as he remembered it as a child. Well-manicured lawn. Lion statues outside of the front door, and a winding front porch with plentiful hanging plants. Mama used to take care of those plants and flowers. Now, Dad had a gardener, and he barely kept up with what was what.

Lennox made his way to the front door and rang the

bell. He had his own separate security code to enter the house, but he wanted his father to come directly to the door. Open it for him. Let him in. He waited for a minute or two, then rang the bell again. He knew Dad was home, despite the long time waiting for him to answer the door. Dad had become a recluse to some degree after all.

Finally, his father arrived. He could see him approaching from beyond the frosted glass of the door windows, crossing the marble floor one stride at a time. A dark royal shade of blue draped the shadowy figure.

Dad paused at the door, as if needing to take a deep breath, then opened it. He stood there in his thick sapphire robe and matching slippers, a gold crucifix pendant around his neck with sparse chest hair showing beneath it. Dad's dark blond hair with wisps of gray at the sideburns was somewhat damp as if he'd recently gotten out of the shower. His slight widow's peak gave him a look of intelligence and wisdom—something Lennox believed was nothing more than a physical stereotypical trait that his father didn't actually possess.

"Lenny, what a surprise." Dad's eyes remained rather small, and his lips curled ever so slightly, as if it took all of his strength to muster a shred of kindness. "What are you doin' here?"

"Was just in the neighborhood. Thought I'd swing by."

Lennox looked down at his father's hand. Long, pale fingers were wrapped tightly around a cold one. He swallowed the unspoken reaction that hung on the tip of his tongue by not saying, *'How many is that so far today?'* Instead, he asked if he could come inside.

"Of course. You're my son."

Dad opened the door wider, and Lennox stepped over the threshold. He looked around as he heard the door close hard behind him, and several deadbolts being locked. Then the beeps and button noises of the alarm being reset. The house smelled fresh, new and airy, as if Dad had just moved in. The marble floors were spic and span, as was the opulent furniture and large frescos that gleamed beneath real gold frames that sparkled as if they'd just been dusted. The place reminded him somewhat of a museum. Not a thing out of place. Not a speck of dust, not a touch of life or essence. So different from the days when he and his sister raced around chasing one another, hollering and screaming for the hell of it, and did cannonballs in the indoor pool to the blasting sounds of rock 'nd roll, country, and rap music.

Lennox's ears peaked as he heard what sounded like classical music playing on low volume. He'd never heard his father play classical music before. *How strange.* It was there, but barely detectable.

"Ya hungry?" Dad asked, his brows slightly furrowed as if he were annoyed about something, but decided to focus on food instead.

Lennox turned to him, his hands on his hips. Their gazes hooked and his stomach clenched, but not from just hunger.

"Yeah. I could eat."

"You're always hungry." Dad chuckled as he made his way past him. "I just had a food delivery. Way too much food for just me anyway. You're right on time."

Lennox followed him into the kitchen. Stainless steel double ovens. Two microwaves. A LED illuminated built-in curio cabinet. State of the art smart appliances. Both sides of the white and black kitchen had large white cabinets filled with some of the most expensive plates and glassware one could buy. He sat down at the hefty irregularly shaped white marble kitchen table with enormous matching scoop chairs. They swiveled back and forth, allowing him to let off a little excess steam.

Dad reached into a brown paper bag soiled with grease stains, and pulled out a hoagie sandwich wrapped in oily parchment paper. It sure smells good, whatever it was. He took out another one and set each on a white plate, along with potato chips and a pickle spear. Without a word, he slid one of the plates toward Lennox, then went to the fridge. Lennox carefully peeled the paper off the sandwich. It was a meatball sub with loads of marinara sauce, jalapeño peppers, thinly sliced onions, and heaps of mozzarella cheese.

"Why'd you order two sandwiches if you weren't expecting anyone?"

"One for lunch. One for supper."

His father poured a tall glass of milk, then shuffled back over to him and set it beside his plate.

"Thank you."

"Welcome." A sad smile creased Dad's face as he reached into his robe pocket, pulled out a cigarette, and lit it. Then, he just stood there, staring at him, sorrow in his soupy eyes.

"What?" Lennox asked between chomps of the hoagie.

He dabbed the side of his mouth with a napkin. The violins in the song seemed to get louder.

"When you were a lil' boy, you loved meatball hoagies. You remember that?"

Lennox thought about it for a moment. "Nah, not really," he said around a mouthful of food.

"There was a greasy spoon down in Benton. It was called Harold's Diner. Long time ago." Dad waved his hand as if it were a simple, fleeting thought. "I'd take you 'nd Silva 'round there and you'd always get that meatball hoagie. Extra sauce and cheese. These aren't as good, but they're a close second." He looked down at his own untouched plate. "I rarely buy 'em now. Then today, I used Uber Eats and purchased two—and here you come. Like it was meant to be. Just a bit ironic is all." Dad shrugged, picked up his beer and chugged it hard. The older man's long throat constricted and his Adam's apple bobbed as he swallowed the piss-colored brew—his medicine for his mental issues and emotional damage. *Am I collateral damage?*

"Yeah... like I said. I don't remember that." Lennox picked up his glass of milk, then took a small sip.

"You were young. 'Bout six or seven or so. I imagine that's not somethin' you'd store in your memory bank. Anyway, your mama wanted y'all to eat healthy, so I'd do it on the sly. I'd whisper to you to tell your mama that we were just going out to get some milk or somethin' like that. We went to that place many times together before they closed. Great food." That sad smile returned to his face again. This time, his eyes watered. "Not a lotta candies, cakes or cookies were in the house. Definitely not greasy, tasty submarines, bubbly Coke, and thick cut steak fries. But you 'nd Silva didn't ever get a cavity, either. So, I guess it paid off."

He looked dreamily towards a large bay window and sucked on the cigarette. Nothing outside but absolute magnificence.

"I remember when Silva and I were younger, we saw you as the fun parent and Mama as the meanie." Lennox mustered a smile as the memories flooded his mind.

"Yeah. A little fun never hurt nobody. Your mama was a pretty serious woman, but she'd laugh with me and *at* me. She had a beautiful smile, Lenny, I'm sure you remember it... and her giggle was hilarious. She had the funniest laugh... said I was the most amusing man she'd ever met. She loved my way with numbers. Found it sexy." He brought his hand to his face, rested his nose against his curved knuckle and shook his head, then tapped his ashes into a nearby ashtray.

"I wish you woulda gotten remarried. You needed someone." *Someone to hold you accountable and stand between you and Grandpa. Be your peace.*

"I've had some beautiful women in my life, Lenny. Before your mama. A few after. None of 'em compared. She was just as lovely on the inside, too." His voice cracked, and he quickly turned away. "So, so smart. Erotic. Witty. Faithful. Trustworthy. Great mother. Wonderful wife. Worked hard. She got that degree, all right. A business woman, an amazing doctor, and damn near a saint. Saints aren't always perfect. We all have a past." He swallowed, then sighed. Took a drag of the cigarette. "She was open and honest with me. I protected her secrets." His voice trembled, and Dad gripped the back of the chair, squeezing it hard with one hand.

"And that's why I could never love another woman the same way. Believe me, I tried. There was no point in getting remarried. I would only compare the lady to your mother, and none of them could compete. Nobody wants to be alone." He pulled the chair he'd been standing behind out and slinked down onto it. He stared at his food on the plate while Lennox ate slowly. His appetite was waning.

"You're right. I've got someone important in my life now, too. Someone I'd protect from everything. Even from someone who brought me into this world if necessary." Their eyes locked. "Why are you talkin' to me about this right now?" He shoved the plate away.

"Because you don't care for me too much, Lenny."

"That's not true. I love you. I just think that—"

"No, no. You think I do everything wrong, and some stuff I did do wrong, but the *one* thing I did right was to fall in love with and marry that woman. Your mother." Dad smashed his cigarette in the ashtray, extinguishing it. "The second thing I did right was to make her the mother of my two children. Well, I guess that's three things right, technically." Lennox picked up the glass of milk and brought it to his lips. "...Your grandfather called me last night."

"I knew you were up to something." Lennox burst out laughing, showing his disgust in a big smile as his heart rate accelerated. He shook his head, sick of it all.

"Stop. Let me finish." Dad put his hand up. "It's nothing crazy. He says he wants to meet with you soon, is all.

Discuss things man to man. Maybe come to a mutual agreement."

"The only thing I can agree with Grandpa about is that we all must pay taxes and we're all going to die one day. Other than that, there is nothin' mutual about us, 'cept my last name. There is only one man in this equation, and it isn't Grandpa. Demons aren't human." He took a big swallow of milk and set the glass down.

"Lennox, you could at least hear Daddy out."

"Me and *your* father have absolutely nothin' to talk about."

"Lennox… I fear he's going to move forward with contactin' your mother's family. Is that what you want? And he won't stop there. He'll make sure it gets back to their neighbors and friends about your mama escorting. He said lust is a terrible sin, and you know how Daddy feels about that sort of thing."

"Lust? That's like a lush blade of grass getting angry at a tree because its leaves are green. You can't be for real? Dad, that old fucker screws a different, random woman almost every day of the week! He's a king-sized pervert, and a king-sized hypocrite, to match his king-sized sexual appetite, at his ripe old age. If it's true that the good die young, he'll live forever. He's probably a vampire. I damn sure wouldn't be surprised."

Dad's complexion deepened as he drummed his fingers against the table.

"I know your grandfather is a ladies' man." Lennox rolled his eyes. *What a nice way to put it!* "I get that, but his beliefs are important to him, son. He believes in God, and he reads his Bible assiduously. My father is far from perfect, but nobody can say he isn't religious. He is very involved in the church. Hell, he puts his money where his mouth is. He owns the 'Christ Pages,' book chain, and—"

"I don't give a shit if he owns the damn old school yellow pages! I don't give a dog's lick on a cat's pink ass about him owning that Christian bookstore chain, all of the donations he gives to the Baptist church, all the speaking engagements at these Christian cult-like conventions he gets paid thousands of dollars to speak at for just a few minutes. That's something to cover the *true* him. The one that looks at the Bible and goes, 'Let me say I do everything in here, but in fact, I do the exact opposite.' In fact, I bet Grandpa thinks he is the second coming of Christ, when really, he's the Anti-Christ. He's completely delusional and insane. He uses religion to control people, and he warps scripture to suit whatever it is he's yapping about."

"Okay, I hear you." Dad gritted his teeth as if in pain. "All of that aside, he's gonna send proof of your mama's past. We can't let that happen. Your mother would roll over in her grave."

"And you think she ain't rollin' around in her tomb right now from the idea of her husband, the father of her children, tryna sell his only son into family slavery?! You think she'd approve?! She hated Grandpa's guts!"

"...But she loved her family, and I'm not tryna sell you at all! If you worked for your grandfather, your struggles would be over and you know he'd never do anything to you! He loves you. He wants you protected."

"Protected like *you*? Are you protected right now, Daddy, or do you *need* protection?" The temperature in the room seemed to plummet.

"Family was everything to your mama! They'll be destroyed if you don't do the right thing. Lenny, please…" Dad put his hands together as though he was praying. "I know you think that—"

"I DON'T WANT TO END UP LIKE YOU! In a big ass beautiful house all alone! Afraid to ever love again, not because you don't want to or no woman is good enough, or compares to Mama, but because of your father's control over you! You know it may drive that lady away, or even better, she'd be just like Mama and stand up to the old man! You don't owe me shit, but to ask me to do this is unreal after all I have done for this family! Haven't I done enough to sacrifice for you?!" He balled up his napkin and tossed it across the kitchen. "I was the father I needed to not only myself, but to Silva." He pointing to himself, his body jerking forward, as his anger unleashed. "I'm the one who risked goin' to prison to keep the bills paid because all you wanted to do was crunch numbers and feel sorry for yourself! You're only semi-sober right now because the day isn't quite over. 'Round ten o'clock tonight, you'll be drunk and your demons will be swimming in the best whiskey and gin that money and your soul can buy! You didn't deserve Mama. And she deserved better than the sorry likes of *you*!"

"LENNOX! Watch your fucking mouth! You're goin' too damn far!"

"I ain't gone far enough! You think a damn meatball sandwich is gonna clean up all the wrong you've done to me and your daughter? Save the day?!" Dad hung his head.

"The neglect from being with Grandpa, helping to run his crooked endeavors instead of coming to Silva's plays, and my football games? Every time I looked out in the stands, I saw my mama. She was supposed to be at work! She had patients who needed her! But no, most of the time she was right there—rain, sleet, or snow. The only time you had the balls to stand up to Grandpa was on the crooked back of grief. Mama died. You cried. Grandpa lied. You absorbed some of her strength, somehow, some way. She must've left you a little behind. A last gift. You used it up too fast, and turned back to your spineless self as soon as things got hot again. Couldn't even stand on business and let Grandpa know that you weren't going to take his shit anymore. YA HAD KIDS! WHAT ABOUT *US*?!"

"More of this!" Dad slammed his fist against the table. "A circular conversation. You think everybody can be some gotdamn Superman?! YOU THINK EVERYONE IS CUT OUT TO MAKE PENNIES AT SOME RESTAURANT OR WORK AT SOME FUCKIN' GYM ALL DAMN DAY, THEN WORK YOURSELF INTO A STUPOR AT NIGHT AT THAT STUPID DANCE CLUB?! You live in a little house in a workin' class neighborhood. Wildes don't live like that! You're exhausted, and what do you have to show for it?!"

"Daddy... I've got love, to show for it. I've got self-respect, to show for it. I've got a plan that God has blessed me with, and made my dream a reality, to show for it! I'm a realist. I'm a peaceful person until I can no longer be. I'm a praying man. I'm somebody's soon-to-be future husband and father, and I take that shit seriously! I'm now a business

owner due to all of my hard work, prayers, and persever-
ance. You're lookin' at the upcoming owner of R.S.S.
GYM – Rain, Sleet, or Snow." Dad's lips parted, and his
eyes widened. "That's right. I finished my certifications. I've
got my degree, finally putting it to use… and I did it all by
myself. No hand-outs. No blood money. I made my OWN
money to pay for them classes, my house, and everything
else. You talk down on my jobs I do to make ends meet.
You make fun of my house – but I paid for it outta my own
pocket. Too bad you can't say the same.

"I have everything I need. This house isn't really yours.
It's Grandpa's because it came from blood money. He
owns you and everything in it. Blood to him isn't just
family, Daddy. Blood to Grandpa means oppression.
Tyranny. Servitude! I don't bend no knee to nobody but
God, and I'd rather be panhandling on the side of the damn
highway in 100°F weather with a fur coat on, than end up
giving my life to a man who sees me as nothin' more than a
step to climb up on! A back to stand on! An ass to kick
when he's mad or bored. I realize somethin' right now
though. I'm sorry for expecting better of you. That wasn't
fair of me. How could I expect you to be a good daddy
when you never really had one?"

Tears streamed down his father's cheeks. He rarely saw
his father cry, and the sight broke him in two. Regardless,
the man needed to hear the harsh, ugly truth. All that
glittered wasn't gold, and a soul was to never be sold.

"You are just like your mama… Good God, you're just
like 'er, Lennox." Daddy covered his face with both hands
and wept.

"...And you're wrong about what you said earlier. I could never hate you. You're my father. You never beat me. Never talked down to me. Never tried to intentionally hurt me. But you're not built for what I wanted you to do. You're not made to move mountains, when you can barely move yourself outta bed, look in the mirror, and face the day..." Lennox took a deep breath and released it. "Now I have to make a quick call and take a piss."

Standing, he shoved the chair hard against the table. He didn't bother looking back at his father as he made his way out of the kitchen, down a long corridor. He passed the first bathroom, then a second. He went around the corner, looked both ways to ensure Dad hadn't followed or one of the maids wasn't in the hall, and typed in the code to enter Dad's office. He hoped it was the same one he knew of and that his father hadn't changed it. The thick wooden door clicked and he stepped inside, closing it softly behind himself. There, on Dad's big black desk, was his laptop.

The room smelled like leather and bourbon. He made his way to the oversized desk chair and booted up the laptop, cringing when the thing made a loud noise. As soon as it was up and running, he put it on mute. One thing about his father was that he relied on everyone else to keep his technology up to date. Dad was old school. If you needed your taxes done or to accept money under the table without getting busted, he was your man—but if you needed a computer software update, he was the last person you'd call. Lennox hoped and prayed that Dad was still rotating the same old five passwords. He typed in the first password Dad might be using.

ACCESS DENIED. That is the incorrect password.

He sighed, and tried another.

ACCESS DENIED. That is the incorrect password.

He knew that if he kept on getting them wrong, eventually he'd be locked out. And worst of all, found out. He said a quick prayer. Tried again.

ACCESS DENIED. That is the incorrect password.

*FUCK!* He massaged his head and mulled the different options.

After a while, he typed: **Aaliyah0110**

The programs began opening, one by one. He sighed with relief, smiling. It was Mama's name, the month and day she was born, of course. He slipped his USB thumb drive out of his pocket and placed it in his father's computer, then opened up several folders on the desktop. His fingers beat against the mouse in rapid succession. One after another, he copied the documents onto the thumb drive. They were encrypted, but he'd worry about that later. Some of the files were rather large. His heart thumped as he grew concerned about being found out. Perhaps their heated discussion had left the man stunned enough that he'd stay put. After a few minutes, most of the files were copied and he ejected his thumb drive and shut down the computer.

He paused when he heard a noise. Looking around the room, he dashed to a small closet where his father kept printer paper, a few coats and what not. As soon as he hid inside, he heard the click of the office door, followed by footsteps. He slumped down in the darkest corner of the closet, careful to monitor his breathing and not move a muscle. He heard the computer boot up. Then clicking. And then his father's voice.

"Hey, Dad. It's me... Mmm hmm.... Well, yeah, I told you that Lennox was here when I thought I saw him outside through the camera, but it turned out to be just some delivery guy. False alarm. It wasn't him after all that stopped by today. You know how my frosted front door is." He laughed nervously. "Afterwards, I did go on and call Lennox since he was on my mind. I asked him about his schedule and what not like you wanted me to, but he was pretty vague. Mmm hmmm... I did... Yeah, that too. I asked casually if he was dating anyone... No... He was vague about that, too. I know you said he's got a girlfriend 'nd all, but it may just be a friend. You know how Lennox is, a bit of a playboy. Chivalrous, too... I understand that, but... okay... yeah, but listen. I know my son very well. Even if they're havin' sex on a regular basis, it may not be as serious as anyone believed.

"I can't because... right... Yeah... yeah... Since he and Silva aren't talkin', that's not an option to try and get her involved to help, so I did think of trying to get someone else to assist instead. I'll continue to try. Eventually he'll open up... I didn't bring it up because he seemed in a bad mood on the phone, ya know?... Mmm hmmm...No, there's no point in pressin' him when he gets like that. He just shuts down... Yeah, it could be... Probably that deal for the fitness center he's trying to open up fell through, like everything else he tries to do, right?"

Dad's fake laughter was almost convincing, but he didn't miss the pain in it. "The bottom line is that he didn't mention anything about anyone confronting her or saying anything, and that's not like him... Right. You and I both know that if he knew, he would have been already there to see you by now...Yes, I agree... He's a hot head when he blows his top... Right!" Dad chuckled.

"Yeah. No self-control! So, maybe he doesn't know after all. Maybe whoever she is, she's thinkin' over the offer and didn't tell him because of that. It's possible. Well, I'll talk with you soon. Bye for now." His father ended the call. A few more clicks on the keyboard, and then the sound of the computer shutting down. Footsteps. Slow and steady. The opening of the office door and then, the closing.

Lennox stayed in place a few moments longer, trying to make sense of what he'd overheard. After a short while, he got to his feet, exited the closet and the office. He returned to the kitchen, where his father sat on the same chair at the table as if he'd never left, his hands clasped on his lap. He noticed his plate and glass were gone. After a minute or two, his old man broke the silence.

"You said you had to make a phone call. Everything okay?"

"Yeah. Fine. I need to get going."

Dad nodded as he stared down at the table. "Well, let me walk ya out."

Both stood at the same time and journeyed quietly to the front door. Dad turned off the alarm system, then unlocked the door. Before Lennox could walk past, he took him in his arms and squeezed him tight, his love pouring through in his grip. Dad stood back, but kept holding his arms.

"Lennox, some things you said today I don't agree with. Some of them I have to agree with because they're true. It hurt me when you said I wasn't a good father." Lennox swallowed and looked away, feeling suddenly warm all over. "Naw, it's okay... you're right. We all have our crosses to bear. It sucks to have your boy not look up to you. Not respect you. I want to work on our relationship, if you'll let me."

Lennox stood there thinking about how his father had finally fallen on the sword—lied to his own father to save him from something, or some*one*. He knew it was difficult for Dad to do, but he did it anyway. For him.

"We can see what happens," he mumbled.

Dad nodded, hugged him one more time, and they said their goodbyes. Once in his truck, Lennox slid his hand briefly in his pocket, feeling for the USB. He headed out to the main road, on his way home. He figured Nadia would come by soon, ready to give him an earful. He had an earful for her now, too. After overhearing his father and grandfather talking on the phone, the puzzle pieces were beginning to come together. Whatever Nadia hadn't spoken of probably had something to do with Grandpa, some offer or even a conversation. Why else would she brought up? It was not Dice, after all. It didn't matter though. Dice still had that coming. He destroyed Nadia's car, so his car got destroyed too. Big fucking deal. He had bigger fish to fry now. He replayed what his father had said on the phone, over and over in his mind.

*Offer? Relationship? I knew he was having me followed, but I haven't seen anyone lately, and I figured he'd follow her too, but... something's not right.* Nadia was holding back... *SHIT. THAT'S IT! GRANDPA MUST'VE CONFRONTED HER IN PERSON! HE OFFERED HER SOMETHIN', PROBABLY SOME MONEY, TO LEAVE ME ALONE. THAT'S IT!!! THAT SON OF A BITCH!!!*

He found himself suddenly speeding as his dander rose, then slowed down as he cooled his jets. When he pulled into his driveway, Nadia was already parked there. The sounds of 'My Love,' by Justin Timberlake, flowed from her car stereo system. He shook his head, parked right behind her, killed the engine, and got out of his truck. Before he'd even reached her, her driver's side door swung open.

She stood there in a white shirt and tight white jeans. With a pair of black and white Chuck Taylors and a gun on her hip. Black hair flowed down past her shoulders.

"Here's the truth! Your grandfather sent a relative of yours to the club the last night. I don't know the guy's name. Told me to drop you like a hot potato and accept a payoff, or live to regret it," she blurted. "That's why you felt like I was acting a little funny. I pulled a gun on him and he was led out back to receive a beatin' he won't soon forget from one of the bouncers. I didn't want to tell you right then, Lennox, because you'd have gone and got yourself killed or ended up behind bars on account of *me!* Look what you did to Dice and LeRon, and those were minor infractions compared to this!"

"YOU HAD NO RIGHT TO KEEP THIS FROM

ME!"

"I was right to want to shield you! I was going to tell you, but not before I calmed down, and we could both discuss it rationally. You should see how you're looking at me right now – it's like your eyes are turning red right in front of me! Don't you see? I had to protect you from *yourself*."

Invisible spools of hot air rolled from his flared nostrils as if he were about to morph into a raging bull. He could practically feel the blood flowing through his veins, and hear his own heartbeat. He became heated all over, his head began to sweat, and his vision blurred with frenzy. It was worse than he imagined. So much worse…

*KILL HIM. KILL HIM. KILL HIM!*

"I'm sorry, but please believe me when I say that I was going to tell you. I know I was wrong to keep it from you," she added, yanking his mind out of his violent thoughts. "but please look at it from my point of view. I shoulda told you sooner, Lennox, but I was scared you'd fly off the handle and then something bad would happen to you. And I… I just got you back! I didn't wanna lose you!" Her voice shook as an angry tear trailed down her face. She spoke clearly, yet the words didn't sound right, almost as if she were speaking in a foreign language. His worst fears twisted around his heart. They stared at one another for a long while. She tilted her head to the side. "You knew, didn't you?"

"You just confirmed my suspicions. Don't you *ever* in your life hide somethin' that one of my buddies or relatives, or hell, the damn mailman for all I care, did to you that was outta pocket! I don't need your protection, Nadia, I can handle this shit just fine. I can't believe this… Get your ass in this gotdamn house! We've got a score to settle."

He grabbed hold of her arm and led her inside his house. Time to get down to business…

# CHAPTER TWENTY-EIGHT

## *No tea, No shade*

N ADIA FELT HER body sway then hit the wall at an awkward angle when she lost her balance on the way inside of the house. She'd broken free and tried to rush ahead of him, talk some sense into him, but it was no use. Lennox slammed his door so hard, the entire dwelling seemed to shimmy and shake like an earthquake. When he faced her again, unadulterated anger shone in his piercing eyes. She pressed her body against the wall for support. He locked his door while she took several deep breaths and briefly closed her eyes. Her heart nearly pounded out of her chest.

"I know you're angry, Len, but I'm angry with you, too." He kept his back turned towards her as he fiddled with the chain on his door. "You had no business crushin' Dice's car like you were in some monster truck show, and puttin' my ex in the hospital, beatin' him down with a baseball bat like yo' name is Babe Ruth. I don't give a damn about either of those men, but I care about *you*. Just like I told you. You know your grandfather would *love* to find you committin' a crime so he can use that as leverage. You just out in these streets running amuck! This is exactly what I was afraid of, and why I didn't tell you what happened at the strip club in the first place!"

He slipped out of his jacket and hung it up in the closet without uttering a single word. That was when she noticed several large cardboard boxes in his living room, some filled with items she recognized from around his house. Before she could inquire why they were there, he took her wrist and led her down the hallway. His house was dark and cold, not warm and inviting as it typically felt when she'd spend time there. It was as if his entire mood had colored the environment around him. Made the world foggy and dreary, dripping in shades of dull, dank gray.

Opening his bedroom door, he flipped on the switch. Light bathed them as it spread from his ceiling light fixture. His bedroom looked pretty much the same as last time, but felt like a completely different place altogether.

Lennox stood there for a while, his chest heaving.

"Sit." He pointed to the bed.

With hesitant steps, she made her way to the edge of his bed and sat down. He began to pace, then leaned against a dresser, crossing his arms and ankles, chin high. She could see his jaw tightening beneath his short, dark beard as his eyes penetrated her with the fury of a million men.

"Tell me what the hell happened. Everything, from beginning to end."

She rested on her palms, leaning back. "First you tell me

why you did what you did today and why you lied to me about that business trip, when *really* yo' ass was in Georgia actin' a fool?"

They must've stared at one another for eternity, neither willing to break the connection. But then he sighed and lowered his head. She'd won this round, even though that didn't make her feel any better.

"Because with some folks, you give an inch and they take a mile. I've had it. Had it with the secrets, the pain. All of it. Your ex wouldn't respect your boundaries. You kept telling him to leave you the fuck alone. I heard it, I saw it. If I did nothing, I am teaching anyone who hurts you that they can get away with it. We teach people how to treat us, Nadia. Contrary to the way us men act sometimes, we're not stupid. We know when a woman we want has a man, or isn't feeling us the way we're feeling her. They didn't have to see me to know I had you on lockdown, and they still played in my fuckin' face!"

"This sounds like it's more about you than me. An ego problem, Lennox!"

"What the hell are you talking about ?! THIS IS A 'DON'T FUCK WITH MY LADY' PROBLEM, GOT DAMN IT!" He beat his chest with his fist, his eyes practically blood red, his voice so loud it ran through her. Made her innards shake. "To them, it's like I may as well not even exist in your life! You're not alone anymore. *NOBODY* rains on my baby. And I mean NOBODY. Why the fuck am I here if I can't protect the woman I love from harassment, threats, and bullshit?! You're crazy if you think I'd let that slide. I'm not about to hand *no* man a second dick so he can fuck my woman over twice! The old me wouldn't have allowed it to go unchecked after the *first* incident. It would have only taken one slick call, one threatening text message or voicemail. They wouldn't even be breathing right now, Nadia, if the old me was in charge still. I had mercy on them. Mercy is not somethin' that came to me naturally. I had to learn how to receive it, and how to give it. I had to get therapy and make an effort to be more like the man my mother was tryna raise me to be, but even the love of my mama wouldn't have been able to stop me if I *truly* wanted them to sleep with the fishes. I saw the tape of Dice and you… what he did to you that night. Every time I think about it, my anger soars. I can't even guarantee you that I may not eventually finish the job. I'm not making any promises."

Her heart rate accelerated while he continued. "It is what it is. They ran out of chances, and I ran out of grace." He shrugged. "They need to talk to Jesus, not me. I'm done turnin' the other cheek. Plain and simple."

She crossed her arms, unable to argue with him—she knew who the hell he was from the jump. Just because he'd matured didn't mean he wasn't still about standing on business. The Wilde blood was strong, and there was no fighting it. She cleared her throat and started talking, running down what had transpired at the club. She began from the time she entered the Sweet Soiree establishment to the moment the man was dragged out kicking and screaming by the security guard.

"…after he was gone, I dried off and left the shower room."

During her confession, Lennox barely blinked.

"From your description of the guy, I'm ninety-nine percent sure of who it was. Sounds like my idiot cousin Sam. A wannabe Jesse James." He scratched his jaw and started to pace the room. "I know why he picked him though, out of everyone. It proves he was bending his rule a little of leavin' women alone. Grandpa's real funny about that, doing anything to women that requires violence. Now in fairness, Sam probably fucked up the orders. He wasn't supposed to approach you like that in the first place, I'm almost sure of it, but Grandpa wanted you out of the way because he couldn't think of another way to hurt me. He knows none of his sons and grandsons would respect him if they believed he was sending them out to rough up some lady. Grandpa is a king-sized chauvinist, but regardless, I've never seen him lay a hand on no woman. All of his abuse to the women in the family has always been psychological, which may be worse." He shrugged. "Grandpa found a patsy is all. Someone he hoped he could slide under the radar, but it backfired. He's gonna try to set me up now because he wants to get in front of my next move. He thinks I'm the same kid from ten years ago who can't control himself. But I control myself just fine—I just plot things out better now."

"I can't disagree with that." She sucked her teeth, re-playing in her mind the news coverage.

"If he doesn't just sit around and wait to see what I do now that Sam has fucked everything up, he'll try something crazy to lure me to him so he can either try to convince me that what I see before my eyes isn't real, or he may even try to kill me. Anything is possible. So that gives us less time."

"Okay, so what's your next move?"

"Well, I told you when I explained my plan that I would be going high up the damn food chain. Grandpa is a shark, so the only way to stop him is to ask God to dry up the ocean. I have been in contact with the FBI. They're aware of my grandfather's shady activities. Known about it for years. Since the police have been of little assistance due to a good percentage of them being paid off to stay out of his way, we can't rely on them for assistance. That's where I come in. It's been up to me."

He reached into his pocket and pulled out a USB.

"What's that for?"

"On this thumb drive are financial records dating back over fifteen years, the majority of them detailing illegitimate and forbidden accounting activities. My father is meticulous about recordkeeping. He has to be, so he can give the information to other family members for debt collection. The extortion payments. The shady tax practices. The gambling rings. My grandfather owns several legitimate businesses where dirty deeds go down, too. He owns hundreds of rental properties and a small national motel chain. Don't even get me started on what he sometimes uses those for. Now, if I present this to the FBI, my father will go down with him. I was more than willing to take that chance. After all, my father allowed that piece of shit to do irreparable damage to his marriage, to his family, and to everything he held dear. I had no hesitation until..." Lennox sighed. "Until he stood up for me today. He didn't even know I was there... He stood in front of the bullet, so to speak."

"What do you mean? What happened?"

Lennox took a deep breath. "I've been painstakingly workin' on this for months. Grinding! I've been meeting secretly with the FBI and giving them all sorts of information, baby—some of the smaller stuff he was dealing with I could verify, but a lot I could not. The big offenses are what they need. Something to sink their teeth into. They've been struggling for years to obtain solid, concrete proof and couldn't even get a search warrant because they didn't have enough evidence for probable cause. My grandfather has the city on lockdown. It's hard to get close to him because he has a thousand fortresses. I knew I could get the evidence from my father's house, though. Like I told you, the plan all along was to get confirmation of him cheating the government, and of him being involved in reprehensible criminal activities. But I, uh…" He shook his head and laughed miserably. "I can't believe I'm second guessing this now. Shit!"

"You don't want your father to have to go to prison."

"No, I don't."

"Lennox, I know you two don't have the best relationship, but the way you're feeling about this now is understandable. He's *still* your daddy, and though you think he's a fraidy-cat, he did for the most part take care of you and your sister." Their gazes linked. Surely he could read between the bloody lines. "In your heart, you feel like you owe him by not punishing him this way. Especially since he's just been doing what he was taught to do. Have you tried to work out a deal with them so that your father is allowed to walk away with no charges if he cooperates?"

"Of course I tried, but that would require him to testify against his father, Nadia, and he'd never do that in a million years. It's one thing to keep the man's secrets, to even lie to him to protect his son—but if he does *that*, become a rat, he'll not only pay with his life, but it could also put Silva in jeopardy, too. Everyone would go down in flames. A lotta innocent people, too. I'm trying to target one motherfucker, but everything he's touched is covered in gasoline. So when that match strikes, people better run. Houston will be burning."

She nodded in understanding, then slowly stood up. She walked up to him, wrapped her hands around the back of his neck, then placed a soft kiss against his lips.

"I've been doin' some thinking since this mess down at the club happened."

"Yeah, I 'magine so." He wrapped his arms around her waist, brought her flush to his hard, warm body, and offered a slight grin before placing a tender kiss on her lips. "What's on your mind?"

"My grandmother told me a story one day. She talked about old medicine, concoctions, remedies from the doulas and Black nurses back in the old days. Some of those medicines helped a woman end a pregnancy. Wasn't approved by no FDA, and wasn't sittin' on no pharmacy shelf either, but they worked. Medicines for a bad back and stomach ulcers, too. Some of 'em were love spells, if you believe in that sort of thing. They had everything, she said, from homemade ointments to make a ninety-year-old man's dick hard, to stuff that would make you think you were floatin' in outer space, feelin' all fuzzy and good on the inside, and it didn't fuck up your mind and give you sores like this shit that folks are smoking and shooting into their veins today.

"A far-out drug made of nothin' more than fermented grapes, seeds, a dash of snake spit, and a bit of this and that for flavor. Some of those remedies made you stay up all night. Some of them made you sleep all day. Some made you lose your inhibitions. Some made you forget everything you didn't want to think about. Others made you aggressive... or horny. Some just brought out the *real* you. She said many times they actually worked because she'd taken her share of them to know. People just had to realize what they were doin', who to get the right stuff from, and how to take the correct amount."

"This is all very interesting, baby, and if I were in a better mood I wouldn't mind the discussion, but what does this have to do with my grandfather needin' to go to Hell without dragging my father down there with him?"

"Well," she leaned in and stroked his hair, tucking a thick cluster of silky black loose waves behind his ear. "Baby, you can hardly catch an old demon with new solutions. You have to trap them in their own depravities. The new shit, like thumb drives, robots, and fancy technology ain't always the answer. Sometimes you gotta open an old ass, creaky crypt to really get to them dusty bones and make them dance. Hell is almost as old as time. Lucifer, the fallen angel, don't dance to new melodies. He waltzes to the sounds of angels playin' harps. It's time to make some music," she whispered in his ear, then told him more. So much more, and soon she felt his face against her own, tightening with a smile…

GRANDPA'S HOUSE USED to be her refuge. The last time she'd been there, she'd left with a new gold Bible, the pages thick and gold-lined as well, and a big, beautiful white box full of apple turnovers and cherry tarts that Grandpa had ordered from his favorite bakery: Baked Brothers Co. Grandpa had been good to her from the moment she'd entered the world. His paternal love, soothing attention, protection, and support were like sweet white sprinkles on a freshly baked sugar cookie. Now, that cookie was stale, dry, hard and crumbling to pieces.

The love remained, yet was fading fast. What a difference the ugly truth makes. Silva sat in Grandpa's grand dining room, her mind filled with fantastical ideas, memories, grief and so much more, resolved to do as Lennox said. Act normal. It had been difficult faking it until she made it, as Mama used to say. After all, she'd never been a great actress, often forgetting her lines in the school plays, but she had played one role well. That of pretending to not be disheartened by life's gut punches. Just like when she was forced to hide her disappointment after having experienced her third miscarriage the prior year. It was rather strange that Lennox had reached out to her on the anniversary of losing her daughter. It had almost seemed like God had stepped in to mend a fence, where another had been broken.

However, Grandpa had arrived with a good word when she'd experienced her last loss. Being the family man that he was, he'd presented her with flowers. He then leaned in close as she lay in the hospital bed, the sheets soaked with her and her husband's tears. She'd been wearing a thick, bloody pad, which only served as a stark reminder of what once was, along with the tremendous emotional pain. He'd told her that one day, God would grant her wish. *Don't give up. God grants babies in the most surprising ways. Miracles happen every day.'* Then, he'd given her a loving kiss on the forehead.

...As a grandmother would. Or so many would think. Grandpa, however, played both parts. She never thought about how odd that had been until that moment. He had a treasure trove of ex-wives, the majority of them still above ground, all grandmothers who were in their adult children's lives, but not one had stepped foot in that house in recent years. Perhaps Grandpa had told them not to? Perhaps they vowed not to...

"Here you go, honey," Grandpa said with a syrupy smile as he handed her a cup of iced tea and sat down with one himself. "I even made sure Mildred added extra lemon and honey. Just how you like it."

"Thank you, Grandpa." She mustered a smile and brought the drink to her lips, tasting it. Mildred was Grandpa's first maid who still came around doing small chores here and there. He didn't have her do too much as she was up in age, but everyone still enjoyed her homemade iced tea and lemonade.

"Now, I know you weren't supposed to come by till next week to talk about my birthday bash, but thank you for poppin' by at such short notice, I just, uh, wanted to talk to you about the—"

"Grandpa, speaking of which, we really do need to discuss your birthday party because I've been working with the event coordinator and she said there are some singing groups and entertainers coming and what not, and the contracts need to be signed. She said she's been waiting quite a while for you to do so. In fact, some of the performing acts are supposed to be contacting you directly today to verify where you want them set up, what you want them to do, and maybe I should just—"

"Silva, that can wait." He waved her off, looking weary. "You make such a big deal about my birthday every year," he smiled proudly, yet sounding rather tired, "and I thank you for that, sweetheart. The parties are always so festive and nice, but this is way more important than merrymaking. We need to discuss your brother."

"Lennox? Why?"

"Well, why not?" He threw up his hands. "I know, I know…" He smiled sheepishly and leaned forward. "Okay, I'll stop foolin' around. There's a specific reason. So long ago you two fell out. That broke my heart." She witnessed the faux frown set into his features. "From my understanding, you still aren't on the best of terms due to how disrespectful he can be. That aside, I need to speak to him about a specific matter, but I'm hesitant."

"Why? Don't you two speak?"

"You see, he and I speak on and off… not often, but a fair amount of times." He tossed up his hands and let them fall loosely against his thighs. "I got word that he might be in trouble again. I need to find out before I pull him into this other situation I'm going to discuss with you."

"Trouble? Well," she sucked her teeth and rolled her eyes, "I shouldn't be surprised. Lennox is always attractin' nonsense his way." She huffed.

"Yeah." Grandpa leaned back in his chair and sighed loudly, patting his stomach. Where one would expect a man of his age to have a bit of a gut, Grandpa's stomach was flat as a washing board. "Some folks just never learn, doll. I mean, I made sure the boy didn't serve a second in jail, you know? Now yes, I know that was a long time ago, and I've let bygones be bygones, but I fear he may be on that same path. Not learned his lesson. Here it is. The bad news." He tsked. "I heard a rumor that he's messin' with a real loose woman who's a known gold digger and lady of the night. He made her his lady. It's serious. It's official. She's of the African American persuasion."

"Well, okay. The whole prostitute insinuation is concerning, and the gold digger part, too, especially since last I heard Lennox has no gold to dig, but her being Black doesn't really matter, does it? I mean, this isn't 1953. So what?" Silva shrugged, then remembered she was supposed to be in character, and slumped back in her seat.

"Oh, I'm not mentioning it as a problem. Just as background info. An understanding, if you will. See, Silva, sometimes when someone has never had anything, they don't know how to behave when it's finally given to them. I realize that some Black folks come from impoverished areas of town, grew up in ghettos, and they struggle—I get it. Sometimes it's because there doesn't seem to be any accountability for their role in their own troubles, but sometimes not all of that is their fault. I've seen racism, hell, we've got racists in our friendly circles and in the family, but this is not about the color of her skin. She's not a good person, sweetheart. Not a good person at all." His eyes turned to inky slits.

"What exactly has she been doing to Lennox?"

"She's been spendin' the little money he has on her—frivolous stuff. To make up for the missing funds, Lennox has been dabbling in get rich quick schemes and is still pouring money down the drain to try and open that gym of his. The bottom line is this: Lennox is gonna run into serious money issues, if he hasn't already. He'll lose his little house. His truck that he loves so much. He's too smart of a guy for that to happen, or so he was until *she* stepped into the picture. It would be a real shame. You know I've tried to get him on my team for a mighty long time."

"Yes, I know. He's being stubborn for some reason. It would be a great opportunity for him."

"It would. He and I need to revisit that situation, for his own sake."

"Hmph. Well, as much as Lennox is someone I never want to deal with again, I wouldn't wish prison on him or him being the victim of a shifty deal falling through, or this terrible woman who's only using him. I hope he's fine, and that's all I can pray for." Her heart thumped hard in her chest as Grandpa stared at her so intensely, it about killed her soul. "What situation did you need to discuss with him besides the money stuff he might have going on?"

"I'm getting to that. Silva, let me ask you somethin'."

"Yes, Grandpa?"

"Are you aware of yo' daddy's drinkin' problem?" He looked so stern. So serious. Yet his blue eyes narrowed and twinkled—like a shark's.

"Yes, sir."

"It's worse than ever. Before, he could manage it well, but in the last year or so, he's been intoxicated early in the day. That's not like him."

"Unfortunately, I think anyone who knows him realizes he has one too many libations, but he seems to function okay."

"Mmm hmmm." Grandpa nodded, his lips in a deep frown. He looked down at his sparkling white dress shoe, bent low, and swiped a speck of dust from it. "Well, unfortunately I think that drinkin' problem led him to do somethin' foolish, honey. Something he can't fix with a spreadsheet or his fancy calculator."

"What do you think he did?" She took a sip of the tea, then placed it down. Grandpa picked up his glass and did the same.

"I think he called his in-laws, in a fit of grief, and they were talkin' about your dear mama."

"Well, that's okay, right? Nothing wrong with that."

Grandpa waved his hand. "Naw, ain't nothin' wrong with talking about a woman you love, no matter how long she's been gone," he offered a tender smile, "especially if you're still on good terms with the family—all the way out there yonder, in Lebanon. But, uh, your father, in his drunken state, called me right after the conversation. Told me that he might have messed up." Grandpa took another swallow of his tea. She clasped her hands together, desperately trying to ignore the tickly sensation from the sweat dripping down the center of her back.

"Oh, dear. Ain't no easy way to say this, sugar." He slapped his knees and shook his head, as if the weight of the world was on him. "Your father was in a panic, Silva. Told me that, uh, he mentioned that your mama used to, how do I say this? Offer personal services to menfolk, if you will." She cocked her head to the side, feigning that she wasn't following his line of thinking. "I know you know about her past... though I've never talked about it with you. It's not fit for conversation. Anyways, he let the cat out of the bag, honey bun. Told 'em that he missed your mama, but she wasn't the saint they thought she was..." The old man's eyes darkened, and a flash of evil showed on his face. "...because she'd been a salesgirl for the sin of lust. A trollop. An exotic, high-paid floozy," he ground out.

Silva reached once more for her glass of iced tea, needing to swallow the scream that begged to come out.

"Oh, no." She coughed into her fist when the liquid went down the wrong pipe. A hateful heat crawled up the sides of her neck and rested against her cheeks, setting her ablaze. "This is disastrous. This is a big deal in her culture. Her religion."

"Yes, I imagine it is! I have tried to brainstorm ways to do damage control, you know? Maybe offer a bit of money so that they can relocate to another one of those little Muslim towns they're in or what not. No amount of money is too much, baby girl, to keep your mama's family safe, and those graves remaining intact, not desecrated. I understand, accordin' to your daddy from a chat we had years ago, that they'd pull your mama right up out of that ground like an overgrown weed, and fling those bones every which way but loose, as long as they were no longer buried there by her respectable grandparents. It would be a pity. A real shame." He shook his head in disgust.

Flashes of the blackmail letter, the damn contract, filled her mind. This ancient piece of excrement parading around town as a man who loved the Lord had written the horrible words to her brother and many of their cousins. How this demonic, decrepit creature sitting before her in his little satin paisley vest with matching shirt, tie, pants and boots pretended to give a damn about anyone but himself was beyond comprehension. He was damn good at being someone that he was not. Had her watching a fictional movie the entire duration of her life. He pretended to be the Disney channel, when really he was a horror movie stuck on replay. Grandpa was an impostor spinning lies as if it were cotton candy on a stick.

"This is one of the pitfalls of lust, but I digress," he continued. "Though I'm no expert, I know Muslims are less forgivin' than us Christian Baptists about this sort of thing, and I'd hate to think about all the repercussions that would fall on those poor people. Your grandparents in particular." He looked rather smug, sitting there pleased as a plum.

"This is a fine mess! Let me call Daddy right now!" Putting on the theatrics, she reached for her purse that was hanging on the back of the chair to get her phone.

"No, No! Your father isn't fit to talk about this, Silva."

"Well, why not? Did you ask Daddy to confirm this

while he was sober at least?" She slid her purse back onto the chair. "Maybe since he was intoxicated when he called you, he's mistaken, Grandpa? Maybe he dreamt it up, or it was some nightmare after a long day of drinking?"

"Well, see, I didn't bring it up to him because I don't want him to go into some deep depression, Silva. You know that your father is, what's the word? Sensitive in nature… Not exactly able to keep himself together in times of trouble. He's a bit of a softie. He doesn't look the part, but he is—on the inside. He's a smart boy, a wonderful accountant, and knows the tax laws like the back of his hand, but when it comes to things like this, well, Scott turns into a jellyfish. And about some nightmare or mistake, naw, I doubt it." He shook his head vehemently. "I know, sober or not, he was tellin' the truth.

"I believe him. I figure after he sobered up, he forgot the whole damn thing, as he does quite often, so there'd be no need to call him and ask, honey, because either he remembers or he doesn't, but the results are still the same. He said it. The damage is done. Now your grandparents will have to live with the shame, but especially have to now worry if anyone else is going to find out. Chances are high, they *will*." He threw her an earnest look. Then, the corners of his lips began to twitch. She rested her hand against her pants leg and balled up the cotton in her palm, squeezing hard. Grandpa looked down at her hand as she treated her trousers like a stress ball, and his smile grew a little wider.

"You're upset… that's understandable, but don't you worry. We'll figure this out. Grandpa will take care of it. I'll make sure your grandparents don't suffer, and everything will be as it *should* be, as if they'd never been told at all. That's a promise." He leaned forward and tapped her shoulder in a reassuring sort of way. "I just ask one thing."

"What's that?"

"That we bring our family back together. Mend it. This has reminded me how important it is to let bygones be bygones, and not allow the past to ruin the future. To not hold our indiscretions over our head. Forgiveness should reign, if you will. I want you and your brother to mend the broken fence."

Those words in her mind now came back to haunt her.

"Oh, Grandpa, Lennox is—"

"Now, honey," He held up his hand as he spoke softly. "I know it's a lot to ask after how rude he's been, and all the damage he caused that I told you about firsthand, but he deserves a second chance, especially in the midst of this crisis. And maybe that's what he needs to turn his life around, you know? A talk with his little sister." He looked downright convincing, making her sick to her stomach.

"…Okay. I'll think about it."

"Don't just think about it, Silva. I need you to *do* it," he stated sharply. "You contact your brother, and let him know that his grandparents over there in Lebanon have been informed of your mother's misdeeds, but Grandpa is gonna make it all go away… as long as he comes on by to see me, so we can talk. Man to man. Finally bury the hatchet. Let God's rain showers wash all of the hurt away." He cracked a crooked smile, exposing all of his pearly whites.

She thought about her mother… then how she'd been

so young and torn to shreds at Mama's funeral in Lebanon. Her family insisted that Mama be flown back home, per her wishes, and that her body be buried within three days—as was tradition. She also recalled the American funeral service they'd had for Mama in Houston, where she had to relive the trauma all over again. She thought about it. Over and over. Harder and harder. Right then and there. A tear rolled down her cheek and then another. She smiled internally... *Convincing, huh? Wilde blood runs deep.*

"Grandpa, I'm going to get some more tea. I have a headache and want to take an aspirin." She rubbed her head as if her skull was throbbing, then moved to stand up.

"No, you sit there and try to calm down. I'll get it. I may not be as young as a baby bird anymore, but I can still soar like an eagle," he joked as he got to his feet.

"Thank you, Grandpa."

"No problem," He winked at her, snatched her glass from the table, and headed out of the dining room, out of sight.

Silva looked around, her heart nearly jumping out of her chest. Her adrenaline soared and her head was *really* hurting now. It was no longer a ruse just to get him away from her. She looked at Grandpa's glass of tea sitting there... half empty. The little bit of ice that was left sparkled in the brown liquid.

*Come on! You told Lennox that you wanted to help! He finally calls you, tells you to do this on your next visit... and he promises it won't kill him. BUT I'M SCARED! I don't wanna kill Grandpa... but I want to make this stop! The way he just sat here and lied on my daddy! His own son! Lied on Lennox again, and on his poor girlfriend who I still haven't even met, but I know it's not true! I know Daddy didn't say that to my grandparents. He would never do that, no matter how drunk he was. How could this man sit here and look at me with a straight face, and tell that horrible lie?! How could he do ANY of this?! I have to stick to the plan... I have to stick to the plan!*

She looked over her shoulder, and up at the camera in the dining room. She'd purposefully sat in a chair that she knew her back would be turned towards. She was lucky for her lot in this family. His security team never monitored her—they let her be. She'd proven she could be trusted many years ago. Grabbing her purse from off the chair, she quickly dug inside of it, removing a bottle that was labeled as Tylenol. She popped it open and took out two of the pills, then a small satchel of herbs ground into a fine dust that was also stuffed inside of the bottle. She set the two Tylenol down onto the table, undid the satchel that smelled a bit like prunes, and made fast work to dump it into Grandpa's tea. Her heart leapt out of her chest while she sweated as if caught in a thunderstorm. A horrible, pouring rain that had no ending in sight.

She looked at the glass, and her entire chest felt as if it were going to explode. She blinked several times and nearly screamed. placing her own hand over her mouth in disbelief. The sooty residue floated to the bottom, but a bit of it rose to the top, looking much like ashes perched atop the soft waves in a swimming pool.

*IT'S COLD! NOT HOT TEA! IT'S NOT DISSOLV-ING WELL! SHIT! SHIT! SHIT!*

She quickly jammed her finger in the liquid as she heard

him approaching, Grandpa's boots thundering and his steps quick as he whistled a little tune. She swirled the stubborn particles around as fast as she could, then pushed the glass aside. Praying the water would stop swirling like a tornado from the whirlwind motion of her finger before he noticed.

"Sorry about that, sweetheart. Took a bit longer. Mildred was in the ladies' room powdering her nose and I told her to put a move on it because my grandbaby wanted another tea, with extra lemon." He chuckled as he handed it to her.

"Thank you, Grandpa, and it's okay. I'll be fine, I think. I hope Mildred's grandson is feeling better. She told me about his cold a couple of weeks ago."

Grandpa sat down. "Gio is doin' much better." He regarded her with narrowed eyes and a scowl.

"Oh boy, you've really taken this hard, girlie. You don't look so well, honey. You're perspiring, and your complexion is all reddened and splotchy. You look like you've seen a ghost and instead of frightening you, it just made you queasy."

"I'll be okay, Grandpa. It's just shocking is all. Sometimes folks are just full of horrible surprises. We tried to so hard to just keep this in the family, but—"

"Well, sometimes the truth has a way of coming out, but on the off chance that your father *was* mistaken, and he didn't say such dreadful things, I'll dig into that after I speak to Lennox. Gotta deal with one fire at a time. Oh," he put his finger in the air, "and don't worry about telling Lennox or your father about this discussion we had until I know what we're dealing with. I will do the talking, okay?

Hopefully by then I'll have more information. You just make nice with him, and tell him that he needs to speak to me as soon as possible. I have to be careful about this, and so do you. Too many chefs in the kitchen spoil the soup."

She nodded in understanding. With a trembling hand, she reached for the pills, tossed them into her mouth, then chased them with the iced tea. Grandpa reached for his glass and leaned back with a great big smile on his face. He took a gulp, and then another, until it was all gone. As the saying went, the truth was sure ugly, and it was cold going down. Just the type of icy drink Grandpa would need to survive his new residence: The pits of Hell...

# CHAPTER TWENTY-NINE

## *Sneak the Sunrise by the Rooster*

"I TOLD YOU if it don't make money, then it don't make sense." Nadia giggled into her phone. "I'm glad y'all had a good time while at it... Mmm hmmm... Yeah, the house is nice, huh? I believe it... Did he CashApp you afterwards or pay another way?"

Lennox looked at himself in the toothpaste-speckled mirror as he gargled mouthwash. His cheeks were puffed with air and liquid as he made sure all of the germs were killed, then spit in his bathroom sink. Turning on the water and rinsing the sink, he'd been overhearing Nadia's conversation for the past few minutes.

Reaching for his black hand towel, he blotted his mouth, hung it back on the cloth ring, and turned off the light. Back in the bedroom, he found Nadia sprawled across his bed with only her satin purple panties on. Long, shapely legs were partially exposed in the folds of his wheat-colored sheets, and out poked one pretty foot with a thin silver anklet around it, toe nails cut evenly and painted a rich dark red. He didn't peg himself as having a foot fetish per se, but he appreciated a lady who took care of herself.

"…For sure. I'll follow up with you… No, thank you, baby!" Her eyes flashed with mischief. "He's a big spender, chile! Yaasssss! … Mmm hmm… I got you, boo… Oh no, sweetie, the pleasure was *all* mine!" She cackled as she ended the call.

He sat on the bed, his back towards her as he reached for his cellphone to re-read the text message from his sister.

Silva: منتهي . غادر مع المجموعة . يبدو نائما. muntahi. ghadir mae almajmueati. yabdu nayima.

She'd written the text message in Arabic—he was impressed—stating that what needed to be done was taken care of, and she'd made sure of it. Speaking and writing in Arabic to one another was a little thing she and Lennox would do as children when they wished to speak privately to one another, without Dad understanding them. At that time, they'd discuss silly things, or plot to sneak from their rooms to play games. Mama, who was fluent in five languages, had taught them her native language when they were babies, and though he rarely got to speak it in his adult life, he remembered it well.

He reached for his iPad and turned on some music: Pinegrove's, 'Need To.'

"Are you ready for what's to come?"

Tears blinded her eyes, surprising him. Watery, dark sanctuaries he wished to drown in.

"You know I am." It was obvious she was nursing a bit of trepidation. Understandable, too. "This is do or die."

She nodded in agreement, then crawled closer to him, wrapping her arm around his neck. His heart nearly burst at the scent of her perfume floating in the air. The cherry-vanilla sweetness was a thing of beauty and seduction. He took her silky form in his arms, squeezing her, finding his solace in a warm kiss. Moving his hand around the back of her head, his fingers sinking in a mass of textured, dark waves, he pulled her to him. He slipped his tongue into her mouth, tasting the wine they'd imbibed, wanting more of it.

His anxiety began to fade like a snowflake melting in the sun. With her, everything felt okay. With her, he could let his guard down. Relax in the presence of greatness. Queen Nadia had stolen his soul, and shot up his despair with double barrels.

They tumbled about, rolling, clawing and scratching at one another. All shreds of clothing were gone, randomly tossed. Animalistic need took over any semblance of higher thought and elegance. The bed was a messy canvas below their writhing bodies, a platform for him to have his way with her. Their eyes locked as he slipped his hand between her thick thighs and played with her tender, sweet pussy. She arched into his touch as his thumb brushed against the silken nub until it hardened against his affections.

"That's it," he whispered in her ear. "Let me make you come. Turn my bedroom into an ocean." She bucked against his touch as he kissed all along her neck, strumming her like a stringed instrument—an evocative, lovely solo song to entertain his ears only. Her forehead creased and her eyes slammed shut as if she were in deep concentration. She trembled against his hand as her orgasm ascended and crashed. When it was over, she took a deep breath, peppered with numerous uneven gasps.

"What's on your mind... and don't lie to me." He kept stroking her, only now, a bit slower, giving her a moment to collect herself.

"It's going to sound silly, but for some reason I just thought of it again. I find it interesting that you were never jealous of me dancin' for men. I've never experienced that before. Guys always said they were fine with it at first, and then they'd start freaking out. You didn't freak out about it."

"Wasn't shit to get upset about." He shrugged. "They can't compete with me."

Her lips bowed at his words. "Yeah, you're right, yet I was jealous of you helping women work out sometimes."

He was taken aback by such a confession. "Really? Why?"

"One time when you called me to come up to the gym so we could go to lunch, I saw some of your clients as I was waiting for you. They were lookin' at me when I asked for you, and I know that look. It was awkward, and I could feel the energy shift. There were many of them. I think you'd taught the spin class that day. Beautiful women... I mean, these were like well-to-do ladies, too. I could just tell. They were born into money, and they could afford everything life had to offer. Yet, as with many warm-blooded creatures, status aside, a good lookin' man can make some women act goofy.

"Not only are you easy on the eye, have beautiful eyes and hair, but you're really nice to women. Old fashioned and traditional in so many ways that turn women on. Of course, you've got all those muscles and things like that. I didn't say anything to you about the whispering, like them wonderin' who I was, and the hatred I could feel when you finally came out from the back. When you did, you immediately grabbed and kissed me. Those women hated me from that moment forward. My reaction, for a split second, was to feel self-conscious. It made me question if I was really the one for you. But then I remembered who I am, and what I deserve. And I *definitely* deserve you."

"Of course you do—you deserve what I am today, and what I'll become tomorrow. You are part of my past and my present. We're walkin' into the future hand-in-hand. You know I'd never entertain any interest from other women. They're my job. You're my choice. It takes more to get me than just a pretty face. I need a woman's heart and soul to be pretty, too. You are what I want, what I need. I want you, and *only* you."

He pressed his lips firmly against hers while stroking her clit in leisurely circles. She moaned beneath him, her body rocking to the rhythm of his fingertips. It was only a matter of time before she had another orgasm. She soon exploded like a million stars. He rose slightly so he could watch her face twist in ecstasy ... a thing of beauty. Tightened forehead. Mouth open, no sound, then a loud moan of pleasure.

She vibrated against him, her pussy slick and juicy, the nectar running down his working fingers and onto the bed.

"I want to play with your ass and eat that good pussy."

They switched positions. Laying down on his back, legs

open, he had her put her ass over his face, and her face near his groin, kneeling on all fours. He massaged her ass as he kissed and licked her pussy. Slippery, velvety folds flattened against his eager tongue. The wet, sloppy sounds her pussy made as he devoured it were melodic tunes. Taking his dick in both hands, she jerked his shaft as she sucked the sensitive head. The pleasure she provided him was unadulterated and fiery. He groaned as his balls tightened.

"I wanna choke on this big, long, fat dick!" she yelled before slurping it firmly. He squeezed her ass so hard, it was turning colors. He motorboated her pussy, his nose compressed against the glossy, plump folds. She began to buck and shake. His heart raced, eager as he was to taste her honeyed cascade all over his lips while it flowed all over his beard.

"Bust off in my mouth, baby! I wanna taste your cum!" she bellowed before her orgasm exploded. She shivered and quaked. He held her steady, sucking, licking and swallowing the streams of clear juice that trickled out of her pink abyss. His leg muscles tightened, and his toes strained as she began sucking him off harder, deep throating his rod.

"UHHHH!" He groaned as he released in her mouth. His ass rose from the bed over and over as he fucked her mouth, shooting his cream… He could feel her tracing his dick with the tip of her tongue, licking up every drop that had escaped her mouth. When she turned and looked at him, traces of his semen were running down her chin and the sides of her mouth. She nodded, smiling. He winked at her, then slapped her ass, making it jiggle. She disappeared into the bathroom for a few moments, then returned all cleaned up. He'd taken that opportunity to stroke his cock into a new erection as he held his phone, looking at porn. She approached him with curiosity in her gaze, got into the bed, then grinned when she saw a video of herself from her old OnlyFans page. He kept watching her play with herself on the video, moaning as he worked his dick into a hungry state.

"How'd you get that?" she asked.

"I joined your OF before you closed it down and downloaded a few videos to keep for myself."

"You coulda just asked me." She laughed. "I have all of them in my collection."

"I preferred it like this," he said with a grunt. "I liked being sneaky about it. It turned me on knowin' I was buying something that I get for free at home."

She burst out laughing and shook her head.

He put the phone down, then turned towards her. She lay next to him, her pussy V'ed open so he could see all the pretty pink and brown folds live and in living color. "Mmmm… that's good… yeah, let me see it…" When he was hard as a rock again, he rolled on top of her. Nestling his head against the crook of her neck, he quickly flattened her to the bed with his body, reached for his dick and…

"Ahhhhh…Ahhhh!" she screamed as he entered her nice and slow. Her pussy pulsed against his deepening thrusts. She breathed deeply, her chest rising and falling at rapid speed.

"I never get used to how it feels when you first put it in, baby. That first stroke makes me almost orgasm immediately," she cooed.

"Your pussy always feels so damn good, baby... So warm, snug and juicy. My dick *loves* it here..." He thrust harder, picking up momentum to the sounds of 'The Rain,' by Cherry Lu. "I love you so much, baby."

"I love you too."

"The first time I saw your dick was by accident." He cocked his head to the side, intrigued. "The toilets in the restrooms had flooded at the Red Rooster, they were broken, and you and some of the other guys were out back pissin' in buckets while the plumber worked to fix it."

"Oh yeah, I remember that day. They had to close down, but we stayed because it was supposed to be fixed soon."

"Yeah. I thought y'all was done. I had some bags of trash to put in the dumpster with me, but you were still back there. You didn't see me. Instead of walking away, I froze, stopping dead in my tracks. You were looking down and pulling up your pants, but I saw it before you tucked it away. I remember thinking, *'I ain't never seen a White boy's dick in person before, and the ones I'd seen in movies and magazines ain't look nothing like this.'*" He burst out laughing, and she followed suit. "I also remember thinkin' how big, thick, and veiny it was... And you had a lotta black pubic hair. I was so turned on. When I got home later that day, I played with myself as I thought about your dick. I had wanted to suck it. See if it tasted as good as it looked."

That was the end of him... He started pumping faster and harder, until there was no way out.

"I'm about to cum in you!"

She wrapped her legs tightly around him as they stared

at one another, falling impossibly more in love.

He sped up, his body a heated inferno. His heart ached as he pressed his chest firmly into her flattened breasts. A beautiful pain. An emotional climax. A sensual heart attack. He gasped as his dick detonated, firing his liquid love within her walls. They lay there, happy and wet. He relished the feel of her fingers running through his hair.

"Lennox." He tingled all over when she spoke his name. "Thank you for always being my friend. Even through those ten years lost, we were on each other's mind. When you fall in love with a friend, that love is deep."

He kissed her cheek, then her soft, pillowy lips.

"I'm never lettin' you go without a fight again, Nadia. Pride and ego are partially responsible for me not trying harder to find you, to figure out why you shut me out. I don't beg for women, but I should've begged for you."

"No, things happened as they should have, Len. You know that. Don't feel guilty about it. We both needed to mature and grow." He nodded in agreement. "Let's say it was a mistake to not pursue one another back then. Playin' devil's advocate. Mistakes we make as young folk many times can be undone or forgiven. Mistakes we make now are far more serious, and I will never make that same mistake with you again. I don't need to be saved, but you're a saver. I've been learning how to let you do what you need to do. I've been learning how to love you the way you need to be loved. You don't need to be saved, either, but sometimes, you let me heal you with advice, sweet words, and my body. You let me inside. You let me get close and see those invisible wounds that nobody can see but me."

He rose up on his arm and lay beside her, resting on his hip. She reached over and caressed his chest as they regarded one another with nothing short of pure admiration and love. Keane's, 'Somewhere Only We Know' began to play. He kissed her forehead, then slowly rolled her over onto her stomach.

He leaned to the far right and opened his dresser drawer. Pulling out a bottle of lube, he slathered it all over his rigid dick until it was good and greased. When he was finished, he closed the lid and tossed the bottle over to the side of the bed. Close proximity in case he needed a little more. Reaching forward, he grabbed one of his pillows that was lying against the headboard.

"Raise up a little, baby." She rose from the bed, and he slid the pillow beneath her lower stomach, forcing her ass and back to arch. Seemingly understanding what was coming next, she spread her legs wider and pushed her ass against his pelvis as he lay firmly on top of her, kissing her shoulder.

He heard her swallow.

"Relax, baby. I'm going to go slow." He smiled down at her as he wrapped one arm around her waist and guided the head of his dick inside her tight ass.

"...Ahhh...Ah! Shit... Lennox, oh God... it hurts...don't rush... don't rush..." She bit into the pillow that was beneath her chin, and gripped the sheets.

"I'd never rush this. Slow and easy... breathe... it's going to be fine... Ahhhh... You've got such a nice, warm ass... That's it, baby... just take the dick... it's going in nice and slow..." He spoke softly in her ear as he guided himself deeper within her tight chasm. He knew she'd had anal sex with former lovers before. They'd discussed their sexual pasts freely. The fact he was quite well endowed concerned her, so he went easy on her.

He inched inside a tad more. She groaned in pain and pleasure. He felt her stiffen, and her body tremble. A deep grunt emitted from her core.

"If you fall, I'll catch you. I got you, baby… feel the pleasure…"

He slowly flattened her beneath his weight, grabbed her left fist which was holding on for dear life to the bed sheet, and intertwined their fingers as he lovingly kissed the side of her face. He felt her instantly loosen beneath him. He rotated his hips in short, slow thrusts. She reached behind herself and spread her ass cheeks further apart for him. His pulse quickened at the display. His heart beat erratically as he slipped deeper within her. She cooed and he groaned, their echoes of pleasure coupling and reverberating. The hollow of her lower back looked so lovely. Beautiful. Like a cello. He glided his free hand along it. *Skin so soft and buttery.* Lana Del Rey's, 'Summertime Sadness' serenaded them.

"Baby! Feels so good! Your big dick in my ass feels so damn good!" she bellowed as she began to throw her ass back, jiggling it, meeting his plunges and thrusts. He whacked her hands away from her ass and held her wrists tight as he navigated himself in and out of her snug passageway. She raised her legs, bending them at the knee towards her back, and gripped her ankles as he rose on his hands, doing push-ups within her. He drove in and out of her ass, breaking her in for a deeper dive. Drops of sweat beat down on her skin as he came and went, his head dizzy from the unbelievable sensation. Her ass squeezed his dick tight as he took his time, being so careful with her dark, tight treasure. He wanted to drive deeper quickly, push hard balls deep, but he paced himself, careful to not hurt her. A guttural growl emitted from his lips, taking him off guard. His head lulled back and he felt his eyes rolling as her sphincter muscles continued to squeeze and caress his ramming shaft.

"FUUUUCK!" The word burned his throat so good as he pivoted his hips, driving his dick further inside of her, slow inch by slow inch. He could feel the rivulets of sweat dripping down his face, neck and chest. Holding on to his composure was a slippery slope—he grasped it by a thread. When he lay down flat upon her back once again, he locked their ankles together. One hand around the front of her neck, the other beneath her, he played with her pussy as he rocked his cock in and out of her until he was almost fully cocooned by her hot ass.

"So deep! SO DEEP IN ME! You're killin' my butt! Filling my butt up! Stretching it with your big, juicy dick. Hurt me, baby! Fuck my ass, baby! Fuck it!" His hips bucked faster and faster until he was slamming into her. He looked at her reflection in the glossy black headboard. Her screams echoed and only stopped when she bit on her pillow, squelching them. All he could hear were muffled groans and cries of ecstasy as his balls slapped noisily against her swollen, wet dripping pussy.

"Oh God! Baby!"

He closed his eyes tight as the bed hammered hard

against the wall. He gripped her neck tighter, his wet, hard body slamming into her soft curves.

"AHHHHH!" he roared as he banged her, his dick draining within that taut, spasming passage. His hand shook so violently against her neck, his entire body a vibration of love and elation. He gripped the base of his dick, carefully slid out of her canal, and watched as his creamy cum dripped out of the stretched hole, and down the crack of her ass. He slowly closed his eyes and swallowed, taking deep, much needed breaths. After a few seconds, he managed to hobble to the bathroom, clean himself up, wet a fresh wash towel with warm water, return to her, and clean her up, too. He tossed it on the floor, got in the bed, his dick still somewhat hard and still on a high, and lay down on his back. His entire body was now shaking like a leaf as he shivered with orgasmic aftershocks.

His heart beat alarmingly fast. His dick twitched and moisture filled his eyes. She rolled over onto her side, then kissed his cheek before wrapping her body snugly around his. Slowly, the beating of his heart went back to normal. His climax had shaken him completely loose… all sense of reality had vanished for a second or two.

They held one another for a long while as øneheart x reidenshi's, 'snowfall' played. They held hands and became falling stars, coming down from a natural high. Saying nothing with their mouths, but everything with their rhythmic breaths that were now in sync.

It wasn't long before he found himself kissing her, just wanting to be close to her in every possible way. They lay together, time passing. The day turned into night. They'd fallen asleep, gotten back up, made love again, and shared a shower which lent way to more intimacy under the rush of warm water and suds. It was now one in the morning, and she was in her bra and panties at his stove, fixing them both some scrambled eggs.

Neither of them could sleep for too long. He'd wake up and stare at her resting, or vice versa, as if they were looking out for one another. Protecting each other from the storm.

"Lennox, are you worried about it?" She moved the spatula across the fluffy eggs as they cooked slowly in butter and cream.

He stood behind her drinking a cup of coffee, then looked out his kitchen window. He knew exactly what IT was.

"No. This has been a long time coming. Worry won't change anything. Only transformation changes things. And it's time for a change."

She sprinkled a bit of salt, smoked paprika, and black pepper on the eggs, then served them up hot on a plate with two slices of lightly toasted wheat bread. The sounds of Atlantic Starr's, 'When Love Calls' played on her phone that she had on the counter. They sat at his kitchen table, across from one another, each with a hot cup of coffee and sweet orange juice. They sat there eating, regarding one another ever so often. Then laughing.

"What are you laughing at?" She asked at one point, even though she'd been cracking up for no reason, too.

"Your pussy queefed a lot when I was fucking you in the shower, and it sounded like the introduction to that old show, Sanford and Son."

"Lennox! Shut up!" she howled, cracking up and turning colors like a prism.

"I kid you fuckin' not." He began to hum the theme song, then make farting type sounds every few seconds. "It was just like that. I was waitin' for a dump truck to pull up, but it was already there… that big, beautiful ass of yours."

She covered her mouth, almost spitting juice everywhere.

"I love the hell out of you, Lennox. You are so crazy… you make me happy." Her eyes sheened over, then she quickly looked away.

"You have no idea how blessed and happy I've been since we reunited." He clasped his hands together. "You know I'd die for you in a heartbeat."

She blinked back tears, then shook her head as if it was simply too much. After they finished their food, he washed the dishes as she sat at the table, playing a game on her phone. He turned on the sink water and rinsed a glass, then set it on the drying rack. He heard a bit of lightning, but it hadn't begun raining yet. *Right now is the time to do this. Yeah. This feels right.*

"Throw on some clothes, baby. I want to take you somewhere."

"Where?" she asked, looking up from her phone.

"You'll see. Come on."

He finished up the dishes while she disappeared down the hall and got dressed. When he was finished, he stood at the sink for a moment, looking at his reflection in the faucet. He pulled himself away from his thoughts, dried his hands, returned to the bedroom, and threw on a black t-shirt, black jogging pants, and a pair of his Jordans. Then, he escorted her out the front door to his truck…

THE RED ROOSTER stood on a ramshackle plot of land, overgrown with tall weeds. The exterior walls were covered in plywood, dirty shingles, and graffiti. One of the windows was broken, exposing an expanse of strange, murky darkness. Lennox rolled down his truck window and leaned out, looking up. The sky above was dreary, full of unspent tears. Dark, bloated clouds clustered together, holding each other tight, squeezing one another as the sky lit up with streaks of gold and silver. He turned his truck off, but left the music playing. 'Lovely,' by Billie Eilish and Khalid wailed through his speakers. He made his way slowly around the truck and opened the passenger's side door.

Nadia looked around, then turned to him, confusion and sadness in her dark eyes, yet she remained quiet. He took her hand, helping her step out of the vehicle. Her left foot extended, covered in a black ballet style shoe. It landed softly on the pebbled ground, and then the other followed. Closing the door behind her, he took her hand in his.

"This is where it all started." He walked with her towards the plywood-covered front door of the restaurant. A rusty chain was wrapped around it. "The Red Rooster is gone. Kyser died, ending a legacy." Kyser had been the owner of the place. He was an old, widowed Jewish guy who'd been raised in the South, and was up in age when he and Nadia worked for him. "It looks the same, yet so different." He peered inside the broken window. Unable to make much out, he used his phone as a light.

They rested their bodies together, side by side, regarding the inside of the building as if star gazing. He could hear their breathing, in sync. The tables inside were all covered in dirt. Some were missing. Some chairs were stacked as if they'd been prepared for business for the following day. He looked at an untouched serviette dispenser, still full of white napkins as if it had just been set out. The horrible yellow and white tile floor was covered in soot, but the menu, written in chalk on a big board, still hung there like some trophy:

*Special of the Day: Steak, cabbage and potatoes.*
*Dessert of the Day: Peach cobbler*

"I haven't been here since my last day way back then." She squeezed his hand. "I have to be honest. I missed it a little. There were some good people here. But mainly, I was missin' you." He turned away from the window and looked into her eyes. "When I look at it now, like this, all run down, it kinda reminds me of me when I left here. Only the ugliness wasn't on the outside, but on the inside. I was full of hurt, but full of promise, too. I got out there and got smacked around by the world. I lost focus. Too much had happened. Too many sins and not enough blessings. I ended up emotionally dilapidated. Just like ol' Red Rooster here. But she still stands..." She smiled sadly at the structure. "Scars, bruises and all. She still stands."

They both studied the sign of the place that still hung

outside on two tall metal poles. Red letters that used to glow with light when the darkness came. Now they were an old, dried-up rust colored, instead of the vibrant crimson from so long ago. A drop of rain fell on his head, then another. They both peered up at the sky. He cupped her chin, made her face him, and the most beautiful smile creased her face. Like an upside-down rainbow.

"We owe a lot to this restaurant." He knocked on the wood. "This is where I met the woman I love. The woman God designed just for me. The lady I had no idea I'd be infatuated with to the point where I thought about you even in my dreams. That infatuation turned to more. So much more."

The rain began to come down harder, now soaking through their clothing. On a deep breath, he dropped down to one knee in front of her, then reached into his pocket.

"Lennox…" she whispered, appearing stunned.

As he pulled out a jewelry box, her eyes grew big as dinner plates, and her mouth opened as if she were going to scream. He opened the black ring box, exposing a solitary blue diamond ring, pear shaped. Like a raindrop. He took her hand and looked up into her eyes. Rain was falling faster now, causing the waves in her hair to flatten against her scalp. The rain webbed between her long lashes and dotted her skin like freckles. She looked pretty in the rain. She was new in the rain. She was home, in the rain.

"Nadia Jazmine Deere, would you do me the honor of bein' my wife? Will you marry me?"

She looked down at him, her mouth slowly closing. A tear fell onto her cheek, blending with the rain, but her lips curled in a smile.

"Yes." She swallowed, her eyes glistening, but not with the rain. "Yes, I will marry you, Lennox."

He carefully plucked the ring out of the box and slid it down her trembling finger. It fits like a glove.

"Oh my goodness, it's beautiful!" Her voice quaked as she looked down at her hand. "I've never seen a blue diamond before. That's what it is, right?"

"Yup. Not a sapphire. That's a real blue diamond. They're not easy to come by, but I got one."

"Len, I hope you didn't spend too much on this." Her smile suddenly faded as he got to his feet.

"Don't you worry about the cost. You just concentrate on when you want to set the date, and what church I need to show up at."

She burst out laughing, then crying. Crashing into his arms, she wrapped herself around him. He squeezed her tightly to his chest. The rain felt so good and smelled so fresh as it kissed them all over. Lightning struck, and she did not jump. Thunder boomed, and she did not move. They looked into each other's eyes, both now soaked to the bone. Billie Eilish's voice played on repeat... the perfect song for a perfect day.

"You're my Bonnie." He smiled, then kissed her nose.

"You're my Clyde." She kissed him back. They stood there, caressing one another until he found himself compelled to pick her up in his arms. He carried her to the side of the restaurant, where the pantry had been, and pushed her back against the graffiti covered wall...

NADIA FELT THE hard, prickliness of the structure against her back. Rain soaked her tresses and made a soggy mess of her clothing. The rain that used to frighten her and dredge up old traumatic memories was now framed in soft kisses, big strong arms and a new blue diamond ring shaped like the tears from angels. Fashioned just like rain. Her body jerked as Lennox tugged at her jeans, forcing them down to her knees. Rain collected in his eyebrows as he regarded her with intense desire. He picked her up in his arms and forced her legs around his waist, then shoved his pants and underwear down past his ass in one swoop. His long, thick, veiny dick bumped against her pelvis, fully erect and ready. She looked down at the small space between them where small raindrops sparkled along his black pubic hair and happy trail. His Adonis belt tightened as he reached between their bodies, grabbed his dick with one hand, and ushered it inside of her.

"Ohhhh..." Her head lulled against the shingled wall of the Red Rooster. She slid up and down the structure, rising high, falling low as he stroked her love with his sword. He lay close to her ear, warm pearls of breath rolling against her lobe, and his breathing grew louder. Gulping air, pinning her tighter against the wall, he piloted her into position, jostling her pussy up and down his hungry shaft. He was viciously sexy without even trying. An all-encompassing experience that made her mind, body, and soul quiver. Their tongues danced as he cupped her ass with both hands, palming them with a tight grip. She graciously endured his severe thrusts. A look of emotional anguish and carnal pleasure spanned his handsome face.

"Look now, I can't wait too long for you to be my wife, baby. I need you now. With *me*. I wanna get married. Don't make the date far away. Let's do it soon."

"I won't keep you waiting, baby. We will!" She held him tighter.

"Good, 'cause I wanna wake up beside you, and go to sleep deep inside of you… *Every* day for the rest of my life."

She sighed as his hungry thrusts grew more demanding. She held onto him for dear life as he beat her pussy to pieces. The wetness and his hard plunges created a sound of their own. A sexual tune that sounded amazing. It felt so damn good. He filled her up and moved with perfect rhythm, killing her blues. She died and went to heaven in his arms every time he made love to her—rolling her hips into his lurches, matching his energy, his vibe, his thrusts, his love.

Their mouths crashed, kissing hard and needy as he cupped one of her breasts and squeezed it. She sighed as he buried his face between her cleavage, then lifted her shirt, sucking her titty over her bra. The wetness of his mouth clung to the lace material, driving her crazy. Wanting more. He tugged at the fabric of her bra, maneuvering the soft globe to fall forward and be exposed. Free in the rain. He took the hard nipple into his mouth, and his low, throaty moan sent shockwaves through her body.

"I love suckin' your big, soft titties," he said around a mouthful. "But I know God didn't give them to you just for my enjoyment. I can't wait to put a baby in you one day, honey. Gettin' married to you, getting a big, pretty house, and having a family of our very own is all I want and need. I've dreamed about this for so long. WITH YOU AND ONLY YOU." He sucked her nipple harder, just as she liked it. Her weak spot. He smothered her mouth with urgency, his love and lust for her pouring out like wine from a glass.

"Oh, shit!" She began to tremble as her orgasm neared. Clutching him tight, she sighed while he pumped his hips in rapid speed within her. He rubbed her right breast and sucked on the left as he went so deep inside of her, it took her breath away. His dick jerked in and out of her, scratching that lovely itch. Her body tingled all over when that good feeling began at her core and radiated to every cell within her body.

"Mmm! Mmm!" He grunted loud with each hard plunge, nearing the end, drawing closer to losing control. She waited for it, wrapping her legs impossibly tighter around his waist. Deep grunts grew louder as he rammed into her, filling her with his liquescent balminess. He slowed then, his rapid jerking now a lulled crawl... She could feel his pulsing dick within her walls. His hip muscles spontaneously juddered as he rested against her. The rain had slowed, and she could feel his heartbeat as he leaned into her, holding her close. After a brief reprieve, they put their clothes back on.

He took her hand and began making his way back to the truck, but then paused. He looked back at the restaurant, the structure sad and forgotten, in an area that few people ventured to. The street was full of dilapidated old warehouses and defunct shops and a lonely gas station that set on the corner. Only a few businesses remained. Once it had been a vibrant area full of working-class people, trying to make ends meet. Lennox leaned against one of Red Rooster's wooden posts, and kissed it.

Nadia kissed his lips, then gently pulled her hand away and made it back inside of his truck. He stood there, alone, looking around. A feeling of love and sorrow imbued him. He looked up at the sky and noted that the rain clouds were letting go of one another, drifting farther and farther apart, and a sliver of sunshine could now be seen in the distance. He'd already begun to dry, though he was grateful for the storm because in some way, it seemed to have washed his sins away. Gave him a new start and a clean slate.

He turned his attention to the ground. Lennox bent low and picked up two stones that were side by side. One was light gray, jagged and rough. The other was dark gray, smooth, with a chipped area, as if something heavy had chopped into it, or something sharp had ricocheted off of it. He ran his thumb over both. After studying them closely, he slipped them into his pocket. Then, he got back in the car and heard the radio playing. Nadia had turned off the song he'd been playing on loop, and now Phyllis Hyman's, 'You Know How To Love Me' took over.

Nadia snapped her fingers to the beat, in the zone, falling into happiness. He laughed lightly, enjoying how joyful she was. She was an old soul with a young groove, and she'd captivated him from the first moment he'd seen her. She was strong, yet soft. She was forgiving, yet not a doormat. She was his twin soul, his soulmate, his gate to heaven, his ticket out of hell. She was the rain and the sun, the lightning and the thunder, and now, she was his beautiful fiancée, too. He turned the engine on, leaned over and kissed her, and took off down the road…

# CHAPTER THIRTY

## *Be Just What the Doctor Ordered*

*...The next day*

NADIA PLACED HER school book aside, then glanced at the clock on her laptop. It was finally time. Mac Miller's, 'All I Want Is You' was playing from her phone. She turned it off, took a deep breath. Clearing her throat, she took a sip of her hot Earl Grey tea sweetened with three teaspoons of honey, and logged into the Zoom meeting. The app appeared on her screen, letting her know that the host was there.

A ball of frenzied tension formed in her gut and clutched her resolve. She'd never done such a thing before, and so much had been happening as of late. Where would she start? How would he respond? Would she say too much or too little? Her nerves warped and twirled around like a spinning top.

Suddenly, a screen appeared on her laptop, and the hard-hitting sounds of Eric B. & Rakim's, 'I Ain't No Joke' began to play. The bass was heavy. Someone important was entering the chat... The screen was black with the exception of a spinning gold king crown with diamonds. Below it read the initials.

S.A.

The crown slowly faded away, and there sat a man who practically glowed. He looked like he was created from AI, but no, he was quite real. His midnight-black hair was coiffed in an old-fashioned pompadour that suited him perfectly, and a thin streak of bright silver was threaded through the side of his shiny tresses. He had on dark tinted glasses, but his eyes were still partially shown beneath them. A sparse, well-trimmed black beard covered his angular and strong jawline. The bridge of his nose was long and thin, and his nostrils had a natural flare. He exuded masculinity and beauty simultaneously. His vitality was absolutely BDE, and she couldn't help but stare. He sat behind at a huge black desk that seemed to almost span the length of the room, his body nestled in a black and red oversized royal chair with gold accents that looked fit for a motherfucking king.

Behind him was a view of the New York City skyline. It was real, not some poster or painting—absolutely stunning, all aglow with sparkling lights. The good doctor was wearing a black jacket over a white dress shirt. Simple, yet well made. The shirt was partially unbuttoned, exposing a bit of dark chest hair, accented with a thin gold chain and a Nefertiti pendant. He raised his large hand and waved, exposing two diamond rings on his long, tan fingers. In his other hand he gripped a fat white cigar.

*Good God almighty. How is a man of his age looking like this?! Looks even better in person than on the author biography of his books. I know his wife is thrilled! Blessed and highly favored!*

She blinked several times, trying to regain her focus, and Dr. Saint Aknaten laughed, as if he'd read her mind. Her cheeks warmed with embarrassment. For some reason, it felt like he'd invaded her thoughts right then and there—as if he had some secret way to delve deep into her subconscious and peruse it like a library. He removed his glasses and set them aside.

"Hello, Dr. Aknaten, I'm Nadia. Thank you for—"

"Pause. Your mic isn't on, baby," came a smooth, deep, rich voice coated in a pronounced New York vernacular and swag. "Turn up your lights, too. I want to see you better, Queen…"

"Oh!" She quickly adjusted the video lighting and turned herself off mute. "Sorry about that."

"Not a problem, love. Now, what was it you were trying to say?"

"I am first… hold on. Let me back up. Let me say," her heart was beating a mile a minute, "I am honored that you accepted my request for a therapy session, Dr. Aknaten. I hope I said your name right."

"You did." He picked up a remote and turned the music down low.

"Okay, good. I, uh, I saw that you are booked for several months out, so I appreciate you readin' my email and doing this for me on such short notice. I know your time is valuable."

"My time is quite valuable, but so is yours. I'm not any less or more important than you. Did it surprise you when I wrote you back?" He flashed a bright white smile.

"It did, actually! I had mentioned to you that I first heard about you from my boyfriend a long time ago. I coincidentally purchased some of your books, and checked out info about your seminars on your website. Oh, and speaking of Lennox, I take it that you received my follow up email about him giving consent to discuss him?"

"Yes, thank you. The patient/therapist confidentiality agreement is important because it's built on trust. Since you two are a couple, I have a little leeway here anyway, but getting his consent was still necessary if I were to be speaking in more than just general terms. Based on your email, that will definitely be occurring. Queen, let me look at you for a minute. Scoot a bit closer to the webcam and look straight into it."

*Look at me for a minute? What for?* She did as requested though, regardless of her trepidation and confusion.

He rested his cigar in the crack of a dark brown ashtray that appeared to be shaped like an ass. She had to suppress a laugh when she saw it, managing to maintain her composure. He leaned forward and clasped his hands, staring at her with such intensity, it was like she was being examined from the inside out. She felt warm all over, as if he was looking directly into her very soul. He stayed that way for so long, not speaking, that she thought his camera may have frozen, or the Zoom connection was faulty. After a short while that felt like an eternity, he exhaled and leaned back in his chair.

"Okay," he sighed, then clasped his hands, "that's good. Continue."

"Um, okay." She waited for an explanation, but he simply looked at her and intertwined his fingers over his knee. "Well, like I said in my email, Lennox is the reason why I know about you. He said you were a big inspiration for him, and are part of the reason he is, in his words, emotionally mature enough to handle a serious relationship, and be a man of his word."

"Yes, your fiancé and I had—"

"Fiancé? He *just* asked me to marry him yesterday, Dr. Aknaten, but I wrote you several weeks ago for this session. How'd you know he was my fiancé now? Did Lennox call you?"

His jaw tightened, and then he frowned. He looked quite perturbed, much to her surprise. His eyes were now level under thick, dark brows. He abruptly leaned into the camera, his body movements swift and antagonistic. She blinked, feeling a bit unsteady as two bright, sunset-colored eyes with traces of gray and copper gleamed right back at her. *Such an unusual shade.*

"If what I said is factual, how is my answer to that question going to help you, Nadia? Is he or is he not your husband-to-be?" His voice was so low, so devoid of emotion, that it shook her.

Her heart began to beat all the faster. For some reason, she was suddenly uncomfortable, feeling like she'd been called to the principal's office, and yet, she couldn't look away from him.

"Yes, it's true. He's my fiancé now, but I just wanted to know how you knew is all." She shrugged.

"Now, let's continue. It's on my website, but I like to give a quick little rundown. I am a licensed clinical psycho-therapist, sex therapist, and psychologist who specializes in human sexuality, family counseling, and interracial romantic relationships, with a focus on Black women with non-Black men. I have a license in massage therapy, sexual healing rehabilitation and treatment, and I also have an accredita-tion to counsel people who have experiences or fantasies involving sexual deviancy. I run an annual private seminar for men who are sex and intimacy addicts, which, for some, falls under the sexual deviancy umbrella. Sexual deviancy, in this case, does not include non-consensual physical interactions. I do not counsel rapists, for I do not believe that the majority of rapists can be rehabilitated, and due to my own bias and hatred of such actions, I am not equipped to engage fairly with men or women who have molested and/or forced themselves upon others without sanction, regardless of the age, race, gender, or creed of the victim."

She could tell that he had the spiel memorized, and yet, she was intrigued with the manner in which he spoke.

"I'm an award-winning author of over twenty-seven

books to date, and have been on many major networks and broadcasts for interviews, or simply to share my expertise regarding some current affairs. I am born and raised in New York City, the South Bronx to be exact, and I am biracial. Half Egyptian—Arab, with no African genetic ancestry on my paternal side. Trust me, I checked and the DNA test proved my father correct despite my desire to claim at least one or two percent African blood." She smiled at that. "My mother was full blooded North Korean, which some people find surprising since most biracial individuals from Korea have parentals from South Korea." She nodded in understanding. "So that makes me, in layman's terms, half Asian and half Egyptian. Now, moving on. You brought up Lennox.

"When I spoke to Lennox over a year ago, you were not in the picture, but I was helping him in regard to some things he was dealing with at the time in his own life, and also to prepare him for you. His future wife." He skipped right over her prior question, and she realized she was simply going to have to be okay with that. The man was not paying her no mind. "As you already know from my emailed response to you, my main mission is to address men. We are the ones, in my informed opinion, who need the most assistance when it comes to relationships— because we are not creators, we are hunters and builders. That is not one in the same. That aside, we have issues with managing our emotions contrary to the stereotype that women aren't able to see things logically.

"Men are naturally domineering—we are designed to be that way. The problem comes in when we abuse our physical strength and leadership skills to control others under false pretenses. Typically fueled by our own insecurities. As men, we are greedy for power and province, controlling, and lack accountability due to the collapse of societal regulations as it pertains to male self-governing. Even some of our convictions and faiths express that women are to blame should a man be weak when it comes to controlling himself. If he feels he's been seduced or sexually stimulated by simply seeing a beautiful woman out and about, then it is the woman whom the blame is placed.

"It's not his fault if he forces himself upon her, men all around this world proclaim. Men of so-called faith. Her ass shouldn't have been outside, or, she shouldn't have worn that dress, or shown her hair due to male temptation. As men, we express our shame, fears and sadness through anger, and are propelled by our sex drives. We want more of what we enjoy, all the time, regardless of the expense to others. This is why my focus is typically on male improvement and regulation. We don't understand ourselves, Nadia, and we don't acknowledge our problems if we are the root cause of them.

"We blame, versus looking within. Looking within would denote failure, and men struggle with admission of failure, because it ties right into our perceived masculinity. Women, characteristically, are much more self-aware. Without acceptance of the truth, there will never be acknowledgement. Without acknowledgement, there will never be improvement as a male, or a community. Excuse me, sweetheart. Hold on a second, please."

"Sure." *Damn. Shit was just getting good. I could listen to him speak all day!*

Saint shifted in his seat, leaned forward and picked up his phone. "Hey, baby, can you bring a glass of wine to my study, please? ... Yeah, that's fine... No, I'm in a counseling session with someone right now, but let him know that I'll call him back later... okay, baby, I love you... Yes, and thank you." He hung up the phone. "Sorry about that. I'll add an extra five minutes to your session to cover it."

"It's all good."

"Now, back to what I was saying. I am a man. I know how we think, the good, the bad and the ugly. Men will listen to me, before they listen to a woman telling him the exact same thing. It's just a sad truth. So, that's where I put the bulk of my energy. Just wanted to shed a bit more light onto that."

She nodded in understanding.

"Thank you again for that consideration. I really appreciate it."

"Of course. Now, please understand that my delivery is often blunt and not sugar-coated. I don't care who the fuck you are. If I believe you need to hear it, I am going to say it." She was silenced by his dark, angry expression. "That withstanding, my job is to help, not hurt, but sometimes when you're trying to fix a broken leg, you have to snap it back into place before putting a cast around it, and that snap of reality, if you will, causes a lot of pain."

"I understand. I'm not overly sensitive, so it's fine."

"Fantastic, but I've heard that before. I am letting you know in no uncertain terms that there is going to be nothin' pretty, enjoyable, or comfortable about this therapy session.

If it becomes too much, you are always free to end the meeting. Just know that if you become a chicken shit and bail, I'm not refunding a damn dime. It's in writing."

"I know." She smirked, getting a kick out of this guy. "I saw it."

"Besides, I live in Manhattan, in one of the most expensive properties in the city." He ran his thumb over his hand, massaging it as he glared at her, his expression somewhat twisted, condescending, as if he knew something she didn't. "I am bougie about the shoes I wear, the cigars I smoke, and fussy as fuck about the foods I consume. I have two sons who eat everything in this house that isn't tied down. One of them is hooked on war video games, and wants everything that comes out on day one. The other one somehow believes he should receive brand new cars fresh off the lot even though he drives like a demon out of hell and has the speeding and parking tickets to prove it.

"I have a daughter who thinks that only expensive name brand clothing that somehow manages to look used up and second hand should be in her closet, and a wife who collects high priced perfumes and those damn Fabergé eggs." Nadia placed her hand over her mouth to squelch her amusement. The man was going clean off. "Xenia, that's my wife, makes annual week-long trips to Paris and London, and she is charitable as fuck, so there's that. I myself am not excluded from the fuckery." He placed his hand over his heart as if about to pledge allegiance to something. "I collect vintage pornographic materials, and you wouldn't believe the going rate for the original copies of interracial dirty movies from the 1920s and 1930s. It's highway robbery, but I have to have them. There's nothin' like a bunch of unshaved, wild hairy pussies on adorable Black queens being pummeled to death by White men wearing Charlie Chaplin Derby hats and suspenders while fucking women right out of their thick ass stockings and pantaloons to the sounds of Rhapsody in Blue by George Gershwin, in the back of a motherfuckin' Ford Model T."

She burst out laughing. "You are hilarious!" He shrugged, then winked at her, showing a gorgeous smile. "I get it though, I understand. We all have our vices. As I said, I'm not sensitive. I'm not bailing. I have tough skin—I'll be okay."

He cleared his throat, then took a sip of what appeared to be water in a gorgeous, chilled wine glass. D-Nice's, 'Call Me D-Nice' started to play. He suddenly looked up from the camera, and she could hear a door opening.

"Heeeey, baby," The man's eyes lit up as if he hadn't seen her in years. It was really sweet. A woman's hand and arm entered the frame, handing him a glass of red wine. "Don't be shy," he whispered. "Give me a kiss." The lady bent down in her silk purple robe and pressed her mouth to his. She was gorgeous. An African American woman with amazing facial bone structure, full lips, thick dark hair that was pinned up in a sloppy bun, and small silver hoops hanging from her ears. A huge blinged out wedding ring was on her finger. The woman turned directly towards the camera and smiled. It was one of the kindest, warmest expressions Nadia had ever seen.

"Hi, Queen. I'm Xenia, Saint's wife."

"Hi Xenia, nice to meet you. I'm Nadia."

"What a pretty name. I'll let you two get back at it. You take care, Nadia."

"Thank you so much, you do the same."

Xenia waved goodbye, but before she got completely out of the frame, Saint smacked her ass. He was staring up at the woman as she walked away, clearly utterly obsessed with his lady. Nadia loved watching them... *They still seem so in love.* He got up, and she could hear him smack her ass again. This was followed by feminine laughter, him whispering something she couldn't quite decipher, and then the sound of the door closing.

Saint returned to his desk, a huge smile on his face. He picked up the glass of wine and took a sip, then another.

"Mmm, this is good. This must be the new merlot she bought. Adding another five minutes to your tally, Nadia. Sorry about that. You shouldn't have to lose time on account of me needing a drink and flirting with my wife. Don't want to short you."

"Okay." Nadia smiled. "That was cute though. Thank you."

"Also," he took one more sip of his drink and set it down, "please keep in mind that I can look at a person and figure out certain things about them fairly easily. That's why I was studying you earlier. That freaks some people out, so I just want to give you a heads up."

"I've been told I'm observant, too."

"Yeah, but you're observant more than likely due to being hunted. You weren't observant because *you* were hunting."

"Hunting?"

"I used to be a gotdamn predator." He said this as if it were obvious.

"A predator? I don't mean to keep echoing you, and I know this isn't what my therapy session is about, but I'm just curious. What do you mean?"

"Predators have to watch prey carefully to see how to capture them. We spend a lot of time listening and learning things about a woman for nefarious reasons. Even just the way a woman walks can tell me a lot. As a teenager who was popular in high school, and later as a well-educated single man, I used my charisma, gift of gab, financial status and physique to ensnare my target. I understood that a woman's brain has to be made love to before her body is ever touched, if you want to make her consumed with you." She nodded in agreement. "To control a woman's pussy, you first need to control her mind. I did it deliberately. That was part of the thrill." A sudden icy contempt flashed in his eyes.

"I see… so you can speak from experience."

"Most definitely. Only a predator can teach prey how to escape from men like me effectively. With that said, I believe in spirit, one Creator, karma, divinity, vibes and energy. My debt to society is to do exactly what I am doing right now… to pay for my sins by offering what I know, assisting men in understanding their nature and controlling that, and helping women heal after dealing with mothafuck-as like me."

"Understood." She sat up straighter.

He moved a bit over to the right, and she noticed a lit stick of incense behind him, as well as a candle.

"Okay, Queen. Here we go… I want you to close your eyes, then take a deep breath for me."

She inhaled, then exhaled.

"Beautiful. Do it again." She did. "Now, open your eyes."

She slowly opened her eyes and looked into his. They were beautiful, seemingly even more so than before. Unusual. Warm. Clear.

He glanced at his computer, then looked back into the camera.

"My diagnosis of you, off the rip, is a Q.L."

"And Q.L. is what?"

"I list it in my book: 'The Queen Wears the Crown.' There are thirty-two types of Queens, variations if you will, but most fall under ten major categories. Q.L. is Queen Lust." Her skin went hot. "A temptress from the top of your fucking head, down to your pedicured feet. Your mind, your soul, your heart make men lose their minds. They stalk you. Annoy you. Beg you for your time. They can even become violent when you reject them. You probably have police reports to prove it. You are aloof, yet show enough sweetness to keep them hooked. You bleed, sweat and cry sex." She forced a demure smile. "From the time you wake the fuck up until your head hits the pillow at night, your pussy is throbbing and gushing, your nipples are rock hard, your mouth full of saliva from anticipating slobbing a knob, and your ass is puckered and greased because men are *constantly* thinking about you. They are sending energy your way, and your body is receiving it. Loud and clear. You have that 'IT' factor. You're a puppet master. Throat goat. Classy, beautiful fucking whore.

"Revenge is held tight between your thighs. You've always had a problem getting men to leave you alone when you didn't want to be bothered, and it's not because you're the prettiest fucking woman in the room, either. It's because you are in fact gorgeous, but more importantly, you are mentally sharp. At times you're vengeful and unforgiving, but you can also be kind and benevolent when it suits you. You have a big heart, but you only show it to a select few. You're not naturally rude, you simply keep to yourself. You're a mystery that everyone wants to solve. You know your way around a dick, and bring men to their knees. You also have taboo sexual fantasies…" She swallowed and stiffened. "I told you not to get your panties in a bunch, woman. We're just getting started. You haven't heard *shit* yet."

He chuckled, then took another sip of his wine.

"You come out swinging, huh?" She laughed. "Okay, that's fine. I don't know how you know this shit, but I'll agree with most of it." She shrugged.

"This is not a bad thing. If you know anything about my background, then you are aware that I am a sex addict. Hence the whole spiel about being a predator. I *know* women. I read women like you're an article in a magazine, without skipping a beat."

"Yes, yes. I can see that. Do you think I am a sex addict, too?" Sometimes, she honestly wondered.

He weighed her with a critical squint. "No. You're fully able to control yourself. You just like to fuck a lot." She tittered and nodded in agreement. "Men who are sex addicts are often attracted to vixens like you. We're attracted to the temptresses. The lust radars. Women who have high sex drives, can handle a big dick, and do it again and again, many times a day. My wife is a Lust Queen, so don't be embarrassed or ashamed, or think it's an insult. It's not. I just recognize one when I see one." He tossed up his hands. "Women like you are usually highly feminine as far as physique is concerned. Your hair and nails are always done. You smell nice. Practice good hygiene. You're comfortable with your sexuality. You also light up a room when you enter.

"You elicit jealousy from other women because you're confident, and the confidence is real. Your self-esteem is high, which men like me would see as a challenge, instead of something to beware of. You're also ambitious, and have your own ideas and goals. However, women like you are often susceptible to predators like me. Why? Because you are looking for love from the strong, protective sort. A man with charisma, one who can make you believe that you're the center of his universe. Lust Queens are actually, Love Queens, but you just don't know it. Lust is simply used as a means to an end. You're trying to replace something you always wanted. Something you never had. It's your biggest weakness: Daddy issues."

She sucked her teeth, then sighed.

"I'll get back to that in a little bit. Back on topic. Alpha men, *true* alpha men, are not intimidated by independent women. We in fact want you to be that way. There are too many men running around here calling themselves an alpha but they fall apart when their woman has multiple degrees, her own interests, and what not. This is super weak. Pathetic. Frail ego shit. It's embarrassing." He snatched his cigar from the ashtray and took a long drag of it. "Remember, a sex addict doesn't always just want sex. He wants to conquer. Break a woman down. We're like vampires. We feed off of your desires and hidden insecurities."

"Do you think Lennox is a sex addict? Did you diagnose him?"

Saint shrugged and tapped ashes into the ashtray. "Lennox isn't a sex addict, but I would classify him as borderline, and I told him such. When being observed and scored, he had more self-control and discipline than most sex addicts possess, but he still used sex as an insalubrious tool. He was still using sex to self-medicate for an extensive period of time at one point in his life. That's why I am mentioning all of this to you." She nodded in understanding. "I taught him how to control his impulses and stop sleeping with women he didn't want to have a future with. Women get hooked on him, Q.L.s included. He's good in bed, right? He fucks you seven ways to Sunday?"

She grinned and turned away, hearing his deep, guttural laugh. "Right... because he knows his way around a woman's body, and he respects you. He wants you to always feel safe, loved, and adored, even when his dick is lodged down your throat and he's shooting cum at your uvula like some water-gun game at a fucking carnival."

Her heart quickened. Somehow, he was roaming the aisles of her mind. A part of her wanted to leave the session, while another part was too intrigued to do such a thing. Saint's eyes hooded as he leaned back in his chair, propping his feet up on his desk. He looked smug. Arrogant. Lovely. All she saw after a while were the bottoms of what were probably very expensive dress shoes.

"Will I be a good wife?"

"I don't know, will you?" he asked with a smirk. "That's a choice, baby girl. Look, your fiancé likes you because of all the reasons I have mentioned, and because you are like his mother, Queen Nadia. Your personality and some of your likes and dislikes are even similar to hers. You captivate him."

She was enthralled by the way he spoke, and his body language. He spoke with his hands and eyes. It was obvious he'd done this so many times, he had it down pat.

"How would you describe the way you view sex as a whole, Nadia?"

"Well, I view sex as ordinary as brushing my teeth, or going to the post office. Despite my profession, well, *past* profession, it doesn't define me. It's an enjoyable part of my life, but not my focus all the time. To me, the human body is natural, and I have autonomy over my own body."

He leaned back, crossed his leg, and chapelled his hands. "In other words, you are capable of seeing sex and intimacy in a healthy way, versus just for commerce."

"Exactly."

He glanced at his computer, then looked back at her. "You explained in your email that you were an OnlyFans model, as well as an exotic dancer, correct?"

"Yes, that's right. Now I'm back in law school though. I retired."

"You retired publicly, but not privately."

"No, I don't give any private tours, so to speak."

"That's not what I mean. Your entire childhood was spent trying to get people you loved to look at you. See you. Notice you. Pay attention to you. Not for ego, but for safety." She swallowed. "It is a part of you." Mac Miller's, 'Fight the Feeling,' the instrumental version featuring Kendrick Lamar, played as he spoke. *He's a Mac Miller and Kendrick Lamar fan, too? Interesting.* "You thought you were taking control of the situation, and any traumas that happened due to the men in your life you believed you could corral those horrors, and force men to submit to you. True or false?"

"True."

"Yes, men paid money to see your body, but really, they gained more than you ever could. They were still using you, baby." Her eyes welled with tears. "You were nothin' more to them than a wet, soft hole to cum on, cum in, or cum to, as they watched you on the pole, or their computer screen. That's why you're still unhealed, Queen, but you've improved... because it's in your nature to never stay stuck. Lust Queens are resilient. You are constantly looking for solutions. That's why you reached out to me. When you look at the men who want to see you shake your ass, you don't actually see them—you see someone else. Now, we've come full circle. You were looking for your daddy..." She sighed, then crossed her legs and arms, holding herself tight.

"And that was the problem. You saw Daddy in *all* of them, and that made you hate your customers even more. You hate weak men. Lying men. Begging men. You're attracted to men who know what they want in life, and how to get it. You like aggressive men. Not so aggressive that they try to define you, or control and rule over you, but aggressive where they mean what they say, and they show and prove. Physical strength. Intelligence. Reliability. This probably plays into even how you get turned on sexually. Fantasies… Say it, baby… You want to be taken."

"Yes."

"This competed with a trauma you endured, but you had the fantasy *before* what happened to you. What happened was, the traumatic experience made you think it was bad. It's not. It's a fairly common fantasy for women to want to be overpowered sexually, but society makes you feel like there is something wrong with you for wanting it. Craving it. You love it when Lennox pins you down. Fucks you hard, sometimes even choking you. You have intertwined potency, virility, a touch of violence, and strength with masculinity. It's not right or wrong. It simply IS." He was quiet for a moment, as if allowing her to absorb his words. "If you voluntarily allow a man to make you submit in the bedroom when you are not the submissive sort, in some strange way, you believe you are getting your power back, and that turns you on a great deal. It's a slap in the face to Daddy, right?"

Her chest tightened and a burning in her heart felt like a slow, horrible burn.

"Nadia, I need for you to not run and hide within yourself. I know what I'm saying is true about you. You know it, too. You struggle with shame and guilt though. I'll repeat it. There's nothing wrong with wanting to be dominated in bed by an alpha male, or any man for that matter. Strong women still want to feel like women, no matter how robust they believe themselves to be."

"Lennox I would consider an alpha, from the way you defined it." He nodded in agreement and sat up. "I'm afraid we'll bump heads a lot because of that. We have minor power struggles from time to time. I don't want that. What's your advice?"

"There's a stereotype that alpha women can't have alpha mates, or that alpha women can't be feminine. There's also this thought process that alpha men can't handle an alpha woman. That's not true. Just don't try to rule over your man. The key is balance." She nodded in agreement as he made his hands like scales. "You're a resilient, strong woman who is about to marry a resilient, strong man. You listen to him though, or at least you try. I imagine you try and pick your battles. Just keep doing that. When Lennox is really pissed off about something you've done, don't try to get in his face, argue, things like that. Give him some space, so y'all can talk calmly. He should do the same for you.

"For instance, I wouldn't classify my wife as necessarily having an alpha woman, or alpha-dominant personality. She's somewhere in the middle, but she is definitely not someone that I or anyone else can walk all over, either. Every now and again, we bump heads, too. The best marriages aren't perfect, Nadia, and occasional disagreements with your mate are normal and natural. It's how you deal with those disagreements that set you apart and determine if your union will last. It's all about give and take, and as long as you both know that you have each other's back and each other's best interests at heart, you should be fine."

"Yes, sir. I understand. Thank you."

"As we move along here, I am going in a different direction. We've established the type of woman you are, what you want, and who Lennox is. Now, I am going deeper. What that means is, I use my education and observation skills to pick up your energy and figure out what you need to hear so you get your life back on track. I'm going to say a lot of shit you're not going to like. It's going to be disrespectful and highly offensive, and no fucks will be given. What I said earlier wasn't shit compared to this. Regardless, when I ask you a question, I need one word answers, and one word answers only. Have I made myself clear?"

"Yes, Sir."

"There's that Southern hospitality." He smirked. "Aren't you just lovely? Here we go..." He zoomed the camera onto his face, offering a cold stare. "Let's start with Nadia, the child... Your mother ignored your emotional desires, but did take care of your basic needs. You feel like you owe her due to this, but you resent her, too. Yes or no?"

"Yes."

"Your father ignored you by abandoning you and your mother, and then when he *was* around, he spent the majority of that time chastising you and degrading you, in order to pump himself up and feel better about what a fucked-up individual he was. He was derelict in his duties. Yes or no?"

"Yes."

"He was a stupid motherfucker who thought himself smarter than everyone else, and gassed his own self up. He had a little charm, a couple coins to rub together, and thought he was the man. He created a whole fucking human being, a female soul, and named her Nadia. Nadia is a name that means hope. That's all he gave you—false hope. He left his baby girl out here on her fucking own with a damaged woman he'd lied to and tricked. Bitter baby mama. Yes or fucking no?"

"Yes."

"Instead of seeing his role in the reason that you, his daughter, became a stripper to essentially gain control over the pain that men have caused you, he showed absolutely no responsibility or accountability. Baby girl was forcing men to pay for a look at her pussy, to lust after you, and you wanted him to know about it because you wanted him to suffer! True or false?"

"...True." She was shaking, trying to keep it all together.

"Stop hesitating when I ask you a gotdamn question that you know the answer to. Trying to keep control of this conversation. Don't play with me, Queen Nadia. I'm not one of your fucking gentleman's club groupies, or Only Fan tricks!" he yelled. "I see *through* you." He pointed at the camera with steely eyes. She blinked back angry tears. "Not all strippers are traumatized, but the great majority of them are and men like me who are sexual predators—because a sex addict is *always* a predator, too, Nadia—seek women like you to dominate and destroy. Y'all are a big prize. We *love* to take you down! It's like getting Wonder Woman to give us dome in the middle of rush-hour traffic. What a high.

"Your mother was a big fish, and your father was out to get that big catch of the day. He wanted to terrorize her. Lennox said that his mother escorted during her college years but in fact it was also a deep-seeded need to break free from her religion's restrictions, mostly imposed by her father. She never told her children *that* part. Your father got this all in motion, the trajectory you were on, but you became an adult and instead of making this a temporary stepping stone to get your money up and bounce, you turned it into a career because you were self-medicating, trying to suppress the trauma. Yes or no?"

"Yes."

"LOUDER! I know you can speak louder than that, damn it! Don't be timid now! You weren't introverted on the stage when you were ripping off your clothes and pumping your hips in a slow grind! You weren't shy behind the camera when you rubbing and sucking your own titties! Do I need to CashApp you?!" He reached in his pocket, pulled out a stack of money and tossed it in the air. It landed all over his desk and the floor. "I'm not a fucking lame, john, simp, square, or a trick! NOW SAY IT! SCREAM LIKE YOU DO WHEN LENNOX IS DICK-IN' YOU THE FUCK DOWN! HITTIN' THAT DRIPPIN' WET TWAT FROM THE MOTHAFUCKIN' BACK! OWN IT!"

"YES!" She buried her face in her hands and sobbed.

"Your father wasn't shit. Most of your ex-boyfriends weren't shit and you were almost sexually assaulted by a man who you rejected, in typical Queen Lust fashion. Making him not shit, too since he was too damn fragile to accept that you didn't want him. YES OR NO?!"

"Jesus… Yes! Yes!"

"You were unable to talk to anyone about that assault, or prove that it happened in the manner that you described to the authorities, and that made you all the more bitter and traumatized. You still blame your father for this. HE *IS* TO BLAME, BUT YOU WERE A GROWN ASS WOMAN *STILL* NOT GETTING REAL HELP, FOR YOUR *REAL* TRAUMAS! YOU WERE SMART ENOUGH TO KNOW SOMETHING WAS WRONG WITH YOU, BUT YOU DID NOTHING! YOU CAN'T BLAME HIM ANYMORE! ALPHA WOMEN STRUGGLE FUCKING ACCOUNTABILITY SOMETIMES, TOO! OWN IT, DAMN IT!"

She glared at him, hating the man behind the camera. She wanted to reach through the screen and wring his fucking egotistical, conceited neck. He leaned in close again, pointing at the camera, and she jumped back.

"Don't you ever, in your fuckin' life, look at me like that again." He gritted his teeth. "*You* chose these fucked-up men for partners as an adult! One after a fuckin' 'nother, you chose emotional and mental bums! They were spiritually void! No God was in them! DON'T GET MAD AT THE MESSENGER. You were no longer a child. You chose losers, users and abusers! And do you know why? YOU KEPT CHOOSING YOUR DADDY OVER AND OVER AGAIN! TRYING TO MAKE HIM LOVE YOU THROUGH TERRIBLE TOM, DIRTY DICK AND

HORRIBLE HARRY! AND WHEN HE DIED, YOU COULD NOT BLAME HIM ANYMORE, AND THAT PISSED YOU OFF! Dead men make poor punching bags! You needed him to stick around so you could keep throwing darts at him, landing on that gotdamn bullseye! DADDY IS GONE. HE WAS NEVER HERE. YOU HAVE TO FACE THIS ALONE! IT'S TIME TO HEAL!"

A tear streamed down her face, and she clutched the edge of her shirt...

"You showed your beautiful pussy, your divine gateway, that wet, sweet hole that is there to please your mate and bring forth life, your lush garden, your oasis, your womb portal, to hundreds of men who didn't deserve for you to even spit on them, let alone see the loveliness of your physical form, and the delightful snatch that is between two warm thighs, made to wrap around your future husband. This is not a condemnation of your past, present or future, baby. Sex is beautiful. The female human body is beautiful. *You* are beautiful. You are loved. You just need to start loving yourself more... Come here... Look at me..." His voice calmed then, and she looked back up at the camera, her face a wet mess. He curled his finger, motioning for her to lean in.

"This is a look in the mirror and for you to understand why you've been behaving badly." He pressed his hands together as if praying. "Not because you stripped off your clothes, but you didn't strip off your ego. You didn't strip off the layers of pain. You held onto anger because it was easier than letting go. You have been dealing with peasants, when you are not only the Queen but run the entire queendom. You fell asleep and forgot who you were. WAKE THE FUCK UP!" More tears budded in her eyes and she shook her head. Her chest heaved so hard, it hurt. "Your body is sacred, my Love. You are Q.L. for a reason. Y'all are rare, baby… It's a compliment. Women like you just aren't born every day. When I speak about you exuding sex, and use the word lust to define you, I am not *just* talking about your body and sensuality. I am talking about people lusting to be like you, with you, or steal what you have. Your essence. Your inner-beauty. Lust isn't always just about sex. It's about wanting what someone has, and wanting it so badly, that they can taste it. You are special. Don't you realize that?"

She smiled and nodded, then wiped her tears with the back of her hand.

"Strangers ask you for help, younger women look up to you, and predators seek to consume and destroy you. You are the light! Light attracts light, and it attracts darkness, too. The sins of the father… Lennox is the first man who had romantic feelings for you that *didn't* remind you of your father in some way. That scared you. You didn't recognize him. He felt unfamiliar. That made you uncomfortable. He was the exact opposite of what you'd seen, and what you were used to. You knew deep down that that big Optimus Prime Megatron Transformer built mothafucka wanted to fuck you, be with you, and just love you," She fought a chuckle in between her tears, and he smiled back at her. "He was crazy about you way back then, and even more so now." He spoke so softly…

196

The man glanced at his Rolex, then flopped back in his chair, grabbed his glass, and brought it to his lips, his wine half gone. They didn't speak for several seconds. He took another taste and set the glass down.

"Your father was a habitual and pathological liar. He couldn't keep his dick in his pants and his mouth off of other women's pussies. As a young lady, your mother, though bright and capable, didn't understand men well, so she was an easy target. True or false?"

"I'd say true."

"One word only, baby. One word." The instrumental version of Mac Miller's, 'Desperado' started to play, the guitar riff wickedly sexy and classic. She had to hand it to the man—he had great musical tastes. It helped her, in some strange way, from feeling even worse than she already did. "Your mother is also intelligent, and intuitive, like you. She's also unpleasant. Nadia, I haven't spoken to your mother, obviously, but I'd venture to say she suffers from depression. When she looks at you, she sees herself and weeps! She hates that you hurt deep inside. Your mother doesn't show emotion in front of you, does she?"

"No."

"Well, I have a secret to tell you. You can choose to believe me or not, but sometimes, when she's alone, mark my words, the tears flow all night long. Some nights that woman cries herself to sleep."

Nadia hung her head and fought tears like her life depended on it. Her stomach caved and her heart kept seizing up. It hurt so bad... so very, very bad.

"She has closed herself off from love. She wants no

parts of it, because it's too excruciating for her to deal with. Your mother was fucked up in the head due to her childhood and instead of dealing with it, she pretended the emotions she felt were stupid, and she buried those emotions somewhere in an imaginary field a long time ago. When she expressed her feelings in the past, they were used against her. Like when she told your father that she loved him..."

Nadia sat up, forcing herself to face the music. She blinked back tears, closing her eyes for a brief moment and promising to get through this. How this man knew such things from reading a damn email and looking at her for a few seconds on a camera was beyond her, but Lennox had warned her... Told her that the man was spooky, and he knew shit he shouldn't.

"And then she turned around and expected her son and daughter to do the same. Cut off your emotions. That was unfair of her. That was abusive. That was neglectful. The Creator gave us feelings for a reason, Nadia. They are *not* pointless. They are *not* useless. They are *not* stupid. They are to be acknowledged, explored, controlled and understood. FEELINGS MAKE US HUMAN. She trusted no fucking body because of past betrayals. Now, that brings us to the final frontier of this session. In your email, you specifically stated that you want to end the cycle. The family curse, as you called it. You need to speak to your mother, and do so with confidence. Now, you are free to speak, Queen." He grabbed his water this time, and took a small sip.

"How do I talk to her about this shit? I've tried, but she doesn't listen."

"She's the only person you tiptoe around. Do what you do to everyone else when you have a bone to pick with them. Don't back down." She nodded in understanding. "Your mother shuts down in the face of wavering, which she perceives as weakness. She wakes up when she stands before strength. She respects when people are direct with her. Do not worry about her responses, receptiveness, or lack thereof when you confront her. She may get defensive, she may not. Either way, don't beat around the bush with her, either. If you say what you need to say, your job is done. Her feelings about it are irrelevant."

She took a deep breath, and then another, trying to slow her racing heartbeat. It had been one hell of an emotional ride.

"I wanted to speak to you a little more about Lennox. I want our relationship to work. I know we both have had a lot of trauma. What advice can you give me?"

He tapped his fingers on his desk to the sounds of 'Soul Sista,' by Bilal. He began to rock back and forth to the music, then lit a fresh cigar.

"Nadia," he placed the cigar to his lips, puffed, then blew out perfect rings of smoke, "the man you are engaged to comes from the same shit you came from. Dysfunction. Trauma. Lust. That's why y'all are so powerful and so sexy together... Sex is a demon and an angel. Sex was all over his mother. Sex is all over you. What drew Lennox's father to his mother was her beauty and natural sultriness. You were created out of lust... Your father was strongly attracted to your mother—so much so that he lied and stole to get her. Now, Lennox's background is a bit different from yours because there are power dynamics at play in Lennox's family. Serious ones.

"Yes, that's true. I have another question. Sometimes I feel like Lennox hides aspects of himself from me. He doesn't lie about it, per se, but he doesn't share it. Like, we were friends and he never told me his mother was Lebanese until we linked back up, or that he was from the Wilde family. He even spelled his last name differently to throw people off the trail."

"Nadia, Lennox feels he has to protect others by not speaking every single truth. Now, I believe if you'd somehow found out back then and asked him directly, he wouldn't have lied, but no, he wasn't just going to give up that information. Lennox is a monster and an angel, all rolled into one. Lennox will *always* be a monster, Nadia, so accept him as he is, but he'll never turn that monstrous behavior towards *you*. He knows better, and he has no desire to, anyway. These are just facts. Just as I will always be a sex addict. I can't change that. My wife accepts it because she loves and trusts me. It's an unfortunate part of loving a damaged man."

"How does she deal with that, if you don't mind me asking?"

He looked at her, smirking, and his eyes sparkled. "I use myself, little bits of my life in therapy sessions, to help make things relatable. I try to steer away from specifics though regarding my private life, especially when it is not explicitly about me."

"Oh, I'm sorry. I guess I thought that—"

"Some days are tough for her. It can be challenging."

He tapped embers into the ashtray. His expression was a bit melancholy as he stared at the ashes. "As a sex addict, I think about sex every day. Think about a drug addict, right? It's the same thing for me."

He puffed on his cigar again, and his eyes turned to slits as he briefly looked up at his ceiling. "It doesn't control me anymore though. Just like in this session. I am sitting here looking at you, a *very* pretty Black woman. My kryptonite. Lennox has excellent taste," She smiled at that. "You have amazing lips, beautiful eyes, and some big fuckin' titties. Trust me, I love me some tig o'l bitties but I am not the least bit sexually aroused." He said the shit so matter-of-factly, it blew her mind. She believed him.

"Wow…" She laughed.

"It's true. I make sure I am in the right frame of mind when I'm working, and I'm always a professional. I can discuss sex in depth without becoming overly stimulated. My wife knows I'm faithful despite my compulsions and obsessions. I do not lust after other women because I have control over myself, Nadia. It took me a long time to get here, but many years ago, I arrived. I have trained myself not to respond to outside stimuli in that manner. Now, don't get it twisted. I *do* find many women attractive, and always will, I'm human after all, but I do not act inappropriately, and don't fantasize about fucking other women.

"I can acknowledge that a woman is beautiful, tell her without hesitation, just like I did with you today. I can see that she has a nice body or whatever, and it will go no further than that." She nodded in understanding. "Besides, I would never disrespect my wife and the mother of my children that way, and I wouldn't want another man to disrespect me or my wife that way, either. I am in a healthy marriage with my soulmate. She is fully aware of who I am, how I behave, what I expect, and what I will and will not put up with. She knows what she signed up for."

Nadia smiled.

"Therefore, my wife helps me get my needs met with the understanding that I am going to need more physical and sexual intimacy than most men. She takes care of it and when she's tired, I just go to Palm Beach." Nadia burst out laughing, and he grinned. "Hey, it's not cheating if it's just my hand," he teased. "All jokes aside, my wife is my helpmate, and I don't think I'd even still be here, alive, if it wasn't for her. Her love has gotten me through some really rough times. I definitely wouldn't be as happy as I am without her. She is my lover, and truly my best friend."

"That's... that's just beautiful. I love that."

He placed his cigar down and looked directly into the camera. "But, uh, make no mistake about it, Nadia. Her husband is sick. I will *always* be sick. I will always be a pervert and sexual deviant. I hate saying that. It doesn't sound good. I like to be seen in a good light, but I also have to be honest with myself. My issues affect her, and that is how relationships work. If we don't heal, we hurt the people we love." She swallowed. "My sexual demands at times can be a bit much, but she understands where it is coming from, and we work through it."

"May I ask how you found out for certain that you're a sex addict? Did you diagnose yourself, or did someone else do it?"

"I've known something was wrong with me at an early age but back then, we didn't have names for these sorts of problems. People would just say, 'Oh, he's just a curious kid,' then when I got a little older and was sexually active, it was, 'He's a horndog,' or if it's a woman doing what I did, people would say, 'She's a fucking nympho.' People laugh it off because it's sex, ya know? People like talking and joking about sex. But this is *real*, and when you have a compulsion like this, it's not funny. There's nothing pleasant about wanting to fuck all day, seven days a week, twenty-four hours a day, if you could. I wouldn't wish this on my worst enemy.

"There's nothing enjoyable about getting angry at your spouse for not wanting to go a fifth round with you when she has work in the morning, or she's tired or sore from all the previous rounds … and you're fucking losing your mind about her telling you 'no' because you're in the middle of a compulsive episode. You're making a scene, trying to make her feel guilty for not allowing you to at this point, cause her physical or emotional pain because you need your sickness fed. She's physically worn-out, or she's just plain tired of arguing with you, ya know?

"These are the things that used to happen early on in my marriage from time to time. Not always, but often enough that it was disruptive. Because see, I had control over it when I met my wife. But then, because I was with her, in a committed relationship followed by marriage, I allowed myself to start having sex regularly again. I was in the throes of my healing journey, and had been abstinent by choice. Well, that triggered something in my brain." He pointed to his head. "I didn't want sex with other women—that wasn't it at all. I only wanted to make love to *her*, but I became obsessed with the sex with her. I transferred my addiction to just one person, but it was still an active addiction. I wanted it continuously, incessantly. It became a new spin off of the original compulsion and there is no way that it is humanly possible to keep up. Plus, mothafuckas got to eat, and work! Live their lives! Do other shit besides lay around fucking all day." He laughed dismally.

"Damn."

"Exactly. I never expected something like that to happen, but it did, and she worked with me through that. The few times these episodes did occur, once I settled down, I felt terrible afterwards because I knew I had said some things in the heat of the moment, cruel things that should not have been said, all in an effort to get my way."

"How do you think you became this way?"

"I know exactly how it happened. I experienced the loss of my mother at an early age. She was hit by a car. I saw her lying in the middle of the street, she was torn to pieces, and it messed me up. There was so much blood, her scream I kept hearing in my mind… My mother was my best friend. I was a mama's boy, through and through. It fucked me up."

"Oh my God, I'm sorry."

He nodded, took a sip of water, then continued. "I was developing. My psychiatrist at the time explained that I was a little boy when this happened, and somehow, in some odd, unfortunate way, I fused my interest in girls and sex with pain and trauma. It's rather complicated to explain, but that's the gist of it. I found a way to grieve by blocking it with something that felt good. Something that would distract me. Every time I would get depressed about my mother, or angry about being poor or whatever it was that was upsetting me at any given period of time, I had this to fall back on now. As inappropriate as it was. In spite of all of this, I am quite self-aware. I knew it wasn't normal to fuck five, six or seven different women in one day, and still want more pussy afterwards. It had to stop." He leaned back, an angry scowl on his face as he folded his arms. "It was also risky behavior.

"It wasn't normal to have an amazing sexual experience with a woman, and then five minutes later, jack off to a porno when I just busted a nut. There's nothing ordinary about that. I was formerly diagnosed by one of the best psychiatrists and sex addiction therapists in the world, Nadia. He spent significant time with me, and I was identified as having a level 5 sex addiction, which is the highest you can get from the chart that he designed, and is still used by many professionals in the field today. It is unusual to get that high of a score, but I did. I was also diagnosed with hypersexual compulsive disorder—level 5 again—and possessing sexual deviancy tendencies, level 4.

"I wanted to do kinky shit because regular ol' vanilla sex wasn't getting me off anymore. There's nothin' wrong with kinky shit as long as it's consensual, and no one is being irreparably wounded." He smiled, and she smiled back. "I love kinky and regular ol' vanilla sex just fine, but if the kinky stuff is *always* the preferred method to achieve orgasm, then it's a problem. My doctor who diagnosed me said I was one of the worst cases he'd ever seen. He even put me, anonymously, in one of his medical textbooks. Patient #0821A-K. How crazy is that?!"

"What medical book was it? I want to read it."

He paused, then burst out laughing.

"I'm serious." She chuckled.

"I know you are. You like to learn... you're a brilliant student, and that's wonderful. I'll send you the link to buy it online. I'm sure it's still in print. Anyway, I became a case study for people all over the world. Me and my dick were a menace to society. I was Darth Vader and my cock was my lightsaber. I was definitely using the force, and I loved the dark side." She stifled a laugh at that, knowing he was for real. "I was in college getting my Masters and PhD, a licensed therapist, which adds another crazy layer to this. I scheduled my life around sexual encounters. Work. Sex. Eat. Sex. Take a piss. Sex. Go to the gym, in an effort to not necessarily stay healthy, but to garner more attention during my hunting of women. To get sex. It was absolutely insane."

"Were you exhausted?"

"ALL THE TIME! But I was also running on adrenaline, which fooled me into thinking I was fine. I would hunt women every waking moment, and even when I was asleep because when online dating began to get pretty popular, I had profiles working for me twenty-four-seven to help catch women to hook up with, too. I'd go to clubs. See women on the street. In the store. At airports while I'd travel for business. Even on phone chat lines before the online dating boom. I would meet up with these women, fuck their brains out, then discard them—like they weren't even human. Most times though, I didn't even have to approach women. They'd come to me, which made things both ten times easier and ten times worse.

"I am a sex addict to my core. There is no cure for sexual addiction, only coping mechanisms and strategies. I refused to become a priest, or abstain forever, so I had to figure out what I *could* do, realistically, to get control of myself—especially once I realized how serious sex is, and how *who* we share our bodies with matters. Sex is a spiritual connection. We form attachments, like wires to people, when we give them our bodies. We become one when we have intercourse with someone. I was out here with women all over the damn city, attached to me. I'd made soul ties because I would get into these women's brains, and then I would fuck these women with skill and passion. I had been inside of them, re-wiring them to fit *me*. Did I know this shit back then? No, but when I did realize it, I knew I needed help. I was hurting people, including myself. You worked in the sex industry, so I know you at least have a basic understanding regarding what I am talking about."

"Yes, I do. There are men who I suspected were sex addicts because they were on my OnlyFans all the time, spending thousands of dollars every month. Or, they'd be in the club practically every day of the week."

"Yes, that's often a telling sign of someone suffering from an addiction. You are not a sex addict, but some of your clients were. It goes with the territory." She nodded in agreement.

"Has things slowed down since you've been married for

quite a while?"

"Unfortunately for my wife, my libido has not lowered or slowed down in the least over the years, but she's okay, and I am satisfied. Now, do you know why I decided to answer such personal questions tonight, Nadia?"

"No, why?"

"Because something told me that if I give you this gift, the gift of personal information regarding my own biggest flaw, it will assist you in something that you'll encounter. Me sharing something with you that only a few people know, in such detail, was important today. I would have preferred not to, but you needed to hear it more than I needed to keep it close to my chest. I don't hide my sex addiction. I talk about it all the time in my seminars, but the particulars of some of the things that transpired in my life and my marriage due to it, well, that's different because it involves other people, and I wish to protect my wife and children from any embarrassment that my past actions could bring."

"I can understand that."

"But, I'm talking about it anyway. With you. Because something may happen between you and Lennox, some-thing out of either of your control, and you need to have patience and show compassion for and towards one another. Something, or someone, that is disruptive or evil may enter the picture, and you two will need to be united to confront and combat it. It may not be an addiction, as in my case, but it will be something that is potentially destruc-tive. Something that is trying to take ahold and control of either your or Lennox's life, and you must resist, and push back. You have to work together on it, just like me and *my* wife." She got chills. "My addiction was definitely disruptive, and it was also evil because it did not yield good fruits. I did not make strong connections due to it. In fact, I did the exact opposite.

"I tore connections apart. I had to use those iniquitous deeds as fuel, and turn them into something positive. That's why I am sitting behind this desk. When the evil disruption comes to your doorstep, because it will if it has not already, I want you to remember this conversation. To every problem, there is a solution. No matter how hard or huge the difficulty seems. I was level five. Level fuckin' five." He held up five fingers. "There seemed no way out, but there was. There is nothing Satan can create that God does not have an antidote for, baby, but it's up to you to find it, and then to use it."

She grabbed a tissue and dabbed at her eyes.

"My antidote was learning skills for self-control, prayer, accepting myself for who I am, teaching, training, and coaching others, and Xenia. She's my medicine. I have this problem, but I have a wife who loves me and is understanding of the situation, and she's seen me grow and conquer it. I can go days, even weeks now without sex if necessary. Before? That would have been unheard of, and quite frankly, impossible. I would attempt celibacy and be successful for a while, but I always eventually fell off the wagon. Our first year of marriage was overshadowed by my addiction. If it is possible to be fucked to death, she was damn near close to that, but once she had our first child, things were greatly improved. She and I make jokes about it now, but at the time it wasn't funny at all. We were newlyweds, and I was stressing her the hell out. She had patience with me, and now, here we are. I am not a problem in that regard anymore, and our sex life is fantastic."

"I love hearing stories like this. Overcoming obstacles. It gives people hope, and you know what? I believe you when you tell me that you sharing something so deeply personal may help me later down the line. In fact, I think I already know what this applies to. Thank you for that."

"You're welcome. So, since you asked me about that, I can use it to go into another point that needs to be made since you wanted my advice about your relationship."

"Yes, please do."

"Lennox is a ladies' man. He enjoys the company of women, but he also respects women. He's also enthusiastic about fighting and violent physical altercations, but he doesn't act on it often. He discovered, unfortunately, that when he physically hurt someone, it felt good and made him forget his trauma for a short while. He wishes it weren't true, and he finds it shameful. Like me, he found a way to cope with it. This is why he's attracted to the gym, Nadia. This is why he is a gym rat, and it is a good, healthy profession for him. He needs it."

She sat there thinking about what Dr. Saint Aknaten had stated. The puzzle pieces were coming together. Damn if he wasn't right.

"That makes perfect sense. Actually, he is right now starting his own fitness center. I'm so proud of him. He bought this old dealership, and they are adding to it to make the area larger. They've already broken ground and the addition is being built. It's going to be really nice when they're all done."

"That's great news. I'm very happy for him. He has to keep moving and burning off steam, if you will. Your fiancé has a lot of rage and physical strength, and that can be quite dangerous if he doesn't have an outlet."

"I know. Believe me," she shook her head, "I know."

"As I told you earlier, I don't believe for a second though, that he'd ever hurt you, or anyone he loves, in a million years. That's control. That's mastery over oneself. He and I spoke about it in depth, and he was one of the more self-aware clients that I've had over the years. I admired that about him. Lennox is a soldier, by birth. He was bred with the intention to destroy." A wave of confusion flowed within her. "It's complicated, would take a long time to explain, but in a nutshell, it's in his genes. He *needs* to hurt things. Someone, long ago, had a propensity to be warlike. A harsh warrior, an iron-fisted ruler, and that gene kept getting passed down in his family, especially amongst the boys.

"The more testosterone the person has, the worse it shows up in them. It's in his bloodline, a family curse, just like what you mentioned in your email regarding your own grandmother's warning. Lennox though, having a good moral compass, wants to mainly focus his wrath onto bad people. He wants to destroy the ugly things in this world and stop bad people from hurting good people. This goes against how it was typically done in his family. He's breaking code, and that may be pissing some people off."

*How in the hell does this man know this?! Lennox obviously spoke to him, 'cause ain't no way.* "He struggles with accepting this about himself because he resents having any violent tendencies at all. He's a work in progress."

"He said you helped him with a lot of stuff, and this was one of them."

"Yeah, I did. I helped him learn how to admit it, live with it, but control it better. When Lennox is in emotional pain, he is susceptible to acting out when he is depressed or angry. It could be excessive drinking to numb it—which from my understanding he has not abused alcohol in years—being promiscuous which stopped soon after his therapy with me, or beating someone up when a warning would have sufficed. Something tells me that this has slowed down, but not ceased." The man leaned back and smirked.

*That's an understatement…*

"I'll just say that he's been a little active."

Saint cracked up at this, laughing loudly. He had a really great laugh, one that came from the belly.

"Okay, okay, that's fine, as long as he is using his coping skills, he'll be okay."

"You mentioned I was like his mother, and he's said that to me several times, too. I wonder though if that could be a bad thing in some way? Like, I want to be this man's wife. Don't want him to subconsciously see me as his mom."

"That's not how this works, though I understand your question and concern. It's not a sexual thing, and it's not a replacement issue, per se, either. Lennox has mommy issues, but in a good way, too. His mother was good to him, but she died too soon. Just like mine did. It was sudden, and he was still quite young when it took place. He was traumatized, and from my understanding, he did not have the support he needed during that time. In fact, he had to step up in areas that he shouldn't have been expected to. He was never allowed the time to properly grieve because he had to take care of everyone else. That resentment and anger built up, and built up, and built up, until it exploded. And that is why he needed help.

"It was the root of his acting out, but you being like his mother, and him wanting someone like her, is about him being drawn to women who are emotionally intelligent, have a desire to learn, spiritual strength, are intellectually sound and gifted, possess external beauty since he is a visual person. His mother was known to be an attractive woman, but more importantly, he wanted a mate with a good heart. Someone who gave a damn about others. Like his mother. Yes, both you and his mother worked in the sex industry, but he is not looking at that sexual aspect, per se. He is looking at it as you both did what you felt you needed to do to reach certain goals, and you both just happened to choose a similar profession."

"I see that, yes."

"He wanted basically a female version of himself, Nadia, because he is quite similar to his own mother. Lennox is a caretaker. He is the quintessential definition of a strong protector. He wants a wife, babies, two dogs and a cat, the white picket fence, all of that, but he refused to settle. It had to be with the *right* person, and the person is *you*." She smiled at that. "It has nothing to do with him wanting you to fill his mother's shoes, or anything like that."

"Okay, thanks for clearing that up." She reached for her tea which had gone cold, and took a much-needed chug.

"I think you two will be magnificent together. You have similar goals and outlooks on life, and you appreciate your differences. As long as you both continue to try to compromise with one another, you'll be fine. Any more questions, Queen, before I wrap this up?"

She took a deep breath and wondered if she should even say it...

"Yes, I have one more. About my father... I want to forgive him, Saint. But I'm struggling. You were right regarding what you said earlier about me and my father. I truly want to be able to let this go and heal."

"First, have a serious conversation with your mother. Then, I want you to speak to your father as if he's here. If that's too difficult, write a letter to your father, and go to his grave and read it to him. Aloud. Say everything that you need to say, and then you must force yourself to let it go. I will send you my meditation book for free. Lastly, I want you to read my book, "Broken Black Highness." It deals with racism, sexism, patriarchy, religious abuse and how this has directly affected Black women in America, and caused you all to be stuck in a never-ending cycle of your pain. Pay close attention to Chapter Seventeen. My wife experienced an absentee father too, okay?" He was speaking softly now, and his eyes shone with warmth and kindness. "I witnessed firsthand what can happen when a woman's father abandons the family. Please read that chapter, and then feel free to follow up with me regarding any questions you may have."

"Okay, thank you so much." She reached for a tissue and dabbed at her eyes again. She felt completely drained, but also, in some strange way, hopeful and rejuvenated. He grabbed his remote and turned the music completely off. Leaning into his desk, he rested his hands upon it.

"Do you believe in prayer and a Higher Power, baby?"

"Yes." She nodded, crying harder. "I do."

"I know you do, or Lennox wouldn't even be with you since that's important to him, but I wanted to hear you say it yourself. I'm going to talk to you, off the record, and say a prayer for you, if that's okay?"

"Okay, thank you so much." She sniffed.

"Close your eyes, beautiful." He spoke softly, his voice deep and warm like a brandy. It was healing. A spiritual balm.

She closed her eyes and listened. Suddenly, music began to play again. Robert Glasper's, 'Better Than I Imagined', featuring H.E.R. and Meshell Ndegeocello. An instrumental version though. Her eyes immediately watered with emotion.

"Listen to the music… think about the man you love. Lennox. Go deep into your memory bank, and ponder how you two met, and how you felt about one another… The beauty of your friendship. It was unique, innocent, and divine." She nodded and wiped a tear away, keeping her eyes closed. "Think about how it feels when he kisses you… his lips against yours… when he lays his head against your shoulder and hugs you... think about how it feels when he is inside of you, making love to you... Deep, deep, inside of you... strengthening your connection, becoming one." She shuddered, feeling the sensation as if Lennox was right there.

"Your bond is beyond the physical. It's made of iron. Evil is designed to try and destroy all that is good. All that is strong. Think about your strengths, Queen. You cause lust. Lust, in the way I am describing it, is a super power, Nadia. Not a sin. Lust, in the way I am describing it, is the unbridled desire of one person, for another person, with the intention of a happily ever after. Your man desires not only your body, but your mind, and your soul. You're not a cheap thrill for him. You're not dealing with a fan or a customer. He's a real man who desires a real woman. Desire spawns excitement and creativity. New life comes forth.

"Most babies are created from sexual desire... and that's beautiful. A desire to be loved, and in love. A desire to be close to someone who makes us feel good physically, and makes us feel special. You make this man feel special. You've brought him literally to his knees, as only a good Queen Lust can. He paid you nothing, and you didn't have to pay with your soul. When he claimed you and told you that he wanted you to be his woman, he didn't want you to take anything off, except for your defenses. He wanted you to let him inside. Not inside your pussy, ass or mouth, but your mind and heart."

She smiled through her tears.

"Lennox wasn't ready when he first consulted me, but he wanted to *get* prepared for his bride. He did what I advised him to do. It took a long time, but he did it. And what do you know? He found his queen. She came back, returned to him, drinking a glass of wine while red and purple lights spun above her head like a halo..." She grabbed another tissue. "...It was the right place, the right time. The Creator saw that he was ready. Nadia, talk to the garden. She can still grow. Write a letter to the sprinkler. He is gone, but you are still here. Then, allow your soulmate to plant a seed in your soil, and he'll vow to never walk away from the fruits of your labor. The death of evil begins with you. Heal for *you*, first. Heal for him, second. Healing hurts. It's ugly, but the results are everlasting. When we heal, we are at our strongest. When we wallow in the past with no plans for recovery, we are at our weakest. We have to feel pain before we can understand and appreciate true pleasure. You and I are here, right now, on purpose.

"Creator, I ask that you help guide this Queen's steps. I ask that you continue to put the right words in her mouth so she can encourage her King, and for her King to do the same for her. I ask that any evil that comes their way is eradicated, cut off at the knees, and all who wish to cause damage to this union be stopped in their tracks. They are like rocks. They are strong in the face of adversity, but they must conquer their traumas. Lennox and Nadia are stones. They've been discarded by people they loved. Trotted upon and thrown away, left to die. But may those two stones remember that when they were thrown in deep water, they rose to the mothafuckin' top. Straighten up and fly right, Queen. Don't be afraid of the rain. Dance in it, for you are the garden of life…"

# CHAPTER THIRTY-ONE

## *Sam I Am*

LENNOX SAT AT his desk, serenaded by the sounds of Foy Vance's, 'Make It Rain'. Tilting his bottle of beer to his lips, he took a few good gulps then set it down on the coaster, mouthing the lyrics to the song while running some software to remove the encryption on a file on the USB drive he'd used at his father's house.

Though he wasn't surprised with his findings, he was disgusted. He moved the documents off to the left on the desktop, then opened his storage cloud. He clicked on the folder his sister had hand delivered to him and watched as the photos and videos populated. Taking a deep breath, he watched each one. He listened to all that was being said, his emotions a roller coaster. He went from rage to sadness, to repugnance, to feeling nothing at all. It was late. He glanced at the time on the computer. 3:12 A.M. Grabbing his phone, he sent a text message to Nadia:

**Baby, are you good? You told me you'd call me afterwards, and it's been a long while. I'm just checking in on you. Let me know what's up.**

He placed his phone back down, closed his eyes and rubbed his throbbing head. Soon, his life would never be the same. His cellphone rang, dragging him out of his thoughts.

"Hey, sexy," he answered. No response. "Baby? … damn…"

Nadia was crying softly on the other end. He could tell she kept trying to speak, but whenever she did, nothing but cries broke through. He sighed, leaned back in his chair, and closed his eyes once again. He remained quiet for several seconds, perhaps even an entire minute. And then, he spoke to her.

"He gets in your mind, and you can't get him out. You now know that from the moment the session ended, you'll never be the same. I warned you, baby. He's ruthless, and they say he handles the ladies a lot nicer than the guys, so that was probably the watered-down version of what I got." He chuckled. "He ripped me a new asshole, then had the nerve to be all nice at the end after basically tellin' me I wasn't shit for like forty-five minutes straight." He heard her laugh a little. "It's alright…it's good for you, like strong medicine. Just process it. You feel bad, but you feel good too, don't you? You have the tools now to start healing. It's hard to explain," he stated with a sad smile.

"Yes… that's exactly it… but… I feel so, so, so much better," she stated between sniffs. "It's like a lot of my pain lifted after we were finished. It was like he'd reached through the screen, and... and made me feel lighter. Cleaner. I don't know. Something just feels different." He nodded in understanding. "He stayed on with me for almost two hours, and didn't ask me to pay more. It only felt like ten or twenty minutes, but we were on that Zoom call a long time."

Lennox nodded. "I'm proud of you, baby. Dr. Saint's good... He knows his shit. Do you need anything from me?"

"No, I'm okay. So, are we still, uh..."

"Yup. I checked everything. You're amazing, you know that?"

"So are you."

"I'll call you when it's time. Try to get a little sleep before I rock 'n' roll. Not much time left before I head out."

"Okay, baby. I'll be on standby. Love you."

"I love you too, Nadia. See you later, baby." He ended the call, placed his phone down and shook his head.

*I wish I could hold her right now. Wrap my arms around her... kiss her... I hate that she's alone, hurting. I don't know what Dr. Aknaten said to her, and she may never tell me the full story, but whatever it was, if you can make Nadia cry like that, then you're a bad motherfucker. I haven't heard her that worked up, since our job at the Rooster. Maybe it's better I'm not there, actually... that way she can process everything in peace? Yeah... it probably is for the best. I'd just be a distraction. She just needs a minute. I know how she feels. It's tough. That mirror is right in front of your face, and you can't turn away from it. She'll be okay...*

After a few minutes, he put all of the documents, photos, files, onto a new thumb drive. As those files were moving over, he backed up the records onto his cloud, then sent full copies to four different people, with instructions on what to do if the worst happened—like him being murdered or taken. He went to the restroom to relieve himself, then grabbed his jacket from the closet. Slipping his .460 S&W Magnum into the holster around his waist, he headed out the door...

MY MAMA TOLD me a story a long time ago. I was just a little boy, but I remember it because it struck me as both funny and creepy. Now, as an adult, I understand more than ever what she was trying to tell me. Everything had come full circle...

Mama said that in her religion and culture, they called the devil *Iblis*. Or if you're learned in the faith, **ash-Shayṭān** ("the Devil") Followed by the epithet, **ar-Rajim** (Arabic: آلرَجِيم, lit. 'the Accursed'). *There once was a small, doll-like man dressed in fine clothing who came into town. He offered gold coins, sweet treats, soft breads, fresh fruits and vegetables that tasted like nothing you'd ever had before in your entire life. He offered to chop wood for the villagers' fires, and he always had a bounty of fine satins and silk. He was small and cute, had an amazing singing voice, could play many instruments, and had the most mesmerizing sparkling eyes. A charming little thing. Harmless for sure.*

*Over time, the villagers grew to depend on him. After all, before he arrived, they were poor, and all he wanted in exchange for his gifts was to sleep in their homes late at night and, on occasion, to receive a home-cooked meal. This went on for quite a while, and the villagers were* now fighting over who had what from the little man, as well as who had the best outfits and the most money. After a while though, bad things started happening in the village, mainly to the children.

At first, no one noticed. One child vanished, then another...

Perhaps the children had drowned in the river they were forbidden to play in? It had happened in the past, so it was not out of the question. But then more children disappeared, and more again. They looked everywhere for their babies, but could never find them. They went on manhunts, and soon they all turned on one another, accusing each other of taking the innocent ones.

All of the offspring were disappearing in the middle of the night. Vanishing into thin air. Nobody noticed the little man in the melee. If they had, perhaps they would have seen that he was growing... he'd been getting fatter, and fatter, and fatter still. In some corner of all of their homes were stacks of gold, candies, fruits, jewelry, silk and satin... but their children were gone. And before one could blink, so was the little man...

The little demon was quite content. It was a fair exchange, after all. The village people had received material goods, his precious time, his lovely singing voice, and his hard labor. The only way he could become more powerful and satiate his hunger was to eat the innocent. Wolf them down whole while the adults counted their gold coins, played with their trinkets, and slipped on their gowns made of fine satin and silk.

Off to the next village the demon would go, and the wicked cycle would start all over again. The parents had been blindsided by glitz and self-indulgence, influenced by overconsumption and insatiability for the finer things in life. So much so, they hadn't even noticed that their most priceless possessions were being stolen and consumed right under their noses. The little demon had gone, and all they had now was *rotting fruit and tarnished rings to show for it. How pitiful. How very sad...*

Lennox pulled up to the house with the neatly cut grass and American flag waving proudly in front of it. It was on acres of land—Grandpa's land. He owned it. All of it. A little structure in the country, in a peaceful part of town. The nearest neighbor was over half a mile away. It was dark outside, the sun not up just yet. He hadn't slept a wink and yet, he felt refreshed. Free.

Inside of his truck, Leon Bridges' 'River' started to play. He leaned back in his seat, bobbing his head slowly to the music as a cool sensation came over his body. As the song still played, he jumped out of his truck and trudged up the driveway of the residence with a bag of supplies. Dropping the bag onto the ground, he stood at the front door, his fingers around his weapon. Chest heaving up and down, flashes of his woman naked and afraid in the shower rushed in his mind. He shuddered as he could practically see her with shower water falling all over her nude body as she gripped a gun, her heart probably pounding damn near out of body...

He wanted to scream. He fisted his left hand, nails digging into his palm, probably drawing blood but he was far too manic to feel a damn thing.

The music pounded in his ears, the lyrics tearing him apart. Turning into a roaring flame, he shot the door, then kicked it in. He raced inside, his body an arrow shooting down the hall until he made it to the master bedroom. The room was dark, but he could see the man in the bed. There was a body next to him, too. Shadows. darkness. A bit of light. The sound of slow movement.

"Howdy, cousin. I understand that you paid my lady a surprise visit. That really creams my corn. I thought I'd pop over and see what's good!"

Lennox heard Sam scrambling, and what sounded like a drawer opening.

BANG! Lennox fired his gun.

The woman started to wail and scream.

"HOLD ON, MOTHERFUCKER! What kinda welcome wagon are you driving? Ain't you gonna say hi to your big cousin?!"

BANG!

The room lit up with flashes of light and the odor of gun smoke.

"…Didn't offer me a drink or nothin'! I'm gonna have to teach you some manners, lil' boy!" Lennox ground between clenched teeth as he beat Sam about the head with the gun, then stopped to choke him one good time. Sam began to convulse, to gurgle and spit up… the sounds of pleasure to Lennox's ears.

In a flash he let go, and Sam gasped for air, trying to speak.

"GOT DAMN IT! FUCK!!!!" Sam yelled as he clambered around in the dark, knocking things over. Lennox wrestled him, beating him to a fine pulp. The lady in the bed was wearing his ears out with all of her cries and shrieks.

He snatched arms, legs, and flesh. Pinching, shoving, breaking bones. Drops of moisture dragged across his knuckles. Freshly drawn blood. Screams and bloodcurdling cries echoed in the bedroom—feminine whimpers turning to moaning wails. Out of the corner of his eye, he caught her reaching for her cell phone on the nightstand.

BANG!

"AHHHHH! AHHHHH!!!" Lennox shot the head-board right above her mass of dark blonde hair. Shards of wood flew everywhere. The woman brought the sheets up to her chin and kept on with her ear-piercing song of fear.

"Well, bless your heart, little lady… SHUT THE FUCK UP!" Lennox roared as he glared at her. He had Sam in a half nelson, pressing the man to his chest so hard he figured he would pass out if he didn't let up soon. "All that carryin' on! And if you try to call anybody, reach for that phone one more 'gin, I'll know before you even say 'help,' and you'll end up just like my cousin here, Kevin Malone from 'The Office.' Ya hear? Do you fucking understand me?"

The woman's screams turned to a low sniffly murmur. She nodded several times, reminding him of a bobblehead figure.

"And as sure as piss ain't lemonade, I will kill this motherfucker faster than a one-legged man in a butt kickin' contest. If you disobey me, and I'll put a bullet in your skull so big, you'll be mistaken for a cherry glazed donut and get licked by the cops when they find your dead body. Fuck around and find out if you want to."

The rage within him was mounting like stacks of leaves. Lennox walked over and locked the bedroom door, then rushed to the woman's side of the bed, glaring at Sam who lay on the floor.

"Sam, if you try 'nd get up, try to be a hero, I'll kill her and you, too. Now let's get you situated, sweetheart."

She screamed when he grabbed the phone on the nightstand, then stomped it hard a good few times with his boot until it shattered to pieces. When he yanked her off the bed, she shrieked to high heaven. Placing his hand over her mouth, he squelched her yells, then covered her lips with electrical tape. He tied her to the bed, wrists and ankles, then returned to Sam, who was looking up at him with nothing but pure fear in his eyes.

"Sam, I think you took me for a fool. You know still waters run deep. Just 'cause I wasn't the loudest in the family didn't mean I can't go BOOM. You and me got some business to tend to. What kinda flowers would you like on your tombstone?"

"LENNY, NO!!! OH, GOD! Don't kill me!" Sam shouted and Lennox stood over him, pointing the gun down at his head. "LENNY, IT WAS GRANDPA! PLEASE DON'T SHOOT ME, MAN! I'D NEVER CROSS YOU ON PURPOSE IN A MILLION, TRIL-LION YEARS! IT WAS GRANDPA! I SWEAR! It wasn't my idea!"

Another flash of light, and more screams, this time from Sammy boy, rent the air.

He dragged Sam outside, bloodied, beaten and bruised, then slapped a thick layer of electrical tape over his mouth. 'Take Me to the River' played on repeat from his truck. Lennox jammed the bastard in the passenger's seat of the vehicle, then made quick work of tying his hands and feet with twine and tape. He hummed to the music as he did, really getting into the groove of things.

"You know Sam, it's hotter than blue blazes tonight. It's a good thing you're wearing only boxers. Wouldn't want you to pass out from the heat, now would we? I want you to see and feel what is comin' your way, boy. It ain't no fun if you aren't conscious to watch the show!" He squeezed the knot around his ankles, drawing a painful whine from Sam. "It's a damn shame it had to come to this… I'm sure Grandpa neglected to explain the danger he put you in by sending you out there to mess with my woman. Now you have to pay the piper."

The poor fool groaned. His eyes glazed over and he was losing strength fast.

"You're home, but the porch light ain't on. Still, you had to know better, didn't you? Wanted to be a big shot and show off. Prove to the old man that you had grit. Had what it takes to be a *true* Wilde boy. So, because of that, you'll have to face the consequences."

Sam started banging his head all around the vehicle. Twisting and turning as if he were on fire. Lennox delivered a gunshot in the air.

"Settle down."

BANG! Lennox shot the gun in the air one more time as he stood right outside the passenger's side door.

Sam kept moving, driving his head into the dashboard, fighting for his life.

BANG!

"MMMMM!!!! MMMMM!!!!" The bastard moaned in agony.

"Yup. I shot ya. You're a hard-headed motherfucker, ain't cha?" Lennox chuckled. "Pipe down. It's just a flesh wound. You'll be all right. Ya hear that, lady?!" he hollered. "Your little half-witted fuckboy toy with a brain made of stale cotton candy just got bit by a bullet! So fuckin' dumb he could throw himself on the ground and still miss!" Lennox slammed the passenger's side door, jumped in the driver's seat, and headed out of there, singing loudly to the music.

He drove slowly but surely until he reached a desolate stretch of dirt road, out in the middle of nowhere. The sky had begun to lighten a bit, but the darkness still had a stronghold. He took Sam out of the truck, grabbed his duffle bag, and dragged him to one of the old trees out there in the big field where the grass and weeds reached up to one's knees.

"Well, this is as good a spot as any. You like tree houses, Sam?"

The bastard's eyes swelled as sweat dripped down his face. Mumbles and murmurs came from his covered mouth—none he could understand.

"This might just be your final resting place. Right here out yonder. If you're lucky though, you'll come out of this lil' situation alive. If you're not so lucky, and it has come to my attention that you're not the lucky sort considering how you got turned every which way but loose by the bouncers in the gentlemen's club, then you'll die here. Alone. I'd prefer the latter. You couldn't find your ass with both hands in your back pockets. No need for you to take up valuable oxygen that someone worthier could enjoy." Lennox stretched and strained as he tied Sam to the tree, arms and legs spread wide.

He reached into his duffle bag, pulled out a camera, and placed it on another tree nearby, pointed in Sam's direction.

"Now see, from wherever I am, I can see you on this here camera, right from my phone. I'll be able to know everything you do. Not that you can do too much. The problem with this area of town, Sam, is it's chock full of cottonmouth snakes, copperheads and bobcats. The grass is too dang high. The moon is still out. That means it's still huntin' time and plenty of hidin' places for critters to crouch down and hide, watch you from a distance before they make their move. A nice warm, bloody body like yours, the scent waftin' in the wind like barbecue? Well, hell… You'll look like a juicy steak, ripe for the chomping."

Sam groaned, and his eyes rolled as if he were lying in the lap of misery.

Lennox heard another vehicle slowly pull into the area. He glanced over his shoulder, saluted the person as they parked, then leaned in close to Sam as he rested his gun against the tree, next to Sam's head. He patted the fucker's chest and sniffed, then bent down to whisper into his ear.

"I have to run a little errand, so I made sure you have a concierge of sorts while I'm away. They'll take good care of you. Now, allow me to let you in on a little something, boy. You were the only motherfucker dumb enough to go on out there and try to have a chat with my girl. You don't go talkin' to a man's lady, 'specially 'bout no business proposition, at her job of all places, without her man's permission. We're family. You don't know much, Sam, but you know better than *that*. You really think Grandpa chose you outta the kindness of his heart to run that mission? Or thought you were the best man for the job? No, sir. He knew damn well that some of the others he may ask would chicken out, or remind him about his rule regardin' fuckin' with our women unprovoked.

"Grandpa don't really give a fuck about you, but he loves your father, another one of his sons he's turned into a slave, so he'll feel some type of way if you come up missin'. Now, technically I bet he ain't tell you to do what you did. Grandpa is a creature of habit, so I figured you ad-libbed a bit, and that's when shit went south. Regardless, nobody but you would be dumb enough to do that. It was a suicide mission. The family, and his little security force, Jasper, Uncle Danny, and all the rest of them know what I'm capable of. Why in the fuck do you think he'd want me, if I'm so damn peace lovin', to help run the gotdamn Zoo?"

Sam blinked several times, his eyes watering until tears started to flow down his face.

"Naw. Grandpa wants his seven wickedest grandsons to join forces with him. He knows how we get down, but we don't want to be ruled by nobody. We're our own men. He calls us renegades. You want to be a 'made' man, huh? You *almost* succeeded though, didn't you? But, you underesti-mated my sweet Brown Sugar. You thought she was gonna offer to suck your little dick or somethin' if you turned 'er loose, didn't you? Figure just 'cause she works there, you can have a little fun with her? Like she's some drug addicted prostitute. You thought she didn't have any loyalty towards her man, or didn't possess any morals?"

Lennox grinned real hard as he glared at him.

"That's what happens when you judge a book by its cover. Make assumptions that lead to your downfall. Now, under typical circumstances, you'd be dancin' with the devil right about now—dead as the day is long. Nevertheless, because you're stupid as hell and I can use you as bait, if you will, I'm going to let you draw breath... at least for a little while longer. Of course, your babysitter could choose otherwise while I'm away. I have no control over what they decide to do to you. It took all of my power, all of my self-control, all of my resolve, to not put three bullets in you tonight, dear Sam.

"One in your fucking heart. Because that was a cowardly thing you did. One in your empty ass skull. Because that was a dumb thing you did. And one in your gotdamn groin, 'cause you got hard lookin' at my woman. Oh yes you did. It turned you on, seein' her naked and all drippin' wet from the water... You wanted a piece of that pretty ass, didn't you?" Lennox grinned. "Now, I've got a piece of you. You stay right here. Relax. Maybe say a prayer or two."

He tapped the man on the side of his head with the butt of the gun, then walked back to his truck. He looked over his shoulder at his captive. Sam tried to scream through electrical tape, furiously attempting to wiggle free, perhaps plead his case, to no avail.

Lennox got inside his vehicle and turned on the radio. Heartless Bastards' "Only For You," came on the air. He turned it up high, enjoying himself. Kicking the truck in drive, he drove past Sam tied to the tree. They met eyes.

Lennox smiled and waved, nodded in the direction of the person sitting in a big truck, then headed back onto the dirt road, driving proudly away under the rising sun...

# CHAPTER THIRTY-TWO

## *A Shred of Evidence and the Naked Truth*

IN ENGLAND, THEY called it afternoon tea. In Grandpa's house, they called it T-minus. The day of reckoning. A ghastly reunion, disguised as a meeting of the minds. The clock had just struck twelve. Lennox parked at the far end of Grandpa's long driveway. As soon as he'd gotten out of his truck, two of his security guards patted him down and his small suitcase was checked for weapons. The guards marshaled him into a black armored truck and drove until they reached the mansion. He was escorted into Grandpa's estate with two guns pointed at the back of his head and 'Rock Around the Clock,' by Bill Haley, greeted him as he entered the house.

"Keep movin' Lennox," barked one of the guards.

"You proud of yourself, Uncle Danny?" The man looked straight ahead like some British Royal Palace guard, hand on gun. "You were adopted, but you're still family. I never treated you any different than my other uncles. We ain't got the same blood, but you still ended up being a damn fool. Pathetic. Blood ain't thicker than water after all."

The sentinels shepherded him into a large sitting room decorated in the Victorian style, in addition to large, antique paintings of cowboys wrestling wildlife and a few hunted treasures: wild boar heads mounted to the walls, their eyes glassy and their horns shining. There was a large antique cream-colored piano in the middle of the room, and the entire floor was covered in an expensive dark blue, violet, and bright red Oriental rug. The room smelled of orchids and cigar smoke. Lennox was led to a small table where two chairs were situated. On the table sat a big, sophisticated bottle of whiskey, two whiskey glasses, a silver eagle-shaped lighter, and two neatly laid out Cuban cigars.

"Sit down." He was nudged in the back with the tip of a rifle into one of the chairs. Lennox took his seat and placed his suitcase by his foot. Through unseen speakers, Barrett Strong's, 'Money' came through crystal clear. He lowered his gaze and concentrated on Nadia, saying her name over and over in his mind. He could practically smell her perfume, feel her lips against his. He fantasized about their wedding and honeymoon, picturing every detail as he sat there in the lion's den. That calmed him, filled him with pride and hope.

Loud, slow footsteps approached, jerking him out of his peace of mind. He kept his head down, the image of his soon-to-be-bride remaining ingrained in his head, and that's where it would stay to get him through this moment.

*Nobody is going to keep me from gettin' married to that woman. I have to be alive, to have her and all we have worked for. We're a team. Ain't nobody bad enough on this Earth to keep me away from my woman...*

A hand touched his shoulder. A heavy hand. A threatening hand. He didn't look up, but straight ahead.

"Lennox... my sneaky, strapping, unloyal *and* unfaithful grandson." Grandpa chuckled light and easy as he took his seat beside him. "How are ya, boy?" Grandpa asked, shifting in his seat. Lennox looked back towards the large doors of the room before answering. The two gunmen were there. Uncle Danny and some nobody. Danny with his back turned, the other staring right back at him.

"I'm doin' mighty fine, Grandpa."

"That's so good to hear. I'm glad your sister convinced you to meet with me. It's been a rough year for all of us." Grandpa grabbed a handkerchief from his pocket and coughed into it. "The cleanin' folks was here today gettin' rid of some old stuff from one of the guest rooms. Kicked up a lotta dust. Not a room that's used too often. My allergies have been flaring lately, and that made it worse." Grandpa leaned forward, his gun on his hip peeking out a bit, and poured them both a glass of whiskey. He then pulled out an envelope from his suit jacket, opened it, and removed a folded stack of papers, placing them down on the table.

"I'm going to get right to it, Lennox. Even though I threatened to do it, I decided not to, out of the kindness of my heart. I haven't told your grandparents about your dead mama's lust problems, how she was climbing on dick after dick for cash. Unfortunately though, and there's no easy way to say this, your father blurted it out to them while he was in one of his many states of intoxication. He confessed to me. The problem is, I'm not sure he remembers, so..." Grandpa shrugged. "Anyway, the threat turned into reality, but not due to me. Now, I already explained to your dear sister, Silva, that I am prepared to fix all of this. Just as I fixed things so you wouldn't spend time in prison. I'm gonna fly to Lebanon and make all of this right as rain. Before we get to that though, you and I need to settle an important matter."

Lennox looked straight ahead. He fixed his gaze on a large oil painting of a red-headed woman with porcelain skin, holding a chubby baby while her cowboy husband trotted off down a tumbleweed covered path.

"The whiskey and cigars are in celebration. Once we complete this today, I'd like a toast. First, we've got to get the business out of the way. This here is a revised contract, grandson." He placed his hand once again on his shoulder. "I'm compromising with you. Something I'm not known to do very often. I've decided to not drudge up your criminal record to the authorities. Well, criminal record that you *should* have had on account of the mess you got yourself in. I had to keep the cops off you for murdering all of those fine folks while you were in college. The contract killin'. I'm sure you remember how I saved your ass, and you didn't even offer me a 'thank you.'" Grandpa sucked his teeth and shook his head. "I took it off the table. Don't want none of my kin servin' unnecessary prison time no how. Plus, it just doesn't look good."

"Yup. That was mighty kind of you, and so unselfish of

you too, Grandpa. You just sacrifice yourself over and over to help others. You're damn near saint-like. Jesus should come down here right now and place a crown of thorns on your head," Lennox stated with a straight face.

Grandpa raised a brow.

"I'm certain that was sarcasm, motherfucker, but I'm not going to entertain your foolishness right now, boy. Don't test me." Grandpa shook his finger in his face. "I'll put it right back on the damn table if I have to, but for now, it's gone, and it'll *stay* gone unless you do something imprudent. You have my word."

"Your word? Well, then I have nothing to worry about, right?" Lennox sneered. "Your word is about as solid as a rushing river. Your word don't mean a damn thing. I'd rather take my chances standing butt naked covered in syrup, honey, and rotten fruit under a bee hive and a hornet's nest that just got whooped with a stick."

They glared at one another.

"I'd like to beat the fuckin' daylights out of you with that same stick or better yet, my bare fists," The old man seethed. "You're unappreciative and sinful! I talked your sister into offering your slimy ass an olive branch. *I* am the reason she even decided to bury the hatchet! I made sure you got your sister back, I offered to fix the shit that your father bungled, I offered to give you a generous salary, a brand-new home and more, and you walk into my house, sit down here, look me in the eye, all while still having a chip on your shoulder?! If you don't sign this contract today, I'll be flyin' over to Lebanon on the first thing with wings tonight. Not to fix a gotdamn thing, but to make sure *every*body in that third world, backwards ass hellhole of a village knows the *truth* about your cock-sucking mama. Capeesh?" Grandpa smiled at him as if he'd just invited him to a big bash with all of the food and drinks money could buy. "Besides, I enjoy travel… and I'm sure some of those underprivileged and lowly Lebanese bitches that live out in the sticks have a real need for some money, and I bet they have real tight pussies, too. I wouldn't mind tryin' one out for size." He cackled. Then, on a dime, he turned real serious as he slid an ink pen out of his pocket and placed it next to the papers.

"I'm sure you think that's mighty generous of you to take a possible prison stay off the table and fix my drunken father's mistake, Grandpa, but see, you crossed the line. Prison, as well as Lebanon, is the last thing on my mind. We need to discuss what happened. What you did… This isn't something that can just be swept under the rug."

"And just what line do you think I crossed, young man?" Grandpa asked with a coy grin, leaning forward.

"You know *exactly* what I'm talking about." They stared at one another a long while, neither blinking nor moving a solitary muscle. "Are you going to man up, or keep lyin' like the fucking rug you're trying to sweep it under?"

"Oh… well, look at you, Lenny boy!" Grandpa beamed. "All outta sorts, huh? Got a bit of gumption today, don't you? Now, you listen here, you overgrown, bubble-eyed, son of a whore. I'm doing you a favor! You're a rancid piece of shit. A Richard Simmons aerobics class teachin' fool! You need to be thanking your lucky stars that I'm not shootin' you down like the dog that you are. I'll give you credit. You controlled yourself from that little misunder-standing you're talking about. Sam and your little lady had a chat is all."

"Oh, it was just a chat, huh?"

"That's right. The chat did not go in the manner I told that bastard to handle it. I don't hurt no women, and I'm a man of my word, contrary to what you just said. I dare anyone else to say otherwise." Grandpa pointed in his face. "I offered her an opportunity. She refused." He shrugged. "End of story. I didn't hurt a curly little heart-shaped hair on her head... or anywhere else, for that matter, and I damn sure didn't order it to be done. You know I would *never* condone such a thing."

"Mmmm, I see." Lennox nodded, then flipped through the papers, one by one. "You know what I find most interesting about you, Grandpa?"

"What's that, Lennox?"

"Your audacity. I must say, you certainly are fearless even when lying your ass off and talkin' out both sides of your mouth, aren't you?"

"Well," Grandpa leaned back in his seat, "I reckon you're right. I do have a lot of gumption. Maybe one day when you grow up, you can be fearless, too. Now, if you don't mind, I need you to—"

"Not so fast. I want to show you something special before I put my signature, in blood, on this agreement."

"Something special, huh? And what's so special that you want to show me, Lennox?" Grandpa snatched his cigar off the table, lit it with the eagle-shaped lighter, and puffed like a dragon. Lennox reached down and grabbed his suitcase.

Opening it, he pulled out a small laptop and a few other items, which he placed on the table. He turned on the computer and logged in. "What's this about? What do you need to show me so badly, boy? The land you bought to start your gym? That old car showroom? Don't waste your breath. Now you got folks building another big ass building on it. Drywall. I already know about it. You ain't got nothin' by me." Grandpa chuckled, rolled his eyes, then sucked his teeth.

"…Yeah. Can't get nothing past you," Lennox mocked as he kept typing.

"This is where you plead with me to turn you loose, right? Show me that you finally achieved your dream and want to run some sweaty, funky place full of fat women who can't stay away from cake and roly-poly men who don't know a day's hard work, all while you go broke to pay the bills and keep the lights on in there? I don't give a shit about—"

"This ain't about my fitness center, but it will involve some mental and numerical gymnastics." Lennox put the USB thumb drive, then turned the laptop screen towards Grandpa. "Solve this math problem. What's one plus one times you're screwed, equal to? You see all those numbers?"

Grandpa leaned forward, squinted, then snatched his reading glasses out of his Western style black and white jacket pocket. He slid the rims on and began to read the screen. After a couple of seconds, his jaw tightened.

"That's a pretty long laundry list of payments you've made to police officers and city officials. Hush money. Comes up to $3,566,691.50, and that's just from the last four years. I've got all their names and addresses. Hell, I even know all about their families and where they like to go on vacation. Now, the—"

Grandpa slid his gun out of the holster. He eyeballed Lennox with narrowed snake vision while setting his cigar casually in the ashtray.

"Where'd you get this? Did your damn father give this shit to you?!"

"Of course not. I got this on my own, and how I did it doesn't matter. Besides, my daddy's got his head so far up your ass, all he can smell is Bengay and bad decisions."

"I know you're not tryna blackmail me, boy... You must have a gotdamn death wish."

"If you shoot me, even kill me, it won't matter." Lennox shrugged. "This information is in the possession of four other people, and will be in the hands of the FBI should I not walk out of this motherfucker in one piece by exactly 1:01pm on the dot. I not only have copies of the payments, but I also have your extortion records involving several casinos. That's just the beginning. There's more where that came from." Lennox pulled up record after record on his laptop, revealing many of Grandpa's devious dirty dinero deeds. The old man plucked his cigar from the ashtray and took a long, hard draw.

"Well, that's just fine, Lennox," he smirked. "That's nice. But all you've done is start a war you can't win."

"Oh, I'm gonna win, Grandpa, 'cause see, the game is already over..." Lennox opened another document, selected a video clip, and pushed play. "Let me turn up the volume so you don't miss any of this."

There, on the screen, was Grandpa lying in the middle of his huge bed, covered in red satin sheets. He was shirtless, sporting only a pair of white cotton boxers and a few large diamond rings on his fingers. A woman was in the room with him, standing by the side of the bed in nothing but red panties. Suddenly, he sat up and smiled. He reached for a glass of wine, raised it in the air and said, *"Hello, fine ladies. Let me see what you have for big daddy."* His voice was slurred.

The tones of many women could be heard within the room. Sweet, feminine chatter and laughter. Then, the rest of them came into view. Six scantily clad women were making quick work of undressing as they surrounded Grandpa's bed.

Lennox took a peek at the man sitting next to him from the corner of his eye. Stoic, he continued to smoke his cigar as he looked at the screen. The sexy women finished disrobing, tossing their lingerie here and there. Within minutes, there was nothing but bubble asses covered in tattoos and silicone titties bouncing up and down. Grandpa was laughing in the footage, having a grand old time, and it wasn't long before one of the women had his boxers down to his ankles and was sucking his cock so good, it made his toes curl. Another woman rode his face like he was a bucking bull. He gripped her hips, bringing her down onto his face as if he were trying to suffocate himself with that juicy peach pie. Grandpa's lips twitched as he readjusted himself in his seat, watching himself in action.

"I had no idea you were so agile, Grandpa. I also had no idea that you enjoyed strippers so much. Wow! I wonder what all those conservative Christian groups you like to hang with, including your religious-based bookstore franchise, would think of you bumpin', grindin' and sickin' that old ass rattlesnake of yours against the big, plump backside of a curvy lady while she sucked on your balls?"

Grandpa swallowed, then reached for the bottle of whiskey. He poured himself a glass. His hand shook ever so slightly as he gulped it down.

"...And as I'm certain you can imagine, if I come up dead, it don't matter. This too, like everything else, will be turned over to the FBI agents who, no matter your efforts, you were unable to pay off. They've been gunnin' for you for years. In addition, this little XXX video will be broadcast all over social media, Grandpa, sent to the local news stations and vloggers, leaked onto international porn sites under the taboo old man young woman orgy category that so many like. Looks like there's a Latina and Black lady that you're enjoying, too, so you also get a bonus classification for your bigoted fans and friends: *Gramps loves interracial rough fucking*, and *Grampa gives illustrious cream pie*. Catchy, huh?

"Of course this will also be sent to the Baptist Christian Church of America, for good measure." The video continued with Grandpa thrusting deep inside some White woman named Sunshine, all to the sounds of 'Party Up,' By DMX. "Oh wow! Look at you go, Grandpa!" Lennox cackled. "You're givin' it to her good! You've got the hydro-pumps. I didn't think you had it in you, ol' boy!" Lennox slapped his grandfather's back as he laughed and pointed at the screen.

"Well, well, well, aren't you a smart little puppy?" The old fucker's chest rose and fell hard and fast. "May I ask how you obtained this footage?"

"Oh, just like the unlawful money trail and receipts, I have my ways. I understand that you paid these girls well, too. You sent them all Cash Apps under an alias, but I've got the account information that the funds came from you originally—just in case you were thinking you could wiggle out of this and say it was a shakedown or some fancy, high tech video trickery." Grandpa slipped his gun back into the holster and sighed. "Rumor has it you were a little discombobulated that evening, out of your mind. A bit woozy, they say. You still managed to test out some of the entertainment for your birthday bash, though it looks like your inhibitions were lowered. I wonder why? Are you a drug user, Grandpa?" Lennox teased. "But I know that you're a serious businessman. This was important! See them first and pick the ones you wanted to dance for you on your special day.

"It's funny how you like gettin' your ass ate, you're eatin' ass, and also fuckin' one of the strippers *up* the ass against the wall!" Lennox chuckled. "Just havin' an ass ol' blast! An Ass-tastic time! A lot of ass stuff was going on that night, but I won't judge you. Sometimes I like to fuck a big, pretty, feminine bubble-butt, too. Problem is, I don't kiss a grown man's rear end, so that makes me unqualified to be hired by the likes of you, now doesn't it?" Lennox winked at him, then grabbed the contract and tore it into little pieces, letting the paper flutter all around like white confetti before hitting the floor.

"Lennox, it's over for you. There's no comin' back from this. You have single-handedly—"

"YOUR THREATS DON'T MEAN SHIT ANY-MORE! I don't give a fuck *what* you do! You're a hypocrite! Living in a den of fucking sin, right there in your bedroom." He pointed towards the doors. "Now, it's time for me to give *you* some credit. You have some stamina, that's for sure. You're like a jackrabbit. Looks like I got it honest! Fucked five women, back to fucking back, and the other two fucked each other right in front of you as you watched and got your jollies off. Impressive for a man your age. So what do we have now on the prohibited checklist, old boy? Fornication, Sodomy, oral copulation, interracial relations some say is wrong too, lesbianism is definitely a no-no, masturbation, a shitload of profanity, barebacking, some lightweight S&M due to the scarf you used to tie one lady's wrists together… a little marijuana was being smoked too, so that's drug use, a bunch of drinking, whoremongering, and those talking points are just the tip of the iceberg. There's more where that came from. Well, surprise, surprise motherfucker, it's my turn to get my jollies off now, too."

"I promise you, Lennox, you will live to regret this. Mark my words."

"The only thing I regret is being born into this fucked up family, but God doesn't let us pick and choose our grandparents, now does He? Legend has it, my whore mama had a whore son who's gonna have a whore wife, and live a nice, sweet whore life. Just a big ol' bunch of hoe bags, ain't we? We're a bunch of wicked, repulsive misfits. Truth is stranger than fiction because last I checked, the *real* whore is sittin' right here beside me. A man filled with lust! 1st Corinthians, 6:18, says, *"Flee from sexual immorality. Any other sins a person commits are outside the body, but whoever sins sexually, sins against their own body.* In Proverbs, 31:3, it says, *'Do not spend your strength on women, your vigor on those who ruin kings.'* Now ain't this something?

"You're this big age, still screwin' women left and right, women of ill-repute as you'd call them, yet you beat me and everyone else with Bible verses for our entire existence. All for you to turn around and visit pound town. Take your dick to the pussy promised land. None of them ladies look like any of your ex-wives to me, dear Grandpa. After this goes viral, I am certain your precious little reputation will be doused in gasoline, lit on fire, struck by lightning, then tossed on a fiery grill down in the pits of Hell's kitchen if you decide to continue to try and fuck around with the likes of me. I don't want no part of your dog, dick, pony, and pussy show. I've told your ass once, I am now tellin' you twice: this top dog ain't nothin' nice!"

"Now listen here you—"

"NO. I'M DONE LISTENING, MOTHERFUCKER! THE DAMN LEASH IS OFF! YOU AIN'T DOG WALKIN' ME NO MOTHERFUCKIN' WHERE! YOUR REIGN OF TERROR AND CONTROL IS OVER!"

Suddenly, Uncle Danny turned from the door and started making his way over, gun in hand.

"Uncle Danny, you better think again or I'll have you handled, too." Lennox pointed in his uncle's direction. The bastard paused, but still kept his gun aimed at him. "Hey,

Grandpa, tell that loser to stand down before I blow the gotdamn whistle on GP!"

"Stop." Grandpa put up his hand for his guard dog to back off. "Go back to your post, Daniel!" Uncle Danny slowly lowered his gun, then backed away towards the door. Grandpa glared at him, his nostrils flared, his complexion red as a beet, and his body shaking with rage.

"And I've got one more surprise for you, Grandpa." Lennox took out his cellphone and pulled up the live cam. He shoved the screen in Grandpa's face.

"What… what have you done?! Samuel! Where is he?!" Grandpa dropped his cigar into the ashtray, his eyes glazed over with what looked to be nothing short of astonishment.

"Your dimwitted grandson, Sam, has to suffer for his sins. Ain't that the family way? Isn't that what us Wilde men are supposed to do, Grandpa? Eye for an eye? You know what's funny? I was just gonna rough him up a little bit, scare him so that he pissed on himself. I figured I'd shoot him in the leg or something if he made a fuss, which I happily did, and then maybe cut off a finger or two, too, just so he wouldn't make the same mistake twice. But then he kept tryna get my attention when I was drivin' him over yonder. I finally took the tape off his mouth to hear what he just had to yap about, and he said a whole lotta interesting things. A whole lot of interesting things." Grandpa's eyes narrowed.

"Like what?"

"Well, for starters, I learned that the kid in my college economics class all of them years ago was planted there by YOU. Ain't that something? I also found out that you set everything else from that situation in motion—that it was all your doing, from the start. Now, none of this can be proven as it happened so long ago and you murdered the only witness, but it's so interesting, don't you think? Seeing as Sam's not smart enough to come up with a lie like that, or figure it out on his own. Not only that, he knew too many particulars he would have been none the wiser to. These let me know for certain that Sammy boy was telling the truth. He got to keep his fingers and toes. Now, here's the deal, Grandpa. This is the agreement that you're going to honor... I'm doing the contracts now.

"I haven't told my father, your dutiful accounting servant, what you did. That you're the reason me and Silva fell out, and you're the reason the cops were snoopin' around the house in the first place, and it was your enemies that I was hired to kill, under the guise of a false pretense which could have led me to going to the big house. In fact, Dad knows nothing of what's going on right now at all. We both know he didn't tell his in-laws about Mama's past life, either, so cut the shit. Another lie used to manipulate and use people. You've gotten away with far too much. It was time to even the score. As you could see, Sam's in bad shape, but I haven't killed him. Understand this though... all I have to do is make one little call and Sam is as good as dead. And guess who'll get the blame?"

"...You son of a bitch."

"That's right. You, sir. King of the stripper orgies. If Sam gets mysteriously killed, please understand that his confession about what you did and how you had me set up was recorded. It, too, was sent to my backup crew before I stepped foot in here. The little lady at his house who's tied up in the bed is going to get her throat slit if you do the wrong thing. She's got nothing to do with this, so that would be a shame, but the person in charge of that operation right now couldn't give a single fuck." Grandpa gave him a strange look, full of hatred. "Guess who's babysittin' pea-brained Sam and happily obliged to help make this happen? Kage the Rage."

Grandpa's eyes widened, and then, they turned pitch black.

"And you know Kage ain't shy around a murder spree. 'Krazy Kage,' as folks call him, is sly as a fox. Guess who one of the four folks are that are ready to post your little sexcapade video all over the damn internet? Roman 'Pretty Boy' the Great." Grandpa's lips tightened. "He's really smart with the World Wide Web, seein' as it's part of his job to make sure shit is right and copasetic on the computer 'nd such. All those stocks and bonds. And guess who's ready to strip down to the last word, dance with the FBI and sing like a motherfuckin' bird flyin' past a pole? Nadia. I'm sure with all of your recent devilment, you know her name quite well now."

"YOU FUCKING FAILURE!!! You betrayed your family for a floozy. A fly by night hooker!" Grandpa slammed his fist against the table.

"You see, Grandpa, I think you know deep down that's not true because if you thought it was, you wouldn't have wasted your time tryna get rid of her. You and Sam messed with the wrong woman, didn't you? She vowed revenge, and she ain't never made a promise she didn't intend to keep. Sunshine and them? The gal who's ovaries you rearranged, and the other lady who you ate like groceries? Those are her friends from the strip club. Pros of the trade. They understood the assignment." The color drained from Grandpa's face. "They got the pat down by your little security team, but the security crew didn't check their asses and pussies. It's funny where you can store a little video-recordin' device right before ready, set, action. Two video cameras the size of quarters, rollin' that beautiful sinful bean footage. Tossed their panties and bras on your dresser, just so—lights, camera, action, motherfucker!" Lennox roared, slapping his knee.

"...I was half outta my mind... delirious. I didn't do this! It was her, wasn't it?! It was your gotdamn sister! You two were in cahoots! I was sleepy towards the end of her visit, and she helped me right into bed... yes! It was her! It was Silva! She'll never be safe because of what you two have done! She'll—"

"Naw, now let's not get carried away here. It was none of her idea. All she did was call me, beg me to meet with you just like you said. Now, because of that call though, she and I did get to talking. I let her know the truth about you. I presented evidence. When she found out about you makin' plans to disrupt things in Lebanon, and I told her about your part in my troubles, as well as the *real* reason I agreed to do those contract kills, well, she decided she was done with you. She's so disappointed in you, Grandpa. Broke her fucking heart."

Much to Lennox's surprise, Grandpa's eyes flashed with remorse. He looked downright upset about Silva being mad at him. He looked so… human. Like a bleeding-heart real person walking God's green earth. The old man lowered his head, avoiding eye contact. *Well hell, he actually does care about her in his own twisted way. I'll be damned.*

"Silva loved you, Grandpa, and you took it for granted. Sadly, she still does, but she found out the hard way that Mama, even in death, is *always* right."

Lennox got to his feet and packed his things away. "It's almost one o'clock. I'd best be leavin'. We wouldn't wanna risk me being late and the Three Musketeers going into action."

Grandpa laughed, slapped the table, and slowly got to his feet. "Naw, I guess we wouldn't want that, Lennox. Question for you… you said four people are privy to your little slideshow you presented today. That means that the Three Musketeers have a companion. Who is the fourth?"

"Oh, I can't tell you that. Gotta always keep one emergency bullet in the chamber."

The two men walked out of the room, side by side while The Big Bopper's 'Chantilly Lace' played through the speakers in the house. Grandpa raised his chin high, his black and silver cowboy boots thumping against the floor. Long, thick, silver hair flowed behind him like a cape, and he moved like the stars had aligned, just so, on his behalf. A king of appearances—the emperor wore no clothes. When they reached the front door, Jasper was close by looking on. Grandpa did the honors. He unlocked it, swung it open, and Lennox was immediately bathed in sunshine. Stepping onto the porch, he turned to his grandfather and smiled.

"I guess this means I'm not invited over for the next

Christmas dinner?"

"Lennox, I'd like nothing *more* than to have you for dinner, but not in the way that you mean."

And with that, Grandpa did a little bow of the head, offered a polite smile, then slammed the door in his face. Lennox made his way down the steps, completing the long jaunt to his parked truck at the end of the driveway. He looked at his watch. 12:59 P.M. on the dot. He immediately sent a text message to Nadia, Silva, Kage and Roman:

*It is done. Codeword: Mama.*

The codeword was so that they'd know for certain that he wasn't dead, and that no one else had his phone pretending to be him. Getting into his truck, he started it up and drove like a bat out of hell. He needed to hold and kiss his baby. After all, the day's activities of hunting prey and confronting an intruder had left him famished, and there was nothing a big dog liked more than to chase and taste a little cat...

# CHAPTER THIRTY-THREE

## *Girl Talk*

"A BOUT THREE DAYS." Mama handed Nadia the basket, then sat down on her living room couch. "She'll be released tomorrow. She told me to tell you not to worry."

"That explains why she didn't call me back. Nana is always trying to sneak back home before I know she's in the hospital. This is the fourth time she's done this to me. Next time she doesn't call me back right away, I am driving straight over there."

Nadia took the basket of homemade jams Mama had made into her kitchen. She then went to sit next to her mother on her couch, hugging her knees next to her. On her television screen was displayed a twenty-four-hour live viewing of swimming fish. Her attempt at a relaxing, laid-back feel.

"Why'd you want to talk to me, Nadia? Ask me to come over here?" Mama cut to the chase. She smoothed her faded, plain black shirt that was a little too big for her frame. Her jeans were dark, with a bit of distress around the knees. Her hair was wrapped in a colorful silk scarf and secured with a knot in the back. Two shiny gold hoop earrings hung from her ears and her full lips gleamed with clear gloss.

"Thank you for the jam. It looks delicious," Nadia began, soon realizing she was going into her usual stalling mode. Dr. Saint Aknaten's words crept into her mind, and she cleared her throat. "Mama, I want to talk to you about some of the things that happened in the past that we never really addressed."

Mama dramatically rolled her eyes and slumped against the couch as if she'd been asked for her left kidney. Nadia continued, not discouraged by the reaction.

"When I was a little girl, I didn't always feel wanted. I sometimes felt you believed I was an inconvenience, or that having me made you unhappy in some way. I know that may not have been true, but—"

"Now what would make you think that?" Mama barked. "I took care of you, didn't I? I never let you go hungry, unclean, or unclothed!"

"Mama, taking care of someone doesn't always mean that someone is wanted."

"Who you know out here takin' care of shit they don't want?! Ain't nobody I know washing their car every week, if they don't want it, or cleanin', decorating and painting a house they don't care about. That don't make a lick of sense."

"I'm not a car or a house. Neither is Nelson, but I'm

not going to bring him into this. I am just going to talk to you about *me*, from my own perspective. You can't compare me to inanimate objects and expect things to improve."

Mama sucked her teeth. "Ain't nothing broken that needs improvement. You just makin' up stuff tryna give me a guilt trip, Nadia!" Mama waved her hand dismissively. "What is this *really* about? You need to borrow some money or something? Now that you've stopped shakin' your tail feather, has the money run dry?"

"Mama, I don't need your money, but what I do need is for you to at least pretend to want to hear my side of the story. You're doing all of this yelling and carryin' on because you're afraid! You fear the emotions that come with these discussions, the same way you feared being the mother that I needed, which caused all of this in the first place."

"Your grandmother told me that you said you talked to some shrink from out there in New York. Now it all makes sense." Mama looked her up and down with disgust. "That man done put a bunch of silly shit in ya head. Next thing you know, you'll be saying he said you were a three-legged clown in some carnival in Peru in a past life, and that you now identify as a circus tent! Pronouns: Barnum and Bailey."

Nadia ignored her mother's interruptions and sardonic jabs once again, promising herself that she'd stay on track. "Do you hear what you're saying right now?"

"Of course I do. I'm not deaf. I'm sitting here, aren't I?"

"Whenever I say something that makes you uncomfortable, Mama, you try to boomerang it. Shift it right back to me." Nadia kept her voice calm, yet assertive. She looked her mother in the eye, never wavering from her feelings or the mission at hand. "You never take accountability, even if you don't quite understand my viewpoint. I'm always wrong, or being silly or overly sensitive, and you are always right, or the only rational person in the room. In your mind, I must be making it up, or I remember it wrong. I'm not making any of this up, Mama, and even if you don't remember my childhood and teenage years the same way I do, it doesn't mean that's not the way it happened."

"Are you finished? Because I have someplace to be." Mama reached for her purse that was sitting next to her on the couch.

"I'm sorry, Mama, that you aren't brave enough to have this discussion."

Mama swiveled sharply to face her.

"What did you say?" she asked in a harsh, raw tone.

"You told me a moment ago that you could hear just fine… that you're not deaf, and you're sitting here, right?" Nadia offered a slight smile as her mother's eyes narrowed upon her. "You can't rewrite my memories for me, and you can't create a false history, either. That's not how this works. What you're doing is gaslighting. Do you know what gaslighting is?"

"Yes, I know what the fuck gaslighting is!"

"Well then stop it, because you're doing it right *now*!"

Mama's mouth twitched as if a tiny invisible electric current was making it jump. She looked stunned. Speechless. Dumbfounded.

"Mama," Nadia placed her feet on the floor and took a deep breath, briefly closing her eyes, "I love you so, so much. I am not saying that you were a horrible mother. I am telling you that there are more things I needed, really, truly needed, that you didn't provide."

"Well, what in the hell do you want me to do about that now, Nadia? I can't build a time machine and go back!" Mama threw up her hands in frustration.

"I don't want you to do anything but listen. That's the hardest thing for you to do. You never want to do it because it makes you feel bad. I feel bad, too. We're just feeling bad together, but we can also feel better together. Please let me—"

"Listen, Dr. Nadia Phil Maury Povich Oprah Winfrey the third, I don't feel bad about a mothafuckin' thing!"

"Well, that's too bad because anyone who thinks they are perfect isn't fit to even have a conversation with a puddle, let alone their own child."

"You are a *real* piece of work, Nadia. You ain't even a mother, so you have no idea how hard it is to raise children, yet you have so much to say about my parenting skills. I went through hell tryna take care of you and Nelson on my own, and you have the nerve to sit here in yo' little sundress and red lipstick, and look at me with those big doe eyes of yours, like we on a movie set. Like this is some soap opera, and I'm just supposed to say, *'Yes, you're right, Nadia! I suck. Can you find it in your heart to forgive me?'* Then I burst into tears, falling on my knees and grab ya ankles, begging you to not walk away." Nadia sat back and shook her head in disbelief. "You touch me with a magic wand, and then we start dancin' and planning a mother-daughter picnic on top of a mountain. This is real life, Nadia. We not White! This ain't The Sound of Music, and I'm not Mary Poppins, either. I had—"

"If you care about me at all, you will be quiet, stop going off on these silly rants and tangents, and give me the floor, Mama!" She lifted her chin, meeting her mother's icy stare. "Taking care of a child's basic necessities is not enough to make them whole, especially when there is no father in the house! You've gone my entire life only addressin' what *you* want to address, picking and choosing what *you* will ignore and give energy to." She pointed her finger at her mother. "I am a person! I am your daughter!"

"And I never said I was perfect. I said that I have no regrets."

"And I'm telling you that I never asked for perfection. I asked for a mama who wasn't scared to hold me! I needed a hug, even if you didn't always understand why I was upset. Somewhere in your mind, you saw that as making me too soft! I needed a kiss on the cheek, just because. I needed to be told that I was smart, that I was beautiful! Instead, I looked for validation out in the world! I needed to be told, 'Everything will be okay,' even when you weren't sure!"

"So now, you wanted me to lie to you?"

"I just wanted you to love me! Not with just your actions, but your words! We have ears for a reason! All children would be born deaf if it wasn't important. You sit here telling me you can hear me, but you ain't never listened to me a day in yo' life!"

Mama gave a black, layered look. She sighed, falling back against the pillow. Staring blankly at the coffee table.

"I didn't call you over here to dissect you, to break you down, to make you upset or feel any type of way. I called you over here to tell you how I feel, what I wished for us, and how I'd like to move forward. I wanted you to come here, instead of me coming to you as I usually do, because I wanted to make sure I had no escape. I didn't want to run away from this discussion. We're more alike than we realize. I do the same damn things you do. I. AM. YOU!" Mama slowly turned back in her direction. "I was a workaholic, just like my mama. I am about making money and saving it, too. Just like my mama. I am ambitious, and I have difficulty with men, just like my mama. I was afraid of true connections and vulnerability. I was afraid to fall in love, just like my mama…"

"I don't think that's fair." Mama's voice shook. Her eyes sheened over, hitting Nadia right in the gut. "I never told you to never fall in love, I told you to not trust these mothafuckas. You chose bad men and so did I, but maybe that's because the majority of men ain't shit. The bucket has slim pickin's, Nadia, and it is nothing more than that!"

"Mama, you and I chose bad men, and it's not because most men ain't shit. A lot of 'em aren't, but I wouldn't say most," she offered with a sad smile. "It's because we attract the 'ain't shit' men. Because trauma has a stench, and vultures can smell it on us. That's how they find their prey."

"Speaking of vultures, your father shares some of the blame don't he, since you out here handing out verbal and emotional ass whoopin's? Because last I checked, he wasn't there for you at all, but he's not available, once again, per usual, to receive this tongue lashing, now is he? It's just me sittin' here being the piñata for both of us."

"This isn't about blame. It's about love. Yeah, my father would be responsible, too, but like you said, he's dead. You and I are still alive though. There's hope. I hope that you'll listen to me. I hope in some ways, after today, we can start fresh."

Mama's face clouded with uneasiness.

"I have something important to tell you."

"What?"

"I am engaged!" She reached her hand out, and flashed the ring. Mama's eyes grew large, and she leaned forward, eyeing at the stunning diamond. "I'm getting married, Mama."

"I ain't even know you were dating anyone. To *who*?" A faint wave of panic could be detected in her voice, taking Nadia by surprise.

"I'm engaged to a man I've known for a mighty long time, but we've reconnected as adults. Well, we were grown when we met, but just young. His name is Lennox Wilde. Mama, it's been quite a ride with this man. He's special. He loves me to the depths of my soul."

Mama looked away. "Baby, that's fairytale stuff. Men are incapable of loving anyone. It's all cosplay."

"Mama, Lennox and I are not fairytales, soap operas or Hollywood stars. We're very much real, and so is our love for one another. We're adults who are trying to process our pain, take accountability for our own actions, and not repeat the same mistakes of the past. We are *both* going through trials and tribulations. We are both trying to grow."

Mama kept her gaze averted.

"Where'd you meet this man? I ain't never heard of him." She slowly turned back towards her.

"At a job of mine before I left for college."

"That restaurant? The Rooster spot?"

"Yes ma'am." Nadia leaned into her mother, and scooted closer. "You and I have our ups and down, Mama, but I'm fortunate. His mama is dead. Been gone a long while. I am so glad that mine is not because I know my fiancé would turn this world upside down to get just five more minutes with her." Mama's hands tensed in her lap. "And here I am, with a mama that is alive, and sometimes it doesn't even feel like we have a true relationship, let alone talk." Mama stirred restlessly in her seat. "I envied his relationship with his mother when I understood how close they were. I dare to say, when he described it to me, I was jealous. He could talk to her! She was strict, but she cared!" A tear streamed down Nadia's cheek as her pain burst. A shower. The rain. "Not a day went by when her children questioned her love for them. I didn't have that with you, Mama."

"I always loved you, Nadia. Always."

"I had a roof over my head, but no kisses on my scraped knee. I had a meal in the oven, but no one was home most days to eat it with me. I knew how to change a flat tire, but no one showed me how to change my life for the better! Yes, you were there, Mama. Some moms aren't. I acknowledge that. Yes, you made sure Nelson and I could take care of ourselves and be independent, self-sufficient, but you also showed us how to *not* trust by example. You showed us how to fester resentment. You showed us how to stay closed off, and emotionally off the grid!"

"I don't want to be blamed for everything! I just... I didn't know what to do! Wanted to protect y'all! I just wanted you safe!" Mama's voice was shrill, chock full of pain. She buried her face in her hand, and cried. A black, soft silence sat between them.

"Mama..." Nadia wiped a tear from her own cheek and rested her hand against her mother's bowed back. "Your son's marriage ended because he's emotionally cut off. He can't connect with folks well. At least, not from the heart. We're not blamin' you. We're... let me rephrase. Nelson isn't here. He can speak for himself so I need to stop trying to intervene on his behalf. He'll have to do that on his own. This is actually about *me*. I'm trying to tell you how *I* felt, Mama. What is so wrong with that?"

Mama sat up and dabbed at her eyes. She took a deep breath, then chewed on her upper lip.

"Mama, let me say it again... I love you so much. If I didn't, I wouldn't even try to talk to you right now. You taught me how to ride a bike. You showed me how to put my head in the sand when the truth was too hard to take, too."

"It would've been funnier if you said, 'You taught me how to ride a bike, and showed me how to ride off from the truth, too."

They both looked at one another, tears and all, and burst out laughing.

"Mama, why are you like this?" Nadia teased, still laughing. Mama shrugged.

"I'm sorry I disappointed you, Nadia. I'm sure there's some things I could have done differently. It's a hard pill to swallow when you know you tried your very best, but you failed. I had a lot going on. 'Specially back then. I... I loved my babies." Mama's voice rattled. "I was just trying to safeguard y'all. Never wanted to cause you no pain."

"Mama, you didn't fail. I'm not a mother, just like you said, but motherhood isn't a test. I know now, as an adult, that you loved me, but as a child, sometimes it just was hard to tell, and that affected me psychologically. I know you were doing it all on your own. I have my own demons to wrestle regarding my father. He walked away and that devastated me."

Mama sniffed, then reached for her hands, cupping them in her own. "Nadia, I've been through some things in my life that I wouldn't wish on nobody. In my day, we ain't talk to no shrinks. Sometimes, we took it to the pastor of our church, but many times, we just kept stuff to ourselves. I'm not the most eloquent woman on the planet. Sometimes I say stuff rudely, I suppose you could say, but I just don't believe in sugarcoating anything. When I'd jump on you about the strippin', it wasn't 'cause I was ashamed of you. It was because I knew deep down, you was mad at me and your father, and trying to punish us. Then the money had gotten good to you, and I felt like... I felt like I'd lost my baby." Nadia paused, measuring her for a moment. "You brought up your brother. I have something to say about that. Nelson's marriage fell apart. We all know that.

"His ex-wife called me one night when they were still

married, talkin' about Nelson hates me and takes it out on her." Mama slipped inside of herself, lowering her head, turning away. Pain showed in her dark brown eyes. Mama wrung her hands, fighting emotions as she did on a daily basis. "Another time, Nelson had been drinking one night, 'bout three or four years ago, and called me hollering and screaming. Told me I was coldhearted and ugly. Said I must've been whorin' around, 'cause I ain't know who his daddy was." A slow tear traveled down Mama's face. And Nadia's, too.

"I wasn't no whore. I never slept around. Nelson's... Nelson's father and I used to be acquaintances. His name was James Avery. James was a traveling electrician. Contractor. He was handsome, handy, and funny, too." She smiled sadly. "We'd go drinkin' together after work on occasion. One night, we'd both had a bit too much beer and liquor. It was the holidays. We were lonely and plastered, so we slept together. A couple months later, I realized I was pregnant. James was in another city by then. I tried for weeks to track him down. Wasn't no cellphones back then. I was thinking about all the things he'd told me about his family, and used that information as leads. Finally, I found his mama. She lived in Tennessee. She said to me, *'What you need James for, honey?'* I responded, *'Ma'am, I worked with James in Houston. I need to talk to him. I'm pregnant with your son's child.'* She replied, *'Baby, I can't help you. I'm old, in poor health, and don't have any money. Can't help with raising no grandkids, and I have more bad news. James can't help you either. James died.'* Apparently, he overdosed. I never knew James had a heroin problem... but he did. I asked some other folks about it, and some of them suspected it.

"I realized his mother didn't seem terribly concerned about having a grandbaby, or maybe she was so wrapped up in grief over the loss of her child, and I so shocked by the news of his death, that we momentarily lost our minds. I got off that phone without leavin' my name and number, without even saying goodbye. I just hung up. I thought about that after the fact, but I was mighty upset. Not just for me, but for my baby yet to be born. Now, here was the *second* child I was going to bring into this world without a father. I'd fucked up again. One man was alive, one was dead, but the one living wasn't doing anything for his daughter, so, he may as well have been in the ground, too.

"I didn't want to tell Nelson about his daddy because I ain't want him to be self-conscious. I didn't want him to feel lesser than. I was afraid of how he'd take it knowing his daddy was gone, and had been a full-blown drug addict. A damn junkie. I ain't want to tell him we was drunk, and not even in a real relationship when he was conceived. Friends, but no commitment. It sounds bad. Real bad. I was raised better than that." Mama's complexion deepened, as if she was living the embarrassment all over again. "I figured if I said nothing at all, he'd be okay. He could make up, in his mind however he wanted about his daddy, you know? He could pretend James was an astronaut, doctor, football player or something... but Nelson eventually just stopped asking me about his father. At the same time, he also stopped looking at me with love and adoration."

Mama's voice broke into a million pieces as the tears poured down her cheeks. "It brought all the bad gunk inside of me up to the forefront! The abandonment from my own daddy, Nadia… it felt the same when I found out James had been messin' with that shit! I felt tricked, just like yo' daddy had done me. I was confused. Too much had happened. Seein' my mama get beat up by my daddy when I was a kid! It never left me. James never laid a hand on me… he was kind. He would bring me lunch, stick up for me when some of the guys in our group would act stupid in our company. He had a real good soul… but he left me, Nadia, just like your father did, only in a different way.

"Didn't matter if he didn't mean to do it. The results were the same. He wasn't there for his child. He *never* got to meet his son, and I now had two children to raise on my own. Nelson looks just like him, too… I saw James every day through our child. He haunts me, but still, it's like he was never here. A ghost that rides on a washed-out memory. Daddies can walk away, Nadia. Mamas have to stay put. The babies end up growin' up, and hating the one that stayed. Just the way of the world… just another day in this thang we call life."

*The sprinkler and the garden…*

Mama faced her fully, smiling sadly. "I wasn't the best mother… I know that now. But I tried to do right by y'all, Nadia. I promise I did."

"And now I understand you better. I admire you so much, Mama. You taught me how to cook a delicious five course meal. You showed me the importance of making my own money to create my financial security. You showed me how to be afraid of the world, and want to rule it at the same time! You are a dynamite woman. You are beautiful.

Strong. Capable. We *both* could have done better. I should have taken accountability earlier for my own choices that I made as an adult. I can't blame you and my father for everything. That's not fair. And that's just reality. You are a tiger in human form, but you had cubs, Mama… If the good Lord's willing, one day, I will be ninety years old. Even then, at that ripe old age, I will still be your baby— because I will *still* want my mama!"

And with that, she wrapped her arms around her mother and squeezed all the hurt away…

# CHAPTER THIRTY-FOUR

## *Old men & Old bones*

N ADIA SAT BESIDE Lennox in the park, sipping an ice-cold strawberry wine cooler and laughing. Lennox loved the sound of her giggle—music to his ears. After such a hard few months, this was the relaxation and love that he needed. A slight breeze blew as they lounged on a large sky-blue blanket, their bare feet exposed and touching. The blades of grass that surrounded them were soft and fragrant, and he found himself pulling some of them up as they drank their beverages, talked about everything under the sun and moon, kissed and vibed out to music. They were in a remote section of the park, on a hill with a slight incline beneath a large tree that shaded them from the sun. It felt like a private oasis.

It was only the two of them enjoying sightseeing and each other's company. People walked around in the distance, some rollerblading or on skateboards. Several tossed frisbees and played with their dogs while a few folks jogged, their headphones or buds in their ears. Not terribly far away was an older Mexican woman selling sweet and delicious frozen lemonade cups. Lennox had bought some in the past when he'd work out in the park on prior solo visits. Sometimes, he'd come to this place just to clear his mind. He turned the music up on his phone. Heartless Bastards' 'Only for You' banged as they discussed Nadia's college progress.

"…So, you know, that's how that goes. I'm definitely glad I am able to move into the accelerated program. That means I'll have less free time though."

"Hey," Lennox shrugged, "it is what it is. Sometimes we have to make sacrifices to get what we want, right?"

She nodded in agreement. "I have to make sure I am there though, for your first day of business. This is a big deal. The grand opening date is still the same for the fitness center, right?"

"Yup, it'll be ready to go. R.S.S. GYM – Rain, Sleet, or Snow fitness center, grand opening! Electrician coming this week to check everything. I wanted the parking lot to have more curb appeal, so they are putting in some green areas, shrubs, and a few more trees. I needed an extra bike rack, too. Silva got me some more benches from her distributor, so that saved me like eight hundred dollars."

"Yeah, that's really good. How's she doing by the way?"

"She's good." He looked around, noticing a few ducks in the lake. "She wants you to call her when you have time. Talk about what type of furniture you want for our new house." Lennox had started packing up his home as soon as he bought Nadia an engagement ring. It was the funniest thing to Nadia when he told her that, but he couldn't help it. He was so excited, he just wanted to be ready to go house shopping with her, get what they needed to start fresh, and be done with it. Best of all, he had the money saved up for a decent down payment. He'd already received several offers on his house, and her lease on her apartment was almost up, as well. Perfect timing. "She sent me an email, too. Had some pictures of different furniture trends. I'm not really into trends, what's in style, as far as that sort of thing."

"I know. Your house furniture and decor are pretty bare bones," she teased. "A true bachelor pad. It's nice though."

"Not to sound sexist or anything, and I'm sure there are some guys who like to do that type of shit, but that's a woman's thing. I leave that up to y'all." He looked off into the distance and saw what appeared to be an argument between an older woman and man. "I want you to be comfortable, so I want you in charge of it. Get whatever you want, arrange it how you want. Have fun." She nodded in understanding. "I told 'er just to give you whatever you asked for." He shrugged. "I don't give a shit. Just give me somewhere decent to lay my head, some place comfortable to sit down to watch TV, play my games and work, and I'm good..." Their eyes met. "...And somewhere nice for our baby to sleep."

"You are relentless." She chuckled, then rubbed her knee. "If I didn't know any better, I would think you were sabotaging my birth control."

"Nah, I wouldn't do anything underhanded like that. That's not cool."

"I know. I was just kidding." She took a sip of her cooler.

"It's just that I'm not getting any younger, and neither are you. You know I want kids—you said you did too, so I figure, why not plan for it now?"

"I do want a child… There's just so much going on with school right now, my grandmother's health isn't the best, the wedding planning, and the fitness center that I—"

"We'll be fine, baby. The finances are good. You heard that from our financial advisor who we met with last week. As long as we stay within our budget, no worries. I paid off your new car. So, no car note. You have a couple more years left to finish law school and if we work together, we can still have a baby while you try to find a practice to work for. Besides, there never is a perfect time to do this. We can always find excuses, but we're a team, it'll be all good. I plan to be a hands-on father, so really, you have nothin' to worry about."

She smirked, then laughed. He smiled at her as he rubbed her back.

"What's so funny?"

"Just picturing you as a father. I know that you'll be really silly… make our child laugh. You'll be a good dad. Protective. I know you will." Her smile faded, and she withdrew a bit into herself. He leaned in and kissed her cheek.

"I promise you, Nadia, I'm going to be there every step of the way," he whispered in her ear. "I'm not going to beg you to have my baby, then leave, or not be there for you and my kids. That's crazy. I want a family, with you, in every sense of the word. Look, I know why you are a little worried about all of this. It's understandable. After we leave the park today, I want you to do what you said you needed to do. If you want me by your side, I'll be there, or I can just stay in the car like we discussed."

"I want you by my side, Lennox. I'm... I'm scared." She swiped at a piece of grass on her leg. "I don't want to get all silly and emotional though. I know, I know." She waved her hand. "Therapy is kickin' my ass, and I *have* to do this, but I still hate feeling so damn vulnerable, Len. I'm getting better though. Just bear with me."

"You are. We both are." He sighed. "It takes time. Do you need Silva's email address?"

"Yeah, send it to me. I told her I don't like that farmhouse, country chic shit. I mean, I said it nicer than that, but not much nicer." Lennox burst out laughing. "I know that's in style, but it's not *my* style. I didn't want to hurt your sister's feelings, but I had to say it. That's all she was showing me."

"She's cool with that. She's a good designer and helps a lot of different clients all over Texas. Grandpa helped her get her business started." He sucked his teeth. "She still doesn't return his calls or talk to him. She's really upset about everything. I know it sounds crazy, but I kinda feel bad for him in that regard. I couldn't believe it, but he looked actually crushed that she knew the shit he'd been pulling all of these years. That man don't love nobody but himself, but he holds something special for Silva apparently. I hated how it went down, but—"

"She needed to be told the truth."

"Exactly."

"It's crazy that he didn't know she seasoned his tea, so to speak. You said he was oblivious?"

"Yeah. He knew he wasn't feeling well, but he chalked it up to some medicine he was taking for his sinuses. His allergies had been acting up for a while, so he took some prescription earlier that day before Silva came over. That's what she told me he said, anyway. He *did* imagine her setting him up with the dancers though, but I cleared that up really quick."

"Yeah, he only probably thought that because she was talking to him about his birthday party entertainment. Have you spoken to Roman and Kage lately?"

"Oh, yeah, many times a week, actually. Kage went to North Carolina for a couple of weeks. I have no idea what for. I think Roman just helped Silva update her website, too. He's a beast. That's not even his thing, really, but he just enjoys doing it as a hobby."

"Oh, that was nice of him."

"Yeah, it was, considering how busy he is. Silva and I are planning to go to Lebanon in the next year or two to visit Mama's family and her grave." He reached forward and stroked her cheek, barely able to keep his hands off her.

"That sounds good. It's been a long while. I love that for y'all." She placed her cooler down, and reached for his hand. Squeezing it. They rested in the soft silence.

"I want you to come, too."

Nadia's eyebrows rose in amazement. "But this is for you and Silva. I would just be in the way."

"No, you're family now, too." He took her hand and kissed it. "I want you there. Please come."

She hesitated, then nodded in agreement. Glue Trip's, 'Elbow Pain' was playing then.

"I need to update my passport though. I think it's expired."

"We'll take care of it right away then, Nadia. You should do that anyway since we're still not sure where we're going on our honeymoon." He leaned into her, cupping the back of her head, and brought her in for a kiss. His heart lurched and pulse pounded as their tongues danced. Tash Sultana's 'Jungle' now vibrated through his body. "Mmmm... baby...I'm so turned on right now. Let me take you."

She slowly pulled away and looked into his eyes. "You better not mean what I think you mean." He felt an overwhelming urge of excitement. "Dr. Saint Aknaten said you didn't have a sex addiction. I think we need a second opinion."

"I don't have a sex addiction, but I *am* addicted to *you.* Come here... Nobody's going to know. Trust me."

He slid off his shirt and tossed it aside, not missing her laser focus on his abs. He folded the large blanket over their legs, covering half of their bodies. She rested flat on her back while he turned onto his side, placing his leg over her body under the blanket and snuggling against the crook of her neck. He slowly closed his eyes, drifted one arm beneath the blanket, and slipped his hand into her loose white shorts, then into her panties. Soft, wavy pubic hair rubbed against his fingertips as he drifted lower until he rested at her moist valley.

He could see her chest rising and falling as he slipped two fingers between her silken lips, gliding them against the soft and tender folds.

"Damn, baby… pussy so wet already…"

He became breathless when she turned slightly towards him, sliding her hand down his chest, then inside his pants. He opened his legs a bit wider to give her better access. She gently stroked his dick, working him quickly into a full erection. Their lips pressed against one another's while 'Both Sides of the Moon,' by Celeste, made the soundtrack to their love. Her fingers dragged beneath his underwear… a warm, soft, bare touch on his lifeforce. His dick twitched in anticipation. She sighed as her valley's sultry wetness resulted from his ministrations.

"Feels good, baby?" he asked, knowing the answer yet still wanting to hear it.

"Yes… so, so good…" she cooed softly.

They moved slowly, their hips bucking ever so slightly in reciprocated affection. She trailed her lips alongside his shoulder as he delved his fingers within her damp chasm. Warm breath bathed his skin as her breathing became labored. A series of slow, needy, deep thrusts of his digits sent her voice to a higher octave. The blanket barely moved and yet, so much action, friction and motion continued beneath the soft, thick fabric. The sweet breeze stirred her dark brown waves and picked up the scent of her perfume, pitching it gently in his face with a burst of floral essence.

"Turn me loose for a second, and just concentrate on your own pleasure," he whispered.

He kissed the tip of her nose, and she smiled. Eyes closed, she breathed harder, resting her forehead against his.

"Let go… let it come. I want my fingers to be soaking wet… I want you to orgasm so hard, Brown Sugar, that it feels like a waterfall gushing in my hand." Light, airy whimpers of ecstasy escaped her mouth as he went faster and faster, thrusting his fingers within her and circling her clit with the pad of his thumb. She shuddered and he kissed her forehead while still plunging his fingers within her wetlands. As she exploded, she buried her face in his chest, hiding her expression of hot, carnal delight. When she settled, she grabbed his dick again, jerking it as they gazed deeply into each other's eyes.

"I love the feel of your big, long, warm dick in my hand… and your big balls, too…"

He swallowed harshly, not daring to blink. She turned him on so much, and he wanted her to see how good she was making him feel.

"I like that," he groaned. "Feels good. Keep rubbing my dick like that."

"You gonna cum for me, baby?"

"Mmm hmmm," he whispered in her ear. "…Keep strokin' me… harder… harder… yeah… yes, like that!"

"Imagine it in my mouth, baby… You love how I suck it…"

"Mmm hmmm! I love how you touch me, baby… and how you suck my dick… you take it deep down your throat… ugh… yesss… I wanna submerge my dick *deep* inside of you!"

She suddenly released him and disappeared beneath the blanket. His eyes strained when he felt her soft hands around the base of his dick, and her hot, wet mouth engulfing him, soon sucking on his shaft.

"Ahhh… FUCK…you're going to make me cum… I'm 'bout to cum… Uh…" He tried to watch his volume, praying his voice didn't carry and bring attention to their situation.

Releasing him, she burst back up out of the blanket, then cupped the head of his jerking cock as he squirted his buttery expulsion into her palms, like a catcher's mitt.

"Ahhh… Ahhhhh…"

As he involuntarily jerked, his hips pivoting and rotating, she kissed his chin, then his cheek while he spent his last dime of cum against her working fingers.

"Ahhh… Shit, girl… That was a surprise…" He could barely catch his breath as he looked up at the pretty clouds floating by in the sky as she cleaned her hands with some wet wipes and hand sanitizer.

They lay there. Spent. Panting. Then laughing. He looked around, placed his finger against his mouth as if to say, "*Shhhh…*" and disappeared beneath the blanket.

"No! No!" she squealed. "Get back up here, Lennox!" she said in a loud whisper. "I'll make too much noise!" She giggled, trying to tug at his arms. Swatting her hands away, he reached his destination.

It was dark underneath, but there was just enough light streaming through the fabric for him to get an eyeful. He pulled her shorts down to her ankles, shoved her panties aside, and eyed her pussy—glistening with honey, and her pink hole there for the taking. Wrapping his arms beneath her legs, he held onto her hips and pulled her to him. He stuck his tongue out and eagerly flicked it against her clit, pausing to kiss and suck all over her pussy. He tented the blanket, opening it just a bit. Just enough to see her face.

"Mmmmm!" He moaned as he ate her. "You're so damn delicious… tasty pussy…"

She sighed, and he could see her gripping the blanket with her right fist. He licked and sucked faster and faster, knowing just what to do to get her off. Knowing just how to touch his baby to make her gush. It wasn't long before she was purring and moaning in response to his oral touch. Her eyes sheened and her body began to shake. He released her, quickly slipping from beneath the blanket. He climbed up her body and pressed himself against her, wrapping his hand over her mouth to squelch her screams of pleasure as her climax edged towards completion. He rose up ever so slightly, looking around once again, then faced her, gazing deeply into her eyes…

"Ahhhh!" came her muffled cry.

He entered her swiftly, and with full force, fucking her in short, hard thrusts until she orgasmed once again. The blanket rose and fell quickly as he continued to fuck her with all of his might. In a matter of minutes he was cumming again, ejaculating inside of her warm, pulsing walls. She pressed on his ass, forcing him impossibly deeper within her. He buried his face against her breasts, suppressing his loud groans until he was completely emptied. When they were finished, they regarded one another with nothing but pure love, then kissed. A few moments later, he looked away in the distance and saw what appeared to be an old man wearing a dark red jacket, with a cocker spaniel at his side. He paused walking, standing still. He seemed rather small, although it was too far to tell, but he had his hand on his hip and was pointing right in their direction.

"Look." He got Nadia's attention as she pulled her shorts up and buttoned them. "Look at that guy over there."

She turned around and followed his gaze.

"Listen. He's sayin' something, Len, but he's too far away for me to hear him clearly."

Then the man raised his arm in the air and angrily shook it. They both looked at each other and burst out laughing. Lennox was laughing so hard, he could hardly catch his breath.

"I guess he doesn't approve. Maybe he needs to get laid, too. Grumpy ass. HOW LONG HAVE YOU BEEN STANDIN' THERE WATCHING? FUCK OFF, PER-VERT!"

"STOP IT!" Nadia giggled. "Don't yell at him, and don't laugh!"

"I'm not!" He continued to crack up, so hard his stom-ach was starting to hurt.

"That vein of yours is poppin' out of your forehead! You're making it worse," she choked out, unable to stop her mirth. "Lennox, I told you! I warned you! We are gonna get in trouble for public indecency! I'll lose my law license before I even get it, all because of *you*!"

"You warned *ME*?! Let me show you exhibit A, Ms. Attorney-to-be. Who was the one who went down on who first?! I had to return the favor. I was just tryna give you a hand job, and you turned it into an entire sexual escapade!"

"And you sho' 'nuff accepted more of what I offered, too! I don't remember you fighting me off!"

They were laughing even harder now, tumbling on top of each other like little children…

"This right here is everything." He gently stroked her cheek, a big smile on his face. "I'm never going to forget this… we just have so much fun together. My lady. My everything. I wanna always be your top dog."

"And I wanna always be your bottom bitch."

"Nadia, come on! That's not funny!" He said the words, but his lips curved in a grin.

She started laughing all over again, and soon enough they found each other in a tight embrace, kissing their cares away…

*…Later that day*

NADIA CLEARED HER throat while Lennox sat down in the half-dead grass. He leaned forward and placed a white flower against the stained gravestone, then stroked her leg, giving her comfort. Standing, she cleared her throat, tears welling in her eyes before she could even get fully started. She dropped the letter as if the muscles in her hands had gone limp. It hit the dirt and pitiful grass that barely grew around Daddy's tomb. Without missing a beat, Lennox picked the letter up and handed it back to her.

She took it, feeling sorrow, resentment, and so many

other things she still couldn't quite put into words.

"Go on, you can do this, baby," he encouraged. Lennox brought his knees up and stared at the grave, offering her quiet support.

She unfolded the letter, took a deep breath, and began to read aloud...

"Father... I titled this father because you are not deserving of the term of endearment of 'Daddy.' I wanted a daddy all of my life. I never received one. For the longest, I hated you with all of my heart and soul. Yes, I am angry. I have the right to be. Yes, I am hopeful and healing, because I need to be. When you met my mother, JoAnn, you promised her the sun, moon and stars. All you actually gave her were moon craters, asteroids, and black holes. I know that everyone sees love in their own way, but I felt no love from you, ever in my life. You were not there physically, financially, or emotionally. It seemed that you wanted to forget us. You wanted to pretend we never existed.

"Then, you became a minister, so full of yourself. You'd think that after you found God, you'd be more loving. Unfortunately, you didn't practice what you preached. The rare times we spoke, you never said words of encouragement. Any exchange we had, you were always fixed on degrading or judging me. You never apologized for how you treated me, either. I'm glad you didn't because it wouldn't have been sincere. You wanted to leave your sins behind, and pretend to be a saint. We all are sinners, Father. Our sins are lessons to learn from, and they make us stronger so that when we are faced with more problems, we know what not to do in the future."

She paused, took a deep breath. Lennox slowly stood to his feet and wrapped his arm around her waist.

"...I loved you. I truly did. In spite of yourself. You didn't just betray me and Mama. You betrayed yourself. You missed out on my entire childhood. You missed out when I lost my first tooth. Took my first steps. But Mama was there. Regardless of her and my differences, she was there!" She paused, sobbing. Lennox pulled her to him and kissed the top of her head. She gathered herself, shook it off, and continued.

"The little bit of money you had when you died went to your new wife and her kids. I've heard I have two sisters and two brothers. Some of those children from your first marriage that you didn't tell Mama about when you got her pregnant with me, and the other one from your third marriage, after you deserted us. I have no idea where these brothers and sisters are. Me and Mama were just told to stay away. As if we were the ones who were wrong. When I was twenty-two, I tried to find one of my alleged sisters on social media. I believe I did, and I was left on read. I tried with an alleged brother, and was told to just move on before being blocked. I never had the desire to try again after that.

"Someone got to them. Lied to them about us. I know who that someone is. Mama and I were made out to be villains, on account of you I'm sure. Father, it is clear to me that you were dealing with things I knew nothing about. Stuff you probably never even admitted to yourself. Pride, mental illness, pain, family trauma and disappointment seem to be abundant in our family. I am begging and praying to God that my future children will never feel the way I did, but I am still glad that you gave me life. I am glad that regardless of the ups and downs I have faced, God used you to bring me into the world. I am here. I am alive. I am… happy.

She swiped at a tear, then went on.

"I have a wonderful man in my life. I am finishing my law degree and was accepted into a special program to complete it even sooner. I'm going to be a wife soon, too. I'm eventually going to be a mother one day, God willing. I am scared to be a parent." Lennox squeezed her. "Children are a beautiful blessing and I want my own, but I am so afraid of failing them. Of making their life hard. Mama had to remind me that being a parent is not all roses. It's tough, and I'm going to make mistakes. I don't mind mistakes, Father. I mind not having accountability. Not having remorse. Not receiving genuine apologies. I mind bringing life into this world, and stomping on it. All flowers need watering. We need the showers. We need… the rain. Sometimes the rain brings pain. Like my tears whenever I think of you. Anything I wanted out of life though, I went after. I have to treat my healing the same way. Sometimes, I was in my own way. Sometimes, I was the problem. I was angry that I couldn't lash out at you anymore when you died. And I was angry that you died, never telling me that you loved me…

"Oh, God…this is so hard! It hurts so bad! He hurt me so badly!"

Her hand shook and she almost dropped the letter again. She buckled at the knees and Lennox caught her, holding her to him.

"It's okay, sweetheart… It's okay." He cradled her head like she was a baby. Let her fall apart against his strong body. She felt so safe in his arms. She cried against his shoulder, soaking his shirt. Her heart leapt in her chest and a wave of dull pain consumed her. She stayed that way for a long time, then slowly pulled away from him.

"I'm going to finish. I *have* to. I am strong enough to do this. I can get through this. I *will* get through this." He nodded and wrapped his arm around her once again. Placing the letter in her pocket, she resumed talking.

"The letter is gone. I am not going to read from it anymore. I'm talking to you one-on-one. Straight from the heart. No script. Daddy… Yes, I changed to Daddy now, because I'm stopping this curse. Letting go of the anger. You were supposed to not just be my father, but my daddy, and I pray in some way, shape or form, even in death, you may have a chance to do that. I don't know how this heaven and hell thing works, and I don't know which one you reside in, but I do know that God is for real. God is merciful. I'm not God, it's above me now, and even though you pretended you were God from time to time, we both know that deep down it was just a cover-up for your low self-esteem and insecurities. I don't know what happened to you, Daddy, but I'm not passing that shit along to the next generation. This curse was born in the darkness, and now, I am shedding light on it. No more physical, sexual, emotional, verbal and mental abuse. No more unnecessary quarrels due to manipulation. No more violence of any kind. No more neglect. No more cruel sarcasm. No more lies and only telling half of the truth, or none at all, because you're ashamed! It stops with me! I deserve better! My fiancé deserves better, Daddy! My mama and my brother deserve better!

"They're going to get a better version of me, because I was not created and put here to grovel in my pain. I am stronger than that! I have business to take care of, and a life to live. JoAnn was a lot of things, Daddy, but weak isn't one of them. I am so thankful for her intelligence and strength. I am so thankful that she and I are getting along better, and she is now open to having the hard talks with me that are long overdue! No, everything is not fixed, it'll take time, but she is willing to listen and share with me parts of her life that she had closed off. Nelson, my wonderful brother, is a damn good man.

"Despite not having the father figure that he too so desperately needed, he is tryna help raise a little girl that isn't even his! Even after his divorce – he knows he is *still* that child's father. That's what real men, do! I wish him healing and grace. We *all* have to do better! We can only do better, when we know better. And now we know. Your grandbabies that I bring forth need a mother who is not too proud to beg for forgiveness!

"They need a healthy mother—in mind, body and spirit—and if I have to go to a local shrink weekly, I will. If I have to pay on a monthly basis to get cussed out and put back on track by that slick talkin', Asian-Egyptian, thug ass, disrespectful nympho with unnerving mind-reading abilities who goes by the name, Dr. Saint Aknaten, so be it! If I have to read five-hundred-page self-help books, join support groups, volunteer at a women's shelter, attend church, take a million yoga and meditation classes for the rest of my days, then sign me up! There is nothing I won't do for myself anymore. It is self-care! It is the psychological soft life! There is nothing I won't do for my mama, except not be true to myself. She sacrificed a lot, and yes, I needed more from her, but damn it, I can't say she didn't try and that is *far* more than I can say for you!

"There is nothin' I won't do for this man," she pointed to Lennox, "because he earned it! When I start to fall, he lies down in front of me and takes the brunt! When I need a crutch, he becomes my fortress to lean on! When I hurt, he becomes my emotional aspirin. When I am disappointed, he helps restore my hope and faith. Real men exist in this world, not just little boys, pretending to be fathers who are afraid to stay put and water their gardens! Broken people make broken homes! Broken homes break children in half! We end up not knowin' if we're coming or going.

"Broken children have to heal, or the broken cycle will continue. I'm not going to let anyone from my past or present stop me from achieving my objectives, stop my healing, and doing what is best for me and my family, Daddy. Regardless of everything, and I mean this from the bottom of my heart, I want you to rest in peace. I hold no ill will towards you. I am releasing it today. The resentment. Gone! The hatred. Gone! The blame. Gone! The forgiveness? I'm workin' on it…

"I want you to know that I am okay, regardless of you abandoning me. God was there. I've been carried a mighty long way. My brother, though younger than me, was a protector, too. I can't stop the rain, but I can trust myself to survive the storm. *You* were the storm, and now, the sun is out, daddy. Ain't nothing that has happened to me, not happened to someone else already that walked this Earth before me. Someone out there survived the same hardships I've endured, 'cause ain't nothing new under the sun. This is my first time coming to your grave, and it will be my last. I am done with this. The sun will not go down on my wrath for another day. I have said what I have to say and now, I am saying, "Goodbye."

She bowed her head while the tears kept flowing, stinging her eyes. Lennox took her in his arms and rocked her. She held onto him right back, wrapping her arms around him. Squeezing for dear life…

# CHAPTER THIRTY-FIVE

## *A Cross to Bear and a Champagne Wedding*

G RANDPA WILDE SAT in his study carving a block of wood. He hadn't done such a thing in years, and being out of practice earned him a few splinters. He bent over, taking his time, being as meticulous as could be. The knife moved deep and slow as he whittled the wood into form. The largest window in his office was open, so he enjoyed the view of his back terrace. The chirping of birds and a nice breeze flowed as The Monkees', 'Daydream Believer' played throughout the house. He paused to swipe a thin strand of his long hair from his face with a flick of his finger. Most of his tresses were pulled back in a taut silver braid that draped his back. Today, he simply felt like doing something new, but something old, too. Returning to his roots.

"As a boy, I used to make things out of wood. I was pretty good at it, too... Somethin' borrowed, somethin' blue..."

In a few hours, his grandson, Lennox Wilde, would be getting married. He smiled big and wide, imagining Lennox's exhilaration on his special day.

"Gotta give it to 'em," he mumbled. "That bastard really pulled that shit off. Surprised me, and that's hard to do. I didn't think Lenny boy had it in him. Well, Lennox, looks like you and that devilish bitch are cut from the same dirty cloth. A match made in heaven or hell. I thought about showing up, doin' something to remind you that I can still get at cha, but I made a promise to you in that contract, and I also have your sister to keep in mind. I imagine Silva's there in attendance, and she wouldn't like that. Now the tables have turned." He shook his head and chuckled to himself. "First it was you on the outs with her. Now, it's me. Can't say I like it over this way too much. Can't say it feels good. I don't deserve this though. I gave that girl everything and was there for her and her goofy husband in their time of need. I figured Lennox would tell her everything when I asked her to reach out to him, sing like a bird, but I didn't think Silva's ass would believe him!

"After all, I've worked on her since she was a little girl. Molding her. Treating her like a princess. I let it be known that he was a paid killer, amongst other things. Whew weeee!" He chortled, though inside, his heart was broken into a thousand tiny pieces. "It don't much matter anymore. A deal is a deal. I told myself, *promised* myself actually, that if these boys found a way out of their contract that met my specifications, I'd leave 'em be. I kinda regret doing that now, but sometimes we have to keep our own selves in check. Checks 'nd balances, if you will. Lennox, you went a little too far. You sure did a number on ol' Sam. Of course, I'm not certain what part was you, and what part was Kage's mentally deranged ass. Now I've got another child not talkin' to me, my son Frederick, and Sam can't talk to me even if he wanted to.

"Fred was mad as hell. He blames me for what happened to his boy. Seems word got back fast that Lennox was on some revenge kick for the visit to his paramour. It happened just like Lennox said it would. Lenny, you sure dropped a bomb on me, didn't ya? Threatening to tell everything to the FBI—even with knowing the risks it would do to innocent bystanders. You had me with a few lady visitors in the throes of passion." He shrugged. "I looked pretty good on that there footage, if I say so myself, but it sure ain't something I want making the rounds.

"Then you added a lil' prize, a little razzle dazzle, by throwing Sam in the mix right there at the end. Like a cherry on top. On second thought, I can't say I blame you. If someone had done what he'd done to my woman, I'd be mighty ticked off about it, too." He grimaced as he stared at the carving, thinking it all through. "I think stringing him up half-naked while Kage shot at a target above his head was a bit much though. Lettin' that snake latch on to his nipple wasn't right, either. Not to mention all the other things that happened... Sam ain't been right in the head since.

"...Well, grandson, I won't lie. You've got a good one there, Lennox. She's pretty as a peach. More importantly, she seems to love you somethin' serious. That woman turned down her own safety, loads of money, and her schoolin' paid in full, all to be loyal to you. I don't believe most women would've done the same. 'Specially with a gun in their face. You go on and live your life, but if you give me any excuse, any at all to come back... I'll be after you so fast it'll make your head spin. I'm focused on the future. I got bigger fish to fry. Now, I'll just concentrate on the others. I think I'll live over a hundred years.

"So, I've got the time... Next on the list is that piece of shit, Roman. I've decided I'm going to start puttin' the pressure on his shifty ass. 'Specially as seeing that he teamed up with Lennox to do his dirty work. Roman, Roman, Roman... my smart-ass grandson with a flip mouth. Always been the kind to talk back and crack a joke at the wrong damn time. Think you're so fuckin' witty and smart, don't you? You're a walkin' contradiction. Women call you beautiful, with your tall height, slender yet muscular frame, naturally sun-kissed skin and blue-black hair, like a raven's feathers. I bet that's from the Indian in our family. I believe my Papi, God rest his soul, said it's from way, way, back... a great-great-grandmother of mine. Comanche tribe, they say. Pops up every now and again in the gene pool. All those good looks don't mean much, boy, because they can't save you from me. You're a charlatan down to your black little core.

"A sick and twisted genius with ways of earning bookoo money. But you're flawed... The black sheep of the Wilde family. Group homes. Foster homes. You're a devious motherfucker, too, and you don't seem to care much about your reputation. Will do anything for the finer things in life. You've got the heart of a thief, and you're soulless. I say, why not put it to good use?" He snickered. "Told me you are walking the straight and narrow now. Horse shit! You've been a fucking problem since the day you were born. Your childhood was a shit show. Your father made some mistakes, and your mother isn't too bright. Blood or not, I never wanted your daddy as a member of the business. He didn't have what it takes. You, though… you're top notch. I get it, you know? How you ended up so messed up in the head. But you're *still* a rotten egg, and you know it.

"You would've been rotten if you came from the 'Leave it to Beaver's' family. Wouldn't have made no bit of difference more than likely. You were a terrible person, and an awful Marine. But you are one hell of a gambler, bluffer, and investor. I heard you can fight, too… got a bit of trainin' under your belt from your stint in the armed forces. All of that could work to my advantage. A nice face to lure motherfuckers in, then… BOOM! Gotcha!" He cackled. "You're going to be mine, Roman… One got away, but the next one I'm taking home and puttin' on a shelf."

He looked at the statue he carved, turning it to and fro. Proud of his handiwork. It was a Christian cross. A beautiful, crudely carved crucifix. *It would look nice on a tombstone.*

He began to sing. "At the cross… at the cross. Where I first, saw the light! And my buuuurdens, of my heart, rooooolled, awaaaaay! It was there, by, faith, I reeeeceived my sight, And now, I am haaaappy, all the daaay!" He continued singing the old gospel hymn, tapping his foot against the floor. "…And now, for my next song, which is dedicated to my grandson, Roman Wilde. A big ol' fuck-up, who so desperately needs his grand-papi to step in and show him the ropes…" He shook his head as anger rolled like the tide within him. "Black sheep, black sheep, have you any wool? Yes, sir, yes, sir, three money-bags full. One for my grandpa, one to keep me fed, one for my funeral, should I end up dead…"

IT WASN'T WHAT most folks expected, but a beautiful surprise all the same. It was overcast on this glorious Saturday, but some sun shone through the clustered clouds, breaking through the gloomy fortress. The Red Rooster restaurant land was owned by some real estate folks from Bakersfield, California, and the area had gone into a seemingly irreversible state of disrepair. Neither Nadia nor Lennox had fathomed purchasing the land or remnants. The idea of being restaurant owners and having to fix up the dilapidated place was definitely something neither were interested in, nor willing to do. However, the notion of prettying her up on the outside and having a ceremony there did.

Could they pull it off? The idea had arrived after Nadia quickly discovered that the places she was interested in having their wedding held were so far booked out, they'd be waiting for years, or the venue was way too expensive, and she didn't wish to stress out their finances unnecessarily. Besides, weddings were just one day. A marriage was forever.

Sure, she'd imagined as a child that her wedding would be in a big church. She'd sport a large white dress that resembled a ballgown, and there would be at least twenty bridesmaids, five hundred guests, and it would be a page ripped out of a fairytale. Now, she wanted something far different. As an adult, she understood that love trumps all. As long as the vows were said, the rings exchanged, the day was special and unique for her and her love, and if it was all sealed with a kiss, she would be satisfied. They found a Christian minister to officiate, and that took some of her planning stress away. The reception was taking place at the Houston Museum of Natural Science, and that was enough money being shelled out as is, but for their actual vows, they wanted something unique to both of them, and them alone. Why not have it where he'd asked for her hand in marriage? The place where they'd fallen in love, but neither would say it...

Nadia sat in the back of the black Lincoln limousine which was parked up the street from the Red Rooster, with the sounds of Buju Banton's 'Boom Bye Bye' playing in the background. She lay back, half sitting up, and half slumping in the large, fancy vehicle with her bridesmaids who were chatting, laughing, and listening to the music, all of them dressed in light blue form-fitting dresses adorned with black and champagne sashes about the waist, champagne colored hand gloves, and blue and black heels with champagne bows on the back. Looking every bit of lovely. Three of the women were childhood friends she'd kept in contact with over the years, and she'd been in one of their weddings as well. Two were strippers she'd been fond of and gotten close to while living in Atlanta, and a couple of them were from Sweet Soiree: Danielle and Sunshine. Lydia came as a guest.

Her Matron of Honor was her cousin, Stella, who'd always been so kind and supportive. One of her few family members who either didn't have their hand out to ask for financial help, or didn't have something slick to say about her mother.

"Okay," the driver said over the noise and rowdiness. "Ladies, we got the go ahead to drive on down the road now."

The women started whistling and cheering, and Nadia's cheeks burned with heat as she grinned from ear to ear. It was showtime.

*I'm getting married today to a man I love with all of my mind, body, and soul…*

"I can't believe it! It's really happening!" she shouted joyfully as her friends continued to whoop and holler in celebration. They moved around the limo, twerking, acting silly and gyrating to the music when the limo driver turned on the song she'd requested to be played as they approached the location: 'Time of Your Life,' by Kid Ink…

LENNOX STOOD BESIDE two tall silver pillars in front of a freshly painted 'Red Rooster' eatery. The inside was still in shambles undoubtedly, but he'd hired some competent workers to fix up the outside, making it look practically brand new—the way he recalled it when he and his bride had worked there so long ago. The sign was back up—glowing and bright, and the front of the restaurant was set up perfectly for a wedding.

Champagne fabric was draped over all of the chairs, cinched with black and blue striped ribbons. They were lined up in front of the place in rows of twelve, where the parked cars used to be. Each chair had a menu on it for when guests arrived, and inside those menus were short biographies of him and Nadia, how they met, and a condensed, sweet version of their love story.

Everyone in attendance had also been passed a napkin from a napkin dispenser in case they anticipated tears. The old Red Rooster logo was embossed on them. Lennox had one of those napkins tucked away in his pocket as he stood beside Pastor Johnson. His groomsmen, all dressed in black and champagne smoking jackets with black pants, talked amongst themselves in the back. The song 'Little Red Rooster,' by the Rolling Stones, commenced.

"I think y'all love birds lucked out. Rain ain't 'sposed to come until this evening," the Pastor stated to him as he gripped his dark red Bible and looked up at the sky.

"Yeah… looks like a fine day for a wedding."

They continued to engage in small talk. The reverend was in mid-sentence, talking about how he'd torn a muscle from an old football injury and needed to try out a new fitness center when the black limousine they'd all been waiting for pulled up.

It looked surreal in that forsaken area, a big, sparkly car in the middle of nowhere. It shined so much one could see their reflection crystal clear. The music switched to 'Genesis,' by Grimes as the driver got out, came around and opened the back. A rush of soft blue tapestry glided from the car like melted taffy floating in the wind. Women with fancy updos, tight curls, bushy afros, dyed braids, and long, flowing hair poured out in various hues of Earth, moving as if in slow motion. Pretty painted faces and feminine fingers grasping white roses, genuine belly giggles, and a parade of enthusiasm showing in their eyes and their smiles.

The groomsmen made their way to the crowd of women, looping their arms around theirs, and prepared to walk down the white lace covered aisle which divided the two sections of seating for their guests. The first order of business, however, was to announce Ms. JoAnn. The tall, statuesque woman stood there dressed in a flowing light blue gown and black low heels. A diamond pendant hung from her neck. Her dark red painted lips curved as she mustered a smile, looking a bit stiff and uncomfortable, though that made her all the more endearing. His best man, Kage, handed her a white rose, then took her arm into his, and together they walked down the aisle.

She gave a short wave to Lennox, and he blew her a kiss

before she sat down beside her son, Nelson. JoAnn and he had spoken in person several times before the nuptials. She'd been over at their new, beautiful two-story house helping around the place, and the three of them had had dinner a couple of times, too. JoAnn was a woman of few words, but a couple of weeks before the wedding, she drove over to his old house when he was loading the last of his belongings on the moving truck. Nadia wasn't around, but she seemed well aware of that. From the reddish hue in her eyes, it looked as if she'd been crying. She hugged him, and thanked him for treating her daughter well. For being a man of his word. He felt her shaking in his embrace. He hugged her tightly and promised his mother-in-law that her daughter was in good hands. Lennox scanned the front row, and his eyes landed on Nelson. Nelson leaned over and kissed his mother's cheek.

The two regarded one another for a long while before Nelson ultimately turned away. Lennox had had the pleasure of meeting Nadia's brother a few months prior at a family dinner, and he'd really enjoyed speaking to him. The guy was funny and down to earth, and he loved his sister a great deal. Nadia's grandmother was sitting next to Nelson—a strikingly beautiful elderly woman with skin the shade of maple, devoid of wrinkles, and possessed a sparkle in her large ebony eyes. Her black-rimmed glasses sat on the tip of her nose. She too wore a light blue dress, and she had on blue shoes to match. After getting Ms. JoAnn seated, Kage spoke briefly with a couple of guys standing about, then came up and stood beside him.

They regarded one another with respectful smiles, then

bumped fists. Kage had on a black leather biker's jacket over his wedding attire. His tattooed hands were adorned with various gold and silver rings. His hair was long in the front, shaved on one side, and straight blonde and silver strands hung over one of his satin blue eyes. He stood tall and at full attention, surveying the area as if he were the lookout for the wedding, too. Perhaps he was… They both had that heat on them in case any uninvited guests made an appearance.

In the front row sat his father, brother-in-law and sister, all sporting expressions of pride. His dad smiled at him as their eyes met, and he nodded in approval. Silva glanced back at the black car, then at him. She was dabbing her eyes with the napkin and the ceremony hadn't even begun. She'd been so supportive—they'd worked hard these last few months to continue to repair their shattered sibling relationship, and rebuild trust. Best of all, Silva adored Nadia, and the two of them were looking forward to getting to know one another even better.

When everyone had gathered and gotten settled, the song changed. Lennox felt a spasmodic trembling in his gut, so he breathed deep a few good times to get control of himself. In his efforts, he became fixated on the partially open car door, and the driver standing there with his snow-white gloves. A big smile spread across the driver's dark brown face as he held the back door open for the one missing member of the marching band.

Lennox could practically taste Nadia as she sat back, unseen and out of view. His stomach somersaulted. He swallowed his emotions in a hard gulp, then checked his reflection shown in one of the freshly cleaned windows of the restaurant, needing a new focus while he got his emotions in check. There he was, dressed in a Sebastian Cruz Champagne Oro Paisley Dinner Jacket, paired with a black shirt, black pants and a black champagne handkerchief tucked in the pocket. His dark hair was coiffed to perfection—the sides cut short, and the top grown out and brushed away from his face. His mustache and beard were neatly trimmed. Pure perfection. He looked rather sharp if he said so himself.

Turning back around, he caught sight of his cousins, who were his groomsmen, as well as a couple of employees from the nightclub and the gym he'd worked at before setting off on his own. Once they were all standing in position, the music faded and the new song playing was 'Happy,' by Pharrell Williams.

People laughed and clapped as Nadia's little cousin, a cute little caramel-skinned girl with sandy brown Shirley Temple curls approached the guests in a frilly light blue dress, frilly white socks, and black patent leather shoes. She was holding a blue basket full of wrapped red and white peppermints like the ones they used to give away after meals at the restaurant. Bouncing down the aisle, dancing to the music, she tossed pieces of the candy here and there. Once she was finished, Lennox's friend's son, a little pink-cheeked boy with short dark brown hair and bright hazel eyes came into view. He held a small-sized carry-out restaurant box which contained the bride's wedding band. He too was full-on smiling and dancing to the music, providing a fun lightheartedness to the vibe.

Once the boy's expedition was complete, the minister smiled at everyone, then raised his hand high.

"Please rise, as we welcome the bride."

People got to their feet and a new song began to play: 'Adore,' by Prince. The limousine door opened a bit wider, now the inside in full view. The driver leaned forward and extended his hand. Nadia stepped one champagne high-heeled shoe out the door, placed her gloved hand into his palm, and got to her feet. Moisture stung Lennox's eyes, but he quickly blinked it away. She was the most beautiful woman in the world to him… Standing there in a champagne-colored gown that belled at the bottom like some princess, she reminded him of Cinderella. He was honored to be her prince, her knight in shining armor.

Nadia's hair was pulled back into an elaborate braided bun, with tiny cream flowers sprinkled on top of it, and a sparkling tiara atop her head. Loose spirals of hair framed her modestly made-up dewy face. *This has to be a dream. I need to pinch myself.* Her brother, dressed in similar attire as the groomsmen, stood up and made his way to her to loop his arm into hers. They grinned at one another, then laughed. Lennox understood the love between a brother and sister all too well. Nelson leaned in and kissed Nadia on the cheek, and then they began to walk forward.

Step by step, they made their way down the aisle, everyone looking at the sight to behold. Camera flashes of light ensued from the professional photographers busy at work, and the videographers and DJ kept busy, too. When she reached Lennox and Pastor Johnson, the latter gripped his Bible with both hands and posed a question.

"Who gives this lovely bride away?"

Nelson stated, "I do." Her brother kissed her cheek once again, then went back to his seat next to their mother.

"Good afternoon, ladies and gentlemen," Pastor Johnson began. "Fine friends, family of the bride and groom, and loved ones alike. We're gathered here today to celebrate Lennox Wilde and Nadia Deere in their lifelong commitment of love to each other." The pastor went on to share a little insight about the both of them, and urged their guests to read the programs/menus to learn more about the couple.

"I've known Lennox for many years. He was my personal trainer, and he helped set up some tents at one of our church carnival events a long time ago. He and I got to talkin' over time and I enjoyed him, and his conversation. I knew he was special from the first time we spoke. Though he isn't a member of our church family, and I've slacked off with my workouts, we've kept in touch, and he's always come and assisted for many of our events. When he called me to ask if I would officiate his wedding, I readily obliged. I am honored to be here today to join this man and this woman in holy matrimony."

Pastor Johnson began the wedding ceremony with a prayer, with all the guests joining in, bowed heads and a resounding "Amen," at the end.

After the prayer was over, the couple were invited to each light a candle. One of the bride's maid's handed one candle to Nadia, and the other to Lennox. On a nearby table, a third candle was standing there waiting to be lit. The table was covered in a red and white checkerboard cloth, and there were forks and knives placed on the napkins, as well as glasses filled with cola.

Lennox chanced a glance at Nadia, and quickly regretted it. He turned away, resisting the emotions that bubbled just below the surface. His heart literally thumped like mad every time he dared to look into her eyes since the moment she exited the limo. They stood side by side, placed their candles together, then lit the third candle that was on the table. Once they were done, they handed their candles to the pastor who hurriedly extinguished them, and set them aside.

He went through the traditional wedding vows, and each of them said, 'I do,' when asked.

"Now we've come to the part where I ask Nadia if she has any words she wishes to share with Lennox. Would you like to speak?" Nadia nodded, then turned towards Lennox. "Go right ahead." They faced one another, their eyes welling.

"You look so beautiful," he whispered. He exhaled a long sigh of joy.

"Thank you," she whispered back. "Everyone, I had written my vows down, but I decided last minute to just… talk to Lennox the way we normally talk. No pretenses. Just love leading the way." She cleared her throat and looked into his eyes. "Lennox, it's so cliché, but in our case it really is true. Today, I am marryin' my best friend. You were there for me when I wasn't there for myself. I was young and didn't have everything figured out. I still don't have everything figured out, but I have a clear direction on where I want to go in life, and *who* I want to take that journey with. The person I want right by my side. That's you. My life partner. I want to take this ride with you, and only you. You are my strength when I am weak. You are my smile when I feel down in the dumps. You're my encourager, and my truth teller when I feel discouraged, or need a dose of reality.

"We've been through a lot separately, and we've been through a lot as a couple—but the mountains we had to climb together were for growth, not because we didn't love each other enough to see the tough times through." He nodded, his heart full and about to burst. "I feel so incredibly blessed to have you in my life. To be able to soon call you my husband. To know that from this day forward, you and I are a team, not just in words but before God. You are my bodyguard when I feel afraid but am too scared to admit it. You just step in, knowing what I need, when I need it. My prayer..." She paused, briefly closed her eyes and swallowed. "Sorry." Her voice cracked. "My prayer is to be a good wife to you. A good support system. A friend in every sense of the word.

"Someone you can trust and rely on. I may not be that young lady anymore that you met in the pantry of this very restaurant, who was cryin' her eyes out over life's misfortunes and uncertainties. But I still have the youthful optimism of a child when it comes to hopes and dreams, and I still get butterflies every time I look at you." The guests aahed, and some patted tears from their eyes. "Today is a good day. The best day. A new start. Today, we are here with our loved ones to celebrate our union, and today, you are here in my heart and I in yours. Forever. We're making a promise. Taking an oath. I love you, Lennox. There are no words to describe just how true and deep my love for you is. Just know that what God put together, nobody, no matter how meek, mild or Wilde," she smiled and winked at him through her happy tears, "can dare to tear us apart."

Their guests clapped and yelled out happy praises.

"Lennox, do you have anything you wish to say to Nadia?" Pastor Johnson asked.

"Yes… yes." He took her hands into his and looked deeply into her eyes. His lower lip trembled and tears streamed down his cheeks. He looked away, then heard voices telling him it was okay, and to take his time. He faced her once again.

"The very first time I saw you here at the Red Rooster, I thought, 'Damn, she's cute as hell!' Sorry for the colorful language, Pastor, but that's what I actually thought." People erupted in laughter, and so did he. Nadia's cheeks flushed with color as she succumbed to the merriment. "But then, we got to know each other, and I saw you as more than just a pretty face. I saw you as a true friend. You used to put music on CDs for me, and we spent a lot of time opening the restaurant together. Just you and me…You intrigued me so much, Nadia. I had never met anyone like you in my entire life. I loved that you had a different background from me, and a different culture too, even though we're both red-blooded Americans. We appreciated each other's differences. Learned from one another.

"You were going through a lot of things… Personal stuff, and for some reason, even though I was going through a lot of stuff, too, I saw it as my job to help you feel better. To make your time here at the Red Rooster somethin' to look forward to. Eventually, our time here together came to an end. Neither of us admitted to one another that our feelings were more than just those of two young adults who'd become compadres. They had grown.

"Strengthened. Developed into a grown man and grown woman sort of adoration. We'd fallen in love, but due to so many things, like being somewhat in denial and other factors, some of them not our fault, the friendship, companionship, all of it, was put on ice. Well, ice melts. The sun came out, and things heated up." A few people clapped and whistled. "Something in the universe reignited those old flames, and I was thawed out fast.

"I ran into you one night, after all of these years, and I went from '*She's cute as hell*,' to '*God, thank you*,'" his voice rattled, "*you brought her back to me*.'" Applause ensued, the emotion on overload. "I told you then, and I'm telling everyone else right here, right now, that I prayed for you, Nadia. I asked God to bring me my wife. Some of my friends said I'd never get married. They said I wouldn't settle down, or I was too picky. I made sure that I had myself together before I made the request. Sent the prayer to heaven. I wanted to be mature enough to be a good man for you. The man you wanted. The man you needed. The man you *deserved*. I had thought about you on and off over the years, and when... when I saw you that night at the club, sitting there alone, looking absolutely beautiful... I knew... I just knew, you were the one.

"They say, if you love someone, let them go. If they return to you, then it's meant to be. Well, this is definitely meant to be. I want to be your husband. I want to be your lover. I want to be your best friend. I want to be the father of your children. I want to be your partner in every way possible. I will be there for you—morning, noon and night, twenty-four seven. We're both independent people, but you have saved me in ways you don't even understand. I've been in love before, but never, and I mean *never*, like this. I didn't even think it was possible to be this deeply in love, but you showed me right quick and in a hurry that not only is it possible, but you were the one to give me such an amazing gift: The gift of your heart." She blinked tears away. "All of your life, you've endured storms. The clouds come, and you dread what's to follow.

"I'm your umbrella." He squeezed her hands as a tear traced her cheek. "I'm your shelter. I'm Noah's ark when that storm turns into a full-fledged flood, and there seems to be no escape. My shoulders are big enough for you and our family without me breakin' a sweat. You can count on me to keep you safe. Protected. You're no damsel in distress, but you're my woman and I'm your man, and that's what a *real* man does. He makes sure his bride knows she's got someone in her corner. Someone who walks in front of her—not to control you, but to take the brunt of whatever is comin' our way." He placed his hand across his heart. "My mama enjoyed a song by SWV called, 'Rain Down on Me.'" The acapella version of the song began to play at that moment. Lennox let it play for a while as he gripped his queen's trembling hands. Nadia began to sob and shake her head. A new smile on her face, but old pain in her eyes.

"My mama absolutely loved this song. I'd like to think

that she's here with us today. Celebrating our day. In fact, I can feel her. She'd love the wife I've chosen, because you're a good woman. Just like her." Tears streamed down his face, and this time, he didn't look away. "Mama had her own storms to endure—everyone does. You never have to face yours alone, Nadia. I'm here today. I'm going to be here tomorrow, and I'll be here forever. When I look at you, because you're so incredibly beautiful and sexy to me, I feel absolute, all-consuming yearning for you, and I make no apologies for it. My love for you is loud like thunder. It's huge, like the ocean.

"When you need a moment alone, I'll give you your space and become a tiny raindrop, giving you room to breathe. However, please understand, when we have a monsoon, baby, some sort of argument or disagreement that has us at odds, we'll always come together eventually and talk, communicate, and work things out, like grown folks do. I've waited all this time for you. I will fight for you. I will fight for us. I'm not leavin' without a battle. It took too long to get here, to make our way back to one another, and ain't no stopping us now. When you have a good thing, you treasure it. God brought us back together because it was finally our time.

"He was savin' our love for a rainy day. And now, that day is here." He took a deep breath, then continued. "You told me once that I was the calm before the storm. When it rains, it pours, but you ain't gotta worry about getting not even one strand of hair on that pretty lil' head of yours wet, Nadia, 'cause now you're safe and protected. Why? Well, that's obvious. Go on and let it rain cats all it wants. They won't land a scratch. Why? Because you've married the Top Dog..." The crowd burst out in applause, laughter, and whistles.

She tossed her arms around him and squeezed. He hugged her right back, so tight, resisting the urge to seal it with a kiss. Taking their rings from the Matron of Honor and ring bearer and repeating the words of Pastor Johnson, they exchanged them, both shaky with excitement.

"I must say, those were some wonderful vows! Just beautiful," Pastor Johnson announced before going into a final prayer. After he finished, he made the closing statements and declaration. "Since Lennox and Nadia have exchanged their vows before God and respected witnesses, have sworn their commitment to each other before us all, and have professed the same by joining hands and exchanging rings, I now pronounce Lennox Wilde and Nadia Wilde, as husband and wife!" People clapped and cheered. "Those who God has joined together, let no one put asunder!" the pastor yelled over the noise. "Lennox, Mr. Top Dog," the man laughed, "you may kiss your bride!" Kage began to loudly bark and howl like some beast.

Lennox pulled Nadia to him and gave her an all-consuming kiss. His heart swelled, his body was on fire for her, and his soul merged with hers. He could hear the cheers and feel the love all around him, and it was the best feeling on God's green earth. He squeezed Nadia, bringing her as close as he possibly could while his body, heart and soul screamed her name.

Reaching into his pants pocket, he pulled out the two stones he'd gathered from the ground when he'd proposed to her. He handed her the one he felt was most like him, and kept the one he believed was most like her. "We're rocks. Rockstars. We're strong. We've got endurance. But even rocks need protection, affection and love. Even rocks can swept away with the storm. Thank you for lovin' me, Nadia, and bringing out the best in me. I promise to choose our love, every single day of our lives…"

She can't stand the rain

It's like tears that turn the iron and metal of love
into rust.

She can't stand the rain

Because it can't drown heartbreak, troubles, and
lust.

He can't stand the pain

It comes as deceased mothers and weak fathers,
hidden in the sorrowful, mourning fog.

He can't stand the pain

But now he can endure it with Queen Lust by his
side, for he *is* the Top Dog.

# EPILOGUE

T HE SOUNDS OF Shaboozey's, 'Last of My Kind' came through loud as Lennox stood on the ladder, removing the painter's tape from the wall of his fitness center. Construction workers, electricians, and even a couple of designers that Silva had hired marched in and out of various areas. He'd done plenty of last-minute changes—his curiosity had sparked. Since he'd gotten back from his week-long honeymoon with Nadia to Taos, New Mexico, things had been full speed ahead. He'd decided to change the name of the place, and a new electric sign was made that read: Wilde Ways Fitness Zone.

He was finally at a place in his life where he was embracing his last name. At this point, for him it meant to conquer, and to be free. Inside the large structure, he had a room set up for yoga classes and a free Lamaze session for expecting mothers. The room was dedicated to his own mother, with her framed photo holding him and his sister Silva as children on the wall. There would be an indoor pool added the following year, and a second attached building for dance classes. Lennox wanted Wilde Ways to become a statewide brand, and was more than willing to put the blood, sweat and tears into it to achieve just that. He climbed down the ladder and looked around. Pleased with the progress. One large area had all of the ellipticals, treadmills, and bikes, as well as a movie-theater-sized screen that showed various shows. There were also small built-in web browsing monitors on most of the equipment offered.

There was even an area set up for daycare services during member workouts, and he'd hired many staff members to run the front desk, aid with marketing, and teach spinning, Zumba and kickboxing classes. In a large closed-in area was all the weightlifting equipment, with a separate shower area, and he also had set up a healthy snack bar and juice center. A lot of money had been poured into this place, but he had no doubt he'd earn it all back and begin making profit in no time.

"Lennox!" Nadia called out to him, holding a stack of notebooks. "Where do you want me to put these?" she yelled over the hammering and music.

"In my office, baby. In fact, come here. I need to talk to you." He waved her over.

Nadia had been a little worker-bee assistant for him, despite having her schedule full due to law school. She was pursuing a full-time accelerated program, and had completed her Juris Doctorate. The woman was kicking ass, and he was incredibly impressed with her resilience, aptitude, and time management. She'd explained the more she does now, the more relaxed her schedule would get over time, so she tackled the time-consuming classes and requirements first. The woman barely got any sleep, but she was definitely determined.

Dressed in a black crop top, black leggings and black and white Nikes, her long dark brown hair parted on one side and tucked behind her ear, she waltzed over and followed him into his office. He closed and locked the door behind them as she set the notebooks on one of his bookshelves. He eyed her up and down, his gaze resting on her cleavage, and then her ass when she turned around to take a seat. He shoved the lustful, seedy thoughts aside, leaned against his desk, and crossed his arms and legs.

"What's up?" she questioned, looking a bit sleepy and exhausted.

"I'm just going to come on out and say it. We received somethin' interesting for our wedding."

"Oh, the gifts from Saint and his wife, Xenia? Wasn't that nice of them?! The engraved charcuterie board and those wine glasses were so pretty, Lennox, and they had our names inscribed on them, too. Saint sent a couple auto-graphed books, and a sensual massage for couples scented oils and candle kit, along with a DVD that he helped produce and direct. DVD? Who still watches those? Anyway, I did! It was kinda porn-ish," she burst out laughing, "but so thoughtful!" They'd just had a chance to open the rest of their wedding presents when they returned to their new house from their honeymoon.

"Yeah, that was nice of them and I'll need to check that

out, especially the instructional movie." He laughed. "But that's not what I'm talking about."

"Oh… what did we get? From who?"

Lennox sighed, grabbed his phone, and pulled up his banking information.

"On the day of our wedding, I saw a sizable deposit. I thought it was a mistake, so I called my bank and asked that they return it to the sender. I had a lot of transactions coming in and going out from contractors and what not. The bank couldn't give me the name of who it had come from, only some agency I'd never heard of. I figured it was just a mistake by one of the vendors. I thought that was the end of it. Then, this morning, I saw that the money was deposited again. Same exact amount. I didn't say anything right away. I was busy, and figured maybe the bank made a mistake. I called the bank a couple of hours ago, and got more information. Long story short… Grandpa Wilde did it." Nadia's jaw dropped. "I know… you don't have to say it. I called him. He didn't answer. I left a voicemail and told him that we don't want his money. He sent me an email in response, well, *us* an email to our joint account today. Obviously, you haven't seen it yet." He handed her his phone.

"No, I didn't." She looked at his phone and began to read aloud:

Lennox and Nadia Wilde,
Congratulations on your recent marriage. I hope that it was all that you wished for. Family is important. Blood is important. I don't have to like you to still consider you family and it's no secret that I don't like either one of you moth-

erfuckers. Despite that, this money is for the new bride and groom. You are in fact family, no matter what, and you have also married. One thing that was in the contract that perhaps my grandson, Lennox Wilde, overlooked, is that no matter the outcome of our business discussions, consultations, and meetings, I am to give a certain amount of money, should that grandson still be amongst the living after said deliberations.

I feel this is fitting for each of my seven grandsons who are currently involved in business negotiations with Wilde Incorporated. There's a reason behind this that I will not go into at this time. Nevertheless, the dollar amount is up to my discretion. My choice. Once the contract is either honored, or null and void, for whatever reason excluding death, the money will be sent.

Needless to say, the contract between Lennox Wilde and myself is null and void based on the events that took place in our final meeting. I am stating, for the record, that in this situation, Nadia Deere-Wilde and Lennox Wilde should consider this a wedding present. It is non-fundable. I wasn't invited to the wedding, and I would not have attended even if I were. Some things are just best left alone. That notwithstanding, Lennox is still my grandson. The offspring of my son, Scott Wilde.

Any children born from this union will be a Wilde, regardless of whether the mother or father like it or not. Lennox let it be known that he is not happy that he was born into this family. That is a shame. What we like and dislike, versus what is fact do not always exist in harmony. That child/children will be my great-grandchild/ren, and as such, they are part of my lineage. No, this is not a way for me to stake claim to the child, as I've done with Lennox and many others, soon after their birth. There is a high probability that I may be dead and long gone by the time any of your children are old enough to come aboard and join my empire.

Lennox and his cousins were to be my last re-cruits. I have nurtured them for several decades, and wished to cash in on my investment, as I am getting up in age. This is what made their participation that much more crucial. I need my legacy continued, and I need to know that my business is in good hands, with the best of the best of the bloodline. Lennox successful-ly disqualified himself, but that does not halt my obligations.

All married couples in this family receive a monetary contribution in order to help forge their new life together. So, on that basis, I am honoring the contract. I am quite aware that the two of you are struggling financially due to vocational and educational ventures.

Nadia Wilde, you now have my surname due to marrying my insubordinate grandson. That makes you family, and I will treat you as such. College is an expensive scam, and that jungle gym that Lennox has pasted and glued together out of clay and construction paper is probably going to be a money pit since most businesses like that fail in the first year, but regardless, you both still deserve credit for attempting to make your own way in this world. Most people want handouts, and you two are trying to earn your keep. Though I despise both of you, you do have my respect.

Now, that brings me to the gift that I have extended to both of you. If you send this money back, right now or in the future, it will just be returned, over and over again. Not only that, but it's also rude to return a present such as this, and that would make me angry. Please don't make me angry. There could be consequences. I would hate to have to re-open my and Lennox's negotia-tions based on this portion of the agreement.

Nadia paused, looking nothing short of shocked. Len-nox shook his head and rolled his eyes. Surely, she wasn't surprised that they were being threatened and given a present all at the same time? What part of, *'This man is dead serious, and bat shit crazy!'* didn't she understand? She continued to read aloud.

> It's best to simply accept the money and put it aside if you don't wish to utilize it for whatever reason. This money has no strings attached. My hope, however, is that you do use it for whatever you need it for, considering the edification of your union, and imminent offspring.
>
> May God bless both of you.
> With my earned respect,

### Cyrus Jedediah Wilde
#### President and CEO of Wilde Inc.

With a look of trepidation, Nadia handed him back his phone. He placed it on top of one of his filing cabinets, then turned back to her.

"How much was it, Lennox?"

He swallowed. "A little over two million."

Nadia wheezed, then slipped out of her chair and onto the floor as if she'd been turned to butter. He burst out laughing and shook his head.

"Get up and stop being silly!" he hooted.

She lay there, looking up at the ceiling as if dazed and confused.

"Oh my God. What are we going to do?!" She jerked her head in his direction. "He threatened you in a nasty-nice way by saying we better not send it back, and though it's tempting, Lord knows we could really use that money, but we can't keep it, Lennox. He'll hold it over our heads and we could risk him finding a way to weasel back into your life!"

"We can, and we will. We just won't touch it right away. I told you that my grandfather has this warped way of thinking. He believes in being a man of his word, he is religious, he is very much into family values, procreation, blah, blah, blah, but he doesn't pertain it to himself. He sees himself as some lord, where the rules don't apply. Anyway, he hates it when someone makes a big promise and doesn't provide what they offered. He's right. That *was* in that contract, in small print, but I honestly didn't think he'd follow through because of what we did to him."

"Well hell, I wouldn't have thought so either, but I knew nothin' about this! I didn't see that in the contract when you let me read it!"

"...It was on the very last page, in small print. Most people would probably miss it. I'm certain that was by design. He's stickin' to it, regardless."

"This is crazy!"

"He's a maniac. A completely insane, unhinged person, but he's also quite dangerous, as you noticed firsthand, so it is what it is. Look," he tossed up his hands, "that's a drop in the bucket for my grandfather. He's a billionaire, okay? This is mere peanuts. He can easily make two million bucks in a month if he wanted to. That's one reason why he literally gets away with murder. He has just about everyone who could help paid off, and if not, he can get them knocked off. He, and the entire Wilde Family, is basically Southern mafia, without the title." She nodded in understanding. "The point is, he knows that's a lotta money to most people, and I have a feeling he gave us a little more because of that shower situation with Sam, even after I got revenge. I think he also didn't renege and gave us the money to try and look better in the eyes of—"

"Silva."

"Exactly. He has a guilty conscience when it comes to her. It's strange. He doesn't give a fuck about hardly anyone but himself, Nadia, but I still haven't figured out why he cares about my sister so much." He shrugged. "Not that it's a bad thing, or hell, it might very well be a terrible thing. Who knows? But there is something about her that he wants protected, and I've not gotten to the bottom of it yet. He actually gives a damn about her wellbeing."

"I imagine you've already talked about this with your sister?"

"Yeah, she's as clueless about it as I am. I can't ask my dad either because he is still workin' for him, and I don't trust him all the way."

"I meant to ask you about that… Does your father know that you got the information from his computer?"

"No. If he does, he's said absolutely nothin'. Like I said, my father is a great accountant but horrible with computers, so he and my grandfather probably suspect that someone who's worked on his computer somehow got a hold of the files, or he got hacked. Something like that. I know they put in extra measures now though so it's harder to obtain anything. Regardless, my dad is in the clear, just as I wanted him to be. I didn't want him hurt in all of this, and, uh, when I realized that he actually did give a damn about me, and what Grandpa was doin'... yeah... it made me have a change of heart." He exhaled sharply. "I didn't tell my father about what really went down all of those years ago with the police and shit. How Grandpa was behind all of it. I'm letting it go." He shrugged. "It's not going to do anything but cause problems, all for things to go right back to the status quo eventually anyway. I've already seen that happen before. My father clearly feels obligated to keep workin' for him. He's an enabler. He and my grandfather are back to their regular, toxic and codependent selves. At least for now."

"Well, you covered your tracks well," she said. "That's good. If he knew that Silva ran our little errand for us, he'd explode!" She cackled.

"You know what's crazy, Nadia? I think Grandpa would feel the same, quite honestly, even if he knew for a fact that he'd been drugged by her so his inhibitions would be lowered, and he could have his little orgy in peace. That would also explain Silva's deep connection to him."

"What do you mean?"

"My grandfather is not stupid. Far from it. He very well may suspect her. In fact, for a split second he did until I cleared her name. He may still after he gave it a second thought, but doesn't care enough to do anything about it. She has some type of hold over him. I saw it in his eyes, and it surprised the shit outta me. Silva honestly felt that love from him, so it wasn't just her being greedy for his money, or anything like that. I was wrong about that aspect. Her finding out he'd been the cause of so much pain in this family gutted her. She cried for days. Anyway," he made his way back around the desk and plonked down in his new leather chair, still covered in plastic, "just wanted you to be aware of this, since he followed up with an email and now has admitted it was him after I attempted to send it back."

"How'd he even get your banking information? How'd he—"

"Nadia. Come on." He sighed. "This is Grandpa we're talking about. If he wants to find out something bad enough, more times than not, he probably can."

"This man is unbelievable. I've heard of some far-out shit, met some demented folks in my life and I thought I'd seen it all, but your grandfather showed me otherwise. After all that has happened, and the emotional toll it's taken on you, Lennox, it seems you could save your cousins the time and trouble."

"What do you mean?"

"Well, you could go ahead and tell your grandfather that if he doesn't leave Kage and all the rest of them alone regarding this workin' for his company business, you'll go through with turning in that video and giving all of that information and evidence to the FBI. All of this could finally be over with." She shrugged and shook her head.

"Baby, no…" He sighed, wishing it were that easy. "It doesn't work like that. I wish it did, but it's far more complicated."

"Well, explain it to me because my ass is ready to go to the FBI, and social media, right the hell now! He sent that fool to my job, wit' a damn gun, and he's just about ruined your family. He's out of control. Something has to be done!"

"Yeah… something does have to be done, but it has to be done in the right way, baby. You're not a Wilde, so this is a little hard for you to understand, but let me break it down like this. For starters, each contract is individual to all of us. None of them are written the same, and they aren't asking for the exact same things, either. The compensation, should we agree, is not always the same, either. Secondly, what happened between Grandpa and me because of this mess was specific to *me*." He pointed at himself. "We have to fight our own battles. I can't fight for Kage, he can't fight for Roman, Roman can't fight for Maddock, so on and so forth. Now, we can help each other, he can't stop that shit, but we can't do the heavy liftin' for one another, and ain't no honor in that. Grandpa only respects you if you stand on your own two damn feet. If you try to ride off of someone else's steam, he won't release you from the contract.

"Thirdly, and this is probably the most important, let's say I did what you said and threw caution to the wind. Let's say I went on with turning in the accounting reports to the FBI, which of course would take my father down, too… but let's put that aside and say I'd do it anyway. And let's say I turned over that sex tape, which would embarrass Grandpa—kinda the entire point, true—and potentially ruin his reputation in the Christian sector that he has attached himself to. Nadia, it would only be a damn speed bump.

"Grandpa has so much pull and power in Houston, hell, Texas and the entire South, period, that he could work from prison and STILL ruin Kage's, Roman's, Maddox's,

Phoenix's, Ryder's and everyone's lives if he saw fit! And believe me, he would, without a moment of uncertainty. The only difference would be now he'd be all the more pissed, and unhinged."

"…Damn." She hung her head and shook it.

"See? And let me tell you something else. Those contracts are set in stone, unless we can find a way out of them on our own, just like Grandpa said. He's got a provision in there—if we can find a way out, he'll let us out, but like I said, each contract is individual. This is no, 'Let my people go,' situation. He ain't treatin' us like Moses." He laughed mirthlessly. "This one act of mine changes nothing for nobody but me. He's serious about this. That man meant what the fuck he said. Nothin' short of death would stop that son of a bitch from still going through with this. The contracts are basically written in blood, but since he put that caveat in there, we have a chance. We didn't make a deal with the devil, but, the devil made a deal with us.…

"Just like Roman and I talked about when I went to visit him a long time ago. This ain't got a lot to do with Grandpa wanting us to work for him. I mean, sure, that is what started it years ago, but right now? This is all about control. It's about power. It's about domination. It's about his legacy and his warped vision for the future of this family. Grandpa takes this family thing, blood ties, to a cult-like level. That man is a narcissist, baby. The worst kind. Only thing is, Grandpa is ridiculously intelligent and has a sense of awareness, which makes him even more diabolical. His downfall, though, is thinking he's smarter than everyone else. He never in a million years thought I'd be able to pull something like this off. He never said that to me, but I can read between the lines. He figured I'd be the easiest one to take down because I don't start any trouble and keep to myself. But he found out real damn quick that he was wrong."

"He sure as hell did." She smiled at him.

"You start some bullshit with me, I'm going to damn well finish it. He's evil down to his damn bone marrow. When Grandpa says he wants you, he wants you, and he's going to do everything he can to get what he wants. Ain't shit you can do about it unless you step to him, one on one, man to man, toe to toe. He don't respect nothin' less."

Nadia nodded, her smile turning sad.

"I get it now. It's fucked up, but I get it."

She sighed and got off the floor, dusting off her knees and butt.

"Well, as interesting as this is, we still have work to do. We can talk more about it at home later tonight. I better finish clearing out that back closet so you can put the towels in there, and—"

"Wait. I have something else to tell you."

"What is it now?" She looked at him with a bit of concern in her expression.

"Speaking of emails, my dick just sent an email to your pussy requesting an emergency meeting. Make sure she accepts the notice. He said he'll make it fast." He curled his finger in her direction and gave her a devilish grin.

"Lennox." She put her hands on her hip. "You are one sick puppy, you know that? I'm not about to have sex with you right now. I have shit to do!" It was obvious she was trying to sound tough, but the smirk on her face gave her away.

Twisting his thumbs around the elastic waistband of his jogging pants, he shoved them down along with his underwear, exposing a throbbing, fat hard-on.

"Lennox, pull your damn pants up. I don't have time for this!" She giggled as she turned to rush out of the office.

Getting up from his seat, he grabbed her by the arm and dragged her over to his desk, laying her down onto her back. She fought the entire time, punching at his chest, laughing hysterically as he yanked her leggings down to her ankles and pulled her shirt up, exposing her bra. Within seconds, he was buried deep inside of her, thrusting away like a piston. She held onto him tight, the music from the main area thumping through their bodies as he made rough, beautiful love to her. Black Pumas' 'Colors' webbed exquisite sounds in his ears as he took her down to the land of pleasure…

She clawed at his shoulders as his hips bucked and pushed, and she wrapped her long, shapely legs around his lower back, keeping him steady as he drove in and out of her with brute determination.

He shuddered when he felt her orgasm burst free… Her back arched and she whimpered with delight. Pausing, he placed a gentle kiss against her soft lips, her body electric, on fire for him.

"My gorgeous wife is so wet right now… I love how that sounds: *'My wife.'* You're so damn beautiful, baby."

He rotated his hips back and forth, then looked down and watched his dick disappearing inside of her, coming back out soon after, slick with her juices. He pulled all the way back, returning only to slam into her hard. Entomb himself within her, to the point of no return. He covered her mouth after she gasped in sweet agony, stifling her screams while he slammed into her a few more times—until finally he fell apart, cumming deep inside of her.

He groaned into Queen Lust's cleavage as she curled into his body, making him whole. A deep feeling of peace overcame him. In fact, he felt right as rain. They rested momentarily, then quietly redressed. When she began walking away to leave, he blew her a kiss, then closed the door softly behind her. He stood there. Looking around. In awe.

He dropped his head and shook it. Moved by how far he'd come in life. Immensely thankful. Everything he ever wanted was materializing. A dream come true. He wanted autonomy over his own life. *Done.* He wanted his own fitness company. *Almost complete.* He wanted a better relationship with his father. *In the works.* He wanted his broken relationship with his sister repaired. *Fixed.* He wanted to fall in love and find his soulmate. *Bingo.* He wanted to get married and plant roots. *Accomplished.* He wanted children. *Fingers crossed, that would be soon on the horizon.* He wanted to be a sprinkler. *Hot damn, he'd found his garden…*

He wanted to nourish that woman. Protect her. Make her always feel loved, respected and cherished. He wanted to water her to quench her thirst for true love, not drown her in the storms of life. She was his harness, when he needed to be yanked back and redirected. Separate, they were not to be trifled with. Together, they were double the trouble. He looked at that closed door, and could hear her talking to one of the electricians. *Nadia has no idea how much she's inspired me. She has no idea how much I love her. She couldn't, because there's no words in existence to describe it.*

At night, she may have been Velvet, but in the new light of day, when the sun shone bright, she was the next beat of his heart.

### ~The End~

Thank you for reading, "Top Dog – Lust." I hope you enjoyed this double novel, which is the first book of the series, and introduces the Wilde family.

This concludes Book 1, Part 2, of "The Top Dog – Lust," but the party has just begun! The second book in the series is called, "The Black Sheep – Greed."

As a reminder, each book in this series is a standalone and contains no cliffhangers. However, since this is a series that deals with relatives who communicate with one another, reading each book in sequence will add greatly to the total enjoyment of the reading experience.

If you enjoyed this book, you may also appreciate some of my other offerings:

# BOOKS ALSO BY TIANA LAVEEN

www.tianalaveen.com/books.html

The Saint Series

The entire Brother Disciples series:
The complete series
BOOK 1: Hear No Evil – The Book of Axel
BOOK 2: See No Evil – The Book of Legend
BOOK 3: Speak No Evil – The Book of Caspian (Part 1)
BOOK 4: Speak No Evil – The Book of Caspian (Part 2)

The Zodiac Series (Capricorn – Sagittarius) 12 stand-a-lone books

The Race to Redemption Series: The 'N Word and Word of Honor

Black Ice
Fire and Rain
Here Comes the Judge
The Viper and His Majesty
Gumbo
Savage
The Fight Within
Tyrant

# AND MANY MORE!

## ABOUT THE AUTHOR

USA Today bestselling author Tiana Laveen writes resilient yet loving heroines and the alpha heroes that fall for them in unlikely happily-ever-afters. An author of over 80 novels to date, Tiana creates characters from all walks of life that leap straight from the pages into your heart.

Married with two children, she enjoys a fulfilling life that includes writing books, drawing, and spending quality time with loved ones.

If you wish to stay up-to-date with her releases, please join her newsletter: www.tianalaveen.com/newsletter

Follow her on social media platforms, as well as visit her website.

Tiana Laveen website:

www.tianalaveen.com

# TOP DOG MUSIC PLAYLIST

Greetings! I typically offer a song playlist in my novels that showcase all of the songs and artists mentioned throughout the novel. I also try to keep the list and digital playlist close if not exact, to the same order that the songs are mentioned in the book(s.) Playing the songs while re-reading your favorite scenes, adds another layer to the reading experience! Give it a try!

HERE IS THE SPOTIFY LINK TO THE MAJORITY OF THE SONGS LISTED BELOW (There are a few songs that were unavailable on Spotify, but they are listed and included below:
https://open.spotify.com/playlist/
75uS2f35m9OBCodWxGQqno?si=27e9cc9c730d40cd

1.  Crystal Gayle – Don't It Make My Brown Eyes Blue
2.  Yuna – Strawberry Letter 23

3. Jack Harlow – Lovin' On Me

4. Rufus (Chaka Khan) – Stay

5. The Beetles – Strawberry Fields

6. Tanner Adell – Buckle Bunny

7. mehro – K3TAMINE

8. Chip the Ripper – Interior Crocodile Alligator

9. The Pussy Cat Dolls – Buttons

10. Kelela – Contact

11. Big Boss Vette – Snatched

12. Ludacris – Pussy Poppin

13. Too Short – Blow the Whistle

14. Garth Brooks – That Summer

15. Justin Timberlake – Until the End of Time

16. Willow Smith – Symptom of Life

17. Usher, Summer Walker and 21 Savage – Good Good

18. JamWayne – No Problems

19. Lorenzo – Make Love 2 Me

20. Intro – Come Inside

21. Art of Noise – Moments in Love

22. The Boogie Boys – A Fly Girl

23. Kano – I'm Ready

24. Dusty Leigh and Bubba Sparxxx – OAB

25. N'Dambi – L.I.E.

26. Tems – Love Me JeJe

27. Kendrick Lamar – Pride

28. Jungle – Back On 74

29. Lucy Chris – Frogs

30. KARRAHBOOO – Running Late
31. Tommy Richman – Million Dollar Baby
32. Marcellus The Singer and Cecily Wilborn – You Baby
33. Sam Smith – Stay With Me
34. MAGIC! – Rude
35. Steve Lacy – Bad Habit
36. Kendrick Lamar – Humble
37. Khamari – These Four Walls
38. Metro Boomin, Future, Kendrick Lamar, DaBaby and Ye – Like That
39. Megan Thee Stallion – BOA (mentioned twice in this book.)
40. Arlo Parks – Caroline
41. Pete Rock – Take You There
42. Smooth – Mind Blowin'
43. G-Unit – Wanna Get To Know You
44. Snoop Dog – Let's Get Blown
45. Kelly Rowland – Motivation
46. Marcellus TheSinger – Until We Meet
47. BadGir – Steppin' Out (featuring King George)
48. Young Guy – Lay Low Play Slow
49. Anycia – Back Outside (featuring Latto)
50. The Moody Blues – Nights in White Satin
51. Cat Stevens – Morning Has Broken
52. Young Guy – Take Heed
53. Jezzy, featuring Bankroll Fresh – All There
54. Doja Cat – Demons

55. Cardi B – Enough

56. Jordan Adetunji – KEHLANI

57. A Boogie Wit da Hoodie – Body (featuring Cash Cobain)

## PART 2/BOOK 1:

58. XXXTENTACION – Vice City

59. Ro James XIX – Already knew

60. Ro James – Take It All (*Not available on Spotify at the time of this book publishing. Please find song on YouTube or Amazon Music.*)

61. Glorilla – Yea Glo! (DJ cut smooth jazz version mixed with Twista's, So Sexy)

62. Janelle Monáe – I Like That

63. Kelly Roland featuring Lil' Wayne – ICE

64. Miguel – Sure Thing

65. Usher – Glu

66. Elvis Presley – Burning Love

67. Neil Diamond – Song Song Blue

68. Shaboozey – A Bar Song

69. Keith Whitley – When You Say Nothing at All

70. Otis Redding – Sitting on the Dock of the Bay

71. Brent Faiyaz – Pistachios

72. Kendrick Lamar – Not Like Us

73. Khruangbin & Leon Bridges – Texas Sun

74. Justin Timberlake – My Love

75. Pinegrove – Need To

76. Cherry Lu – The Rain (*Not available on Spotify at the time of this book publishing. Please find song on YouTube or Amazon Music.*)

77. Keane – Somewhere Only We Know

78. Lana Del Rey – Summertime Sadness

79. øneheart x reidenshi – snowfall

80. Atlantic Starr – When Love Calls

81. Billie Eilish and Khalid – Lovely

82. Phyllis Hyman – You Know How To Love Me

83. Mac Miller – All I Want Is You

84. Eric B. & Rakim – I Ain't No Joke

85. D-Nice – Call Me D-Nice

86. Mac Miller – Fight the Feeling (featuring Kendrick Lamar)

87. Mac Miller – Desperado (The instrumental version)

88. Bilal – Soul Sista

89. Robert Glasper – Better Than I Imagined (featuring H.E.R. and Meshell Ndegeocello)

90. Foy Vance – Make It Rain

91. Leon Bridges – River

92. Heartless Bastards – Only For You

93. Bill Haley – Rock Around the Clock

94. Barrett Strong – Money

95. DMX – Party Up

96. The Big Bopper – Chantilly Lace

97. (Duplicate song was mentioned.)

98. Glue Trip – Elbow Pain

99. Tash Sultana – Jungle

100. Celeste – Both Sides of the Moon

101. The Monkees – Daydream Believer

102. Buju Banton – Boom Bye Bye *(Not available on Spotify at the time of this book publishing. Please find song on YouTube or Amazon Music.)*

103. Kid Ink – Time of Your Life

104. The Rolling Stones – Little Red Rooster

105. Grimes – Genesis

106. Pharrell Williams – Happy

107. Prince – Adore

108. SWV – Rain Down on Me

109. Shaboozey – Last of My Kind

110. Black Pumas – Colors

*If any of these songs on this book playlist appeals to you, please purchase and download a legal copy of the song/ album in order to support the artist(s.) Thank You!* ☺